Praise for *Frat Girl*

"A sweet, subversive deconstruction of frats and feminism, Kiley Roache's debut will have readers sighing and snorting at Cassie's adventure into fraternity life and finding her own truth."
—Christa Desir, award-winning author of *Bleed Like Me* and *Other Broken Things*

"Refreshingly honest and intelligently written, *Frat Girl* is filled with relevant topics and written by an author to watch!"
—Julie Cross, *New York Times* and *USA TODAY* bestselling author

"In her debut novel, Roache has created a narrator with a strong, relatable voice as well as a cast of nuanced characters full of pleasant surprises and believable personal growth."
—*Kirkus Reviews*

"*Frat Girl* is a telling tale of feminism, fraternities and freshman year.... Compelling, creative and cleverly written."
—*TeenReads.com*

Books by Kiley Roache
available from Harlequin TEEN and Inkyard Press

Frat Girl
The Dating Game

frat girl

kiley roache

ink yard press

Recycling programs
for this product may
not exist in your area.

ISBN-13: 978-1-335-49904-2

Frat Girl

This edition published by arrangement with Harlequin Books S.A.

For questions and comments about the quality of this book, please contact us
at CustomerService@Harlequin.com.

® and TM are trademarks of Harlequin Enterprises Limited or its corporate
affiliates. Trademarks indicated with ® are registered in the United States Patent
and Trademark Office, the Canadian Intellectual Property Office and in other
countries.

InkyardPress.com

Printed in U.S.A.

To the friends I've made in college:

You're feminists.

You're frat boys.

But most important, you're family.

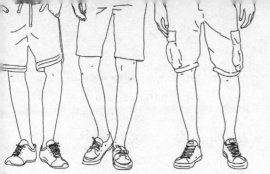

chapter one

THE STEVENSON SCHOLARSHIP WAS MAGIC. IT HAD the power to make a $60,000 annual bill disappear. It was the difference between a community college and the school of my dreams. Between spending the next four years in giant lecture halls with the same kids who partied their way through high school ignoring me while I studied alone and they skipped class for beer bongs and wet T-shirt contests, and joining the most elite group of young men and women in the world. Between spending the next chapter of my life still in the Midwest—land of marrying at twenty-two and popping out 2.5 kids—where half the people would assume I was going to college only to get my "MRS degree," and flying away to California to study feminist and gender studies at one of the most progressive places on earth.

But I needed a project. The scholarship was funded by tech billionaire Greg Stevenson. You know, the one who created an empire by night and studied by day when he was in college just ten years ago.

My online application was picked from among thousands, and the interview rounds went better than I could have dreamed. I was one of two finalists left and would be pitching my project to the board, including Stevenson himself, in a few days.

I wasn't terrible at public speaking, so I wasn't too stressed about presenting my idea.

The problem would be not having one.

"I'm so fucked," I say, sitting at my desk and scrolling through Facebook, like I might find inspiration there.

I turn to my best friend, who is sitting, her ass halfway out my open second-story window, chain-smoking Marlboros.

"What's the other person doing, again?" she asks.

The official emails didn't tell me who my competition was, let alone what they were doing, but I searched Twitter for the name of the scholarship, and, lo and behold, my competition is the type to Tweet his every movement, from trying out a gluten-free diet for fun to humble bragging about how #blessed he was to be a Stevenson Award finalist.

Two hours of stalking instead of working on my project later, and I knew he was a CS major from San Francisco who'd already created two moderately successful social media apps. I also knew waaaay too much about his cat, Ashby.

"It's got to be another app, right?" I say.

"Well, I'm assuming it's not poetry," Alex says, swinging her combat-booted foot, casting a shadow on my baby-pink walls.

I pull out my phone and turn my whole body toward her, sitting cross-legged on my desk chair.

"He Tweeted yesterday at 11:06 a.m. 'working on a new project' and then two hours later 'coding by the pool. Could I be more #SiliconValley #California!?!'"

Since the fund is run by Stevenson's charity, not his company, they supposedly invested in all sorts of projects, but there was a clear favor toward the technical, money-generating kind.

"So he's the same idiot that school is made up of." Alex takes a long drag and blows smoke out the window, toward the quiet suburban street below. "You're something different. Sell that."

"Yeah, I'll just tell them I want to do something different. I don't know what, but different."

"Welcome to being a humanities major." She shrugs.

Alex and I have been best friends since the Model UN conference I attended freshman year, when I was waiting for another young Republican in a suit to give the opening remarks and instead she bounded onstage: pink-haired, tattooed and brilliant.

She's a year older than me and the only person from our town to go to an elite school before me. In fact, she's at the school I'm so desperately trying to find a way to attend: Warren University.

Before college she went to the giant public school with metal detectors at the entrances—the same school my parents paid the archdiocese an obscene tuition to keep me safe from—where she got straight As in all APs and tried every drug ever invented. "God, imagine how smart she'd be if her brain was fully functioning," our friend Jay once said.

Dirt-poor and knowing equally about 'shrooms and Sophocles, she didn't exactly scream typical Warren University student. But she was everything they want to be. They dress like her at Coachella, but she's been going to the thrift store since fifth grade, when her dad was laid off, not since vintage came back.

We've been at this all week, spitballing stupid ideas fueled by coffee (me), cigarettes (Alex) and rosé (her all day, me once I give up).

"What's up, nerds?" Jay leans against the door.

"I'm watching my future slip away from me," I say, putting my head in my hands.

"Ugh, drama much?" He flops down on my bed. "Just be like me. Go to IU and have blonde girls with Delta Delta Gamma tank tops stretched over their double Ds try to claim you as their very own gay best friend while you fuck their closeted football-player boyfriends behind their backs."

I wish I could. Well, at least the attending-IU part. I had messed up pretty royally when it came to applying for schools. My mom hadn't gone to college, and my dad "didn't have the time to waste" on helping me, so it was just me and a guidance counselor with three hundred other students to help.

So when I went to college night and the Warren representative stood up in his gold-and-blue suit and said they meet 100 percent of financial need, I believed him. I applied early, and when I got my acceptance, I saw no reason to try anywhere else.

But then the financial aid letter came. And the people who sat in a boardroom in California saw meeting my need in a different way than me and my mother did, bent over bills in our cramped kitchen. They included the restaurant franchise in their assessment of what my parents "owned," but it wasn't like they were about to sell it to meet my tuition.

By that point, it was too late to apply anywhere else.

But I don't want to talk about all that right now. I turn to Jay and roll my eyes. "My gender and orientation prevent this plan, but thanks for your input."

"Yeah, I think that's just you, Jaybird," Alex chimes in from the window.

He rolls his eyes. "It's overrated anyway." He props himself up on his elbows, swinging his feet up and down alternately. "Is angst-y time over? Because I'd like to enjoy one of our last nights together before we all grow up and our souls die, Wendy Darling."

"He's right—not thinking is when I think my best. C'mon, bring the wine." Alex steps up on the windowsill and pulls herself onto the roof. We grab the bottle and follow.

Lying on the roof of my parents' compact house, we stare at the stars and city lights. We listen to trains go by and point out planes coming into the airport a neighborhood over. We pass around Two Buck Chuck Rosé and sip from the bottle. And I try to think about anything except for getting out of here on one of those planes. About the pitch in three days that will decide my fate.

I take a sip. "Seriously, though, the school's in goddamn Tech Town, USA. What gender and sexuality studies project will make them happier than a million-dollar app idea?"

"A million-dollar app that just allows people another way to socialize?" Alex takes the bottle from me, takes a long pull and continues. "I mean, I like socializing, but, please, like the best and brightest people in the world don't have better things to do?"

Jay snaps his fingers in agreement.

Alex pauses just long enough to nod at him. "I mean, I'd prefer world-class minds to be endeavoring to understand who we are and why we are here and what this place—" she waves her hands, sweeping into her sentence the suburb around us and stars above us, and almost spilling the pink wine "—means, not creating apps that make it easier for eighth graders to send each other tittie pics."

I take the wine back and think about this as I sip the hypersweet concoction.

"You could start some sort of nonprofit for girls in tech," Jay says.

"I looked it up—there are already like five student groups there that do that. Plus I know almost nothing about coding."

"You could learn."

"Yeah, but if they're gonna give someone this much grant money, they kind of want you to be able to produce something for them pretty quickly. Not like, I'll get back to you when I learn how to code."

"Truuuuue." Jay nods solemnly.

We lie silently for a while.

"Maybe Warren is too much of an old boys' club to want a major gender project," Alex says.

"Maybe that's why they need it," Jay retorts.

"They're trying to get better," I say. "They suspended that frat." While I'd procrastinated, I'd read article after article about the controversy surrounding Delta Tau Chi.

"Put them on probation," Alex corrects. "And it's just a PR move. There's so much money in that frat, they're not really changing anything."

"What'd they get in trouble for?" Jay asks.

"They're sexist, homophobic pigs." Alex lights up a cigarette.

"No, I mean—"

"Creating a hostile environment for women." She takes a drag before continuing. "There's some rule with housing and Title IX. They had signs all over the house with sexist jokes on them."

"Signs?" he asks.

"Yeah, they threw a party for International Women's Day. Had signs over the kitchen about it being a woman's true place, signs in the bathroom about period pain being punishment for being so bitchy, and don't even get me started on the ones near the bedrooms."

"That's repulsive." I'd never heard the details; the articles I'd read said only that they'd been misogynistic. But Alex had been there. Well, *there* as in Warren. I doubt she'd attend some godforsaken frat party.

Jay runs his hands through his jet-black hair, considering this. "I mean, not to defend the douche bags, but it's not technically supposed to be an environment for women, right?"

"That's not an excuse." Alex sits up.

"I'm not saying *I* would make the joke. I think they're assholes for saying it. But how can you get in trouble for creating an environment that's unwelcoming to women when your charter is to be a boys' club? I mean, no one would really know if a frat was a toxic living and learning community for a woman unless one tried living there."

"Maybe *I* will," I say.

I was just trying to make a joke before this conversation devolved into one of their ridiculous arguments, which always get way too heated, considering they always represent the far left and the farther left.

For half a second they laugh politely, but then the banter goes on, fading to buzzing in my ears.

I stare down at the street below, the street I danced down when I got my acceptance letter. I'd met the mailman at the curb for five days straight until finally, *finally*, that letter I'd been dreaming about arrived.

I was ecstatic to tell my parents that their daughter was going to attend the most exclusive school in the country. I hadn't even told them where I'd applied, not wanting to get their hopes up.

I'd pictured hugs and tears. I'd pictured champagne.

But I should've known.

Should've known the response would be that there was no way they were about to spend that much money so I could get a piece of paper that would hang uselessly in my husband's house.

I told them not to worry, about the 100 percent need thing. But when the second letter came and it was time to go to the bank for unsubsidized loans and second mortgages, I should have known they'd say it wasn't worth the trouble.

I should've known my dad would say, between beers, "Hell, your mom didn't even go to college, and she seems perfectly content."

And that my mother would nod and extol the virtues of 1950s-style housewifedom in the twenty-first century. The satisfaction of a life filled with aprons and diapers and Xanax.

What my father doesn't know is enough of the latter or a bottle of white wine will get her talking about how she always wanted to be a veterinarian growing up. "Coulda done it, was top of my high school class, you know," she'd tell me between hiccups. "What am I now? Is this *it*?"

I thought I'd study hard and do well and avoid her mistakes. I wasn't about to get pregnant and married at eighteen. I hadn't even stopped working long enough to have a boyfriend.

But I should've known what was coming. I should have known years ago when my father went to alumni meetings to protest women being accepted into his alma mater.

Hell, I should have known when I was seven, eating ice cream earned with straight As, and my father said, "You are so smart. It's too bad you're not a boy."

Or all those times he said he wished he had a son to carry on the family business (because apparently you can't run a Chili's franchise without a Y chromosome).

Or to be a legacy in his stupid frat…

"Oh my God! Ohmygodohmygodohmygod." I scramble off the roof, back through the window and practically run to the computer, where I start searching, typing, printing.

I work for fifteen minutes before I even sit down.

I hear Jay and Alex climb back through the window but don't look up.

"What—"

I hold up a finger, cutting Jay off. "Hold on—I don't wanna lose my train of thought."

When I turn around, Alex has pulled the pages from my printer.

"What is this? Delta Tau Chi?" Her eyes widen, and her excitement radiates from her as if her pink hair is made of fire. "Oh my God, you are not!"

Jay just looks confused.

"Can you really?" she asks.

"As far as I can tell, there's no rule anywhere. I think it's just usually assumed or implied. But they're on probation for telling sexist jokes, so what are they gonna do, kick me out of Rush when there's no rule against it?"

"Can someone please tell me what's going on?" Jay says.

"I'm joining a frat," I say.

"Not just any frat, but the douchiest frat on campus," Alex interjects.

I nod. "I'll go undercover and write a personal account of *real* culture inside a frat house. Show how terrible and sexist they actually are, so no one can deny it anymore. End them."

"That's crazy," Jay says, but he's smiling.

"I think it's simultaneously the best and the stupidest, riskiest idea I've ever had."

"That's why I love it." Alex's purple-shadowed eyes absolutely sparkle. "How can I help?"

"Hand me those papers. And get some coffee. We have thirty-six hours."

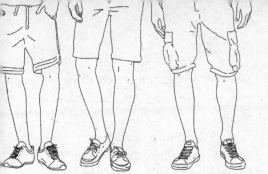

chapter two

Dear Cassandra:

Congratulations, I am pleased to inform you that you have been selected by the Stevenson Fund to receive the Stevenson Scholarship for Study and Research for this year. This scholarship was established to promote a life-long practice of simultaneous scholarship and creative endeavors, because we at the Fund reject the premise that your career begins only after graduation or that academic pursuit should ever cease. The award value and other information about your scholarship are provided below.

We were very impressed by all you have done in your academic career, but even more by your potential for growth and future success. This is not simply a prize for what you have done; rather it is an investment in your future. The Fund provides you with a full-tuition scholarship in exchange for equity in any and all entities you create during your time at Warren University. Tuition will be granted each year upon the submission of a renewal application, and on the condition that you maintain a GPA of 3.0 or higher and keep on schedule with all projects.

Our goal is to help you make a difference in the world. We believe in your vision and leadership, and aim to grant you as much creative independence as possible, but there are certain criteria you are expected to meet.

With the help of a project coordinator at the Fund, Madison Macey, you will create a plan for the completion of your projects. But you must meet the deadlines you set for yourself or risk losing funding. The exception would be extensions you request with the help of your PC and that are approved by the Fund board.

Please fill out the attached forms as soon as possible, at which point the amount of your scholarship for one year will be sent directly to Warren University. It will be placed in your student account on hold status awaiting the completion of the first round of tutorials with your project coordinator and the creation of a preliminary four-year plan. Please send this to your project coordinator (address listed below) in two weeks' time.

Congratulations, and best wishes for a productive and successful academic year.

Sincerely,

Rupert Jones

Vice President

Stevenson Scholarship Fund Board

I STARE FOR THE THOUSANDTH TIME AT THE LETTER that had changed my life. The result of an all-nighter, followed by the scariest twenty-minute presentation of my life. Then the waiting and checking the mail, and the waiting and the pacing, and the waiting. And then, one morning I opened the mailbox and the waiting had ended, and it was time for screaming and crying and calling my grandmother and getting absolutely obliterated on cheap champagne with Alex and Jay.

After reading over the letter for the umpteenth time, I fold it neatly and place it in my empty desk in my new dorm room. I want to hang it on the wall for inspiration like I'd done in my room at home, but I have to be low-key about the scholarship or people will ask what my project is. It's the same reason there wasn't a press release from the university, and why I didn't get to attend the Fund's banquet in New York City. I have a fake backup project about the experience of female athletes, but I'm not about to bring it up in conversation. Which honestly doesn't make me much different from the other kids on scholarship in a land where most kids arrive at school in Audis and Teslas, if not by helicopter. (Okay, I've heard of only one person doing that, but *really*...)

I shut the drawer and turn to inspect my new home, a rectangular room with twin desks, wardrobes and beds. Everything I own is in duffel bags and boxes around me.

After all the movies I've seen about moving into college, heading off on your own, getting into your first apartment, taking on the big world with wide eyes, I expect...something.

But all I really feel is that it's kinda stuffy. It's like I'm waiting for all the deep, life-changing emotions to finally arrive. In the meantime, I'm just in a much too hot, nondescript room without air-conditioning on a late-summer afternoon.

The building is the oldest on campus, like two hundred years old, and it takes me a while to pry open the window. Doesn't do much to affect the heat anyway.

"Pretty bullshit they don't give us air-conditioning," my roommate says, returning from the bathroom down the hall and slamming our door, disregarding the *open door, open friendship* rule they kept telling us about during orientation events.

Warren has a really strict roommate policy, forcing everyone to enter randomly so all the kids from elite schools don't pair up and leave kids like me—who know zero of the two thousand other students in our year—stranded.

Which is how Leighton Spencer got stuck rooming with me instead of one of her ten close friends who also got in.

She's a pretty, wiry track runner—"not here, in high school, but I could if I wanted to"—with a platinum-blond ponytail and a ten-minute answer about where she's from that includes three European cities and the most selective boarding school on each side of the United States. And she scares me absolutely shitless.

"I started hanging some stuff up while you were gone. I hope you don't mind." I glance at my Christmas lights, Warren pennant and vintage Beatles poster. "If there's anything you don't like, I can take it down."

She flops on the plasticky blue mattress she'd claimed by the time I'd arrived, her Louis Vuitton luggage stacked around her, untouched. "It's your half of the room—why would I care?"

"Thanks." I clear my throat.

All my decorations are up, and all my shirts, pajamas, underwear and socks are placed in their respective drawers, by the time she eventually gets up to hang a rainbow of cocktail dresses in her wardrobe and starts taping Polaroids above her desk.

"Do you mind if I play music?" I take my speaker out of a box my mom labeled "Cassie's dorm stuff" (so specific and helpful) and set it on the desk.

"If it's not pop."

Okaaay, then. I scroll past the boy bands and choose an indie alternative band I heard at Fountain Square.

She looks up as the first song starts. "I actually like this band. Where did you say you were from again?"

"Indianapolis."

She turns back to her things.

I look at her pictures. Leighton vacationing in the Maldives, at home in Hyde Park, leaning on a balcony with the Eiffel Tower in the background, Leighton with three different boys in a series of repeating shots. There are also a bunch with a dark-haired girl, laughing candids, posed with her hand on her hip, meeting James Franco.

I think of Alex.

"Is she your best friend?" I point to one with the girl.

"No." She scoffs. "I'm not friends with girls—too much drama. That's my sister." She rolls her eyes. "I mean, half sister. That's why we don't look alike. She's at Dartmouth. Pi Phi."

She stares at me for a second too long and then turns back to her wall, trying to figure out how to hang up her map from Urban Outfitters that still has the USSR on it. *Edgy.*

"First hall meeting!" someone shouts, knocking on our door. "Come on out, frosh!"

I open the door to see a tiny redhead ringing a cowbell and wearing a very bright T-shirt with a button that says, "I ♥ Frosh."

A group of people are huddled awkwardly and silently in the hall. Leighton stands in the doorway, as if debating whether she should go outside for this at all.

"Welcome to Warren!" the overenthusiastic redhead says. "I'm your RA, Becky Scott. I hope you are all just loving meeting your roomies! I think we might just have the best hall ever this year, and I'm really excited to go on this journey with all of you! But first I have some presents!"

The presents turn out to be all the free shit Housing gave her, and soon I find myself with the weirdest assortment of objects I have ever held at once.

There's a rubber duck with a mental health hotline number stamped on its butt to represent "Duck Syndrome," the

idea that the high-stress environment of an elite school com-
bined with the Californian desire to seem chill creates a group
of students who act calm on the surface but are paddling for
their lives underneath.

Welcome to college, I think. *That's comforting.*

Next come the rainbow stickers with the words *This is an
inclusive community!* across them. And your choice of glittery
or black ones that say, "Of Course I'm a Feminist."

A muscular guy about the size of Hagrid from down the
hall opts not to take one of these. "Those are who's messing
with my frat."

"Aren't you a freshman? How are you even in a frat?" My
hand flies to my mouth—that was *not* in character.

"Yeah, but I'm a football player." He looks at me like I'm
stupid. Maybe I should've noticed his T-shirt, which also
broadcasts this affiliation.

"All football players rush DTC," he says.

"Oh."

Next there were the condoms. I blush despite myself, used
to my Midwestern Catholic school and the oxymoron that is
Abstinence-Only Sexual Education, which is a little bit different from liberal California. I mean, this stuff *shouldn't* be
taboo; it's a health issue. Still, I can't bring myself to grab one
in front of these people I just met. I feel like a bad feminist.

The football player has no problem taking multiple boxes.
Classic. He's my favorite type of antifeminist, the sexually
prolific guys who don't support gay rights and think the very
women they fuck are "slutty" for being available. The hyp-
ocrites who are all right with the sexual revolution when it
means they get laid but not when it means oppressed groups
expressing their sexuality.

The meeting disperses, and Leighton is still in the doorway,
apparently not wanting anything rubber, duck or otherwise.

"Hey, I'm gonna put this on the door, okay?" I say as I struggle to peal the backing off one of the feminism stickers.

She seems about to give another grunt of indifference, but then the words register.

"Yeah, no, I'd rather you not." She wrinkles her perfect little nose.

"What?"

"It's not a good look."

"Yeah, I wasn't sure about the sparkles, either. I could grab a black one?"

She just stares at me blankly, turning her head to the side so her blond ponytail swings.

And something clicks. "Leighton...are you not a feminist?"

She shrugs. "Are you?"

"Yeah..." I resist the urge to add "of course."

"Whatever, just don't put it on the door, okay? I don't want any guys to see it and think I'm like that."

Like what? Sure of your own inherent worth no matter what kind of reproductive anatomy you have? The type of person who's for equal pay and against the human trafficking, abuse and inequality that so many women are victims of? Are you worried a sweaty frat guy might not like you because you think women in Pakistan should be able to go to school, or women in Saudi Arabia should be allowed to drive or there should finally be more Fortune 500 CEOs who are female than who are named David? Do you think you'll seem bitchy and shrill if you support women voting or getting to go to college?

I think all this but just say, "I have to use the bathroom."

Splashing water on my face, I think, *I am so fucked.*

If I can't change the mind of a bright, athletic girl who has every reason to demand her accomplishments not be diminished because of her sex, how am I going to change the minds of a group that basically benefits from a patriarchal system?

I dry my face with shitty industrial-style paper towels and look in the mirror.

And I remember: I don't have to convince them of anything; I just have to listen, record, write and publish, then watch their whole system go down in flames.

I throw the sticker in the bathroom trash and walk outside.

"Hey there!" a peppy voice says when I'm barely out the door.

That's the thing about the first week of freshman year—people are *dying* to make friends. Especially at a school like this, where it's incredibly rare to enroll alongside another person from your high school. Unlike Leighton, most people get dropped here, cut off from everyone else who used to define their lives, the single goal that guided them through high school—*get into a good college*—achieved, and have absolutely no idea what to do with themselves or who they even are.

It's like they ooze desperation: *I really want to know about where you're from and your potential major that you will definitely not stick with. Love me. Please!*

I'm not saying I'm not victim to the loneliness and anxiety, too, but when you're about to embark on a complicated social experiment, you can't really make legitimate friends.

For a lot of the students on this campus, the ones who introduce themselves with a suffix of Greek letters after their names, what I am about to do would be social suicide. The ones who will want to cheer me on are probably good people, too good for me to want to lie to them as much as I'd have to.

Which is why I've planned to make friends only within my frat (such a weird sentence still) and those who are directly connected to it (the sister sorority or whatever) and steer clear of lying to more people than necessary.

Still, I don't want to be rude...

I step the rest of the way out of the bathroom and take in

the pretty Asian girl with winged eyeliner and hipster glasses smiling at me. "Hey, what's up?"

"Not to be weird but I heard what your roommate was saying. About the stickers. What bullshit!"

I smile. "Thanks. I'm just glad someone else thinks it's crazy."

"Where are you from?" she asks.

"Indiana."

Her eyes light up. "No way! That's so cute."

"Thanks?" I say.

"Do you live on a farm?"

"No I, uh, live in Indianapolis. It's the fourteenth-biggest city in America."

"Oh, of course," she says, waving her hand as if to dismiss the picture of me with pigtails going out to milk the cows she had started to conjure.

"That's cool, coming to such a different place, though. I'm from SoCal, so it's only a few hours away for me."

I nod knowingly, even though I just recently learned that "SoCal" means Southern California and not, like, Very California.

We look at each other for a beat.

"I'm Cassie, by the way." I reach out my hand.

"Jacqueline Wang. Jackie."

And it's silent again. "What are you majoring in?" I ask, hating myself for becoming one of the Eager Freshmen.

"Physics or CS. How about you?"

"Gender and sexuality studies."

I brace myself for the *They have that here?* or *What will you do with that?* I've come to expect.

But she just raises her eyebrows. "Maybe you can bring back some books to educate Leighton, then."

I decide one real friend can't hurt.

But now the pressure of small talk is on. I look down at my shoes. I look back up. "Do you play any sports?"

"Yeah, climbing."

"Like rocks?"

She turns her head to the side.

God, I am such an idiot.

"Uh, yeah," she says.

"That's so cool."

"Yeah!" She smiles. "We should go sometime."

"Yeah, that'd be cool." I kick myself and hope she doesn't think "cool" is the only word I know.

"..."

"..."

"Wellll… I gotta go," she says, breaking the silence. "I wanna finish unpacking tonight, because I plan to fill an entire wall with postcards. But come by my room later!"

I smile and wave and wonder if I should take her up on that offer, if I *can* take her up on that offer. I debate if I should call my project coordinator to get approval first. And then I hate that I even thought that.

Approval for a friend, what am I doing?

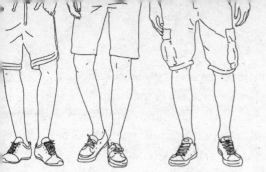

chapter three

LIKE A TYPICAL FRESHMAN GIRL, I'M SPENDING MY first night of college trying on outfit after outfit, making countless trips to the hallway to look in the full-length mirror.

But unlike a typical freshman girl, I am not obsessing over my outfit for the first day of class. I picked that—a white boho blouse and olive shorts—in about 2.5 seconds.

I am probably the first girl in history to spend her first night of college obsessing over what to wear to fraternity Rush. Not exactly the trails I thought I'd be blazing when I was seven with a poster of Sally Ride on my wall or when I was fifteen and carrying one of Gloria Steinem's books everywhere I went.

But I keep the endgame in mind: one year of investigative journalism in a frat, and I renew my funding. I get to go to college at the best school in the country, and I get three more years of gender-related research funding toward what I really want to do, whether that's the wage gap in American tech or women's education in the Middle East.

Setting the winning outfit on my desk, I recheck the pile of syllabi I printed out earlier for my classes tomorrow.

I glance at the clock: nine thirty. Leighton left to meet a friend a few hours ago with no indication of when she'd be back and a clear indication that I was not invited.

Which is fine, it's not like I particularly *want* to be friends with *her*, either. But it would be nice to at least be civil with my roommate.

I walk down the hall to find Jacqueline's door open but her room empty. She wasn't joking about the postcards. Half of her back wall is covered in photos of far-off cities. The photos end in a jigsaw shape, with the rest of the wall blank. On the floor I see painter's tape and a pile of even more glossy postcards.

There's also a poster of a girl stepping off the curb onto a New York street, empty after the rain. It's dark save for the city lights, reflected on the wet pavement, blurry like they're running together. Her back is turned, and all you can see is her wavy hair and her arms raised like she's dancing or celebrating.

For a second, I can see my life if I were a normal student. I would want to befriend people like Jacqueline, to sit around in her art gallery of a dorm room, talking all night about books and movies we love and places we want to visit. I could introduce her to Alex—they would love each other. We could go for late-night burgers in Alex's beat-up Saturn and see concerts in the city.

Music erupts from a room down the hall. A gem that combines "bitches," "money," "ass" and "pussy" with the sound of…maybe Transformers having sex?

I can't see the listener, who apparently also doesn't believe in "open door, open friendship," but a large sign on the door reveals that he's number 82, Duncan Morris.

My Hagrid-size frat "brother." *Fabulous.*

I return to my room, slamming the door. I turn the lock and grab my phone, dialing Alex's number furiously.

"Hello!" her voice rings with joy.

"I miss you."

She laughs. "I miss you, too. How are you? How's your dorm? How are you liking college? Tell me everything!"

"Eh, it's okay. I've spent most of the day unpacking my room."

She laughs. "Fair."

I stare at the window, at the dark outline of a tree.

"How's your roommate?" she asks.

"Um, she's okay, too."

"Just okay?"

"Yeah, I mean she hasn't been mean to me...but she 'doesn't like to be friends with girls.'" I do my best Leighton voice.

"Ew."

"I know."

"Fuck that shit." There is a clattering sound on the other end of the call, followed by laughter. Alex giggles before seeming to remember our conversation. "Um, how's your room, minus the slightly unhinged person living in it?"

"Fine. Pretty small. The beds are uncomfortable, so I think I'm gonna get one of those topper things."

"I did that last year," Alex says. "What's nice about the house is we can get whatever furniture we want because it's owned by the alumni and not the school. Also we can paint the walls!" Her voice gets higher and louder. "I think I'll do one black and then write quotes in silver Sharpie."

"That's gonna look awesome."

"I hope so. Or at least that it turns out better than any of the paintings I did this summer. What a bunch of train wrecks."

"Oh shut up. That one of Jay's dog was MoMA material, and you know it."

We both laugh. I lie back on my uncomfortable bed and close my eyes, and it almost feels like home.

"Can we hang out tonight?" My voice is weak.

"I wish, but there's a mandatory event at the house. Bonding activities or whatever. I'd invite you to come along, but it's all rituals and secrecy and stuff."

"Yeah. I understand."

Although the members of DTC might not realize it, Warren housing and social life do not live and die by the frats.

While there are fourteen houses with ancient letters on them, there are far more without.

Some are ethnic themed: French House, Black House, Native House, Casa. Others are "learning-living communities" organized by major.

The remaining houses are the lit clubs. Alex lives in one of those.

And let me tell you, they could not have created more Alex-y housing if they tried.

The five lit clubs range in hipster level from Urban Outfitters to basically a commune.

The house members are connected by a "literary fraternity" so they can have official events together. All of them practice free love, "mind-opening" drug use and vegetarianism to different degrees.

Alex lives in what I'm already sure will be my favorite. Most people at Dionysus spend meals and homework time fully clothed, but there's definitely lots of house-cest to go with the communal stall-less showers and sleeping rooms. Like, there are no bedrooms, just rooms to hang out in and a giant screened-in porch with forty bunks and hammocks.

Not totally my speed, but better than dorm life with Leighton. "Can I just come live with you instead?"

Alex sighs. "I wish. But hey, at least you don't have to live in the land of freshmen for too long."

"Yeah, but then what? I move into the land of assholes and creeps?"

"Aw, c'mon, Cass—they're just people. Not all Greeks are evil, you know."

"We'll see about that."

I hang up the phone and sigh, searching my room like something to do or a new friend might appear.

On my first night of college, I go to bed at ten o'clock.

———

All throughout my first day of classes I can barely focus. As soon as the last one ends I run back to my dorm to start getting ready.

I shower and put on a lot of makeup, but nothing too bright or dramatic. I want the boys thinking I'm not wearing any, that I'm supercool and not at all vain. Idiots.

I put on a short, tight but simple dress made of T-shirt material, the type of dress a guy would pick out for a girl. I don't want to wear anything that looks girlie or frilly, but I need to look hot. The fun, sexy party girl who you forget is a girl except for when you think about fucking her.

After slipping on red-and-white high-tops, I plug in my straightener. A ponytail would be too tomboyish. And curling my hair would look like I tried too hard. (Boys don't understand that all heat tools take the same level of effort.)

While I can't seem too *much* like a girlie-girl, I also don't want to seem like one of the boys, because then I'll lose out during Rush to *real* boys. To these misogynist dickwits, I will never be a better man than a man. So I need to use my assets. I need to be like one of the guys, but *with boobs*.

It's disgusting.

I check the campus map three times before I leave. I can't show up with it—looking like a stupid freshman will be an automatic loss of Rush points or whatever it is.

"Hey, Cassie, where are you headed?" My RA, Becky, pounces as soon as I make it to the lobby.

"Out." I push through the old, heavy doors.

Well, I've been on campus about a day now so it seems about time to cement my social group for four years. I make my way toward The Row, winding between palm trees and sandstone buildings. There are a few other people out and about, but mostly campus is pretty empty.

A large fountain that looks like a demented tree sits empty, turned off because of the drought. *Am I supposed to pass that?*

I try to remember the tour I took when I arrived on campus.

Okay, yes, I definitely passed the math building before, although all the academic buildings do kind of look the same.

I glance around.

Shit, I definitely did not pass this weird modern art statue before. I would have thought it looked like a giant bug and laughed for sure. I would never have forgotten that.

There's no way I'm not going to be late now. Fuck, fuck, fuck.

Why'd I have to go to the biggest freaking campus in North America?

I pull out my phone. *Please, please, pleeeeeasse. Oh, cool, it's at 20 perc—*

And it died. *Awesome.* I live in Silicon Valley, but that won't stop my iPhone from jumping from twenty to zero whenever it feels like it. I fight the urge to throw the $600 piece of hardware at the weird ant statue.

"Are you all right?"

I turn around.

The beautiful boy in pastel shorts and a white polo button-down looks at me with concern in his eyes. *Wow, those eyes.*

Deep brown in a way that held mysteries, but lined with the most beautiful, long eyelashes. I've often heard people say that since girls wear mascara, good eyelashes are wasted on a boy. I respectfully disagree.

They were eyes that made me want to trust him, even though we'd never met. I was transfixed by him.

I cleared my throat. "Yeah. I'm just late, lost and my phone died."

"Where are you going?"

"Rush."

"Oh, me, too! I didn't know sorority Rush was happening now, too."

It's not. Actually, it happened before school even began. "Um…"

"Well, I'm not sure where The Row is, either, but my phone's at fifty percent, so you can come with me."

He smiles, and I melt.

I know I should stay focused, but I really do need help…

"That'd be great. Thank you."

He reaches into his pocket and pulls out his phone. Ooohhh, he has nice arms, too.

Shit, he's looking at me. Act normal, Cassie.

I make myself smile and probably look like a serial killer.

He looks from his phone to the path in front of us and then back again. "Okay, I think that it's…this way."

"That's not very encouraging." I laugh. "But I guess it's better than what I have."

He smiles. "That's fair."

"Lead the way."

We walk in silence for a minute, just the sound of our footsteps. I try to think of something interesting to say.

"So what classes are you taking?" he asks.

"Rhetoric, Intro to Gender Studies and Sociology 101."

"Oh, I'm in that one, too!" His eyes light up.

"Really?"

"Yeah. I was really excited about the description, but today was kind of boring."

"Oh my God, *I know.* But hopefully it will get better."

"I have faith." He checks his phone again, and we take a right.

My red-and-white high-tops kick up dust from the dry California ground. By the main buildings, the lawns are still well watered and manicured. But back where the students live it's all cracked ground and sparse dry grass.

"I feel like I'm gonna look so sweaty and gross," I say. "And I hate that I have to care, because of how superficial these things are."

He turns his attention from his phone to me. "I think you look really great."

I laugh. "I wasn't going for that. I'm just trying to have an objective conversation."

He tilts his head to the side. "What do you mean?"

"Like, I'm a confident person. I'm not fishing for compliments or needing you to say that. I have eyes and a mirror. I understand the difference between good hair days and bad ones. Me being made-up and my makeup melting off."

"I didn't think you weren't confident. I think you *objectively* look good."

"Well…" I glance away briefly. "Thank you."

"Even if your makeup is melting off a little bit." He reaches out and brushes a stray eyelash off my cheek. "But now you get to make a wish."

My whole body feels like a live wire. Our eyes lock and I'm scared to look away, for the moment to end, but also I'm scared if I don't I will make it weird and—

"Continue on Galvez Street." Siri, the third wheel I'd forgotten about, ruins the moment.

We both look away, and I try not to giggle as we proceed forward. The silence turns from sexually tense to awkward.

He clears his throat.

I look at him.

There's a pause.

He doesn't look up from the path when he says, "Um…do you wanna exchange numbers? So we can talk about sociology and stuff?"

My heart picks up. "Yeah, sociology and stuff."

He hands me his phone, and I type in my number, checking it three times. I go to text myself his name and…

"I just realized, I don't know your name."

A movie-star smile spreads across his face. "Jordan Louis."

"Cassandra Davis," I say.

He reaches out to shake my hand. "Very nice to meet you, Ms. Davis."

We hold hands and eye contact for a second longer than we probably should.

I can feel myself blushing and look down quickly to hide it. "Um, here you go," I say, handing back his phone.

"Thanks." He examines his screen for a second. "Hey, it seems like we're pretty close…well, I mean to where I need to be. Hopefully I'm leading you in the right direction."

"Where are you rushing?" I ask.

"DTC."

"Yep, that's right near where I need to go."

But my heart sinks as I say it. Because even though I have no right to be emotionally invested in this person I just met, he's tall and has pretty eyes and a heart-melting smile, and he was my knight in shining armor, and now odds are I'll have to spend the next year lying to him. Which sucks. I should tell him—no, not about the project, just that I'm rushing DTC, too, that we're now competitors, and even if we both got in, anything between us would be incredibly complicated. But part of me just wants a little bit longer where he's just a cute boy and I'm just a girl he's flirting with. So I fake a smile.

We arrive at the house, the letters looming over us.

So this is DTC. It's a lot bigger than the other frats I've seen on campus. There are huge white columns, like this may house some sort of system of government and not sixty boys who probably, as a collective, couldn't do a load of laundry. There's also a big balcony across the third floor from which a brilliant Warren student is trying to lower a cooler on a rope to his brothers below.

Guys in matching bro tanks and a rainbow of pastel shorts are scattered around the yard. Some are seated at a folding table that, if I had to guess, is usually used for beer pong, with a poster sloppily duct-taped to it with the words *Sign in here!* written in black Sharpie. Others are just standing around out front drinking canned beer from Warren koozies and yelling weird inside jokes and chants at one another. A bunch are staring at me.

I turn away from the house.

He looks at me. "Do you know where your sorority is from here? Or I can look it up?"

"I got it, thanks again." I step backward and almost trip over my own feet.

"I can walk you there."

"No…you go ahead in. I know how to get where I'm going from here."

"Are you sure?" He seems genuinely worried about leaving me.

"Yeah, definitely."

He looks at the house and then back at me. "Okay. It was good to meet you. I really hope to see you again. Good luck."

"You, too."

He turns and walks toward the sign-in table. He's almost there when he turns back and yells, "Text me, Cassie." He winks at me before he turns away.

I smile despite myself. It takes quite a guy to pull off winking like that.

I raise my hand to wave and smile. *Don't worry, Jordan*, I think. *You'll definitely be seeing more of me.*

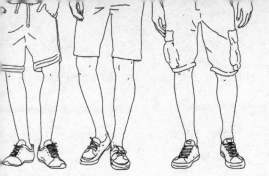

chapter four

I WATCH HIM AS HE SIGNS IN, LAUGHING AND smiling and chitchatting with the actives. Man-flirting, as I like to call it. Even from a distance, I can tell they like him. Of course they do; he's the type of person who's magnetic, who kills the first impression, makes it seem like he cares about you, even when all you've done is say hello.

He disappears into the house, and I shake my head, like I can physically scatter the thoughts of him.

Focus, Cassie, focus.

I walk down the block and decide to loiter for a bit so I don't walk in right after him. Taking out my dead phone, I pretend to type.

Okay, if I wait any longer people will start to notice.

With a deep breath, I walk forward, beer-goggled eyes tracking me.

"Hi," I say as I approach the sign-in table.

An athletic-looking boy with blond hair and a cutoff shirt

highlighting amazing arms looks up, unfazed. "Tri Delts don't have to sign in. Go ahead."

"I'm actually here to rush."

He looks at the other guy, a lanky white dude with a backward baseball cap, and back to me.

"DTC," I clarify.

"Uh…okay." The blond guy looks back to his friend, who shrugs. "Sign in here, I guess."

They whisper as I quickly jot down my name and cell and check the legacy box. My handwriting is neat, but not too girlie. I don't dot my *i*'s with a heart or anything like that.

I smile sweetly as I set down the pen and make a break for the front door before they can figure out how to stop me.

Inside is pretty similar to outside. Guys trying to impress one another while drinking beer that undoubtedly tastes like water at best and piss at worst.

I am the only female.

This could easily be extremely awkward, but I can't afford to let that happen. I smile and walk forward, giving off an air of confidence I don't really feel.

The first two rooms are furniture-less, and one has a giant fireplace with a composite photo above it of all these fuck-bois in suits and ties.

Lipstick on a pig.

The next room is almost as empty, except for a large wooden bar piled high with thirty racks of the usual suspects: Pabst Blue Ribbon and a bunch of Lights—Coors, Keystone and Natural.

I grab a Natty and head back to the other room.

"Hello, everyone." An older guy steps onto a makeshift stage at the far end of the room. There's a slight ruffling sound as everyone turns to look. The boy smiles, and his blue eyes sparkle. "My name is Peter, and I'm honored to welcome you to the Delta

Tau Chi house. I know some of you are still filtering in, and that's all right, but I just wanted to take a second to say hello and hopefully put you at ease." His eyes scan the room as he speaks, like he's talking to each of us and none of us. "Some of you may understand the Rush process, but for others this may be new…" His eyes reach me, and he falls silent for a second. He looks at the floor, and shakes his head before looking up with a picture-perfect smile and beginning again. "Basically we'll spend this week hanging out and getting to know you guys, and then we'll vote and some of you will be asked to join us on a Rush Retreat this weekend. After that we'll vote again, and those young men will be invited to pledge. If you have any questions at all, feel free to ask an active—that's what we call current members. Thank you. Have a great night."

He steps off the stage to light applause, and people return to their small clusters of conversation.

Do I walk up and introduce myself to someone? Or hang back and let them come to me, like I'm too laid-back to do the whole ass-kissing thing?

"Hey there." I turn around to see a short but muscular guy. His hair is spiked, like he's trying to pick up a few inches any way he can.

"Hi," I say.

"I'm Jackson," he says.

"Cassie."

I switch my beer to my left hand so I can shake his with my right. "You a freshman?"

"Yeah." He smiles, like he doesn't know that answer should be given timidly. I nod and look past him, trying not to be rude, but knowing I should be talking to upperclassmen. I'm working right now; I don't have time to chitchat.

"What's that, a Natty Light? Interesting choice."

"Thanks." I give him a smile. "I've always thought that,

of the shitty beer, Natty is the best. It knows what it is and owns it. It tastes like water, but who cares, you barely paid anything, and we all know taste's not why you're buying it." I take a sip before continuing. "Now, other cheap beers, they put this fake 'beer flavoring' in, because it's too cheap to naturally taste like beer. But that fake stuff is what tastes so bad. They should just admit what they are, an inexpensive, tasteless beer, you know?"

He looks at his own Keystone, his eyebrows drawing together. "I guess so."

He starts to say something else, but from across the room I catch Jordan's eye, and everything else fades to a blurry buzz. He sees me, too, and looks confused, if not kind of…heartbroken.

Do I go say something?

No, we just met. There's no way that sad look in his eyes is about me, right?

Someone taps my shoulder. "Excuse me." I turn around to see the boy from the stage. My blond friend and baseball-cap guy from sign-in loiters behind him.

"So sorry to interrupt. I'm Peter Ford, chapter president. I was wondering if we could have a quick word."

Whoops, already in trouble.

I nod and turn back to Jackson, raising my hand in a small wave before following Peter up the stairs.

He looks like he'd be president of a frat. Much better dressed and carrying himself with more confidence than the rest. Charismatic and handsome, the type of guy adults would say was going places but with a little bit of player still mixed in. Like the college equivalent of JFK.

"That was quite the analysis of beer," he says as we climb the stairs.

I shrug. "I like to party, but I'm also a huge nerd, what can I say?"

He laughs. "Well, welcome to Warren Greek Life," he says, spreading his arms.

And for the first time, I feel a small bit of hope that I might actually like it here.

We reach the top of the stairs and pass a calendar that features a photo of a different topless model every month. August's is licking a popsicle in a way that...well, let's just say it wouldn't be the typical way someone might enjoy an ice-cream treat.

Aaaaaand my brief feeling of hope is gone.

Peter gestures for me to enter one of the bedrooms. The blond and baseball-cap guy follow, and finally Mr. President himself. He closes the door behind him and crosses his arms.

I glance around this room. Luckily there are no sexy calendars, just an American flag and a Warren ROTC poster. The rest of the room is pretty minimalist: navy bedding and a desk stacked with books and a large protein powder container. It's a very *boy* room.

The two henchmen flop onto the bed. I take the desk chair.

"Is this some sort of stunt?" Peter studies me.

"No." I stand up and straighten my dress, pulling on the short hem. "Um... I know this seems weird, but my dad was a DTC, and he always talks about it being the best time of his life. He didn't have any sons to carry on his legacy, and he kind of raised me as a boy because of it, buying me video games instead of Barbies, and playing catch instead of going to the daddy-daughter dance." From the DTC alumni websites, I know that the whole legacy thing is a huge deal. Like, if I was Chase Davis instead of Cassie, they'd be in big trouble for denying me a bid.

I clear my throat, and they don't jump in, so I continue. "I know that if I want to party in college I've got to go Greek..."

Everything I know about Alex and life in general is counter to this, but one of the DTC frat members tweeted it once. "But I've always been friends with dudes more than girls, and, honestly, shotgunning beers and throwing amazing parties sounds a lot better than wearing pearls and baking cookies."

These aren't *all* lies. It's true that my dad was a DTC, but he would definitely not be a fan of me doing this. And I do happen to like a lot of things gendered toward men—beer, baseball, *Call of Duty*—although I also like boy bands, Nora Ephron movies and cheesy prom-posals.

"Are there rules against it?" Peter asks the two boys on the bed.

"No," I interject, holding my head high. "I checked." I smile to soften it. I figure the name of the game is to have enough alpha confidence to demand their respect but enough softness so as not to rub against their perception of how a woman should behave.

The mission is to find out how living inside the environment of a frat house is for women, so when I'm inside I will *be* a woman, a real human person. I will be, as much as possible, "myself" as I would be if I wasn't conducting this experiment, so I can get the most accurate result.

But first I need to get inside.

So, not unlike a lot of people here, I will lie my way through Rush. *Hi, my name is Cassie, and I will be reading for the role of frat boy's wet dream.*

It feels kind of gross, like I'm betraying my sex. Or like I'm playing a character out of some porno.

But I remind myself of the higher cause, buckle down and silently repeat, like a mantra: *pizza, beer, video games, boobs.*

After extensive research on Reddit and Urban Dictionary, these are the things I decided.

I will be a size four but eat burgers and pizza.

I will not be a bimbo, like the rest of those dyed-blonde, fake-tanned sorority girls. But I won't be smart enough to threaten the boys' ego or intelligence.

I will be feminine looking but not stereotypically feminine.

I will drink cheap beer like water.

I will get fucked up, and seem to be queen of all drinking games, but somehow never be an emotional or sloppy drunk.

I will like nerdy things like sci-fi movies but look more like gold-bikini Leia than the female equivalent of Peter Parker.

I will be sexual but not. Always down to talk about masturbating or threesomes but never do either. I will be flirty and hot, but never have sex myself. Otherwise I risk being demoted from "guys' girl" to "group-ho."

I will love sports and action movies. And I will know more about all these things than the boys do, even if I don't always show it, so I don't become a "fake guys'-girl," which is the worst offense, because then they'll know I'm just doing this so they'll like me.

And then there's the most important part: to give no fucks.

To be the kind of girl guys would let into their frat, you need to "not care what anyone thinks" and "do what you want," while making sure what you "want" is to do everything in a stereotypically masculine way.

The whole idea of this cool girl is to hollow a woman out to just her body—the part they see the most value in—and then fill her with the things they think are worth something.

The title "one of the guys" is an honor. And it's sexist as hell.

I flutter my fake eyelashes and look up at Peter with a sweet, mischievous smile, like I'm considering sharing a secret with him and him only.

On the inside, I'm trying not to vomit.

"Well, in that case, I don't see why not," he says.

The blond guy looks shocked. Baseball-cap guy is laughing his ass off.

"You'll have to earn your bid like the rest of them, but I don't see why you can't try," Peter adds.

The blond stands up. "She'll mess with the rest of Rush, distract the other pledges."

Peter turns to me. "Don't do that."

I laugh. "No problem."

"There'll be sorority girls here, so just don't draw too much attention to yourself, and the other rushees shouldn't even notice."

I nod.

"Good luck, pledge. Now get your ass back downstairs. It's members-only on the second floor."

chapter five

"ONE OF THE GREATEST HURDLES FOR SOCIOLOGY is the Hawthorne effect, when subjects alter their behavior because they know they're being studied. The effect referenced in the name comes from a study about productivity, when, as you might guess, workers picked up their pace when they knew they were being watched."

My Sociology 101 professor, an eighty-year-old woman in a navy pantsuit, slips off her reading glasses, and looks out to the class, an auditorium of freshmen (mainly) and seniors (more than there should be) who almost forgot they had to fulfill this requirement.

"This is a bit like how cell phone usage might go down in this class if there was a team of scientists filming you instead of just a half-blind old bat at the front of the room. But then again, I still see, say, you there in the third row with the blue phone case."

Everyone shifts in their seats. The boy in question turns red, and a few people laugh.

"Tell your mother I say hello. I do hope the only person you felt the need to contact during my class is the woman who brought you into this world. Otherwise, do put it away."

He sheepishly slides the phone into his backpack.

"Now, where was I?" She puts her glasses back on. "Oh, yes. The Hawthorne effect. So now, knowing this, it makes sense to conduct some studies covertly, although, that of course carries its own array of risks..."

The door in the back of the room swings open, but luckily, Professor Abbott is too engrossed in her notes to notice.

I see someone walking down the aisle out of the corner of my eye, but I am too terrified of my tiny, fierce professor to look.

"Excuse me," a familiar voice whispers.

My heart skips a beat as Jordan shimmies past the rest of the people in my row and settles into the seat next to me.

I steal a glance. He's fishing through his backpack for a notebook, so luckily he doesn't see me staring. He's wearing a checkered button-down and light blue shorts, impeccably dressed for a nine o'clock class. And he looks *good*, like so good I have a weird feeling in the pit of my stomach. I was hoping he wouldn't live up to the memory I had replayed in my mind as I lay in bed the night before. But instead he's even more beautiful than I remembered. I'm painfully aware of how close he's sitting to me, scared I'll give myself away, like he'll hear my breath catch or my heart race.

He looks over, and my eyes dart to the front of the room, where Professor Abbott is rambling on about things that honestly would probably be very helpful for me to know. But I can't focus, can't hear anything but my own heart beating wildly.

I keep my eyes forward as he leans over and whispers, "You could've just told me you were going to DTC."

I glance over. "I didn't know what to say."

He stares at me like he's trying to figure something out. Then he shakes his head and turns to his notebook.

He doesn't say anything for the rest of class, taking notes in tiny, neat handwriting and meticulously organized columns.

My own notes are an appalling scrawled mix of cursive and printing, sometimes veering off the lines.

When the lecture ends, he leaves without saying anything to me.

Okay, then, bye.

I head out into the fresh air and feel a bit better in the California sun. I cut through the sandstone quad, past the dry fountain and toward the coffee shop.

I am here, I keep telling myself, but it doesn't seem real as I walk through scenery I'm used to seeing on postcards.

I grab a cappuccino so I won't be too dead for my first meeting with the professor who will be helping me with my independent study.

My project coordinator, an uptight blonde from the Upper East Side who's constantly checking one of her countless social media accounts on one of her two smartphones, is not my favorite person. We've had several Skype meetings, and she is always wearing designer business wear and telling me that this topic "is so hot right now" and "will generate so much buzz" once we go public. That's her favorite word, I think, *buzz*. She truly sounds like a bee during most of our calls. It just worries me that she doesn't seem to care what people will say about the project as long as they're saying something.

But I do have to give it to her; she hooked me up with about the best faculty adviser in the history of ever. I've been a fan of her for years, reading her entire body of work the summer I first heard about her, and impatiently anticipating the release of everything she's done since. One of the top women's studies professors in the world, and she's going to sit for an hour a week and listen to me rant about frats. I almost feel bad for her.

The imposing door in front of me opens. A beautiful, tall black woman smiles at me. She's wearing a patterned dress that complements her headscarf. She looks polished and smart, but also like she exudes sunshine. A bit different from the salt-and-pepper-haired old men in heavy black and navy suits who teach so many of the classes here.

"Hello, I'm Dr. Eva Price."

I know. I've read all your books. "Cassie Davis."

"Would you like something to drink? Coffee, water, juice?" she asks as she leads me into her office.

There is a grand dark-wood desk, and ornate bookshelves overflowing with easily hundreds of books, as well as vases and boxes covering every available surface.

Most notable are the pictures on the wall behind her desk, so that when she sits she's flanked by photographs of her at the Fruitvale Station protests, holding a sign outside the Supreme Court during *Roe v. Wade*, meeting Malala on the floor of the UN, deep in conversation with Nelson Mandela, shaking hands with the president of the United States. *Jesus.*

She sits, and so do I, feeling about an inch tall. There is no way she should be taking on my project. She's light-years too big for this.

"Well, I'm going to make myself some tea, if you don't mind." She grabs a mug off her shelf.

Speechless, I nod. It's always odd to see larger-than-life people do such mundane things.

She settles into her chair. "So, I know this is the last thing you want to hear right now, but as feminists— You do consider yourself a feminist, yes?"

"Yes, of course."

"Good. I always like to avoid the whole 'feminism means

equality' conversation when I can. You do not understand, Ms. Davis, how exhausting it is to have to urge young women to align themselves with a movement that simply fights for their dignity."

She takes a sip of her tea. "So, as I was saying. As feminists, I don't know if this is exactly what we want to or need to be getting behind right now, and I know that's scary to hear. But I think as a researcher, an activist, or a writer, that sort of self-reflection, continuously asking yourself, *Why am I doing this? Is this the best way to go about it? Is this what the cause needs right now?* is endlessly important.

"When it comes to creating a just world, you have two main fights, in my opinion. There's the legal and the social. Do you know the slogan 'the personal is political'?" She gets up and scans her shelves, finally grabbing a book and handing it to me before she sits back down.

"It comes from second-wave feminism," she says. "The idea that we aren't just fighting for the vote, which we had by that time. It meant that the issues women continually face in personal relationships, like gender roles in the traditional family, are a huge social problem and not isolated incidences. It's similar to the philosophy that microaggressions—those little acts of prejudice, like asking a biracial person 'what they are' or touching a black woman's head in public because you want to feel her natural hair, or assuming all Hispanic people are Mexican—can add up to become a major contribution to the continuation of systematic oppression."

She pauses, probably to see if I'm still following, so I nod.

"And while I don't think people are wrong when they say that these little things are unjust, I sometimes worry that people will think the fight is over if we talk about them too much. Like they think all that's left of racism is a rude comment about my hair being frizzy when there are people of color being shot by police and imprisoned at alarming rates. Because as much as it bothers me that working women still spend more time doing housework than their husbands who work the same or fewer hours outside the house, there are still places in the world where women can't vote or safely seek an education. So, which battles do we choose?"

"Why can't we…uh, do both?"

She nods like I've made a comment as articulate as hers, when in reality I'm struggling to even say anything. "That's the problem with the social side, right? Because the legal one is clear, you just get the votes. But the social aspect is so controlled by humans and the ways they react. You can't force people to act a certain way, so we have to play the game a little bit or else people won't listen. For example, in 1955 a pregnant teenager gets kicked off a bus. That could've been the beginning of the bus boycott. But that's not very good PR, to have a pregnant teen as the face of the movement. So they wait. As a feminist, that enrages me. But they were right. In 1950s America, that movement had enough challenges without adding to it. So they wait for Rosa Parks, a grandmother, and the world is changed. But no grade-schooler will ever be in a skit about Claudette Colvin.

"You think only the bad guys have to spin, but when you are trying to change the world, you have to remember that social systems are made of people, and you have to sneak in change like giving vegetables to a child, make it easy to swallow at first. Because if you're too blunt with the privileged, they will shut you down before you begin. So we have to worry about what our movement looks like, unfortunately. We have to care what people think of feminism, so it's not written off."

She pauses to pour herself a second cup of tea. "If it was up to me, fraternities wouldn't exist. It's that simple. I think they're bad for almost every marginalized community—

women, black people, LGBTQA people. But…do I want the next piece of academia with my name on it to say that? Or to say something about education for young women under the Taliban? Am I shying away from it, even though it's important, because it may be controversial? That would be bad. Or am I shying away from it because there are more important things to focus on and I would needlessly push away those who might otherwise be allies? I just don't know."

She's quiet for a while, sipping her tea.

"So, um, with all due respect…" I catch myself nervously playing with the hem of my skirt. I fold my hands in my lap. "Why'd you take on my project?"

"I'm a researcher, Ms. Davis, so I don't say no when I'm unsure. I investigate. In this case, you seem better suited to investigate than I would be, but I *would* like to help you. I guess what I'm saying is, I'm not asking you to go in there and find out if this system is messed up. I need you to go in there and find out if the system is messed up *enough* that we need to make it our next priority. Is that all right with you?"

I nod furiously. "Yes, absolutely."

"Excellent. Let's get started." She stands, leans down and picks up a large crate, setting it down on the desk with a thud.

"I had one of my assistants compile the research on fraternities, women and minorities, and women and minorities on college campuses more generally. I suggest you get started as soon as possible."

I pick up an article off the top; it's from CNN.com and entitled "Are Frats an 'American Apartheid'?"

"I also have arranged for a series of interviews with average Warren students. They won't find out what the study is about until they have decided to participate and signed a nondisclosure agreement, of course, to maintain the objectivity of the study. And while you'll be involved, you obviously can't be in the room without giving your cover away, so we'll figure out something with that. But I thought it'd be best to have the greatest breadth of information possible for background."

I nod.

"Let's do our due diligence, pay attention to nuance and see exactly what this problem is and what the best course of action may be."

Her words still ring in my ears as I practically skip across campus, pulling out my phone to text Jay and Alex.

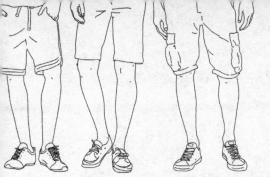

chapter six

I'M LEANING AGAINST THE BACK PORCH OF DELTA
Tau Chi, sipping a Natty and looking out at the lake, when a
familiar-looking guy walks up to me.

"Hi, I'm Marco," he says. He's tall and athletic looking,
with tan skin, beautiful in an all-American way, with broad
shoulders and a strong jawline.

"Cassie," I say. I don't think I know any Marcos, but I can't
shake the feeling that I've seen him before.

He has a clipboard full of questions, like all the other actives, but slips it under his arm.

The Rush party has just begun, and people are mostly still
milling about, some aggressively kissing ass, while others seem
to be working up the courage to talk to an active. I went for
the "this is all beneath me" vibe and have been just hanging
out.

"Are you having a good time?" Marco asks.

"Moderately," I say. "How about you?"

He smiles. "Yeah, this time of year, everything feels very forced, you know?"

I nod.

"Things should be fun and simple." He reaches out and tucks a strand of hair behind my ear.

"Torres!" someone across the way yells. "Where's the vodka?"

"My room—fridge!" he yells back.

And I realize how I know him. I've seen that name on the back of a jersey. I'm talking to the quarterback of the Warren football team.

"Shots?" he says, turning back to me.

I shrug. "I'm more of a tequila girl, but I'll settle."

He raises his eyebrows. "Tequila it is."

My phone buzzes, and I'm looking down to check it when he says, "So, Cassie, have you ever done body shots?"

I look up, and for a second, although my mouth is open, no words come out. "I—"

"Hey, Marco." Peter is walking over to us, smiling.

He pulls Marco aside and whispers to him.

"Really?" Marco says.

Peter nods.

"Well…" Marco says, walking over to me, "I've just been informed you're not a Delta but a possible pledge, so I guess I should be vetting you instead."

I want to say, *Instead of what?* But I know the answer and have no interest in making the moment more awkward than it is.

"Okay, then. Let's do this." He pulls out his clipboard and flips the pages. "Um, okay." He scratches his head. "Well, the question I'm supposed to ask all the pledges tonight is, 'Where did it happen?' Meaning, uh, like where did you fu—make love for the first time. It's, uh, meant to be ambiguous to mess with the pledges, so they aren't sure how to answer. But, uh, we can skip over that."

"No, it's fine." I wave my hand. "I don't want to be treated any differently than anyone else."

"Uh, okay."

"It hasn't happened yet for me, but the first time I did… like, other stuff, it was in a car."

He raises his eyebrows and nods, giving off an aura of professional interest. "All right, then. Sooo…what teams do you root for?"

After I tell him my preferences—football: Colts; hockey: Blackhawks; baseball: White Sox—we cover my favorite cheap beer: Natty; nice beer: Corona, with lime; and drinking game: "Does shotgunning count? Okay, then Rage Cage."

"Kate Upton or Scarlett Johansson?" becomes "Channing Tatum or Chris Hemsworth?" and I ask why not both.

"Ass or boobs? Um, let's say abs or arms?"

"Hmm, I feel like that's not quite equivalent."

"I know, right?"

I try not to laugh as I watch the genuine struggle of this athletic god as he flips through the pages of his questionnaire, trying to figure out the heterosexual female equivalent of ass versus boobs.

He calls in backup, and before you know it, we've got a running back, two wide receivers and half the d-line gathered around. The other freshmen are throwing daggers.

"Some girls like nice hair, like the boy-band types," one guy says.

They all nod in agreement.

"You'd be surprised how insane girls can go about calves," another suggests. "That's why I never skip leg day."

"Calves or hair? Is that for real what we're going with?" Marco asks.

"No, no, no," star wide receiver Donald Stewart says. "Y'all are being ridiculous. You know as well as I do that it's all about the D. We might not like to admit it, but you know it's true."

I almost spit out my beer.

"Hold on." Stewart holds up his hands. "I'm texting my girlfriend." Everyone leans in. "She says, 'What is wrong with you?'" He stares at the screen indignantly. "Nothin', baby, just trying to value your opinion, my God."

"I think women focus in less on one feature," I say. "So it's hard to compare. I think as a girl you kind of find someone attractive more as their entire appearance, and also, like, their personality, the way they carry themselves."

"Yeah, why *do* we focus on one thing so much?" Donald says. And for a second I think they might be about to have a breakthrough, to realize the difference between appreciating the sexuality and beauty of people and objectifying them and reducing them to one body part.

"Why do we even have to pick between ass or boobs?"

"Yeah, why not *both*?"

Aaaand they missed the point.

"We should start a revolution."

"Hashtag assandboobs?" I say drily.

They all laugh.

"What's going on out here?" Peter steps out onto the porch.

"We're changing the world," Marco says.

"Ass and boobs, Mr. President," Donald says with dreamy eyes. "Just picture it, ass *and* boobs."

"Get back to your freshmen." He shakes his head in dismay but is still smiling.

———

I'm barely back in my dorm when my phone buzzes. It's a text from an unrecognized number.

J: Freshman! It's been great to get to know you. A few of us are going to get sushi/go sake bombing tomorrow at 8. Meet @ the house but don't tell anyone. We don't need a dirty Rush violation and neither do you. Keep it real—Jake (I'm the Rush chair always wearing a hat)

Yes! One step closer to a bid and, in turn, securing my scholarship.

I lock the door, then grab my laptop on my way to bed. From my desk, someone—and by someone I mean Leighton—could read over my shoulder if they opened the door. But when I sit on my bed I can position myself against the wall and gain some privacy.

I open a private browsing session so nothing shows up in my history and go to the Stevenson website. I log in using my password and a verification code sent to my phone, and open the folder for my field journal entries.

The journal was Madison Macey's idea. The Stevenson people loved the personal experience part of my proposal, and they want a lot of my voice. What it's like to piss in a bathroom that has urinals, how the guys eat, and so on. The color of the story, as they say. "The fluff" is what Price calls it.

No Files Uploaded. Well, at least for now.

Entry 1, I type.

Entry 1: The fraternity Rush process seems wholly superficial. Perspective members compete for the attention of actives by "bonding" over objectifying women, whether it be ranking the school's women's sports teams on attractiveness or debating the virtues of Kim Kardashian's rear end vs. Nicki Minaj's.

Potential New Members (PNMs) also recount their sexual exploits to impress the actives, who seem to value the number of women a PNM has slept with as a good indication of whether he will fit. The phenomenon of "Eskimo brothers"—a term used to describe two men who have had intercourse with the same woman based on quasi-historical misunderstandings of Inuit practices of polyamory by young men throughout the country—seems to be the pinnacle of this ranking system.

Drinking to extreme levels is also valued, second only to sexual prowess.

Sororities are often invited to these events and encouraged to speak to PNMs in a move that seems to associate interactions with these women as a possible benefit of membership. Rush posters often advertise sorority guests alongside food—e.g., the lovely ladies of KAD and sushi, or Pi Beta, steaks and cigars.

An hour later, I submit my entry and close my computer.

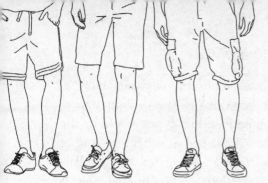

chapter seven

"I DON'T THINK I CAN DO IT." I STARE UP AT THE
rock wall, arching toward the ceiling.

The sun is just beginning to set beyond the windows that
make up the opposite wall, and it's casting a pink-orange glow
on the stone surface.

People scramble up and down, hopping between footholds
that seem way too far apart.

"Nonsense," Jackie says. She looks different without her
glasses and hipster clothes, wearing athletic shorts and a tank
instead. "You're gonna be a natural. I can tell by looking at
you."

I look at her and the biceps that seem almost comical on
her petite frame. I turn back to the other climbers. Some are
her teammates, using the same blue-and-gold gear she's strap-
ping herself into. Others, like me, have rented gear from the
gym, but they're all lean men with beards and women with
remarkable arms—your classic granola-eating climber types.

People who are actually naturals at this.

"Have you seen me?" I turn and flex my nonexistent muscles.

She laughs. "I'm serious, you think it'd be all about upper-body strength, like the big bodybuilder types would be the best. But petite girls are actually the most suited, because of their low center of gravity. You've got to have the right balance of flexibility and core strength, and traditional athletes don't always have that."

"Hmm, a sport I actually have the possibility of being good at."

She smiles. "Exactly."

She explains the basics as she straps me into my harness. "Okay." She pats me on the shoulder. "You are good to go."

By the time I've managed to get both feet off the ground, albeit only about a foot up, she's strapped herself in and started scrambling up the wall like some sort of small forest creature.

"C'mon, you can do it," she yells down to me.

I stumble my way toward the top. Jackie scales the entire thing and rappels back down before I make it halfway.

She starts up for a second time and catches up to me at about the three-quarter point.

"I'm stuck." I readjust my feet by a few centimeters; they feel like they might go numb. My fingertips scream, sick of supporting so much of my body weight.

"See that red one, at about your knee?" she says.

I nod but don't turn toward her, my eyes on the rocks.

"That's your next step. It's kind of small, so you're only going to be able to fit one foot, and you're going to want to move on quickly."

My eyes dart from the red rock to my feet, then to the ground far below. "Shit. Maybe I should just rappel down."

"Nah, you've made it this far—no way this one will be hard for you."

Grunting, I lift my right foot to the tiny red rock. All my

weight on my right toes, I push myself up and then grab higher rocks with my left hand, then my right. I scramble to get my feet onto two bigger rocks a bit above the rest.

"Nice!" Jackie climbs up to my level.

"You sound so excited. I thought you said that part was nothing."

"Are you kidding? That's the hardest part of this course! Took me three tries to get past it."

I roll my eyes and keep moving.

We both tap the ceiling before rappelling back down.

"This is actually pretty fun, once you get past the part where you think you're gonna die," I say once my feet are back on the ground.

"I know, right? It's a pretty cool workout. A great place to think, you know? I like how metaphorical it is. Making progress, reaching higher."

"Yeah. I guess so." I hadn't really thought about it as something so...deep. It was just a sport, after all. "But you don't actually go anywhere."

"That's true. But that doesn't mean it doesn't matter." She reaches down to adjust her harness. "Like, there are these Tibetan monks who make these amazing sand paintings, spend weeks with their backs bent over them, working in excruciating detail. And when they're done, they wash them all away. That's climbing—you have all this progress, you reach higher just long enough to take a breath, and then you come back down."

I took up at the wall, at the almost-gone sun, then back to her.

"But that's also life." She places one foot on the wall, ready to go again. "You try so hard to live as much as you can, to grow and change and develop, and maybe inspire the same thing in the people around you, but you know that either way, you and everything you do and everyone you meet will be dust in the end."

She starts climbing again. I stand there for a minute, dumb-founded, before I follow her.

I hate how snobby it makes me feel to say it, but I would never have had a conversation like that with the kids at my old school. They were plenty smart, but not in a daring way, in a get-good-grades-to-get-a-good-job way.

Sure, they knew more when they left school than when they started, about the mitochondria being the powerhouse of the cell, and the green light representing Gatsby's desire, but they had the same opinions on politics and religion and life as they did freshman year and, for God's sake, as their parents had before them.

It's not a lack of intelligence; it's a lack of curiosity. There was none of the thirst for knowledge like you can see radiating from people like Alex, like Jackie.

I wanted to be like that. That's why I left. I needed to look for more than what the kids talked about at home—who was dating who and where the next my-parents-are-out-of-town party would be—I just knew if I stayed much longer, I'd suffocate. But I wasn't sure if I'd ever be smart enough to have anything real to say.

We make it to the top again, and I take a deep breath.

"You're right—this is pretty amazing."

"Again?" she asks when we reach the ground. She smiles, and it lights up her whole face.

"I have to go soon," I say. "I have dinner with a family friend at eight," I lie.

She nods and picks up her water bottle, the official one all the athletes are given, a status symbol. She raises it to her lips for a second, then scrunches her nose. "Empty."

We leave the climbing area and head to the general gym.

"Ugh," she says as the glass door closes behind us.

"What?"

"I forgot the athletic gyms are closed today because of training limits. Which means all the meatheads are at the Muggle gym."

I look around the room, and sure enough, the whole place is littered with giant men lifting weights. Not exactly your typical Warren student.

We push past all the scrawny freshmen loitering at the edge of the room and wait in line at the watercooler.

Jackie is reaching for the faucet when a brick wall of a guy steps in front of her.

"Hey, dude, there *is* a line!"

He doesn't turn around.

She reaches up to tap him on his shoulder. He swats behind him, like Jackie's hand is a fly, before looking over his shoulder. I recognize Duncan, the football player from down the hall. "What?" He takes out one earbud.

"There's a line."

He laughs and continues to fill his bottle. "I'm in the middle of varsity conditioning. I think I need it a little more than you and whatever elliptical crap you're doing."

My jaw drops. I turn back to Jackie.

"For your information, I'm an athlete, too," she says, then stands taller and shows him her water bottle.

"Okay." He laughs. He screws the cap back on his bottle and then pulls out his phone, taking his time to select a new song while he continues to block our way to the water, his chest in a sweat-stained shirt like a wall.

Finally he steps away, shoving his phone back toward his pocket but missing and slipping it into a fold in the fabric instead. It clatters to the floor, ripped from his headphones, and slides across the linoleum to my feet.

Duncan turns around, panicking.

"Don't worry—the screen didn't crack." I step forward to

hand it to him. I glance at the screen for only a second, but long enough to see that the song he had chosen was by One Direction.

"Nice taste in music." I press the phone into his hand.

He turns white as a ghost. "You can't— Oh my God." He grabs my arm and pulls me farther away from the watercooler. "You can't tell anyone." His voice is earnest.

"What? That you were super-rude to us? You didn't seem bothered by that a minute ago."

"About, you know, that playlist. My sister bought the songs, and, I don't know, I just kind of like them, but my teammates can't know, okay? So don't say anything."

He seems genuinely freaked, so I resist the urge to laugh.

"Yes, sure, calm down. I'm not gonna tell anyone. I really don't care."

"Okay, thank you." His shoulders drop half an inch as he relaxes.

"Whatever." I walk back to Jackie.

God, masculinity is fragile.

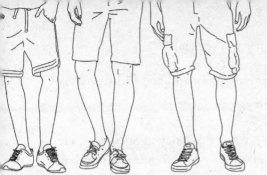

chapter eight

RUSH CONTINUES TO PASS WITHOUT A HITCH. WHEN
the first weekend and the first round of cuts comes out, I'm
one of the few who receives an invitation to the Delta Tau Chi
Rush Retreat. Luckily, the email invitation also mentions that
the members of Pi Beta will be joining us, so hopefully I will
be able to continue inconspicuously, or, at least, less conspicu-
ously than if I was the only girl.

When I was at Catholic school, "retreat" meant three days
at a sleepaway camp, holding hands, praying, lighting candles
and sharing secrets.

I have a feeling that's not what we'll be doing.

It's six thirty in the morning and cool, because the sun hasn't
burned off the haze when we line up to get on the buses.
They're big yellow ones, rented from the local elementary
school.

Four actives are loading countless cases of beer through the
handicap entrance in the back.

I spot Jordan as I'm climbing on board, and I instinctively smile and raise my hand to wave.

He looks away.

Jordan hasn't spoken to me since that day in Sociology. He always comes in late and sits as far away from me as possible. I'm not quite sure what I did. I mean, I get we're competitors now, but that doesn't seem like a reason to treat me like a pariah. We could both end up here, and then what?

So maybe he isn't mad. Maybe he isn't anything.

That's not only more likely; it almost seems worse, that he isn't mad but just doesn't care at all.

Which is fine, I guess. It gives me the chance to stay focused, to play my role perfectly.

I lose him as we pile on the bus, me sitting near the Pi Betas but still with the DTC guys.

"This is *so* much better than our house retreats," a bottle blonde with a blue Pi Beta tank stretched across her white-bikini-clad, fake-tanned breasts tells her friend.

"I think we just went to get our nails done my year," her brunette friend answers.

"Ugh, you are so lucky." She flips her hair. "We sat in the house basement, where we had to recite some weird poem, and then we passed around a candle and told first-kiss stories."

"Oh my God, I remember that!" a girl behind me yells. I turn instinctively. She has bright red hair and porcelain doll features.

A sorority with a white girl with brown hair, a white girl with red hair and a white girl with blond hair? *Now that's what I call diversity.*

"Good thing we do ours after Rush," the blonde says. "Otherwise I would have been, like, fuck this shit."

The brunette nods in agreement.

The blonde turns toward me, leaning across her friend. "I'm sure yours will be a lot better."

"I'll make sure of that," the redhead says. She pops up from her seat behind me and leans on the back of mine. "I'm Pledge Mom!"

Suddenly I'm surrounded by Greek letters and hair bows. The smell of tanning lotion and cheap beer is making me nauseous.

I open my mouth to explain, but the words elude me.

"Hey, I'm so sorry, cuz this is so rude of me, but what's your name?" Blondie asks.

"Cassandra Davis. Cassie." The words stumble out. I should explain I'm not pledging, but how do I?

"Cool! I'm Kelley, I'm the new president." She splays a French-manicured hand over her heart. "My apologies, I'm still getting to know all our little babies."

"Oh, I'm not a—"

"Oh! Are you the girl who transferred from the Cal Alpha chapter?" The redhead practically bounces up and down with every word. "I didn't mean to call you a frosh."

"My brother goes to Berkeley, too!" the brunette adds.

"No, I go here."

Kelley nudges her friend. "Katie, don't be rude." She leans over her to me again. "Welcome! She just meant, like, you used to go there."

"No, I'm a freshman, I'm just—"

Something changes in her eyes. The pageant sparkle drops out of them. "Wait, you *are* a Pi Beta pledge, right?"

"Uh, no."

They look at each other, their heads turning exactly in sync, like they share one brain.

The blonde purses her lips and turns her head to the side. "Not to, you know—but, um, who invited you?"

"The guys," I say. Not a lie. I was actually invited quite formally, with a letter slipped under my door.

The one behind me sits so quickly the cheap bus seat makes a weird swooshing sound.

The others shrink away from me, back into their own side of the aisle.

"Classic DTC—Warren girls aren't hot enough for them," the brunette tells Kelley.

Like I can't hear them.

"Always on to the new blood." Kelley cuts her eyes at me. "It happens every year with Rush. The upperclassmen always warn you, but the sophomores never listen. The events become all about the *hot new girls*, and the actives end up standing there like, hello, we're still here. At least it used to be *our* littles, though. Now they're just shipping in girls to fuck."

Ew, ew, *ew.*

I want to defend myself but don't even know where to begin. That I'm not trying to sleep with them. That I'm not even trying to be friends with them. That I'm just trying to expose the fucked-up-ness of a system that has these girls saying stuff like that.

We used to be the whores of this frat, and now what are we? Just the madams?

So much for sisterhood.

They're part of an organization that's supposed to lift up women, not pit them against each other, and for what? To get the attention of some spoiled undergrad drunk off his ass and threatening to fight everything that moves, knowing Daddy can cover the legal fees?

I turn silently to face the front of the bus.

The doors finally close, and people start to pass the beer around. Some DTCs fiddle with the radio for a bit, struggling to get anything but static.

Music erupts from the speaker just as the overloaded bus lurches forward.

I chug beers and take shots of Fireball like a pro at eight in the morning as we head down the 101.

Someone yells something about shotgunning, and I stand up.

Someone else hands me a can of Natty.

"Does anyone have a key?" the guy in front of me asks. He has coifed hair and is wearing expensive brand names, even though we're all dressed for the beach.

"Here, like this," I say. I hold up my can and use my canine tooth to make a hole, just like Alex showed me once.

His eyes go wide like quarters. "Did anyone else see that?" he asks, turning around to address the crowd.

"Do it again!" he says, handing me his beer. I laugh, a feminine, sly laugh, not at all like my naturally loud, brash one.

I do it again, this time with an audience. After I bite it, I make the whole bigger with my thumb carefully so not to cut it, and then lick the beer off.

"Yes, that's my Cassie! Killin' it!" Marco yells from the front of the bus.

I blow him a kiss.

"All right, let's do this," I say, handing the boy his beer back.

I don't need to look at the girls to know they're seething. I catch myself smiling. God, their game is messed up, but it's pretty damn thrilling to beat them at it.

The alcohol starts to go down easier, and soon we're all standing and dancing, and the world is a swirling, beautiful, bright place. God, day drunk is the best.

The music cuts off in the middle of a song. Some people sit down; others just stand there, drunk and confused.

A skinny black guy in a Warren baseball cap stands at the front of the bus, a radio-style microphone in his hand.

"Aaaaattennnnntion, passengers. So, we're currently expe- riencing some technical difficulties, by which I mean Carter tripped over the aux cord when he went to throw up in the trash can that he—" our unofficial cruise director looks down "—seems to have missed anyway. All right, cool. We're work- ing on getting the radio back, but in the meantime, this is DJ Chase coming at you. Here's 'Trap Queen.'"

And then he not only sings every single word, but also mimics all the little electronic sounds.

Everyone kind of looks at one another, and then there's a silent agreement to roll with it.

We stand and dance again, and I can't stop laughing at Chase imitating Fetty Wap's voice, and how ridiculous and fun this shit show of a bus is.

They get the music back on after Chase's fifteen minutes, and everyone claps as he stands on his seat and bows. The bus driver starts to yell at him in Spanish, and he sits down sheepishly.

The shotgunning guy turns around. "What's your name again?"

"Cassie," I say, over the music.

"Sebastian." He shakes my hand.

"So how are you liking Pi Beta?"

I open my mouth to answer, but before I can, a shrieking sound rips through the bus. I turn around to see a member of Delta Tau Chi standing on his seat and urinating outside the window.

What he doesn't seem to realize in his apparent bliss is that the pee is coming back in the window a few rows back and spraying on a couple of traumatized Pi Betas in a rainbow of ruined designer bikinis. They scramble out of their seats, squealing.

"OMG, Vivian, that's your boyfriend! Do something!"

A petite blonde pushes through the aisle.

"The motherfucker's interned for NASA. I can't believe he doesn't understand that his pee will catch the wind."

The music cuts out, and Chase is back on the loudspeaker. "Attention, Mr. Harris, please sit down and refrain from urinating further until the bus has come to a complete stop."

We finally arrive at the beach, and there actually is a lot of peeing in the bushes by the guys and, God bless, a few girls who squat in the parking lot.

The guys unload the kegs, and when someone says we forgot cups, I get a fabulous idea.

That's how I end up doing a kegstand in a bikini as thirty people cheer me on and count (fifteen seconds, not bad for my first try) until I shake my head and am helped back to the ground, half laughing, half coughing.

I'm playing this role better than I ever thought I could.

And then something weird happens.

I realize I'm having real, genuine fun.

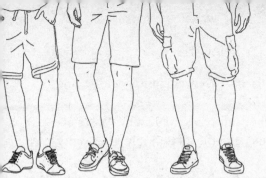

chapter nine

RUSH RETREAT LEAVES ME HUNGOVER AS SHIT FOR my first interview session.

I sit with my head in my hands in a room with cold metal walls and industrial lighting, and try to focus on not dying.

The room—"your home for the next year," as Professor Price referred to it in her email—is empty save for a stark metal desk and a big window on the opposite wall, a one-way look into the room on the other side, where study participants will see only a mirror.

I drag a small recycling bin from the corner of the room to the desk, just in case. I'm really hoping I don't throw up in this Nobel Prize winner's trash can, though. Even if my hangover was acquired in the name of our project.

There is no part of the project proposal that specified Fireball shots, you idiot.

I can't believe I actually thought that was fun yesterday. We laughed and laughed, but nothing was clever; nothing was actually funny. We weren't friends. We were just people getting fucked up near each other.

The digital clock on the wall reads 10:02 a.m. We're already almost an hour behind, and there's probably still twenty minutes until we begin.

Outside, volunteers from Price's class are having the subjects sign forms, taking down their information and lining them up in the order they'll enter.

They're being paid twenty dollars an hour, plus a free catered lunch.

Price stops by briefly to ask if I need anything before leaving to catch a plane and save the world.

I alternate sipping coffee, to try to bring myself out of the fog, and water, to try to hydrate and flush some of the toxins out of my body.

Exhaling, I open my MacBook.

So far, when I log in to my project portal there are only my journal entries and my notes on the books and studies about frats Professor Price has been having me read. Technically, that's all the Stevenson people wanted, but Price demanded funding for the interviews, because sneaking into one frat and having only their stories is not science, she said—it's reality TV.

I like it because we can see what they actually do versus what they say in the interviews. It's only a piece, but an important piece to develop a real picture of what these communities are like.

The idea is when the findings go public, people can read through my journal entries, with Price's scientific findings and commentary interspersed or in a sidebar. Keep the human element up front, Madison says. But then use the facts to show this isn't just me ranting, Price always qualifies.

I glance at the clock blinking on the edge of my screen.

I may as well work on the Kardashian element while I wait for the science.

In her most recent email, Madison told me my updates so far were "totally fab!" but asked if I could write an introductory entry.

Introduction:

I, Cassandra Davis, an eighteen-year-old girl, a freshman at Warren University and self-declared ardent feminist, am about to join a frat.

I'm doing so with funding from the Stevenson Foundation in order to study the culture of fraternities, which have long been a bastion of the university system, but have also become a center of controversy in regard to diversity in sex, race, sexuality and socioeconomic status. My study will focus on sexism and the treatment of women by these groups.

The fraternity I have chosen is Delta Tau Chi, the oldest frat in existence at Warren. The chapter is currently under probation for creating a "hostile environment for women." This is based on complaints last year about a party with a misogynistic theme.

But DTC has long been the center of the social scene on campus, and the incident has not altered that.

My intent is to get proof that this wasn't an isolated incident but rather evidence of a toxic culture. To find and expose the truth.

In order to ensure that the members of the fraternity do not discover my intent, no one knows about my experiment. Not my parents, no one in the frat, no one in any vicinity of Greek Life and no one in the administration. The only people besides myself who are aware of my project are my Stevenson project coordinator, Madison Macey, who lives on the other side of the country, and the renowned women's studies expert Eva Price, who is organizing interviews with students in and out of Greek Life.

That is, until you read this, and then the world will know, every friendship I've made here will end, and I'll become the most hated woman on campus.

I highlight and delete the last sentence. I don't get to care about the social life or reputation of "Cassie Davis, party girl who joined a frat and is aggressively fun." She's just a character, and the real me is just an observer, a scientist, an actor, a spy. My college experience gets to be nothing more than one giant social experiment. But considering the boys who thought an important get-to-know-you question was "Ass or tits?" and the girls clawing at each other for those idiots' attention, it seems like a small price to pay to end the madness.

A message pops up on my computer.

StephanieB@warren.edu: Ready when you are.

It's from the research assistant who'll be inside the room, asking the questions. She knows only about the interview portion of the experiment and thinks that's it.

She'll read from a script Professor Price and I developed, but depending on how the conversation turns, I can message her follow-up questions or deviations.

To her, my name is just "Observer 2." (Price gets to be Observer 1, of course. When she's here.)

I slip on the large black studio-style headphones and type back.

Observer2@warren.edu: Good to go.

The first interviewee is a quiet Hispanic girl. She sits directly across from Stephanie but keeps looking nervously at the mirror.

I smile instinctively, wanting to make her feel more at home. But, of course, she can't see me.

It turns out she's a freshman and, having skipped sorority Rush, has had no personal experience with Greek Life.

"My mom warned me against going to the frats, though. She read an article."

Her interview takes all of ten minutes.

Not the most valuable interview, but general opinion is important to get, too.

Great job! I message Stephanie. One down!

Hundreds to go, but at least not all of them today.

Person after person sits in the chair across from Stephanie. There was a lit club guy with sleeve tattoos who didn't understand why this study was occurring in the first place. "Do you realize how many more important issues there are? You guys should be talking about fracking, not this bullshit!"

With that, he got up and left. I wonder if he'll still help himself to the free lunch.

Then there was a junior, a member of a frat—not DTC—who wanted to talk at length about brotherhood and philanthropy, but was unable to remember if there were any racial minorities in his frat during his three years at school.

There was a young woman who, without hesitation, said that she loved to go to the frats on weekends for parties, but never alone. At which point I had to stop myself from yelling through the glass how royally messed up it is that she has to be on guard at a place where she's supposedly relaxing and having fun.

After a while everyone starts to blur together. I watch people rotate in and out of the chair until I'm dizzy. Watching the window starts to feel more like I'm watching TV, but really boring TV, like C-Span or something.

I watch for hours and hours, and my headset starts to hurt. The same barrage of questions starts to echo in my head.

Do you understand that this study is being done on a voluntary basis?

Are you or have you ever been part of a Greek letter organization?

Have you ever been to an event hosted by such an organization?

What are your perceptions of Greek organizations?

Do you believe them to be communities that are hostile toward women? Can you tell me about an experience where you found this perception to be true?

Can you think of one where the opposite happened?

How often do you feel the generalization holds true?

Have you ever been sexually assaulted? If so, by a member of a Greek organization? By a nonmember?

I'm drawn out of my trance when someone I recognize settles into the chair. She's one of Alex's lit club friends. A child of some of the original San Francisco flower children (a flower grandchild, if you will); her name is Lavender.

I wouldn't say that we're close friends, but we definitely know each other.

A chill goes down my spine. It's different when you're watching someone you know without them knowing you're there. With strangers, there's a sort of mutual anonymity, but the next time I see her at Dionysus, she'll have no idea that I know whatever thoughts, whatever secrets, she's about to reveal. The mirror is starting to feel like a weird idea.

When Stephanie reads the opening statement, about how this study is regarding the culture surrounding Greek Life, a huge smile spreads across Lavender's face.

She folds her arms across her chest. "Well, I can tell you now you won't need to conduct these interviews for long."

Why's that? I type.

Stephanie repeats my words.

"It's clear isn't it? I mean, it's been clear for years. Probably since these goddamn things started. They're terrible. Sexist, racist, literally anything that ends in -ist, they're probably that. Honestly, I think they should get rid of the whole thing."

Stephanie looks to the mirror. Then back at Lavender. "So, um, I'm assuming you've never been a part of a Greek organization?"

She's trying to go back to the script.

Lavender just looks at her like she's insane.

"I—I mean, have you ever experienced any of those things that you just mentioned, at a Greek organization?" Stephanie asks.

"Are you kidding me? I'd never set foot in one of those places."

"So you don't know anyone involved with Greek Life?"

"God no, and I'm better for it."

I place my head between my hands. *Can't do much with that level of proof, but thanks, Lav.*

"Are we done here?"

Yes, please.

When the interviews are finally over, I drag myself back to the dorm and do homework until Leighton bursts through the door at 8:00 p.m. and declares she's going to sleep.

That's her pattern: stay awake for days at a time partying, or stay in bed for a week, going to sleep at seven or eight and then spending most of the day watching Netflix.

Her sleep schedule flips back and forth between rock star and retiree. I have no idea how she plans to pass her classes.

I start gathering my stuff to go work in the lounge downstairs.

"How was your weekend?" Leighton asks.

I look up, trying to mask my surprise. "Um, it was pretty

fun," I say. "I had a good time Saturday, but maybe too good of a time, considering how I felt today."

She nods knowingly and wraps herself in her white Ralph Lauren duvet, so only her thin face peeks out.

I sometimes feel like she's a small child, but with expensive things. Like something broke when she was shipped off to boarding school at the age of nine. The work has transitioned from multiplication to linear algebra, and the fun has transitioned from toys to drugs and boys, but I'm not sure if *she's* much different.

While so many of us are homesick and getting used to living on our own, calling our parents crying when we have a cold or get a bad grade, Leighton has a Post-it taped to her desk that says, "Call parents! At least every two weeks!"

"I'm jealous," she says to the ceiling. "I can't wait for the frats to be done with their dumb recruitment so we can have real parties. Now it's all about flirting with the little boys instead of us." She scoffs.

"Did you rush a sorority?"

"Yeah." It's like I can hear the *duh* in her voice. "Kappa Alpha Delta." She adds this like it should mean something to me.

"But you moved in at the same time as me?"

"I stayed at my house in the city during Rush."

"Oh." *But I thought you didn't like girls?*

I expect the conversation to end here, this being the longest Leighton and I have ever talked.

"Why do you ask?"

"I don't know…that doesn't really seem like your thing."

"The baking cookies and shit?"

"Yeah."

"Doesn't matter. Not going Greek? That's like social suicide. I *had* to be Delta, like, it's top house, *hello*, and if I didn't get in, oh my God, I'd be transferring." She rolls over on her side, facing me. "Luckily it all worked out."

She smiles and cuddles up to her pillow. The happy look falls from her face like she's flipped a switch. "That is, it will all have worked out once the fun can actually start."

I nod.

She closes her eyes, and I think she might be asleep. And then her eyes flicker back open.

"I mean... I'm sure you'll be fine, though." It's like she just processed that she insulted me. "Maybe you can do deferred Rush? Actually, I can ask my recruitment chair about you, if you want," she says.

"Thanks, Leighton, that's very sweet." I don't quite know what to say. But I can tell this is a very big favor in her messed-up view of the world.

She's supporting an exclusive social system and the ranking of cliques...but at least she's offering to help me into her own toxic clique.

I shake my head.

I throw the notebook in my hand back on my desk and decide to go to bed now and work more tomorrow.

Because there is no way I could write a coherent thought about Greek Life right now even if there was a gun to my head.

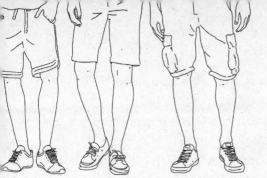

chapter ten

THE COFFEE TASTES THIN AND WATERY, LIKE THE KIND
you get on an airplane, and the headphones press into my ears.

It's just another typical day in the lab, and with my computer on the desk and the one-way glass in front of me, I'm flipping through old notes and only half paying attention to the current interviewee, a girl named Lily with a pixie cut and light blue dress.

"Do you understand this study is being done on a voluntary basis?"

"Yes."

"That it will be recorded, and that portions of your interview may be published, although your name will be changed?"

"Yes."

I chew on the end of my pen and look through the window, thinking her headband is cute. It's really more of a scarf she's tied around her head.

"How old are you?"

"Twenty-one."

"Are you currently part of a Greek organization?"

"No."

"Have you ever been a part of a Greek organization?"

"Yes."

I shuffle through my papers, trying to find the transcript of an interview we did a week ago with a football player and Sig Nu where he kept referring to women as "biddies."

"How long ago did you leave?"

"About two years ago."

"Have you ever been sexually assaulted?"

There is a pause. "Yes."

I drop my pen and look up.

"By a current or former member of a Greek organization?"

She turns her head and looks at the mirror, at me. After a second, she turns back to Stephanie. "Yes," she says, her voice barely making it across the room to the mic.

I grab the computer and pull it onto my lap.

STOP, I type.

Stephanie clears her throat, stalling.

I'm so sorry that happened to you, I type, and Stephanie parrots it. If it's not too much to ask, could you tell me as much as you feel comfortable with about what happened?

Lily shifts in her seat. "Um…sure. So, I was at a party at—at one of the bigger houses three years ago, my freshman year. I'd been there a few times for events. I'd made it into a pretty good sorority, one of the top houses, you know? My mom was a member, and she's superbig with all the alumni stuff. I didn't really fit in with those girls, but…but that doesn't matter. I'm getting off topic. So anyway, I didn't have that many friends among the girls, like real friends, you know, that would have your back, but it felt like I was safe, right? Because I was with my sisters. So I guess that made me feel like I could get really drunk, you know? But it's not like I was really drinking that much more than anyone else. I mean it was a frat party, so..."

She exhales. "So we'd had the pregame with them and I'd started drinking pretty damn early. But I didn't black out." She holds up her hand. "That's really important to know, that I remember everything. Not that it would excuse anything if I didn't. But I'm just saying I remember everything he did, and there're no parts I'm missing, so this should be good evidence, right?"

Stephanie nods.

"So right. I'm pretty drunk by the time other people start to get to the party. I see this guy I'd met a couple times at other events. He's older, and seemed pretty nice the other times I'd seen him...

"I'm that level of drunk when you're feelin' good but not like superdrunk anymore, and you've convinced yourself that you're gonna sober up any moment so you need to drink more.

"So he starts talking to me, and pretty quickly I ask if he knows if they have any more alcohol, since the kegs were running out. It's pretty common at these things to have the bad alcohol in the main room, and then people, like upper-tier Greek Life people, they can go into the back rooms and drink better stuff.

"So he nods and leads me off, and I'm thinking we're gonna go to a room with like ten or twenty people in it, my sisters and his brothers, that kind of thing.

"And then, well, yeah..." She looks at her shoes. "The room was empty. He, uh, he locked the door and pushed me onto the bed and started kissing me, and, ugh, at this point I just, like, think he's gotten the wrong idea. That maybe I've been sending signals that I wanted this, that maybe this is my fault."

She laughs, and it's a hollow sound.

"So I kind of start to push against his chest, lightly at that point, and saying things like, 'Hey, let's go back to the party' and 'I'm not really in the mood' and 'I don't really want to right now.' Trying to be *nice*." The last word sounds like she's spitting.

"But he keeps advancing and shushing me. So I start pushing harder and saying no, like a forceful no, and I start to realize he doesn't really care what I'm saying.

"And that's when I panicked, when I knew what was happening.

"And I yelled, but it's so loud at those things, people probably couldn't hear me. Or, I mean, that's what I'd like to think."

She wrings her hands. "He, um, he raped me, and then he left. He went back to the party."

Her face is pale, her lips almost white.

"And I just left, walked across campus alone. I kind of, uh, shut down. I should've called the police right then, I guess, or told someone, but I just went home. The pain was gone, but only because I felt, like, nothing. Not like I was okay, but the opposite. Like my mind could not handle what happened and just stopped.

"And I showered, which apparently was a bad move."

She's quiet for a long time.

"Did you tell anyone?" Stephanie finally asks.

"Not for a while. I didn't know how to tell my 'sisters' or whatever, you know, because I was this quiet freshman they only put up with because of my mom, and he was in one of the best frats on campus. I mean, maybe they would've believed me. In retrospect, of course they would have—they weren't monsters. But then..." She shakes her head, and tears bead in her eyes. "I was just so confused and so mad I didn't know what to do."

The room is quiet.

"And it got pretty bad, and I—I ended up in the hospital,

and they made me talk to someone. But she kinda sucked. But they wouldn't let me quit counseling if I wanted to go back to school, so they switched me to Sasha instead."

She smiles, weakly. "She kind of rocks. So I ended up telling her, and getting better, you know, and quitting the sorority and finding new friends, good friends, and some of them are in sororities even."

She touches the scarf. "That really helped, talking about it. Telling someone. I can live now." Her voice is tight.

She slides off the scarf. "It's kind of warm in here, huh?"

"Yeah." Stephanie stands. "We can turn on a fan, if you want. Or take a break? Get some water?"

"No, I'm fine." Lily straightens her back. "What's your next question?"

"We really don't have to—"

"What is your next question?"

"Would you like to see them gone?"

"What? The frats?"

"Yeah."

"I don't care."

"Why?"

"Because fuck that. Because I was raped and they want to change his fucking housing to deal with it? Are you kidding me? He wasn't playing music too loud after hours—he attacked me. I want him in jail. I want him hung, for God's sake. Not his club disbanded, boo fucking hoo."

"Some people think frats create misogynistic environments."

"The world is a misogynistic environment. He was in math club, too. Do you think if they get rid of that, it'll make up for what happened to me? Getting rid of the frats is a fucking cop-out. Something big needs to be done. It's not a frat problem—it's a human problem. It happens everywhere, in the army, at work. Hell, you wanna talk about misogynistic environments, I worked at a tech start-up last summer and let me tell you—"

She stops abruptly and exhales. "Sorry, I'm getting worked up. The point is talking about how abolishing frats like that will get rid of assault or misogyny, it's…reductive. And kind of insulting."

Stephanie glances toward the mirror, which she isn't supposed to do. I frantically type a question—But if there's a victim that thinks it will help…?—and Stephanie dutifully asks it.

"Then burn them fucking down."

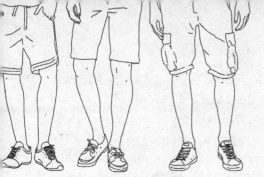

chapter eleven

STEPHANIE LOOKS TO THE WINDOW FOR HELP, BUT my brain is short-circuiting.

Lily clears her throat. "You know what? Sorry, but are we done here?"

"Um..." Stephanie turns back to the mirror and so does Lily, and she looks like she's screaming behind her glassy eyes.

"I just really..." Lily looks around for help, but the room is empty except for the unhelpful Stephanie. "I can't keep talking about this."

I stand too quickly, and my chair clatters to the floor behind me. I remember the computer and pull it toward me, typing frantically. I need to know if she's okay, if he was caught. I need to help her.

But the girl is getting up from her chair and wiping tears from her eyes.

This stupid system is too slow. I drop the MacBook on the steel table, cross the room and push open the heavy door without thinking.

There's the flutter of a blue dress at the end of the hall before it disappears behind a door marked "Women."

I practically sprint down the hall, my patent leather flats slapping the floor. A door to my right flies open. It's Stephanie, headed to get the next interviewee, like nothing happened.

Her eyes grow wide as she looks at me, the door swinging shut behind her. "You aren't supposed to be out here."

But I don't stop.

"Come back!" she yells after me. But I'm already at the bathroom door.

Lily is braced over the sink, looking like she might be sick. "Hi."

"Hi?" She turns to take me in, her eyes scanning me, trying to figure out if she knows me.

"My name is Cassie Davis. I was, uh, behind the mirror."

"Oh." She stands up. "That's a little…"

I swallow. "I know. I'm sorry."

"No, it's fine, I, uh, I knew someone was back there. I just didn't think it was someone so…" She gestures vaguely, a tissue in her hand.

I nod, although I have no idea what she means. Her eyebrows furrow. "Are you supposed to follow me into the bathroom?"

I step back. "Uh…probably not. I'm not here, like, officially." I gesture behind me. "I can go if you want." My fingers brush the doorknob.

"No." She bites her lip. "Please, I just…need someone. If that's okay. Not that— It's just… I'm just—"

My hand drops from the knob. "No need to explain."

The door swings open behind me. "Observer 2!" Stephanie says.

I step in front of her. "Will you just give us a—"

"No, you can't."

I look from her to Lily.

"It's fine," she says. "I don't want to get you in trouble."

"Just give me a second, okay?" I exhale. "Stephanie, can I speak to you in the hall?"

"I guess…"

I step forward, closing the door behind me to give Lily privacy. "Really?" I say through gritted teeth.

Stephanie is even more frazzled than I would have expected. "You're not supposed to be out here. And you're definitely not supposed to be talking to subjects outside the interviews." She emphasizes every other word by waving her clipboard.

"She needs me."

"It's against all the rules. If you break the rules, you can't keep being part of the study."

"Then I quit," I say without a pause.

"What? I'm—"

I head back into the room, swinging the door closed before I hear what Stephanie plans to do. I lean against the door so she can't follow and turn back to Lily.

"I'm sorry," I say. She just looks through me, so I keep talking. "And I'm sorry about earlier, about this whole thing—that was probably not easy to talk about."

"You think?" Her voice is sharp.

I look down. I'm never good in situations like this. Alex is always better, with her bits of gritty wisdom, quotes from old songs and beat poetry.

"Are you okay?" I ask, not sure what else to do.

"No." She licks her lips, wet with tears. "I mean, I am. I mean, I just don't know." She laughs manically and sits on the floor.

I reach for the paper towel dispenser and quickly hand her a piece. "So you don't ruin your dress."

She nods and takes it, slides it under her butt. I hand her another one, to wipe her face, then sit down beside her.

"He's in jail now." She dabs her eyes, looking up to the ceiling, a smudge of watery charcoal liner below her lashes. "My case was still being *processed*, whatever that means, when a girl walked in on him attacking her roommate. Since there was a witness, the case went pretty quickly."

For a second there's just the sound of a leaky faucet and two heartbeats.

She twists the paper towel in her hands. "Doesn't really make it better, though." She exhales and looks at me. But there's nothing to say. "I mean it's not— I try to not let it ruin my life, because then he's hurt me twice, you know, and I won't give him that. But sometimes when I talk about it, I still, you know, I get—" A tear slides down her bright red face. She swipes at it aggressively. "Shit, I'm crying again."

I take her hands. She exhales, and it sounds jagged. "It's okay," I tell her. "You're okay. Breathe."

I can hear Madison Macey screaming through the receiver. I can't make out everything, but I've heard enough snippets— "our investment," "Cassandra," "risk everything," "basic academic procedure"—to get the idea.

Professor Price's assistant sent me in midway through the call, at which point I was immediately keen to leave, but she gestured for me to wait. So here I sit in the chair in the corner and stare at my hands, trying to make myself as small as possible.

Professor Price gives one-word responses, and no indication of her opinion on the matter: "Yes." "Sure." "That's reasonable." "I see where you're coming from."

She doesn't look over at me, instead just making brief notes or spinning in her chair and glancing out the big window. I turn back to my hands, studying my bracelet and chipped nail polish.

"All right, I'll let her know. Thank you." The phone snaps back into its cradle.

I look up. Professor Price is leaning back in her chair, still looking at the phone.

"Well, you're in quite a bit of trouble." She looks at me for the first time since I entered.

"I can expl—"

She waves her hand to silence me. "They're right. The fact of the matter is you violated the rules of the study and risked the exposure of the entire project."

"The project is meant to help people like her. She was distressed and I talked to her. How does that risk—"

"The interviews are meant to be held in a vacuum. Talking to subjects outside the interview is a betrayal of their trust."

"But what happened to her didn't happen in a vacuum. This isn't data to her. It's recounting the worst experience of her life!"

"But your actions almost made her pain in doing so useless. The Stevenson Fund just threatened to cancel the whole project. Then she would have told her story for nothing."

"But isn't this study, all this work, meant to help people? How can we put technical requirements ahead of the actual human beings this is supposed to be about?"

She sighs. "Professionally, I have to disagree with you. If we bend the rules, create gray areas, then we can't trust our data or conclusions." She pauses. "But personally, I understand why you did what you did."

"I—" I don't quite know what to say. "Thank you."

"Don't." She purses her lips. "I defended you, but they're

still mad. To them, the personal interaction is the most important part, and they feel that if the interviews become a liability, they should be stopped. I talked them down before you came in, saying I would have major qualms about supporting the project if the entirety of the literature was an eighteen-year-old's journal, and they agreed to let Stephanie continue the interviews, and you can watch them on video after hours."

"What? So I can't ask follow-up questions? I can't interact with the subjects even from behind the window? That's ridiculous. Can't we call them back, ask again—"

"Cassandra, I don't think you understand. They threatened to pull all the funding. You violated your contract. They could void your scholarship, end the whole study. It's best for you to tread very carefully from this point on."

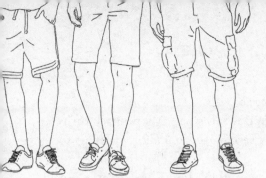

chapter twelve

"WAKE UP, BITCH! WAKE UP!"

I roll over, groggy. Although I usually don't like to respond to derogatory names, the voice is so loud I don't really have a choice. It's coming from down the hall, and probably not directed at me, but still...

I'm reminded of when my little cousins used to say, "Hey, stupid!" and then laugh for ages when I'd turn around.

I sit up. The room is still dark; no light is coming through the windows yet.

"What the fuck?" Leighton says.

I reach for my phone and click the clock button: 4:30 a.m.

Leighton's lamp clicks, and light pools into the room.

She pushes her sleeping mask up into her disheveled blond hair and looks at me with dazed eyes.

"Pledge! Pledge! Pledge!" The chanting continues down the hall.

"Ugh, oh my God, it's the goddamn frats rolling people out," she says.

"Rolling what?"

"C'mon, Morris, let's gooooo!"

So it's the football player down the hall. My stomach turns to knots. *What if I haven't been chosen for a frat?* My life is so weird now.

"Oh my God, I forgot you didn't know anyone in a frat here," Leighton says, sliding out of bed. "When clubs and shit pick you for membership, they sneak into your dorm and wake you up superearly and kind of kidnap you."

She walks over to our sink, getting herself a glass of water. "If it's, like, chess club, they'll come at eight and then just take you to get doughnuts or something, but the band wakes people up at four and then makes them take shots and run naked through campus. I hear the lit clubs make you go to class on acid."

"What do frats do?"

She shrugs, yawning. "How the hell should I know? Do I look like I have a dick?"

Just then there's a quiet knock at the door.

"Hello?" I say.

Leighton looks confused but reaches to unlock the door anyway, opening it slowly.

"Um, Cassie?" Marco peeks his head through the door.

"Yeah?"

He lets out a sigh of relief and steps farther into the room so he can actually see me.

"I'm, uh, supposed to roll you out. Put on your shoes and let's go!" He says the second part a little louder, like he's remembering how this is supposed to go.

I climb out of bed, looking around until I find my Converses under my desk. Leighton gapes at me, then at him, her properly raised, sorority girl socialite brain short-circuiting.

Marco stands there in the middle of my room, avoiding

looking at me, taking in my pink bedding and Christmas lights as I slip on my shoes.

My face warms as I realize I'm wearing only booty shorts with "Warren" across the ass and a thin tank top with nothing underneath.

"Okay." I look up. "I...also need to put on a bra."

"Oh, uh, okay. I'll—" He kind of spins awkwardly in a circle. "I'll wait outside."

He disappears into the hall, closing the door behind him.

I quickly root through my drawers for a simple nude bra, slipping it on under my shirt.

"What—what the—what was that?" Leighton stutters.

I readjust my shirt and turn around. "I'll explain later. See ya!"

As soon as I'm out the door, Marco pushes me forward. "Let's go!"

And that's how the weirdest rollout in DTC history happened.

I stay tight on Marco's heels as he runs down the three flights of stairs to the lobby of my dorm.

When we arrive, Morris is standing there in plaid boxers and flip-flops, along with three more actives I don't recognize.

"Let's go, pledge—let's go!" one of them yells at me.

I pick up the pace but can't help smiling.

They have us stand on the lawn in front of the dorm.

"Turn around!"

We face the building.

The world goes dark as one of the actives pulls a blindfold over my eyes. He grabs my arms like he's planning to handcuff me and ties my hands behind my back.

The rope digs into my wrists as they spin me by my shoulders and then start leading me forward.

"Shit!"

I hear the unmistakable sound of someone hitting the ground.

"Get him up," one of the actives growls.

"Uh, you need to step down here," the active leading me says.

I step off the curb carefully.

"Someone call Peter and tell him we're ready," the same voice, clearly the leader, says.

Ready for what? I know it's not worth asking. They won't tell us.

I shiver.

Here's the thing no one tells you about California, especially drought-ridden California: it's like a desert, even the parts that aren't technically deserts. Sure, it reaches a nice seventy degrees every day, and we shouldn't complain. But that doesn't mean it won't get as cold as, say, forty degrees, at, I don't know, four thirty in the fucking morning. Which, when you're in shorts and a tank, is pretty damn cold.

Finally I hear a car approaching. The engine still running, it stops in front of us, the smell of burning gasoline mixing with the damp, cool smell of morning before the dawn.

I hear the sound of car doors opening, and then someone picks me up, carries me a few feet and throws me into what can only be the back of a van.

I'm lying on the floor—there doesn't seem to be seats back here—and I can hear and feel other people already here.

Someone lands next to me with a considerable thud. Has to be Morris. It probably took all four of the actives to lift him.

The doors slam and the car takes off, screaming down the street as AC/DC's "Highway to Hell" blasts louder than I ever thought could be possible.

And let me just say that I've been to rock concerts and a number of raves with Alex and thought the volume was totally fine. I am eighteen, not eighty, and I do not complain about loud music.

But this is *loud*.

Whoever is driving is definitely speeding and likes to take turns hard, causing all of us to shift around, bumping into one another.

"Who else is here?" I don't know if they hear me, and if they reply I can't hear them over Brian Johnson's vocals.

The song ends…and starts again.

Oh my God. Where are they taking us? And exactly how many four-minute intervals away is it?

The third time it's annoying.

The sixth time I want to claw out my eardrums (but alas, my hands are tied).

The eighth time I'm singing along to every word.

When we finally stop they've played the song easily ten times. The music cuts off and leaves my ears ringing.

I hear the door open and then, "Let's go, pledge bitches!"

People start to push. I sit up and scooch forward on my butt till my feet are over the edge. I hop out, and my feet crunch on gravel. I sway for a second, then steady myself.

"Hurry the fuck up!"

I walk forward carefully, and someone bumps into my back, almost making me fall.

Actives are yelling at us, helpful guidance ranging from "Turn right and walk straight!" to "Follow the sound of the footsteps of the pledge bitch in front of you." Oh, and then there's my favorite: "Don't fall, you asshole!"

The eternally helpful list of every vulgar insult in the English language continues.

We walk forward onto grass, which becomes progressively thicker, until the grass ends and I'm pretty sure we're in a forest of some sort. Branches scratch my legs, and I pray I don't walk into a tree. The ground starts to slant downward.

And then I hear a splashing sound.

Where the hell are we? We easily could've driven the thirty-plus minutes to Half Moon Bay, but that's developed, I doubt there would be much forest. I guess we could be by a lake, but I can't think of one that's close enough, at least not in this drought. I mean, except for...

Oh my God. It occurs to me that we might still be on campus. That they may just have driven us in circles for forty minutes, blasting that godforsaken song.

Those insane geniuses.

"In the water!" someone yells.

We walk forward without question. *What if they don't tell us to stop? What if this is some sort of bizarre human sacrifice?*

"Stop!" someone yells when I'm up to my knees in icy water. "Turn around."

I do.

"All right, pledges! In a minute an active will hand you a beer and a key. When I say go, you must shotgun your beer. The last to finish goes for a swim. If you start early or take off your blindfold, you go for a swim. If you talk back, you go for a swim. Getting the picture?"

No one says anything.

"Pledges, when I address you, you will respond, 'Yes, sir.' Now, did you understand the instructions?"

"Yes, sir!" everyone yells in unison.

I think I may have joined a cult.

Someone splashes my shorts as they approach. They untie my hands and place a can in my left and a key in my right.

"Go!"

I cut into my can and liquid sprays out at me. I shove the

key in my waistband and raise the can to my mouth, holding it up with one hand while I fully open the top with the other.

Beer rushes into my mouth, and I chug as fast as I can. Around me, I hear cans splashing the water as pledges finish and spike them.

C'mon, c'mon, c'mon, Cassie.

Finally liquid stops flowing from my can.

Yes!

I throw it down and wait to hear someone after me, but there is only silence.

Fuck.

Multiple arms push me down, and my feet slip on the muddy bottom. I'm under for only a second before they pull me back up by my armpits.

I lick my lips; the water isn't salty. I stifle a laugh. There's no way this is anything but the lake behind the DTC house.

I cough, but before I can catch my breath, another can is being placed in my hand.

"Again!"

I reach for the key, but my fingers feel only the damp fabric of my waistband.

Panic spreads through me. I grope for it, wishing I could take off my blindfold and look. But there's nothing there; it must have fallen out when they dunked me.

"Fuck."

Thinking fast, I lift the can to my mouth and bite down with my canine tooth. Luckily the can is flimsy and collapses immediately under the strength of my jaw.

Yes!

"Fuck yes, Davis! That was badass!" someone yells from the beach.

I make the hole bigger with my thumb and finally shotgun. I'm better this time. But of course my late start means I'm behind everyone else.

They dunk me again.

And again we shotgun.

This time I'm ready to bite it right away, but I cut my thumb making the hole bigger.

Which is fine. I'm shivering badly now, but I've gotten used to the water enough that I won't mind going under.

But this time they don't just push me under. They hold me there, pressing down on my head. I want to scream, but I'm already out of air, and anyway, there's no one to hear me under the water. My lungs burn, and I start to count: twenty, twenty-one, twenty-two...

I try to remember how long humans can survive without oxygen.

I reach up for the hand holding down my head, scratching with my nails. I think I may pass out when they finally pull me up.

I start to fall forward, but hands hold me up.

"That's three times in a row, pledge! What do you have to say for yourself?" The yeller is right in front of me, like a drill sergeant. I can feel his breath on my face.

I turn and spit, because there's lake water in my mouth, but also because I like the effect.

I smile like this is all just good fun to me, not verging on torture. "I don't know. I guess girls just take longer to finish."

A murmur spreads through the pledges. No one laughs at my joke, and I guess the sound of a feminine voice has shocked them even more than the words I said.

"No talking back, pledge." He barely finishes speaking before I'm underwater again.

But this time is shorter.

When I come back up there are a bunch of voices speaking in the line.

"A girl?"

"Is that allowed?"

"Is it some sort of prank?"

"A pledging thing?"

"No talking, pledges! Again!"

I shotgun immediately, but a few people are still whispering about the shock of hearing my voice.

Which is just enough delay for me to break my losing streak.

I hear the splash, and then more yelling. "You lost to a girl, pledge! How does that feel? She's like five feet tall! Get yourself together!"

We go again, then again.

After six I hear someone throw up in the lake we're all standing in.

I try to push away the image so I don't throw up myself.

After eight, I finally hear Peter's voice say, "All right, let's bring it in."

"Take off your blindfolds," the drill sergeant says.

I reach up and pull mine away. It's light out now, and I have to blink a few times before my eyes adjust. I was right; we're standing knee-deep in the campus lake, staring at the house.

"Welcome to DTC, gentlemen," Peter says from the hill. "And, uh, lady."

The boy from the bus—Sebastian I think—stands in the water with us. So he was the dunking drill sergeant. "That's all. You can go now, pledges, but be at the house at eight o'clock tonight."

I can already tell they'll have a good cop–bad cop thing going.

"And try not to be belligerent in your classes," Peter says.

The actives turn to leave, and the pledges visibly relax.

People clump together into groups of three or four or five, chatting and laughing.

Except for me.

This is supposed to be the time when we forge friendships over the shared pain. Where the strong bonds of common struggle are forged or whatever.

And I'm sure that's true for the rest of them. They pat each other on the back. Tell each other they did well if they're dry. Or they'll be fine if they're soaked.

Or laugh about how crazy fun that almost-torture was.

Or, of course, talk about the crazy girl pledge.

No one addresses me; they just speak about me.

They stare at the girl in the clingy wet tank top.

The girl in the frat.

I decide not to hang around. After picking up a few floating beer cans on my way out of the lake, I climb the hill silently.

As I reach the top, I turn back around for a second. The rest of my pledge class, a group of thirty or so athletic-looking, mostly white guys, is still having a good ol' time.

I make eye contact with Jordan.

Who is staring at me like the rest of them.

I turn back around and head home.

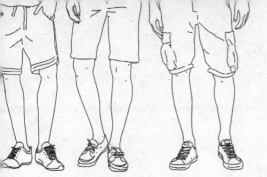

chapter thirteen

MY MIND IS SWIMMING AS I WALK BACK TO THE
dorm. I kneel on the cold tile floor of the hall bathroom and
make myself throw up three times. The online alcohol education class we took said throwing up won't always sober you
up, depending on how much you've already absorbed, but I'm
hoping this will at least help me not get worse.

There's no way my body will be able to handle as much alcohol as the guys, some of whom are twice my size.

I drag myself back to my room and climb into bed. I really didn't want to miss my gender studies class today. We're
talking about educational disparities between boys and girls
around the world, and I've read the guest lecturer's book three
times. But I can't exactly show up drunk.

I lie in bed, watching stand-up on Netflix and eating snacks.
I try to chug water to fend off the hangover I know is im-
minent.

Around the time I finish the collective works of Aziz An-
sari and switch to Sarah Silverman, Leighton comes home.

"You joined a frat?" she says before she's even in the door.

I pause my computer but don't look away. "Yeah."

She doesn't say anything for a long minute, and I start to wonder when it's socially acceptable to hit Play.

"Are you a lesbian?"

"What? No."

"Good, I put on my room application that I wouldn't live with one of those. Like, looking at me naked and shit."

This girl is ridiculous. I open my mouth to explain how absolutely fucked up that thought is, how it's homophobic and unacceptable. How it would be ignorant from someone raised in the Deep South, but is appalling and inexcusable from someone raised in the most liberal places in America and Europe. Someone who's attended world-class institutions and given every reason to not be an effing bigot.

But I'm too tired.

"That's nice, Leighton." I close my computer. "Can you turn the light down?"

She clicks off the overhead and switches on her laptop.

"Are you hungover?"

"Yeah."

"It's four in the afternoon."

"Yeah, well, I got drunk at five this morning."

She laughs. "I want to be in a frat."

"You'd love it," I say, my voice empty. This conversation needs to end.

"Maybe I can come hang out with you sometime."

I think of the first week, when she would leave to hang out with her friends and act like I didn't exist. Of every day but these last two, when our conversations wouldn't last beyond five words.

"Knock yourself out."

She rummages around the room for a bit, changing into workout clothes.

"Also you should know you're all over Twitter," she says. The door slams.

I reach for my phone, quickly sign into Twitter, and, sure enough, she's right.

It doesn't seem like anyone has figured out who I am, but word has definitely spread about the girl who was rolled out for DTC.

I use different search terms, like "girl in frat," "chick in frat," "DTC Warren," and have no trouble finding comments about me.

The tweets range from the simple:

Heard there was a chick in a frat?

Who's the bitch who rushed DTC?

To the supportive:

You go girl #girlindtc

Way to teach those guys to stop being so exclusive! #girlindtc

Remember that our sex represents 1/100 of the most funded club on campus, but it's a good start. Way to go, whoever you are. #girlindtc

To the cruel:

I didn't get a bid, but I guess I didn't show off the right ASSets.

Didn't know we were literally supposed to suck dick for a bid.

THAT WHOLE HOUSE IS GETTING LAID! We should've let girls rush years ago.

That rush room debate must have been hard. Most guys get one word: nice, cool, or fun. She probably got 3: tits, ass, pussy. Smh #chickindtc

Basically my timeline looks like "Greek letter vagina what?! Man and woman friends?! It hurts my caveman brain."

I refresh the page. The lovely football player from down the hall has tweeted.

#girlindtc lives down the hall from me. Her name is Cassie Davis

Thanks, man. And thus the last few minutes of my normal college experience ended.

People are even less polite on the anonymous forums.

On Yik Yak my name goes from "girl" and "chick" to "whore," "bitch" and "dyke." People think I used my femininity to get in, or that I lack it completely.

I scroll through, dizzy. It takes up 90 percent of the feed, the rest being recycled internet jokes from people seeking easy up votes. When it comes to the buzz around campus, it's just me, me, me.

There's one comment that sticks with me even more than the cruel ones. It's from a woman.

It's great to see fraternities taking a more inclusive turn, but I worry that they'll use 'but we let a girl in!' as their defense for ridiculous/sexist behavior in the future.

Then she links to a tweet from the official DTC account talking about how it has taken "the historic step" of being the first fraternity to admit women. Acting like this is Seneca Falls, when all they're doing is letting me play beer pong with them.

I wish I could comment back to this girl, tell her I'm not their tool. That I'm not going to naively be their puppet, that I'm going to take them down from the inside.

I set down my phone, having read quite enough for today. Quite enough for a lifetime. I feel like people will be camped outside my door soon, like on TV when there's a scandal and you see the reporters crowding all exits, hoping to catch a glimpse of their quarry, who's hiding out from the cacophony of voices and blinding flashbulbs.

But there's no one outside my door. My generation is made up of strictly digital vultures.

I wake up to my phone buzzing.

A: You've gone mainstream!

The text is accompanied by a link to the website of *America Weekly*, one of the most popular magazines in the world. I click on it:

Amid rising controversy among fraternity systems about hazing, discrimination and sexual harassment on campuses across the country, one school is making headlines for a very different reason. Delta Tau Chi fraternity, which made headlines last year when an investigation was opened into the environment they create for female students, has just accepted the first female pledge to an American fraternity.

It's so surreal, I can't keep reading. I am literally in the news. I scan down and see my name, followed by the words "was unable to be reached for comment."

Shit.

I check my email, and sure enough: *America Weekly, Huff Post, Buzzfeed, Seventeen,* NBC, *Jezebel,* Fox News, *Maxim. Maxim?*

I close my eyes and breathe deeply. I should run any comment by Professor Price and Madison Macey first, to avoid compromising the integrity of my project or losing my scholarship.

I'm drafting a joint email to them both when I get a second text from Alex.

A: You've gone international!

BBC had apparently picked up the story.

I let out an involuntary kind of growling sound and text her back quickly.

Me: this is not funny

A: of course it is

A: and it's exactly what we wanted to happen right?

Right.

I'm staring at my phone, waiting for an email from Professor Price or Madison Macey to come in, when an email from someone else pops up.

From: peterford@warren.edu
To: cassandradavis@warren.edu
Subject: Fame
Yoooooo

Pledge, you are famous!

remember when talking to our friends in the press that we don't haze or engage in underage drinking
speaking of...
Just wanted to give you a heads-up for tonight
Wear a sports bra and like full panties (idk what they are called, but like the opposite of a thong)
You'll thank me later
Don't tell anyone I sent you this
Tell kathie lee and hoda I say hey
—P

What the hell have I gotten myself into?

Before I have time to consider this, the next email comes through.

From: price@warren.edu
To: cassandradavis@warren.edu
Subject: No comment to the press yet
Don't say anything yet. Stevenson people will want you to, but the project, not the buzz around the project, comes first.

I nod, even though she can't see me.

I type back. Will do, thank you.

Turning off my phone, I set it on my desk before leaving for the house (with a sports bra and spandex on under my tank and yoga pants, which is a little bulky, to be honest).

I walk down the hall and see that Jackie's door is open; she's sitting at her desk working. Behind her the postcard wall is finished and looks absolutely dazzling.

"Hey, girl," I say as usual as I walk by.

She doesn't respond, and I assume she didn't hear me, which is fine. I'm gonna be late anyway.

I'm almost to the stairs when her voice echoes down the hallway.

"You're pledging a frat?"

I turn around. "Yeah."

"Why? To make a point?"

I take a deep breath. "No, for real."

She scrunches up her face. "Then why?"

"I, uh, tend to get along with guys better," I say, just as I'd planned and rehearsed for moments like this. "Girls are too much drama."

I avoid her eyes. The words don't sound like mine.

"That's some shit, Cassie." She exhales. "That's some internalized misogynistic *shit*."

"What?"

"I'm gonna lose my only friend on the hall because she wants to go live with the most sexist human beings on campus?"

"You're not losing me." I'll only be three blocks away, and I'll come back—as much as my class and pledging schedule allow anyway.

"You're right. I'm not losing you. I never had you. You weren't the person I thought you were."

She closes the door, disappearing into a million faraway cities, while I'm left in the blank-walled hallway.

It's hard enough to see strangers hate you on a screen, but that was nothing compared with this.

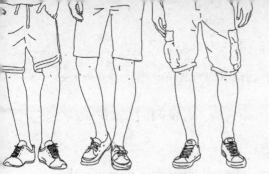

chapter fourteen

FOR THE FIRST TIME I ARRIVE TO THE HOUSE BY THE
lake to find the door closed. There are no welcoming people
on the lawn or the balcony. There's no music spilling out from
open windows; in fact, the windows are all closed and covered
with blinds, curtains or, in some cases, what seems to be tinfoil.

If it wasn't for the bigger-than-I-am Greek letters still above
the door, I would've thought they had packed up and moved
away.

The rest of my pledge class is waiting on the porch, some
sitting on the steps looking bored, others pacing, even more
scrolling through their phones.

I don't see Jordan. In fact, the only one I know by name is
my friend from down the hall.

A few guys nod as I approach, and one even says a quiet
"hey."

Duncan doesn't look at me.

"Thanks for the tweet, man," I say.

"Hey, you can't pull a stunt like this and then resent the attention."

"Should we go in?" someone else says before I can respond.

Everyone kind of shrugs.

"They said eight, right?"

Just then the door opens. The lights are off inside, but the late summer dusk lights up Peter's face.

"Come on in, guys."

I follow them into the dark, empty front section of the house.

"You're late, pledge bitches," a voice says.

Two other figures are waiting for us.

All the rowdy, obnoxious boys from Rush Retreat pile into the room silently.

"All right," Peter says. "As most of you already know, I'm Peter Ford, and I'm the current president of Delta Tau Chi. I hope you enjoyed our wake-up call this morning. If you didn't, you can leave now. As you know, hundreds of young men rush DTC every year, and you are one of the chosen thirty we have allowed the privilege of pledging.

"After tonight you will officially be pledges of the Cal Beta chapter of Delta Tau Chi. This does not mean you are yet a brother. At the beginning of the next semester, the actives will vote, and if you complete your pledge tasks properly this semester and are voted in, you will be initiated into the brotherhood. It is not an easy path that lies ahead. If you don't want to take on the honor and responsibility of membership, you know where the door is."

I look at him like I'm listening intently, when I'm really just trying not to roll my eyes.

"All right, then, down to business. As you all probably already know, we are on probation. That means even small mistakes can get us in a lot of trouble. There will be an email going out to all of you in a few minutes with my cell phone number. If you ever are in trouble, you do not call your mother. You do not call your RA. You call me. I can't emphasize enough how incredibly dead you'll be if we lose our house because one of you idiots over-or underreacted to a situation while you're blackout drunk."

He gestures to the other actives. "Marco here is your social chair. You're gonna wanna be nice to him, because when there's a sorority girl you really start to like, he's your wingman. And Bass…" He turns around and Sebastian, the drill sergeant from this morning, steps into the light. "Bass is your pledge master, or 'new member educator,' if anyone from the university ever asks. He is here to welcome you, and by welcome, I mean make your life a living hell."

A smile spreads across Sebastian's face that makes me shiver despite the stuffy room.

Peter turns to Bass. "I think that's about it for introductions, so I'm gonna let y'all take over now."

"Okay, pledges, welcome to bid night," Marco says.

Peter disappears behind a black curtain that has recently been put up, dividing the main room in two.

"What are you wearing, pledge?" Marco steps toward a boy wearing basketball shorts and a freshman orientation T-shirt.

"That's the geediest thing I've ever seen," Bass says.

Only about half the room seems to know what he means, but my extensive research pays off. GDI, which stands for God Damn Independent, was a term originally used by those outside Greek Life to answer the question of what frat/sorority they were part of. It was typically used by those who, like the lit club members here, are very social but chose not to go Greek. But soon after its advent, Greeks started using it in a derogatory manner, pronouncing the acronym phonetically and implying that the GDIs wanted to be a part of Greek Life but weren't cool enough to make the cut, so they were trying to spin their lack of affiliation.

The pledge opens his mouth, but no words come out for a solid thirty seconds.

"Take it off," Bass says.

"What?" The boy's eyes go wide.

"Down to your boxers." Marco steps back and looks at the rest of us. "You know what? None of you are dressed in a way I want associated with this fraternity."

"Everybody strip," Sebastian says.

"Let's go."

"Pile your clothes by the door."

The first to listen to this order are the ones who had shown up in tight-fitting or cutoff shirts, which they take off to reveal six-packs.

I hang back for a second with those on the scrawny or chubby side of GQ, who seem considerably less excited about this whole idea.

Marco isn't paying attention to those of us who are loitering but is yelling at those who are already half-dressed to line up, while making rude comments about their bodies, which is not encouraging to those of us who are already reluctant.

I know I'll have to do it, too, that this is what Peter was warning me about…and I will, I will—I just don't need to be one of the first. No need to draw attention to myself.

"You, too, Davis," Sebastian says. He's leaning against the wall where people are piling their clothes. I want to ask why he singled me out from among the rest. But I know why.

His words seem to hang in the almost-silent room. All eyes turn to me. My face burns, but it's not the coy blush they undoubtedly assume it is; it's rage.

I cross the room and slip off my tank and then my yoga pants.

The sports bra covers way more than a regular bra would,

and the athletic spandex shorts I'm wearing as underwear are equivalent to a pair of cutoff yoga pants. It's an outfit someone could conceivably exercise in on a warm day.

Sebastian shakes his head. "Who told you about tonight?"

"What?"

"Who told you secret information about pledge rituals?"

"No one. What are you talking about?"

"So I'm supposed to believe that's what you normally wear under your clothes?"

I look around at the guys, most of them wearing loose-fitting boxers that go practically to their knees. I'm less covered up than most of them, but of course he doesn't care what *they* look like.

Making them strip is a show of force and power, meant to remind the pledges how vulnerable they are to the whims of the actives, to establish where they rank.

I'm just an added bonus, a nice view for the actives while they torture the rest of the pledges. It makes me want to scream. I just bite my lip and make a mental note. I have to keep my head down until I can use my real weapons.

I start to walk to the other side of the room to line up, but then turn back around. "I don't know if you've ever seen a girl undress in real life or just in videos, but we don't typically wear thongs and push-up bras every day."

"Don't talk back, pledge." He pushes off from the wall, turning to the rest of them. "Speak only when spoken to by an active!"

Marco opens the curtain, and noise erupts from the back half of the house. We file into a large, dark room, where the actives are standing on tables around the edges, wearing all black and banging pots and pans.

They're all screaming, some saying, "Pledge, pledge, pledge!" Others are impossible to understand.

They're all clearly intoxicated.

Once we're all in the room, they begin a rousing rendition of a song that's 30 percent Greek letters, 30 percent swear words, 30 percent references to drinking and drug use and a token 10 percent references to brotherhood.

Have you ever been stone-cold sober and half-naked in a room full of almost blackout drunk guys screaming out a song you've never heard but they know by heart?

It's a new level of awkward.

I feel like I'm at a concert on another planet.

When the song ends, one of them starts chanting, "Shot list! Shot list! Shot list!" Soon more of the actives are laughing and joining in.

Marco says something, and two people shine flashlights on him like a spotlight. I don't know if it seems more like a cult or a bunch of small children trying to tell scary stories.

"Okay, everyone shut up. Pledges, time for the ancient and sacred tradition that is the shot list. The scrolls, please." He reaches back, and someone hands him an iPhone.

He types on it for about a minute before he looks up. "...all right! Here we go."

"So here's how the shot list works. Throughout pledging, actives can add you to the shot list when you do something. You get shots of Fireball—" Marco reaches under a table and pulls out a red handle "—as a reward when you do something good. However, when you do something bad, you get a shot of Taaka."

In case you've only ever drank like a civilized human being who doesn't despise their liver and don't recognize that last word, Taaka is plastic-bottle vodka that's cheaper than dirt but tastes worse.

It tastes the way nail polish remover smells.

When the devil sees people committing murder or cutting

you off in traffic and cries tears of joy, those tears are made of Taaka.

"We'll do this every week until initiation. Your points will also be tallied so we know who the top pledges are when it comes to picking participants for certain events. Do you all understand?"

"So it's kind of like the house points system in Harry Potter?" someone says.

"Yes," Marco says. "So for that, Pledge Nerd will get a shot of Fireball for demonstrating an understanding of the system and a shot of Taaka for making such a dorky comment."

We pass the bottles back as Marco continues.

"Parker, for throwing up in the water everyone was standing in, a shot of Taaka." He grins. "Parker, for rallying and winning the next round of shotgunning, a shot of Fireball."

The bottles are passed to Parker, but Marco doesn't stop. "Jackson, for the geediest Instagram caption ever."

Every active in the room yells, "Hashtag blessed!" in a level of unison that was clearly well rehearsed and is quite impressive, considering the collective level of intoxication.

"We almost took your bid back for that one, Jackson. A shot of the ol' Russian."

He continues like this, reading roll, the names followed by crimes and praise, while the handles are passed. Finally they run out, at which point Sebastian is ready with new ones.

There's a lot of Taaka for stupid comments made during Rush or social media posts they found, as well as for antics after leaving this morning.

One guy gets a Fireball shot for having a girl in his bed when they went to roll him out this morning and another gets Taaka for taking ten minutes to wake up.

And then Marco says, "Davis."

I step forward.

"For being a badass bitch and joining not just a frat but the best motherfucking frat in the country... Fireball."

The actives cheer, and although it's probably my imagination, they seem louder than they were for everyone before me.

Someone hands me the handle. It's half-empty. I pour myself the first cinnamony shot.

I toss it back. It burns a little in my chest but tastes like candy.

Marco steps closer. "Davis, because I got an angry text from every sorority on campus today, one shot of Taaka." But his smile makes me think he might just be glad I pissed them off.

God save my soul, I think as I stare down the liquid evil. I try to toss it back quickly to minimize the pain, but I gag and think for a second that I may throw up and earn myself three more.

But thankfully I don't. My eyes water and I wrinkle my nose, but in the dark I don't think anyone sees.

The guy after me asks for a chaser, and Bass laughs before adding a Taaka shot for the question.

"Louis."

I turn around. And there he is. He must have come in after we were already in the room.

I look at him in a way I shouldn't. Because this is supposed to be a moment of brotherhood and bonding, and I'm trusting the guys around me—even though I know it won't hold true for all of them—to stand in the same room as me in these skimpy workout clothes and not sexualize me but see me as one of their comrades.

But when Jordan stands up, wearing tight Calvin Klein boxer briefs, I can't tear my eyes away from his amazing washboard abs and the way they meet his hips, making this kind of triangle thing...

"A shot of Taaka for being late."

I turn back around and force myself to stare toward the front of the room.

I shake my head, refocusing. I'm working right now, and just because the Fireball is catching up with me, that doesn't mean I get to let my mind or eyes wander.

They continue through the list, and the actives start to yell out last-minute additions according to our behavior during the meeting.

By the time they reach the last few people, there are three empty bottles on the table, and everyone is moving and speaking in a way they think is more fluid but is really more jolted.

"All right, pledges!" Bass yells to get our attention.

He and Marco exchange a look. "We've just realized what a terrible job we've done welcoming you to campus," Marco says.

"They probably don't know where anything is," Sebastian says.

"Heck, after the first party they'll probably get lost doing the walk of shame."

"Well, shit, we can't have our pledges stumbling around the quad."

"I guess we'll have just have to give them a little tour."

I've learned enough in the last few hours to know when they start speaking like they're in some sort of twisted skit, things are about to get pretty bad for us.

"Pledges, outside!" Marco calls.

We walk outside, and I'm very aware of how half-naked I am standing on the lawn.

For a while we just wait as all the actives other than Marco and Bass leave. And after that, we wait some more. Maybe that's the joke, to make us stand here all night, waiting to be told what to do.

"See, Marco, I think the problem with this pledge class is that they already think they can run with us."

Marco shakes his head in disdain. "Just got your bids and already you think you can represent these letters!" He points toward the house. "You have no idea what these letters even mean yet."

"They mean nothing," someone nearby mumbles. "They're a random collection of letters from another language."

Sebastian snaps his head toward my side of the group. "What's that, pledge? Who's talking back? I do not think I told any of you to speak."

The crowd rustles as everyone looks around, trying to communicate with their eyes and figure out who the unlucky one is.

"Step forward, pledge, or the whole class goes down with you."

The boy walks forward.

"Three shots of Taaka for Pledge Smart-Ass." Sebastian pulls a plastic handle from his backpack.

"On your knees."

Pledge Smart-Ass kneels, and Sebastian pours the awful liquid straight into his mouth.

"Get back in line."

The pledge scrambles up and returns to the group.

"Like I was saying," Marco continues, "you think you can run with us, but you have to learn to walk before you run." A huge smile spreads across his face. "And you have to crawl before you walk."

"On your hands and knees!" Sebastian yells.

Everyone gets down. Luckily the grass isn't muddy, thanks to the drought. We crawl down the sidewalk, two or three across, in a long line. The concrete is a lot harder on my hands and knees than the grass.

"Cassie," someone whispers.

I turn around; it's Jordan.

"Yeah?" I face front again, trying to seem unaffected.

They keep yelling at everyone not to talk. Jordan catches up until he's beside me and ignores the order. Under his breath he says, "You could've told me."

"Told you what?"

"That you were rushing the same freaking frat as me."

"What do you mean? I saw you at a ton of the events."

"I assumed you had a boyfriend here."

Oh.

"Well, I don't." My voice is indignant. Although I guess it's not *that* out there for him to think it. And that might explain some of the glaring in Soc 101.

"Title IX and Futbol, no talking!" Sebastian says.

I turn to Jordan. "Is that us?"

"I guess we have our pledge names now," he says.

"Futbol?"

"I'm on the soccer team."

That doesn't seem half as bad as mine.

"Title what?" he says.

"Nine," I answer. "The amendment that enforces gender nondiscrimination in schools. It's why girls sports have equal funding."

"Ah," he says. "Like, *girls in sports, what's next, girls in frats?*"

"I think that's the joke," I say.

We continue on in silence, over concrete, gravel and asphalt. And it hurts; it hurts *a lot* considering how drunk I am. This is going to be awful tomorrow.

I look down and flip my hands over; they're bloody and raw.

We crawl for easily fifteen minutes, while the pledge masters periodically stop and pick someone out of the line to kneel and drink, sometimes with reason, sometimes not. Finally we reach our first stop: the Kappa Alpha Delta sorority house.

The members are standing in front of their house, dressed in all black. I spot Leighton, but she avoids my eyes, whispering something to the girl next to her.

Sebastian has us line up, kneeling in front of a sorority girl armed with a handle for each one of us.

They pour Malibu rum into our mouths and chant.

"Drink motherfucker, drink motherfucker, drink motherfucker, drink."

Then we're crawling again.

We arrive at another sorority house, and although I'm already quite intoxicated, I start to notice a pattern. They have vodka, and the girl who offers me a beverage takes a personal approach.

"Oh, perfect," she says, walking up to me. "The famous girl-who-joined-a-frat."

Their president counts down, and right as they're supposed to pour the booze in our mouths, she whispers, *"Slut."*

I know a second too late what's about to happen. Instead of pouring the liquor into my mouth, she splashes me with it, like this is the *Real Housewives of Warren.*

My eyes burn, and I try not to scream, instead letting out a kind of whimpering sound through my clenched teeth.

"Oops." She walks away, swinging the bottle and almost skipping.

My vision is blurry as we get back in line, but I manage to find my way. I end up next to Duncan. *Perfect.*

Keeping my head down, I blink furiously and try to bring the sidewalk into focus.

Little dark dots appear as teardrops fall to the pavement.

"Are you *crying*?" he asks.

"No, my eyes are just watering."

"Sure." And I can hear it in his voice, the *this is why we don't let girls in* tone.

"She poured vodka in my eyes," I say matter-of-factly.

"On purpose?"

"Not all the attention is good."

After three more sororities, they leave us drunk and bloody in the middle of the main quad. As far from my dorm as I could possibly be.

"Be at the house tomorrow at six for move-in," Marco says before they leave.

"Do you want to walk back?" Duncan asks.

I nod. It's silent and awkward as we make our way across campus, but at least I'm not alone.

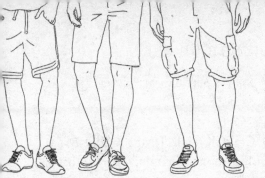

chapter fifteen

Entry 6: Hazing

Hazing is presented as necessary to turn the pledges "from boys to men" but seems to be more of an excuse for current members to exercise dominance. This pattern speaks to the toxic hyper-masculinity of such organizations: associating dominance with masculinity and, in turn, submission with femininity.

Most tasks involve drinking to extreme and dangerous amounts—often chugging beers or taking shots for punishment. Demonstrating an impossible alcohol tolerance seems to be seen as a show of strength. Other forms of punishment—such as push-ups or wall sits for an extended period of time—are examples of testosterone-fueled competition.

Other pledge tasks emphasize humiliation, especially in front of women—such as crawling half-naked to every sorority on campus.

Humiliation is also clear in the verbal abuse hurled at pledges during any interactions with actives. Most of these insults seem to imply the pledge is womanly and therefore weak. Examples include "don't be a pussy," "do you have a vagina?," "don't be a bitch," "are you on your period?," etc.

I CLICK SUBMIT AND CHECK THE TIME. I DID MY project entry and homework as soon as I could, worried that at any moment I would get an email summoning me to the house. But when my phone does buzz, it's to say that the actives have an event with a sorority and only the top pledges are invited. I, of course, am not one.

I check my syllabi and realize that for the first time since maybe my first night here I have neither homework nor rushing to do.

I text Alex on my way out of the dorm.

It almost caused a lot of problems when I told the Stevenson people about Alex. Especially since I had mentioned no one from my high school was at Warren and they had assumed that meant I wouldn't know anyone, and therefore all my social interactions could be focused toward the project. They wanted me to pretend I didn't know her. I argued that for my mental health I should be allowed to have at least one friend outside the experiment. That was not an adequate answer. It was actually Alex's idea to bring up social media and the fact that there was no way to erase my friendship with her from my past.

Even so, she had to sign a nondisclosure agreement about her knowledge of the project so far, and I was supposed to keep her separate from the project and spend as little time with her in public as possible.

It sucks to live five minutes away from your best friend and not get to hang out with her all the time. But whatever, it's more than I'd see her if I was at college on the other side of the country.

The door to Dionysus is open, but I still knock once before

I walk in. The main room is empty, all the furniture gone, though a gorgeous vintage chandelier hangs from the ceiling. A beautiful Indian girl in a knit crop top and high-waisted shorts is standing on a ladder and hanging string lights radiating out from the chandelier like rays from the sun.

"Is Alex McNeely here?"

The girl opens her mouth to answer, but another voice yells over her.

"Cassandra Beatrice Davis, is that you?"

"Not my middle name," I say as Alex half hugs, half tackles me. She smells of flowers and cigarettes. Of course, she's known my actual middle name for years, but she finds shit like this hilarious.

"I like your hair," I say. It's back to blond. Short and full, but with a hint of darkness at the roots, and cut asymmetrically, like a punk rock Marilyn Monroe.

"Thanks!" she says. "I miss the pink, but I'm glad I can wear red again." She's already taking advantage of that, clad in a maroon slip dress. She's radiating energy, in full-on Happy Alex mode. The thing about Alex is that she's either a walking party or a brooding, smart-but-cruel cloud, depending on the day.

"How are you?" she says as she leads me toward the dark wood staircase.

"I'm famous," I say drily. I spent the day getting death glares from everyone in my FemGen classes. The kids in my dorm either refuse to talk to me or want to talk my ear off, which is almost worse, because it risks my cover.

We reach the second floor. All the doors are open to what were bedrooms in the building's past life as a frat house, before Kappa Sig got kicked off campus. Now they're sitting rooms and studio spaces. The sound of an old record floats out into the hall. Some people are perched on couches poring over textbooks or staring at laptops, their faces illuminated in blue light. Others are sitting in the hallway drinking craft beers, having given up for today.

Alex nods to them as we pass, and I give a shy wave. The staircase is bare but for a large poster of the original *Moby Dick* cover art. Someone has placed a Post-it note above the *Moby* and written "S my" in Sharpie.

We reach the third floor, and I follow Alex down the hall and out onto a large balcony full of students smoking cigarettes and drinking wine. This may very well be the only place on campus where you'll find people drinking out of glasses and not red plastic cups. There's a cluster of bottles on a wrought iron table. Probably not some of Napa Valley's finest, but, honestly, I'm just impressed it's not boxed.

A cute boy with dark-rimmed glasses plays Arctic Monkeys from a Jambox, and a few people chatter in French.

"This is my best friend from home, Cassie. She visited last year," Alex says to the group.

I kind of recognize some of them, but others are complete strangers. They all turn. Some nod, while others wave or say a quiet "hey." Many speak with varying degrees of European accents.

Someone hands me a glass of red wine, and I sip as Alex lights up a cigarette. She once told me she had so many international friends because the only kids who smoked actual cigarettes on campus were "trailer trash" like her and the kids who grew up "somewhere between Heathrow and JFK." I replied by telling her she'd just quoted something someone said to Jessa, who I think is the *Girls* character she would be, if this was a *Buzzfeed* quiz. She looked at me like I had three heads.

I sip the bitter liquid and look out over the lake. On the other side, the lights from Delta Tau are barely visible through the trees. *My new home.* I purse my lips and look away.

The moon reflects off the water, a wavy mirror image of itself.

"So you're a freshman, then?" a skinny boy with sleeve tattoos asks.

"Yeah." I clear my throat. I sound nervous. I hope no one recognizes me, or asks if I'm *that* Cassie, the one who's all over social media.

"Well, we don't support underage drinking here at Dionysus," a black girl with violet hair and a slight British accent says.

I go to set down my glass, but she shakes her head no and winks, flashing a dazzling smile at me.

"God, I love first semester," the boy playing the music says. "Groups of thirty freshmen walking down The Row."

"And they all wear those lanyards," a blond French dude says. "No matter where they're going."

"All wearing Warren T-shirts, just in case they forget where they are."

"Blackout drunk at Delta Tau, probably."

They laugh, and I wait for someone to bring up, well, *me*. Not me, the girl they just met, but me, the girl who, did you hear, rushed a frat.

"Lining up at the bookstore, like they haven't heard of Amazon."

Everyone laughs, and I make myself smile, feeling like there's a spotlight on me. Or maybe a neon sign above my head that says, "I'm New Here," with a flashing arrow pointing down.

"Classic McNeely, letting all the riffraff in," the tattooed boy says.

Alex flips him off; she's laughing, though.

"Don't listen to them," the guy playing the music says. "They just give you shit because they're jealous they only have two years left and you have four."

A lanky boy with a bow tie nods. "It's the best. It will go by really fast, so enjoy it."

The purple-haired girl shakes her head. "It's not the best—you sound like a football player."

The tattooed boy bows his head and snaps his fingers in agreement.

"Everyone here acts happy because that's what they're supposed to be." Alex pauses to light a second cigarette with her first. "It's sunny, and we're the smartest and will make the most money. How could you not want to blow rainbows out your asshole?"

"Oh, shut up, like this isn't still amazing," music boy says.

Alex shrugs. "I love some things. But I don't love others, and I'm sick of feeling like I have to pretend I do."

"Amen!" someone yells from the other side of the balcony.

Alex blows them a kiss. We're both silent for a bit, looking out over the lake.

"How are you really feeling about the…move?" she asks quietly.

I close my eyes and shake my head. "I'm just glad I'm here at all. I'm that much closer to doing the work I really want to."

"Yeah?" Alex takes a last drag of her cigarette and puts it out on the balcony ledge. "What exactly is that?"

"I don't know," I say. "Honestly, there are so many problems in the world for women, and I don't know how to solve any of them. I guess I kind of trust that I'll know when I graduate, but maybe that's putting too much faith in a school with a fancy name and huge tuition." I trace the edge of my glass with my finger. "All I do know is that you and me put up with a lot of sexist bullshit growing up, and we had it light-years better than most girls in this world. So I have to do something. That something right now happens to be stopping frat boys."

She shakes her head. "If the so-called brightest minds in the most liberal pocket of America can't get their shit together, God help us." She turns around and calls across the balcony, "Hey, Poppy, if I leave ten bucks on your desk, can I take a bottle of rosé?"

"Yeah, for sure." The purple-haired girl laughs. "It only cost two, so that's a pretty great deal for me."

We stop in the kitchen to open the bottle and then head outside to one of the hammocks in the backyard.

I lie down, and she takes a long pull before climbing in next to me. "If it's too full, we'd spill," she says.

I nod knowingly. She cuddles up next to me and hands me the bottle. The wine is sweet; it tastes like spring.

The hammock sags and squishes us both toward the middle, which might be uncomfortable with someone else, but Alex and I don't have many boundaries anymore.

"Your boob is comfy," she says.

I laugh, and she reaches for the bottle.

"This sucks," I say.

"What?"

"Lying my way through my college experience."

She rolls her eyes while drinking the wine. "Oh, shut up," she says, the bottle still inches from her lips. "You get to go to Warren for free, and you'll be a published scholar before you graduate. So quit whining."

I exhale and look up at the stars. "That was a bit harsh," I say, then turn to her and steal the bottle back like a little kid fighting for a toy.

She shrugs. "That's what I'm here for."

"I know I'm lucky, but…but also it's like I don't get to have genuine interactions with people. A school like this is stressful enough with a support system. I don't get to have friendships. I get to have social experiments."

"Yeah, but I mean, that's kinda the price of living in a place like this for people like you and me. You're living a more literal lie, but do you think my friends here are the type I can talk to about money or about my mom? I mean sure, I have fun, but I learned to drink in a trailer park, not the kiddie clubs of New York. Last year I kept telling myself it was fine, you know, people to drink with are people to drink with. I have you and Jay to have meaningful talks with, and the rest of these guys are just for fun while I learn enough to take their corporate baby asses down in court."

She looks up at me. "Did I tell you I picked a major? I'm doing this interdisciplinary program thing in philosophy and law for social justice. Which is what I think of when I have to listen to kids talk about how annoying it is that ISIS is too involved in the Maldives now, so they have to vacation in Hawaii instead. Sometimes learning how to fight the good fight means I have to be the pink-haired girl in the land of Vineyard Vines. Bring it on."

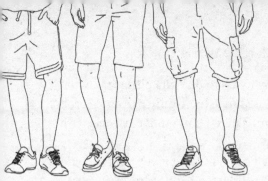

chapter sixteen

MY ALARM RIPS THROUGH THE ROOM, AND I WANT to kill everyone associated with DTC because they scheduled us to move into the house at 6:00 a.m.

The games don't stop.

Peeling myself off the bed, I slip on a shirt and athletic shorts. The hot dude-like dream girl is dead; time for them to live with a real woman.

My stuff is piled in bags and boxes on the floor, but I decide to just bring one bag now, show my face at this ungodly hour to avoid the shot list, but do the real grunt work later.

I step over the rest and glance at Leighton, who is still sleeping soundly. *It's been real.*

I grab my phone, and it lights up like a fireworks show. There are more alerts than I would've thought possible. Texts, tweets, Facebook messages, Snapchats. From my friends, family, acquaintances, unsaved numbers.

I scan a few but decide to answer them later.

The only one I open is from Sebastian. It's the official

pledge ranking, deciding who has to do extra pledge tasks and who's excused or even invited to actives-only parties. I scroll down, and down and down. There I am, number twenty-five out of twenty-five. *Lovely.*

I pause in front of Jackie's door, shifting my weight. I could knock, but she's probably still sleeping and wouldn't want to hear from me anyway. Even if she was willing, what would I say?

———

When I get to the house, everyone looks about as happy for me to be there as I feel.

"Let's go, pledges! You need to be moved in before house-cleaning at nine. Your names are on your doors."

The first two doors I pass feature nomenclatures like Bambi and Man Tits, so I doubt I will find "Cassandra" on any of them.

Most of the pledges are placed three or four to a room clearly meant to be a double, but when I find the door with "Title IX" written in large letters, it leads to a single.

It takes me only fifteen minutes to unpack my first bag, and the bare mattress looks tempting. But no level of tired would convince me to sleep on this frat house bed before I douse it with disinfectant and get at least a mattress pad and my own clean sheets as a barrier.

As I close my door I notice the room across from me has a real name: Sebastian Elliot. Perfect. Clearly I'll be getting special attention when it comes to terrorizing the pledges.

After five short trips, everything I own is officially in the frat house that is now my frat home. What a joke.

When I went to the room for the last load, Leighton was awake, if still in her silk pajamas.

She kind of just stood there for a minute and then wrapped her arms around me. I slowly raised my arms to hug her back, disoriented.

"I'll visit soon!" she promises.

I just nod and grab the last box.

As it turns out, my room in the frat used to be a storage closet. I have a twin bed with a set of drawers underneath, and a simple desk and wooden chair. There's a whole foot between the desk and the bed, so the chair can't come out fully and I have to kind of slip in from the side. Luxurious.

But at least this room doesn't come with a Leighton.

The desk has one drawer that locks, presumably for my computer, phone, headphones, cash and other valuables.

I fill it almost completely with all my paperwork for Stevenson, books about Greek culture and reports on fraternities.

I'm sitting cross-legged on the floor, unpacking my clothes, when someone knocks lightly on my open door.

"Hey, neighbor." I look up to see Jordan leaning on the door frame. "Can I come in?"

I smile. "Sure."

He steps inside, and due simply to its shoe-box size, we end up standing pretty close together.

"I see you've unpacked the essentials," he says, picking up the bottle of tequila from my desk.

It's the only thing besides my clothes that's not still in a bag or box.

"I didn't want the glass to break."

"Of course." He smiles, and his eyes sparkle. "We should break into it later," he says, sitting down on my desk.

"Yeah, definitely," I say. I stare at him for a second, trying to discern if the invitation was to join the guys in a classic night of drunkenness and brotherhood, or something more intimate.

I look away.

Get it together, Cassie. It's tequila, not a fine wine. He's suggesting a rave, not a romantic evening.

I reach for a bag, pulling it onto my lap and opening it. Unfortunately, it's the one with my bras and underwear. I grab a single pair of socks and place them in a drawer, hoping he doesn't see me blush.

"This is nice," he says. I look up to see him checking out my room.

"It's a bit small," I say.

"Yeah, well, at least you're not sharing a room with three other guys."

"Very true." I laugh, hoping he doesn't notice that I set down a practically full bag and reach for another. Luckily this one is T-shirts. I grab a stack and shove them in a drawer. "It may get kind of lonely, though."

Of course, that will be less because I don't have a roommate and more because I'm the fucking feminist living undercover in a frat house.

"Well, I'm right down the hall, so you can come visit anytime."

I open my mouth to answer, but before I can, another boy comes barreling in.

"C'mon, dude, we're moving the furniture. We need you."

"Oh, sorry, be right there." Jordan slides off my desk. "I'll catch up with you later, Cass."

I nod and turn back to my boxes. I bite my lip to keep from smiling too big or, God help me, giggling at the nickname. T-shirts, sweats and underwear successfully in my drawers, I turn to the wardrobe.

Opening the door, I find a half-empty thirty-rack of Natty and a hanger bar slanting at a sharp angle.

I pull the beer out and stand on the floor of the wardrobe, so I'm basically inside it.

Grunting, I pull on the higher side of the bar. It screeches and slides down half an inch.

Well, then.

There's a light knock and the sound of the door opening.

"Hey, you're back." I step out of the wardrobe and perch on the edge of the bed.

But it's not Jordan.

Bass looks confused. "How's unpacking going?"

I swallow. "It's all right." Why is he really here?

He makes himself comfortable, sitting on my desk like Jordan did.

"Do you need something?" My voice is high.

"Just trying to get to know my pledges." He picks up the tequila, inspects it and then sets it back down.

He peels at the sticker on my laptop: "Of Course I'm a Feminist." I'd put it there the first night of school, just to prove a point to Leighton. I'd forgotten about it.

"Interesting…" He doesn't look up at me.

"Hmm?"

"Feminist, huh?" This time he does look up.

I swallow and nod. "Uh, yeah."

"Brave to set foot here, let alone accept a bid." He tilts his head in a way that sends a chill down my spine.

He starts opening and closing my drawers.

"Can you not?"

His hand is poised over the locked one. "What? Don't want everything to be out in the open, then don't move into the house."

He seems to have forgotten about the last desk drawer and crosses to my dresser, pulling a red lacy bra out of the top drawer, as if to prove a point.

He throws it at me. "Buy something push-up for events. If we're gonna have a bitch in DTC, she's at least gonna be hot."

I stare at the lingerie in my lap as the door slams.

What the hell have I gotten myself into?

My phone rings.

Taking a deep breath, I brace myself and hit the green answer button.

"Hey, Mom."

"I've been trying to reach you all morning, sweetie." Coming from her, the last word sounds more like a slur than a term of endearment. In classic Midwestern fashion, her words sound nice until you catch her tone.

"Sorry."

"You sound hoarse. Are you hungover?"

"No." *I mean, not really.* "I'm just tired, Mom. I've been up since six." I walk over to the window, looking down at the boys below as they lug their things into the house.

"And yet you haven't had time to answer any of my emails?" She means texts, but there's no point in correcting her.

"I've been unpacking."

"Right, into your *frat house*." It's clear that in her mind, prison would be preferable. "Speaking of, darling, I was watching Fox News this morning, and they were calling you a crazy *feminist*, which is ridiculous, because I know I raised you to be a lady and I don't want California changing you."

"Yes, Mom, don't worry. My opinion on feminism hasn't changed." *I'm just as radical as you didn't know I was when I lived at home and pretended I was a good little passive Catholic girl.*

"Now, tell me—do you find yourself attracted to girls? Because I read this article the other day, and—"

"No, Mom, I still like guys. And *feminist* is not the same as *lesbian*." *Not that it would be bad if I was a lesbian, although she would undoubtedly think so.*

"Okay, I just wanted to check. Your grandmother will be

calling me any minute, and she will *not* be happy. Think of the stress you're putting on her poor heart."

I wonder if one day I can call my own daughter to tell her that her behavior doesn't comply fully enough with my vision of appropriate gender roles, continue the tradition.

"Well, good luck with that, Mom. Tell Grandma I love her, talk to you soon. Loveyoubye!"

I hang up and set my phone on the windowsill. I'm only halfway through a box of books when my phone buzzes again. This time it's only a text.

Alex: turn on channel 10

I pound down the stairs and into the TV room. Two actives are chilling with their feet on a coffee table that looks like it's lived a hard life.

"Can I use this?" I point to the television, which is currently off.

They shrug, and I click the remote.

I'm not used to the channel lineup here, but as it turns out, 10 is MSNBC. A woman is speaking ardently while a scroll runs across the bottom of the screen that says, "No, Fox, she is not a feminist."

"I'll tell you, Bob, when I said I wanted to see more women in heavily masculine environments in Silicon Valley, this is not what I had in mind. A young, traditionally beautiful girl moving into a frat house? I doubt they picked her for her ideas. This is not progress."

"So are you saying this move is antifeminist?" Bob asks.

She blinks at the camera. "Those are your words, not mine, but I would definitely not describe this Cassandra Davis as a feminist. In fact, if anything, she is a classic straw man feminist. Demanding things we don't even want. Equality doesn't mean you let us into your misogynistic organizations. It means you get rid of them."

If only they knew. That's what I'm *trying* to do.

I shut off the TV. Not exactly what I'd dreamed of when I thought I would be on TV for my research one day.

"Don't listen to that bitch," one of the actives says.

"Yeah, it's chill that you're here."

My heart starts to swell.

"Shit, be proud you aren't feminist enough for them. No one likes a shrew."

Well, that took a turn. I walk back to my room and plop down on my just-made bed.

This is not how I wanted my life to be. I'm one of the people who should be on TV saying the kinds of things that newswoman was saying, not living with people who think *feminist* and *shrew* are synonymous.

I get up and lock my door, then pull out my computer.

As soon as I'm logged in to the secure site, I start furiously recording every detail I can remember.

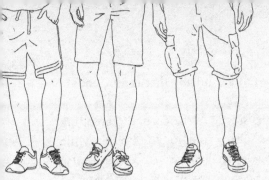

chapter seventeen

I ADJUST TO LIFE IN MY NEW "FRAT HOME."

Every morning I wake up and step over beer cans and half-empty Taaka handles on the way to the shower. I always wear shoes when I leave my room, because a grimy film seems to cover everything in the house.

I carry Lysol in my shower caddy and try to air out the gross boys-locker-room smell before I shower.

Sometimes there are girls with messed-up hair and mini-skirts loitering around, and I offer them my comb and their choice from the thirty-pack of toothbrushes I picked up at Sam's Club.

Then I head off to class, saying a quick hello to the athletes coming back from practice, and those with more questionable hobbies who are waking up wherever they collapsed the night before.

When I return I am always greeted with the loud sounds of gunshots coming from *Call of Duty* in the main room or a yell of "pledge," followed by some sort of profanity.

And at night I fall asleep to the lullaby that is 50 Cent vibrating throughout the house.

I spend my waking hours sitting in the corner, pretending to read the same few pages of my sociology textbook while listening for material for my journal entries. And I get plenty: how sex is often seen as a conquest; a guy "got head," or if he is often successful, "slays." Saying someone has sex often is a compliment for a guy—"he pulls"—while a sign of weakness for a girl—"she gave it up."

"I mean it's not bad, but we know most of this already." Madison Macey's voice is staticky over the phone. She's on Bluetooth driving through LA and has interrupted her thoughts on gender with bouts of swearing at other drivers.

I crouch beneath the window of the listening booth I've reserved at the library. I can't exactly take calls like this in the house, but even here, in the soundproof booth, I feel like a fugitive.

"Know what?"

"Intense drinking, power dynamics and dominance when it comes to sex—this is not shocking or new."

"So?" I run my hand through my hair. "I mean it's my findings so far. And although it's the stereotype, I'm not sure if it's been illustrated with an academic study like this. And even if it has, more proof for a theory is worthy research, right? I mean, isn't that part of the social science process, to gather more evidence to support the prevailing assumption or to disprove it? We can't, like, change the facts just to make it novel."

She sighs. "'Frat Just What We Expected' is not headline making, Cassie. I want something new, something that raises eyebrows, turns heads."

How about that rolls eyes? "What exactly do you have in mind?"

"Well, first of all, you aren't in the story at all. It's all I heard this, I heard that. Push it a little more, engage with them. I want to see *you* in the story. Fuck. Sure, asshole, just cut me off, fabulous."

I move the phone slightly away from my head to spare my ears the cacophonous honking. When the noise subsides, I cautiously bring the phone back to my face. "But I'm just the reporter—it's not about me."

"Of course it's about you. Otherwise we'd just have a bunch of hidden cameras in there, not a coed." She pauses. "You're replaceable, Cassie. Remind us why it's important that it's *you* in there, *embed* yourself. When I read your next entry, I want to be blown away."

The line goes dead, and I wonder if she's done with me or just driving through a tunnel.

Embed myself. I wish it was as easy as she made it sound. But it's hard to engage with people who mostly don't seem to want me in their house at all.

Not that they don't like the idea of me. For God's sake, the Warren chapter and the National Organization for DTC wrote press releases about the great example they've set by welcoming me. Their Google News tab has gone from talk of probation to talk of awards.

But the reality of me actually living there, actually being a member and not a talking point, seems to be an inconvenience they forgot to consider. Everyone seems to view me as an annoyance at best, an intruder at worst.

I'd like to think the actives are no meaner to me than they are to the other pledges, that this is just the reality of pledging. But then again, I never budge from the bottom of the pledge list, except for the one time I was second to last to a dude named Pledge Bambi.

But that doesn't explain the way the rest of the pledges treat me.

I can hear them most nights, from my window, drunkenly yelling as they gather outside the house to romp around campus, to have nights they'll look back on when they talk about their glory days.

Everything I've read about frats tells me this is the time when we should bond over our common pain. The people who defend hazing under the guise of "tradition" always say that creating adversity makes people come together.

But my pledge brothers don't seem to want to forge any sort of bond with me.

The only one who seems to want to interact with me, besides the ones who want to torture me, is Jordan.

I can't tell if he likes me or just pities me, feeling bad for the kid always sitting alone.

But he starts inundating me with invitations.

He pops up at my door at least three times a day, smiling like I'm his long-lost best friend.

"Hey, Cassie, do you want to study sociology?"

"Hey, Cassie, do you want to get lunch at the student center?"

"Hey, Cassie, do you want to sit with me at dinner?"

"Hey, Cassie, do you want to go to this party/social/sorority mixer where everyone but me will hate your guts?"

"Hey, Cassie, will you come out of your room so I can stop worrying about my charity project and get back to hanging out with my real friends?"

Okay, so those two aren't exact quotes per se.

I take him up on the studying and eating, and he becomes the only one who can draw me out of my room for anything but class or mandatory pledge events. Granted, he's the only one who tries.

And that scares the shit out of me.

Because he's the only one I *want* to try. Which is a bad

thought, because I should be focused on the experiment, on interacting in a purely research-based way with these people I hate, not spending the day waiting for a text that sets off butterflies in my stomach, or to see his beautiful face at my door.

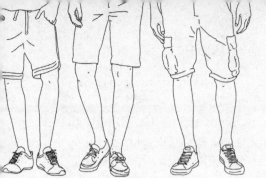

chapter eighteen

"WELCOME TO YOUR FIRST HOUSE CLEAN." PETER stands in front of the whole house, all of us assembled in various states of undress and hangover. I rub my eyes. The kid next to me—Pledge Bambi, who I've just met—yawns. Well, at least until Peter's eyes fall on him, and then he snaps his mouth shut and stands up straight. I look at him out of the corner of my eye. He *is* pretty tall and lanky. Not to mention his baby face and big eyes.

"I want to see all of these cans recycled, the kitchen restocked, dishes washed, the floors scrubbed and vacuumed—including the bathroom."

The crowd emits a collective groan, but Peter continues unfazed, rambling about disinfectant and no-streak window cleaner.

I scan the room. Examine the half-congealed pot of mac and cheese on the floor underneath the only still-upright table. The sea of empty beer cans that makes the floor hardly visible. The not-so-empty beer cans spilling onto the tile. Oh God, at least I *hope* all that yellow liquid is beer.

I look up to the ceiling, trying not to throw up. Is that...a *bra* hanging from the fan?

"All right." Peter claps his hands and smiles. "I think that about covers it. See you in a few hours." He spins on his heel and walks toward the door. The other actives do the same.

"Well, this sucks," Bambi says. The rest of the pledges mumble in agreement while dispersing.

I head into the kitchen to grab a few trash bags before making my way to the TV room, which has hopefully been hit less hard by the trash tornado than the main party rooms.

A few people had the same idea as me, including Jordan, who's in a white undershirt and penguin pajama pants, hair perfectly disheveled.

I clear my throat. "I, uh, come bearing trash bags."

"Thanks," Jordan says, taking one, but he seems distracted.

I lean down to pick up a few cans of Natty Light, shoving them in my own plastic bag, extremely aware of the tiny sleep shorts I'm wearing, which are basically just boxers.

"I can't figure out why this couch is like this," Jordan says.

I stand up and walk over to examine it. Half the couch is a darker green than the rest, seemingly soaking wet.

"I know!" A guy I don't really know very well—I think his name might be Alan, or maybe Aaron, walks up. His eyes are wide in wonderment. "I fell asleep there, and I woke up soaking wet. It was *so* weird."

"Do you think one of the actives threw a bucket of water on you?" Jordan asks.

"Wouldn't he remember that?" I say.

"Nope," Alan/Aaron says with a stupid smile. "I was so blacked that whatever it was, I slept right through."

"Jesus," I say under my breath.

Jordan rubs his chin, examining the couch like it's a clue

in a murder mystery. "Do you think…" He turns to… Al—let's just call him Al. "Could it be, uh, pee?"

I squeal despite myself and jump back from the couch.

Al turns bright red. "It is *not* pee."

"Okay, okay." Jordan holds up his hands to calm the witness. "There must be a reasonable explanation for this."

"Like a leak?" I suggest.

We all look up.

"I don't know," Jordan says. "The ceiling looks fine."

"Well, maybe it dried," Al says.

I scrunch my nose. "I don't think—"

"What's in the room above?" Jordan asks, already on the move. He stops when he reaches the bottom of the stairs. "Cassie, run up the stairs and walk forward on my instructions."

"Yes, sir," I say, dropping my bag of tin cans and running past him toward the stairwell.

"This is a serious investigation, ma'am. I do not appreciate your sarcasm."

I roll my eyes as I race up the stairs, but a smile sneaks onto my face. When I reach the top, I yell back downstairs that I'm ready.

"Okay!" he yells back. "Step forward as I count. Take one step!" he says in a booming, dramatic voice.

I laugh and do as I'm told.

"Two! Three! Four!" We step forward together, a floor apart. He stops when he gets to twelve. I take in my surroundings quickly before sprinting downstairs.

"No dice," I say, panting as I rejoin them. "Just a bedroom, no bathroom or water fountain."

The color drains from Al's face. "Maybe—maybe a pipe burst."

"And what, targeted only the couch you were on and then resealed itself?" I say.

"Face it, man." Jordan shakes his head. "The investigation was airtight. You peed."

"I did not pee!" Al looks around frantically. Duncan passes by the door. "Hey, dude, come in here," Al calls. "You're my roommate. Tell these guys, how many times have I blacked out? I don't *pee myself*, right?"

Duncan leans into the room, his body so large it's like he is supporting the door frame instead of the other way around. "Uh…yeah, you do. Like every time you drink."

"What?" Al goes ghost pale.

"Oh my God," I say, backing up. "Oh my God, and I almost touched it."

"Yeah, dude." Duncan sighs. "You didn't know that? Why do you think I gave you the bottom bunk? I'm almost three hundred pounds. Do you think I like climbing that little ladder?"

"Wh-what? Why has no one told me this?" Al asks.

Duncan shrugs. "We thought you knew."

"How did you *not* know?" I ask. "What have you thought before when you've woken up soaking wet?"

"I—I don't know." He shakes his head. "You black out and you wake up and things are weird. I thought maybe I'd spilled water on myself, or that they did as some sort of prank…"

I stare at him. "But the smell?"

He shrugs. "They pee out the window out of laziness a lot, so our room just kind of always smells like that."

I struggle to comprehend that and try to think about what side of the house their room is on to avoid walking near their window as Al continues to grapple with this new knowledge of himself.

Jordan pats Al on the back. "It's gonna be all right, man.

But, uh, cleaning this room? We're gonna leave this one up to you."

"Good luck." I smile shyly as I cross the room. I walk up the stairs, hoping I can wander a bit and avoid cleaning until the worst has been dealt with. I nod to the naked calendar as I walk past. This month is Carmen Electra. And then I stop in my tracks.

The hall is empty, and quieter than it has ever been, but something else is off. All the doors are shut and presumably locked. Except for one.

Okay, Madison Macey. You want embedded? You want an inside perspective like never before? How about a tour of the president's bedroom?

I look around, but no one else seems to be on this floor. I pat my pocket, making sure I have my phone, as I slip inside and slowly close the door behind me.

The room is just as I remember it from Rush. Much plainer and light-years cleaner than the rest of the house. American flag and ROTC poster. Bed made with military precision. Books stacked neatly on the desk near a desktop computer.

I walk over to the desk and click the mouse. The computer lights up, but it's password protected.

I glance at the door. I could try for the password, but I could spend hours doing that and get nowhere. And I probably have only minutes.

I open the top drawer. Pens, playing cards, highlighters, phone charger, condoms, Post-its. I close it and try the larger drawers on the side. The first one is full of spiral notebooks and thick volumes with titles like *The Spread of Nuclear Weapons* and *Political Order.* I close it and open the next one. Lying flat is a file with "Pledges" written across it in neat handwriting.

I set it on the desk and flip it open, feeling as if I should be wearing gloves or something. I glance toward the door.

The hairs on the back of my neck stand up as I flip through. First a copy of the flyers they'd posted around campus. Then photos of each pledge, seemingly from their Facebook pages, along with a few sentences about each.

Joe Walsh: Asshole, but legacy. Yes.

Duncan Morris: Football, automatic yes.

Ben Worthington: Awkward, but his dad gives hella money to the alumni association. Yes.

Chris Lewis: Pretty boy. No.

I take a picture on my phone and flip the page to see myself at prom smiling. I remember Jay snapping that picture as I laughed and blew him a kiss.

Cassie Davis: Opportunity. Yes (Pending).

Opportunity? For what? PR? Or…ew…like sex? And *pending*, what does that mean? Was that pending a vote during Rush? Am I still pending?

I flip through the rest of the pages, looking for more. But there are no more notes about me.

The last page is an Excel printout. Pledge names on the x-axis, active names on the y.

It seems to be the system they use to create the pledge list. Who's rewarded by invites to exclusive parties, who's punished with shots.

Most people get pretty similar results across the board. Those who go out often or play sports get high marks from everyone. Duncan has sevens and eights. And Alan Morris (so it *is* Alan) gets sixes and sevens. Although once this peeing thing breaks, he'll probably drop.

Others are less luckily. Ben "Bambi" Worthington gets twos and threes.

I find my name and trace a line across the page. One, seven, three, eight, three, four, six, two. I seem to be the only pledge where there's no agreement.

Even more interesting are my votes from the executive section. Marco Torres: eight. Sebastian Elliot: one. Peter Ford: zero.

What the hell? He must really not want me here. There isn't another zero in the goddamn chart.

I snap a picture, close the file and put it back where I found it, then slide the drawer closed quickly.

The next and largest drawer is full of similar files, but upright. The other one must belong here, but Peter must have taken it out recently.

I flip through them quickly. *Budget, Alumni, Nationals, Housing, Rush.* About what I'd expect. *Initiation Material, Emergency Contacts.* Then…

My fingers freeze over the last file, whose tab is bent, so I almost didn't see it.

Cassie Davis.

Why in God's name is there an entire file devoted to me?

"Ahem."

My head snaps up, and I see Peter, hand still on the doorknob, staring at me.

I pull my hand back like I've touched fire and stand up straight.

"What on earth are you doing?" he asks.

"I, uh…" I glance around. "Aren't we supposed to clean in here, as well?" I look for anything out of order, but find only a single pen on the desk. I place it in a mug carefully before looking back up at him. I tell myself to smile.

"No, it's just the common spaces." He steps forward, studying me.

I step back, my hand brushing the wall.

"Didn't you listen to my speech this morning?" He steps between me and the desk, clicking the drawer closed with his heel.

I laugh nervously. "I did, but you know me…" I make a stupid face and bonk myself on the head. "Dumb freshman."

He shakes his head. "Sometimes I wonder why we let you idiots live here."

Yeah, you even gave me a zero.

"Get back to work, pledge. I don't think the first-floor bathrooms have been cleaned yet."

Ugh. First-floor bathrooms are the ones open to the public during parties, which undoubtedly means vomit.

"On it." I smile as I walk past him.

The door slams as soon as both my feet are in the hallway. The lock clicks into place immediately.

So much for finding out what was in that file.

chapter nineteen

"NO, NO, NO. CULTURAL RELATIVISM IS THE OPPOSITE of ethnocentrism."

"What?" Jordan turns his head and stares me down. "Are you kidding me?"

We're lying on his floor, sociology books and notes spread around us, trying to study for the midterm over the sounds of Nicki Minaj floating up the stairs and through the half-open door.

I giggle. "No."

"So it's not true that..." He picks up his notebook. "And I quote from the lecture—'cultural relativism is judging one society by another's standards'?"

"Not according to the book." I hold up the giant volume.

"What the...?" He looks at me like this bit of information has shaken his entire worldview.

"Yeah, I know. I'm thinking there was supposed to be a 'not' on that slide."

He sits up. "So you're telling me that because of a *typo* I have memorized the exact opposite of this *key* concept of sociology?"

I glance up, considering this. "Yes."

"Ugh." Jordan scrubs his face. "What a joke."

"It's okay. At least you found out before the midterm." I give a cheesy smile and a thumbs-up. "What's next?"

"Um…" He flips through his papers.

A ringing breaks the brief silence. I reach for my phone instinctively, but it's not lit up.

"Hello." Jordan pops up, and suddenly I'm looking at his ankles. "No." He begins to pace. "Now is fine. I—I've been trying to call you for a while."

A few boys rumble down the hall, yelling something about celebrating their math midterm being over.

Jordan's attention snaps to the open door. "Yeah." He clears his throat as he crosses the room and shoves the door shut. "Yeah, I understand that, Mom." He turns around to pace the other way.

I gather the papers around me to give him space to walk.

"But how do you think it makes me feel, or Sara, or, God, Dad?"

I look up at him, but he doesn't look at me. Should I leave? He's between me and the door again but not making eye contact.

I stand and step forward.

"Hold on a sec." He turns to me, covering the receiver. "No, stay. Sorry, I'll just be a second. You don't have to leave."

I collapse back onto the floor.

"You know what, Mom, I have midterms, and I really can't talk about it right now." He hangs up the phone.

"Are you okay?" I ask.

He shakes his head. "Yeah, it's just a lot of bullshit." His eyes are fixed on his notebook. "My parents split up last year, when halfway through my mom's pregancy with my, I guess, half brother, my dad found out it wasn't his. She's with this other dude now and all mad we don't like her fiancé, like we don't all remember how they got together." I can tell he's trying to be matter-of-fact, but his words are laced with tension.

"Oh my God, I'm so sorry."

"Yeah, whatever, it's just drama. Every family has it."

I think of my parents. Barely talking when it's not "Get this from the grocery store," "I need these cleaned" or "Have you seen Cassie's report card yet?" Or, more often, fighting. Burned dinners and messy rooms turning into red-faced screams and tears. Cries of "I'm not your servant" and "I didn't sign up for this when I took those vows!" Drunken recounting of dreams that died on the vine. Hatred and resentment of a choice made in a time of white tulle and tears of joy. I think of my father sleeping in the den. Of my mother crying herself to sleep.

I clear my throat. "But I mean…if you want to talk about it, I'm here to listen."

"Thanks." He smiles briefly.

We're both silent for a while.

"Honestly, it doesn't make any sense," he says. "Cultural relativism should be when you judge things *relative* to other cultures, for God's sake. That's what it sounds like, any—"

His phone starts to ring again, but he slides his notebook to cover it.

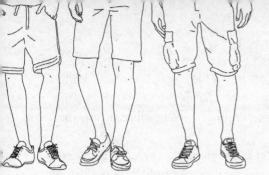

chapter twenty

SHOES SQUEAK, ROPES SWISH AND HARNESSES
click as athletes with biceps and Nike shorts, and granola types
with blond dreadlocks glide up and down the climbing wall.

I sit on bench near the equipment room, where I've been
for thirty of the forty-five minutes since I got here. I twice
made it halfway up the course I've been stuck on for weeks
before quitting.

I watch Jackie go the last few feet to the top, making climbing look elegant, like a dance.

Her black ponytail shines as she rappels down the wall. As
soon as her feet rest on the mat, she unclips. This is very unlike her. Every week I've watched her, she follows the same
routine. She likes to do each course three times in a row before moving on, but she's done this one only twice.

She turns and moves quickly, almost aggressively. And it's
not until it's too late that I realize she's charging toward me.

"Enough." She folds her arms, smearing chalk on her elbows.

"What?" I ask.

"What do you mean, 'what?' What the hell are you doing here?" Her voice is loud, and a few heads turn. "Here, c'mon." She grabs my arm, fingers digging in, and pulls me into the equipment room.

She turns on me as soon as the door clicks shut. "I've seen you here, like, four times. You barely ever climb. You just lurk."

"I—" *That's because I'm really here trying to work up the nerve to talk to you.* I look down, embarrassed. "I'm scared to fall."

She shifts her weight, her arms folded again. "That's bullshit. This is classic you. Don't half do something. If you're going to do it, do it. But don't, *don't*, make everything gray and muddled."

I don't think she is talking about climbing, either. Our eyes lock for a second, and her resolve softens just enough that I think this may be my chance.

"I'm sorry. Okay? I should've told you, about—about this whole thing. I just didn't know how to do it right...so I just didn't. And then it was too late because you knew and I didn't know how to fix it." I tell the truth as closely as I can.

She scoffs. "You know what your problem is?" she says. "You have no discipline. Don't want to do the difficult thing. Like you have perfect form, great potential, but you barely practice. When you're here, you just lurk around, make me feel guilty, distract me..."

"Jackie."

"What?"

"I don't come here to climb."

She exhales loudly, sending chalk and dust from the old equipment into the air.

I continue. "I keep coming here trying to figure out how to tell you that I'm sorry. To ask you to be my friend again."

She unfolds her arms. "Can I be your friend again and still think some of your actions are stupid?"

I nod. "For God's sake, I think my actions are stupid a lot of the time."

She half smiles. "Well, I'm not about to be friends with a quitter, so you better get back up there. It's the green one, by the way. On the far left. You skip it every time. The trick to that course is half steps, horizontal movement. Things can't go straight up all the time."

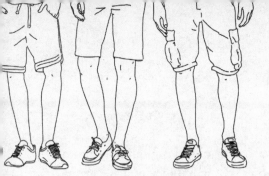

chapter twenty-one

"FIRST ALL-CAMPUS TONIGHT, BITCHES. IF YOU DON'T get this all set up in time, you will know a new kind of hell." Sebastian weaves through the room, refusing to help while he yells at everyone to work faster.

There have been plenty of mixers and smaller parties, but now it's time for the first real *Animal House*–esque, old-fashioned Frat Party of the Year. An all-campus party, meaning that in theory anyone who goes to school here could be invited. But, as always, there will be a list, and it will be an all-Greek-members or ridiculously-attractive-people-who've-become-friends-with-Greek-members party.

"Are you finally gonna come to this one?" Jordan asks me as we lug the sixth keg inside.

I shrug, which basically consists of me moving my head to the side, because I'm still struggling to carry the keg and walk backward.

"Why do you never go to any events?"

"I do. I was there a few nights ago."

"Not the mandatory pledging ones. I mean parties and stuff."

"I go." My voice is higher than usual, giving me away.

"So why do I never see you?"

Maybe because I'm in a corner observing, pretending to text while really taking notes on the number of drinks consumed, number of women hit on, number of songs that glorify violence against women.

I exhale. "I guess I'm just hesitant to go to parties where everyone hates me."

"Not everyone hates you."

"Have you *seen* Yik Yak?" I glance behind me as we move through the door, which is propped open with a full handle of Taaka. "Because I'm a bitch trying to take down Greek Life, a girl hater trying to take down sororities, an asshole apologist who hates women, a lesbian trying to convert straight sorority girls and a slut trying to sleep with the whole house. And none of those things plays well at parties."

We set down the keg. "I don't know. I think the last one would play pretty well with the guys at any party."

I elbow him and take off to unload the rest of the car.

"Hey, that actually hurt!" he yells after me. He holds his arm as he catches up to me. "I don't hate you, and I'll be there." He smiles that smile I can't help but see when I listen to sappy love songs.

"I'll consider it." I look down, biting my lip.

"Let's go, pledges!" Marco is sitting on the roof of the back porch, yelling through a megaphone and watching as pledges string lights, build a DJ booth and unload industrial quantities of alcohol.

Jordan and I grab cases of Taaka and Southern Comfort from a junior's car and set up plastic shot glasses in the main room.

As usual, the good booze will be in the actives' bedrooms,

but there's always a buttload of the cheap stuff for the masses. The level of organization behind the chaos, vice and debauchery amazes me.

"They take this so seriously," I say as I arrange plastic shot glasses on the table.

"Yeah, well, what do you expect? It's Warren," Jordan says.

"I guess I expect them to channel all of this energy into something a little more...important."

He shrugs. "I mean, they do that, too, right? Like our Rush chair is teaching my computer science section, and our president has interned for the actual president. It's just that they're also perfectionists about this stuff. You know, work hard, play hard, Cass. Excellence in everything, whether it's school, career, athletics or partying. Plus, partying burns off some of the stress."

Or maybe they're just a bunch of assholes trying desperately to prove they aren't nerds just because they care about school.

"Marco, don't forget to remind all the sorostitutes!" Bass yells as he walks past us into the kitchen.

This term bothers me in so many ways. They throw it around all the time, directed not only toward random girls but also their girlfriends. It's an insane word to use. Not only is it offensive to women but specifically to women who are a part of their own system.

And as much as I hate to admit, it bothers me almost as much that they didn't go with sororiwhore or whoroities. They were right there.

"Cassie," he says as he cuts back through the room. "Make yourself useful—text your lady friends to increase the ratio."

Oh God.

The ratio: the true mark of a good frat party versus a bad one. Not how many people black out, how many drinking games are won, how many mediocre hip-hop songs are played or, God forbid, if anyone has fun.

Nope, it's the ratio of how many potential people to sleep with per person trying to fuck. And in this hyperheteronormative environment, that means how many hot girls per guy.

"Okay." I roll my eyes but text Alex anyway. Not for them, but for me. So I can have one real friend at this party.

I look up from my phone to see Jordan's eyes on me. He looks away, his face turning red.

Well, maybe two real friends.

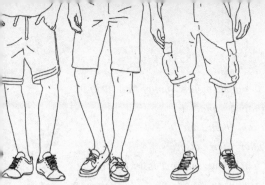

chapter twenty-two

Entry 18:
Much of what scholars would characterize as sexist and misogynistic speech around the house seems to be viewed as "just joking," not as seriously intended, much less hateful, comments.

When called out, fraternity men defend their comments to the author and other women who visit the house by pointing out that all friends tease each other, and that true equality means they can make fun of female and male friends alike.

However, there are notable differences in the exchanges between men and those that include women. In male-to-male exchanges, jokes tend to target the individual, pointing out his unique flaws.

While male-to-female interactions also may include this type of "teasing," they frequently also include a broader—no pun intended—focus, where the target of the insult is not just the female to whom the joke is directed but all females.

The men make jokes about their male friend being stupid because he failed a math test.

The men make jokes about all women being bad at math because their female friend failed a math test.

Male friends "need to calm down, bro."

Female friends "must be on their period."

The insults directed at females are distinct from teasing between male friends. When friends joke back and forth with each other, there is a constant reversal of who is insulted and who is doing the insulting. The balance of power is always changing. When insults are directed at all women, they reassert a long-entrenched imbalance of power.

THE DOORBELL RINGS RAPIDLY A BUNCH OF TIMES

in a row. I x-out of the Stevenson site quickly and shut my computer. I check my phone, and sure enough there is a text from Alex.

"I got it!" I yell, racing down the stairs and hopping past the last few, although the dudes lounging around in the common room aren't exactly racing me, and the guys in the other room, where beer games have already begun, probably can't hear over the music or want to leave their station.

"Hey!" Alex says as soon as I open the door. She envelops me in a hug that smells like perfume and hairspray. She's wearing a red leather minidress and has done her hair like Marilyn Monroe.

When she steps inside, heads turn and half the guys stand up at attention, as if royalty has entered.

She walks forward as if she doesn't even see them, leading the way although it is technically my house. "Oh my God, you would not believe what is going on at Dionysus. This girl cooked dinner the other night and told us it was veggie burgers but it wasn't, and—"

She pushes the door to the main room open with a manicured hand.

"And, like, half the house is vegan, so everyone is *pissed*..."
She keeps talking, but I zone out, taking in the room full of
guys playing twenty-one cup, which is like beer pong but
with three players on each side and continuous action. My
eyes linger on Jordan, who's at one of the tables, raising his
arms in celebration as his shot glides around the rim of a cup
before sinking.

"It's so ridiculous, right?" Alex asks. "Cassie?"

Jordan turns in our direction, and I wave. He looks nice,
in jeans and a blue sweater. Noticeably better dressed than the
sea of guys in tanks.

His eyes light up. "Cassie!" He runs over and sweeps me into
a huge hug. "You're here!" He sets me back on the ground.

"Yeah," I yell over the music, smiling. "And I brought my
friend Alex."

"Oh, hi." He turns to her. "I'm Jordan, Cassie's, uh..." He
looks at me, a question in his eyes. "Frat brother, I guess."

They shake hands, and he looks her in the eyes politely, but
his eyes don't linger like the other boys'.

He turns to me. "You look great."

"Thanks." I'm wearing my favorite jeans, made to look distressed, faded in just the right places to flatter me.

"I always fought with my mom, because she would never
let me buy the kind with the holes in them." He laughs. "Saying why would you pay for them already like that."

"Uh..." My phone vibrates in my pocket but I ignore it.

His eyes go wide. "Oh, but no, I think they're cool!" I smile
to ease his nervousness. Alex cackles.

A Ping-Pong ball bounces past him, but he doesn't take
his eyes off me.

"Look alive, Louis!" someone behind him yells.

"Oh, sorry." He chases after the ball but then walks back

over to us and just stands there holding it. "Do you guys need anything, beer or wine, water?"

"Jordan!" The two guys at his table look pissed.

"Oh my God," he says under his breath. He looks around, but most people are engaged in their own games or conversations, except for one guy, who's just in the corner watching. "Bambi!" Jordan waves him over.

Bambi looks behind him like there might be someone else here named after the same Disney character before stumbling toward us.

"You're in, man." Jordan holds the Ping-Pong ball out to him.

Bambi shakes his head vigorously. "I've never played before."

"It's not a deadly weapon—just try your best." Jordan folds the Ping-Pong ball into Bambi's hand.

"Okay." He stands up straighter. "On it."

My phone buzzes again. *Who could this possibly be?*

"So, right, beer? Wine?" Jordan asks.

"Are we talking wine in a bottle or wine in a box?" Alex asks.

I pull out my phone.

Alex: omg

Alex: he's hot

I roll my eyes and type back.

Me: Shut up it's not like that

"A bottle…" Jordan says. "But just a twelve-dollar bottle."

Alex laughs. "Hey, I'm used to Two Buck Chuck so that is glamorous to me." She pulls out her phone and types quickly.

Alex: You've got to be kidding me.

Alex: have you seen the way he looks at u

Alex: Get it gurrrrl

Me: Stop. Also there's no way he doesn't know we r texting each other you dipshit

"Cassie?" Jordan asks.

"Huh?" I click the lock button quickly and look up.

"Wine? It's in my room."

"Oh yeah, sure."

We're halfway up the stairs when someone yells after us. "Dude!" Marco stumbles forward, out of breath, and grabs Jordan's arm. "Santa Clara DDG just got here. What are you doing?"

Delta Delta Gamma, or DDG, is a sorority with no house here, but it's top house there.

Jordan blinks at him.

"Jordan! Santa Clara *DDG*."

"Okay, man, one sec." Jordan gestures over his shoulder. "I just have to—"

"Dude!" Marco shifts his weight impatiently, like a small child who needs to pee.

"Um…" Jordan turns to us. "You guys wanna just grab it from my room? It's on my desk." He looks at me with hopeful eyes. "Catch up with you later?"

I nod.

He disappears down the stairs, following Marco, who's rambling about how hot the girls from Santa Clara are.

"Nice to meet you!" Alex yells when he's clearly out of earshot. We stomp our way up the rest of the stairs. "Boys *suck*," she says. "Oh my God, Santa Clara DDG, Cassie, they are so hot! I don't know anything about them but the Greek letters plastered across their tits, but I heard their name and I came immediately!"

She disappears into Jordan's room and reemerges with a bottle of pink Moscato. I laugh. "Don't say that stuff too loudly here."

She rolls her eyes as she takes a long swig of the wine. "I don't care." She wipes her mouth. "I'm just here to see you and get drunk on their booze."

We make our way downstairs. The boys and a collection of what I can only assume are pageant queens are playing games of Rage Cage, a game where you have to bounce a Ping-Pong ball into a cup before the person behind you does the same and stacks their cup on yours, forcing you to drink so you can add a new cup to the game.

The girl next to Jordan is having the darndest time sinking her ball, and she keeps touching his arm and asking for help. He seems more than happy to show her proper technique.

Everyone is smiling, laughing and having a grand ol' time. But I can't help but notice that the conversations consist only of "Go! Go! Go!" "It's your turn!" "Yes!" "No!" and, of course, "Drink!"

Drink, drink, drink, drink, drink.

The games wind down as the crowd grows. People stumble in, everyone barely dressed and already drunk. Someone turns the music up and the lights down, and soon everyone is dancing, on tables, moving wildly and recklessly between partners, a kind of raw animal energy filling the room.

"But I want to daaance," Alex says as I lead her out of the room. She swings the empty wine bottle in her hand.

Having had only a few sips, I'm less inclined to make a fool of myself in public.

We sit down on the fringes of the party, on a couch in a well-lit hallway that leads to the first-floor bathrooms.

I half listen to Alex tell the same vegan burger story for the third time, before going in-depth on the controversy surrounding the lighting plans for her first student art show in San Francisco.

"You'll come see it right?" she asks. "Even if the lights are so bad you can't see any of my paintings?"

"Of course."

"It is during finals week, so I understand if you can't—"

"Dude, I wouldn't miss it."

She smiles and rests her head on my shoulder.

I watch people stumble in and out of the main room, sweaty and shiny, girls with shoes in their hands, makeup smeared and eyes bright.

I watch Duncan Morris watch a girl, say something to another guy, then down the rest of his beer before walking toward her.

He says something, and she looks up and smiles. They speak in each other's ears to be heard over the music, and after a few words, she kisses him. A few more sentences are exchanged before he leads her up the stairs.

Romantic.

"Cassie, I'm tired." Alex stretches out on the couch, resting her head in my lap.

I pet her hair. "Dude, you probably don't want to sleep here…" I think of the Pee Incident and shudder.

She sits up slowly, yawning. "I should go home."

"I'll go with you." I think of all the times I've been warned to not walk alone at night, especially on campus, especially when drunk.

"You can't go with me." She moves her hand in a sloppy gesture. "Because then you would have to walk back here alone." She taps my nose at the word *you*.

I can't help but giggle. "You're pretty great, Alex."

"Wha' can I say." She shrugs, and for a second I think she may fall over. She pulls out her purse. "Lemme call Dionysus, get them to walk me back."

Ten minutes later I take her to the door, squeezing past Sebastian as he works security, which seems to be mostly him judging how much cleavage girls' outfits show off. He's holding a clipboard, but I doubt there's much on there.

"Excuse me." I push through the crowd. "I'm trying to get out—let me through."

Eventually I'm able to hand Alex off to a girl with a nose ring and a guy with silver hair.

"Thank you," I say.

The girl shrugs. "No problem, she'd do it for me. Here." She holds her phone out to me. "Give me your number, and I'll text you when we get back."

I wave as they walk away, Alex launching yet again into the Vegan Scandal Story, this time to an even less receptive audience.

"Dude, we were *there*," the guy says.

I laugh.

"Cassie!"

Huh? I look over my shoulder to see Leighton, in heels and a sparkling dress that looks like solid silver molded to fit her body, arguing with Sebastian.

I walk over. "What's going—"

She attacks me from the side, almost tackling me. It's not until she kisses me on the cheek that I realize she's hugging me.

"Told you Cassie was my roommate, asshole."

"Uh, yeah," I mutter.

"She's with you?" Sebastian asks.

"Yeah, sure," I say.

He hands her a wristband and we go straight inside, garnering a groan from the line behind us.

"Oh my God, that was awful," Leighton says, her smile dropping as soon as we are past him. "I went to cut the line, and he was being sooo rude to me. He wouldn't believe I was in KAD—can you believe that? And of course none of my sisters were answering their phones."

"Yeah, Sebastian can be kind of a prick." We move through the house, into the crowded main room, where The Weeknd is blasting and the lights are flashing.

"Do you want something to drin—" I turn around, but Leighton is walking quickly the other way through the crowd. A whoosh of blond hair and clicking heels.

Classic.

I push through the rest of the dancing crowd and out the back door. The cool air coming off the lake is a welcome change from the sweating, steamy party.

A boy I've never seen before, with great hair and a striped shirt, stands at the other end of the porch, rummaging through his pockets.

The door clicks shut behind me, and he looks up. "Hey."

I nod in response, walking forward to sit on the railing.

He steps forward carefully. "You smoke?" He pulls a cigarette out of a squished pack and holds it out to me.

"Nope." I press my lips together.

"Uh, me, either." He shoves the pack back into his pocket. "I don't even know why I have these."

I crack a smile.

He winks and sits beside me.

"Connor," he says, holding out his hand.

"Cassie."

He raises his eyebrows and nods, as if I've told him something interesting. "So tell me, Cassie…if you don't smoke, what are you doing out here? Hiding from someone?"

"No," I answer too quickly. "I mean, it was just a bit much in there. So loud."

"Yeah." He fidgets, like he's holding an invisible cigarette. "DTC can be a bit much. I'm not a big fan of their parties."

"Thank you, I'm so sick of fra—"

"Our parties are so much better. Classier," he continues, not seeming to even notice I tried to speak. "Have you made it out to Sigma Alpha yet?"

"Nope." I look back toward the house. The windows are so steamed up you can see only flashing lights and shadows. "I tend to, uh, get enough frat here."

"Is your boyfriend in DTC?"

I furrow my brow. "No."

"So, no boyfriend, then, or just not here?"

I turn back to him and smile politely. "No boyfriend."

He nods approvingly, and it's not until that moment I realize he's been flirting with me. I thought we were just having a conversation, the first half-normal conversation I've had with anyone I've met at one of these parties, but of course he has an agenda.

"So are you in a sorority?" He slides a bit closer to me.

I lean back, but there's a pillar behind me. I could stand up, but I don't want to insult him, and it's not like I don't mind being close to him. He's not bad-looking, after all. It's just a bit… I glance toward the house but still can't see anything inside except the blurry shapes of dancing figures. Disorienting.

"Uh, no, I'm not."

He frowns. "That's too bad. You should've rushed. You're

pretty cute." He pokes me on the arm playfully. "You could've been a Delta." He smiles.

"Uh…thanks?"

He leans forward, and before I can react his lips are pressed against mine. I'm frozen, not really kissing him back, but not pushing him away.

The sound of the door pulls me out of my trance.

I lean back. "I…" My sentence fades from my mind as a familiar blue sweater catches my eye over Connor's shoulder. Jordan is standing in the doorway.

We lock eyes for a moment. Connor says something, but it doesn't register.

The way Jordan is looking at me, his brown eyes like that, it's almost like he's…heartbroken.

But that can't be right. Because right behind him in the doorway there is a girl and she is in a little black dress, and she's looking at him so dreamily and now he is taking her hand, and probably leading her back to her dorm.

And there is no way that look in his eyes is for me.

There is no way he cares that I'm here kissing this boy.

And yet…

He shakes his head, and the look is gone; his eyes are blank.

"Hey, Wright," he says, looking at us. "Nice!" And then he disappears, whispering something to the girl that makes her laugh and playfully hit him, and I don't know what else I expected. He's just another frat boy, after all.

I turn back to Connor. "You know him?"

"Yeah," he says. "We have a class together."

"Oh." I try to sound like this information is nothing to me, like my question was just polite.

"So…" His eyes meet mine.

He leans in again, and this time I kiss him back.

chapter twenty-three

I WORK ALL DAY ON MY JOURNAL IN THE RARE QUIET
as people sleep off their hangovers.

I feel like the night before left me with enough material to focus on recording my observations rather than, uh, interacting with my subjects, so I plan to lock myself in my room for most of the day. But by eleven I desperately need to sneak downstairs for some food.

I'm walking down the hall when the door next to mine opens.

Jordan is still in the blue sweater from last night, along with red plaid boxers. He looks at me for a second but doesn't say anything. No invitation to study or eat or watch stupid TV, no overly friendly smile.

I pass him silently, and I know something has changed; something is broken, ended before it even started.

My stomach growls at the smell of bacon as I make it down the last few steps.

Pablo, the chef (yeah, I know, these fuckbois have a personal chef; the world is a very unfair place) has prepared a brunch that makes me want to cry. I decide to brave the idiocy of conversation for the deliciousness of quiche. (Yeah, that's right, this frat eats like this is the Hamptons, probably because that's what most of them are used to.)

I pile bacon, fresh fruit, pancakes and a variety of mini quiches onto my now multiple plates while I wait for my omelet to be ready.

Sitting down at the end of the long table in the main room, which people were dancing on the night before, I try to enjoy my bubble of brunch bliss before it's ruined with a sexist/racist/homophobic comment. *Spin the Frat Wheel of Fun to find out what one of these highly educated idiots at the other end of the table will say first.*

Duncan glances down the table as I sit but doesn't say anything.

"Did you end up getting with that girl again, the one from Wednesday?" Marco asks him.

Duncan turns back to the guys. "Nah, I wasn't feeling it." He takes a sip of his coffee. "Got with her roommate, though."

Jesus. I turn back to my food. *Even one of the ones who seemed like he might be half-decent.*

"God, that must have been an awkward walk down the hall," Marco says.

He shakes his head. "I wasn't about to have sex in a sorority house. Are you kidding me, man? All that estrogen around, probably wouldn't even have been able to get it up."

That makes no sense. I focus on my omelet. *Happy, happy, good food.*

"Dude, don't you live in a quad?" Marco sees no reason to stop shoveling food in his mouth while he talks.

"Yeah, yeah, he does. My quad," Bambi says.

"Eh, dude, shut up. You were asleep." Duncan forklifts eggs into his mouth.

"Yeah, until I was woken up by 'Ohhh yes, Duncan, harder, like that, don't stop, don't stop.'"

They all laugh—even me, but I feel dirty doing it.

Peter sits down across from me and nods. He's the first person who seems to even care I'm here.

We eat in silence for a few minutes while Bambi continues to reenact the *When Harry Met Sally* diner scene.

Peter practically inhales his food. I've never been a self-conscious eater, but wow, there's something about a boy eating in his natural habitat that is next level.

"Nice hickey, Cass," he says through a mouthful of food.

My hand goes to my neck.

"You're fine," he says, standing up. "It's freshman year—have some fun. Just not with the other pledges, okay?"

"That's a rule?"

"Let's just say some of the leadership would not be happy. Your being here is kind of a divisive issue already."

"Okay..." It's not like I was going to. And if I was, the only person who interested me seemed more interested in that black-dress girl anyway. But even if I *was* interested, it seems like an odd rule.

"What about gay guys?" I ask.

He stares down at his food, suddenly looking very unlike his Kennedyesque self. Much more like a puppy that just made a mess. "That hasn't been a problem."

"You've *never* had a gay member? The whole time you've been a frat? How is that possible? Like, twelve percent of people are gay."

He opens his mouth to speak, but before he can, Sebastian joins us and answers for him.

"No, we haven't, and we never will."

"Why?" My word is so loaded I'm worried it may sink before it gets to his ears. There's no reason he could supply that wouldn't be appalling.

"Listen, I don't have a problem with it. I just don't wanna see it, don't want it in my house."

"What do you mean? Bambi basically *watched* Duncan have sex last night. Are you telling me that'd be different if Duncan was getting with another guy?"

He doesn't blink. "Yeah."

I want to slam my head against the table. If it was two girls, I'm sure he'd love to watch.

Sebastian gets up to get more food.

"Are you gonna do anything about that?" I ask Peter.

"What? He's on the exec committee. He has the same veto power I do. If he wants a no intra-house dating policy, we'll have it."

"Why don't you call him out? Even if you can't stop him, you should tell him he's being a homophobic asshole."

"Do you really think it would change his mind?" Peter scrubs his face. He looks tired.

"Double Ds, I swear!" someone down the table shouts. Duncan.

I glare at him.

He doesn't notice, just keeps gesturing in front of his chest while the others look on. Sebastian returns, staring at them with pride.

"Hey, idiots!" Peter yells down the table. "Don't kiss and tell. Have some class."

They fall silent, Bambi squirms in his seat, and Marco rolls his eyes.

Peter heads to the kitchen to refill his plate.

"Easy for him to say," Marco mutters once Peter's out of earshot. "We've all seen his fuckin' ten of a Delta girlfriend."

"Yeah, and it wasn't like he didn't have a rotation of girls coming in and out of the house before they got together," Sebastian adds.

"But I never told you about them." Peter emerges from the kitchen with another heaping plate.

Bambi turns white.

"You *are* aware that I can hear your big mouth from a room away, right?" He sets his plate down. "Bambi, pull yourself together. I'm not gonna hand out shots when everyone's hungover, okay? My God."

"You didn't need to tell me, asshole," Bass said. "I could just sit in the courtyard weekend mornings and watch them climb out a first-floor window. That was the best part. They'd all leave at seven thinking they would be unnoticed."

"Could've just slept in," Bambi says.

"That's what I told them." Peter takes a sip of coffee.

This whole conversation is making me lose my appetite. The very girls they try to get back to their rooms or congratulate their friends on fucking are mocked when they decide to say yes. And these girls, what kind of emotional turmoil are they putting themselves through, making a choice at night and then having to hide it not even twelve hours later?

But it's not just the guys who are guilty of thinking we should have to climb out the window. We're the ones doing it.

It's what has always made me uncomfortable about sororities. They have such strict rules about not drinking and not allowing men to set foot in the house, but anyone who's had any experience with sorority girls—or, in fairness, any girl on a college campus—knows that alcohol and boys are a huge part of the social scene.

But God forbid you talk about these things with your "sisters." It's all "do as I say, not as I do." It's passive aggression mastered and tied up with a bright pink bow.

But for God's sake, it's okay to get drunk every once in a

while, and you should be able to do it with the girls you call your sisters. And it's human and natural to want to have safe, consensual sex, whether that's with a long-term boyfriend or a hot stranger, depending on your personal beliefs and situation at the time.

So why the fuck do we keep acting like someone will sew a red *A* on us if we have a little fun?

As the great prophet (Tina Fey) tells us in the good book (*Mean Girls*), "You all have got to stop calling each other sluts and whores. It just makes it okay for guys to call you sluts and whores."

The Greek culture of hypocrisy creates this culture of sex and partying being guys-only activities, so they have all the control: frats are where you go to drink and have sex. Your own home is where you lie about those things.

And here's the worst part. When you associate shame with any sexual behavior or any use of alcohol, you have no way of knowing when there's a problem and things go too far.

It happened at my high school back home. We were all "good" Catholic teenagers, but everyone who was dating had sex, and they all lied about it. So my friend Gabby thought her boyfriend's behavior was normal. That what he did in the back of his Chevy Impala that one night wasn't something to be talked about, but it was fine, because even though everyone said they didn't want to, she'd heard everybody did it anyway, so it was normal, right? It wasn't until two years after they broke up that she realized she'd been raped.

And here are these frat boys, laughing at the fucked-up culture surrounding sex. There's so much I want to tell them. But I can't exactly tar them because of what happened to Gabby back home, even though you can draw lines from these little everyday sexist insults to the normalization of true trauma.

Fuming, I stand up to wash my plate. I dump my extra food

in the compost bin and then rinse my dish. I grab the sponge, scrubbing at a bit of food that just won't budge.

"Easy there, Cassie."

I turn around, wiping my forehead with my arm, since my hand is soapy. I know my face must be bright red. Duncan is staring, waiting to wash his plate after me.

I give him a look and turn back to my work.

"Jesus, you're in a mood this morning," he says.

"I—" I shove my plate into the sink with a clatter. "Do you think it's cute?" I turn on him. "Do you think it's charming? Do you think it puts me in a good mood to hear you guys talk about women like that? I mean, it's one thing to—to parade your carousel of women in and out of here, but at least have the decency not to mock them the next morning."

"I wasn't—"

"Whatever." I push past him, out the door.

"Cassie." His voice is pleading.

I stop walking. "What?"

"It's not because I like it this way." He rinses his plate and sets it down delicately. "I've never actually been on a date before."

I turn around. "How is that—"

"I went to an all-guys school and spent all my time playing football. And then I came here, and all these girls just…" He sighs. "It's easier to just flirt with someone at a party who won't even remember your name if they reject you than to ask out a girl you like."

Oh.

My phone dings, and I reach for it instinctively. He shrugs and walks out.

I open the email; it's the pledge rankings. Duncan is at the top—again. And Bambi and I are fighting for dead last, also again. My score is so low, I'm probably at risk of being dropped before initiation.

"Duncan, wait!" I chase after him, up the stairs. "Do you want me to set you up on a date?"

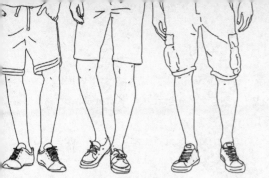

chapter twenty-four

"YOU WANT ME TO GO OUT WITH *WHO*?" JACKIE asks over the phone.

She's downstate for a big climbing competition. I'm sitting in the main quad, surrounded by tourists, old people studying maps and parents taking pictures of their babies in Warren onesies, and prospective students, aggressively asking tour guides about their SAT scores.

"That guy we, uh, met at the gym that one time, Duncan? And I don't want you to really go out with him. Just...pretend to. So he can practice."

"Will *he* know it's a pretend date?"

"No."

"*Cassie...*"

I stand up. "But I'll be there, too." I pace back and forth in front of a stone archway. "*And* you get a free meal. You don't have to kiss him or anything. Just go to dinner with him, show him he can enjoy having an actual conversation with a woman, then peace out at the end saying you have to take a call. I'll let him down easy saying you're…on and off with your ex and trying to work it out. Or whatever. Something that has nothing to do with him."

She sighs. "Okay. But I want Italian. Not some chain place, either. The good stuff."

I smile and sit back down on the steps. "I can arrange that."

She exhales. "And he can hold my hand, but no kissing. Not even on the cheek."

"Okay."

"God, why am I doing this?"

"Because you looove me," I singsong into the phone.

"You should know I'm rolling my eyes," she says.

"Don't care."

"All right, I gotta go." The background noise builds, shouts and clapping; she must be at the gym now. "Text me the details."

"Yes!" I pump my fist as I hang up the phone.

Three retirees with cameras turn around and stare.

"I, uh, got an A," I say.

They nod knowingly and one woman says, "That's wonderful, darling," while the others return to taking pictures of palm trees.

———

I'm standing in the strip mall Mama O'Malley's proudly calls home, by the car Duncan and I came in, when Jackie is dropped off by one of her teammates. She stalks across the parking lot, wearing a white sundress, leather jacket and a scowl.

"You look nice," I call out.

She only half smiles in response.

Once she has reached me, I say, "He's inside getting our names on the list."

"This whole meeting-in-the-parking-lot really adds to the prostitution feel of things." She doesn't stop her progress toward the door.

I walk quickly to catch up with her. "You're not a—"

"I'm a date for hire."

"Point taken." I pull open the door.

We step into the brightly lit restaurant, greeted by the stereotypical Italian music, loud conversation and toddlers' screams.

I scan the room. Most of the tables are booths, about half of which have high chairs pulled up to them. On the wall there are big framed close-up photographs of tomatoes and wheat.

And an honest-to-God poster from *Lady and the Tramp*.

"Great," Jackie says, slipping off her coat to reveal the thin white straps of her dress, which look beautiful against her tan skin. "Really classy."

I smile sheepishly. I may have picked it by Googling "Italian Restaurants Near Warren."

She looks around. "There's no coat check, is there?"

I shake my head.

"Cassie!" Duncan is sitting at a booth, waving to us. He's wearing khakis, a slightly wrinkled button-down and a navy blue blazer. It's weird seeing him wear anything but a T-shirt and Warren basketball shorts.

"Hello, I'm Duncan Morris." He gets up and shakes her hand vigorously.

She nods. "Jackie."

"After you." He makes a sweeping motion with his arm.

She slides into the booth.

"Isn't this place great?" he says as we sit down.

"Yeah," I manage. Jackie just makes a noise.

"I like the dogs." He points at the poster. "Reminds me of my brother."

"I didn't know you had a brother," I say.

"Yeah." Duncan smiles. "He's six."

"Hey there." A woman with a gray ponytail passes out plastic menus. "My name is Annie. I'll be your server tonight." She smiles tiredly. "I'll give you a second to look things over while I grab your breadsticks."

A pudgy toddler at the next table spikes his sippy cup at the ground, causing an explosion of chocolate milk. Annie sighs and heads over.

"So…" Duncan says as she walks away. He's staring at his water, ripping the edges of his cocktail napkin. "Cassie said you're an athlete, too?"

"Yeah." Jackie clears her throat. "I climb."

"Cool." He looks up. "I always wonder how you win those things, like I get how you get to the top or not." He laughs nervously. "But is it about your form or how fast you go?"

"It's really complicated." She takes a sip of her water.

I kick her under the table.

Her eyes go wide, and she coughs, covering her mouth to avoid a spit-take. She sets down her drink. "And you play football, right?" Her tone is kind of bored, but at least she's talking.

Duncan finally breathes. "Yeah."

"I can't even imagine doing that." She shakes her head and raises her eyebrows as she turns to her menu, which features something called "Italian Quesadillas" that may have something to do with cheesy bread.

"Yeah." He nods. "I get that. They say when it comes to your head, it's the equivalent of being hit by a car every twenty or so tackles." He runs a hand through his hair.

"Why would you ever do that?" she says incredulously.

He shrugs. "I get to go to school here."

"Oh." She bites her lip, her face flushing. Her voice quieter, she asks, "So…where are you from?"

"Whoa, sorry about that." Annie swoops in. She sets down a large basket of shiny breadsticks. "It's been crazy tonight. What can I getcha?"

"Garden salad," Jackie says.

"Is that all?" Annie asks.

"Yep." She smiles politely as she hands her laminated, picture-filled menu back.

"Fettuccini Alfredo," I say.

"Good choice." Annie winks at me as she takes my menu.

"Uh, thanks."

All three of us turn to Duncan, who's still studying the menu. "Can I get a Caesar salad, an order of the sausage ravioli, a fettuccini Alfredo also…and is it possible to get more breadsticks?" He looks up at Annie.

"Sure thing, sweetie." She takes his menu and walks away.

Jackie and I sit in stunned silence, mouths gaping.

"What?" Duncan says. "I've gotta put on fifty pounds this year."

"Wow," I say. "That's a lot."

"Yeah," he says. "But I'm gonna need it when I go up against the USC line next year."

I nod, pretending I know what he means.

"God, I wish I had to gain weight for my sport." Jackie leans forward to rip a breadstick in two, leaving the bigger piece in the basket.

"You'd think that," Duncan says. "And if it was five or ten pounds, I'd agree. That's just eating a little more and a little worse. But I have to keep eating long after I'm full. Like, when I go in to watch film with the team, they hand me five peanut butter and jellies, and I'm not allowed to leave until I finish them."

"Jesus," Jackie says.

We discuss hometowns, families, high schools and pets. Well, mainly they discuss. I just throw in a question here and there to keep things moving. But as time goes on, it's harder for me to get in a word.

Jackie is laughing at Duncan's retelling of the Alan Peeing Incident, when Annie returns with our five orders.

"Be careful it's—"

"Shit!" Duncan says, grabbing the plate before she can finish her warning. He turns bright red. "I mean fuck—I mean... oh God."

"—hot." Annie laughs and sets down the rest of the plates.

"I am so sorry." Duncan turns to Jackie, eyes wide.

"Why?" She furrows her brow.

"Because...you're a, um, girl. I shouldn't swear in front of you."

Jackie looks at him like he's insane. "I don't fucking care. Say what you want."

Duncan stares at her, stunned, as she shrugs and reaches for the other piece of breadstick.

I enjoy my pasta silently as they discuss the intricacies of the Warren athletic system.

"I'm gonna run to the bathroom," I say when Annie comes to collect our empty plates.

"I'll go with you," Jackie says. Duncan stands quickly so she can slide out of the booth.

Jackie fixes her makeup while I wash my hands.

"Thanks again for doing this," I say.

"Oh." She clicks her lipstick closed. "No problem."

"I didn't exactly want to set a DTC up on a real date." I laugh. "Couldn't do that to a girl with a clear conscience."

She stares at me for a second, lipstick in one hand, purse in the other. After a second she turns away, shaking her head as she mumbles, "Jesus, Cassie, they're just people."

"What?"

"I mean, I don't love frats." She struggles with the zipper to her clutch. "But that doesn't mean everyone in them sucks. Like, Duncan's really sweet." She slides the strap of her bag over her shoulder and looks up at me. "Believe it or not, I actually kind of like him."

"What?" The automatic faucet shuts off, but I stand frozen, my hands dripping into the sink.

"Yeah." She walks past me toward the door. "You know what, you can still leave if you want, but call off the ex-boyfriend fake-out or whatever. I think I want to finish my date."

I'm left standing in the empty bathroom as the door swings closed.

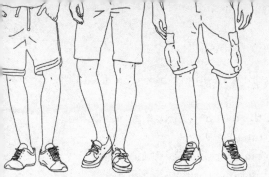

chapter twenty-five

MY DOOR IS SHAKING, AND THERE IS A BANGING from somewhere close. I awaken with a jolt, sitting straight up in bed. The room is pitch-black, and my heart is racing.

Oh my God, what are you supposed to do when there's an earthquake? I never learned this. I'm going to die because I'm Midwestern.

"Let's go, pledges—wake up!"

So it's not an earthquake; they're rolling us out again. Stumbling out of bed, I check my phone: 3:30 a.m.

On a school night. *Fabulous.*

I throw on a bra and shoes, and head out into the hallway. Pledges are emerging from their rooms like zombies.

"What's going on?" I ask the zombie who's double the size of the rest.

"I have no freaking idea," Duncan says. "All I know is I have practice in four hours."

We collect on the lawn in front of the house, waiting for orders. The morning wind bites at my skin, exposed by my thin tank top. Some of the guys are in just boxers; at least I'm better off than they are.

A whistle cuts through the darkness. Sebastian is standing on the doorstep, looking smug.

Behind him Marco is in neon workout gear and a backpack, like he was already planning on getting up at the asscrack of dawn to jog and wanted passing cars to spot him.

"All right, pledges, let's start running!" Marco takes off down the steps, cuts through the disjointed crowd of pledges and onto the road.

"You heard the man!" Sebastian says. "Go!" He whistles again.

We run in a pack, athletes near the front, Bambi and I near the back. My flip-flops slap against my feet and cut between my toes, so not meant for this.

Sebastian continues to blow the whistle with every step we take, and my head begins to pound.

I wonder if we're going to make the rounds to the sororities again. The thought of more Taaka in my stomach, let alone my eye, is revolting.

But we turn away from the sororities.

Oh, so main quad. Hopefully we won't have to vandalize anything too priceless.

But we pass the turn toward the quad and continue to run straight.

"Where are we going?" I ask Duncan, but even as I say it I realize the answer.

We file onto the lawn of Sigma Alpha, shivering, as Marco walks to the front of the group.

"All right pledges." He swings his backpack around to the front. I'm not sure what I'll do if they ask me to drink. I have class in a few hours and really need to stay sober, but I'm worried if I say no they'll reprimand me—meaning more shots. He reaches into the bag and pulls out some sort of flag. He unfurls it and holds it up so we can all read what it says. "Alpha Sigma Sigma" is written in huge letters, with the first letter of each word in extrabig type. "The first one to climb that pole and replace their stupid flag with this gets out of housecleaning for a week."

I look up at the flagpole that reaches as high as the second-story windows.

Well, fuck.

The varsity athletes step up immediately, of course. They fight for a while about who gets to go first. Marco finally settles it based on pledge points.

And one by one, they take the flag and walk up confidently, each guy easily pulling his body up halfway using his overly muscled arms before he loses his grip and slides back down.

And then I remember what Jackie said. *You think it'd be all about upper-body strength, like the big bodybuilder types would be the best. But petite girls are actually the most suited, because of their low center of gravity. You've got to have the right balance of flexibility and core strength, and traditional athletes don't always have that.*

What would she think if she knew when she said it that she'd be helping me pledge a frat?

I stand up. "I'd like to try."

Everyone turns to look at me.

Marco shakes his head, but Sebastian looks amused.

"Well, then, get up here, Title IX."

"Excuse me, excuse me, excuse me," I whisper as I make my way through the crowd of boys, who are all sitting down now and refuse to move for me.

Marco hands me the flag while the crowd chatters and laughs. I look down at my shoes and pause for a second before sliding them off.

"A ho's natural habitat!" one of them yells, but it's impossible to know who in the dark. Scattered laughter follows. A stripper joke, *charming*.

I look back at them, these blurry faces of my so-called brothers, and feel so alone. My heart races, and the metallic taste of adrenaline is on my lips.

Now that I've taken this risk I cannot afford to fail.

I turn back to the pole, take a deep breath and close my eyes for a second. I visualize myself reaching the top to roars of congratulations from an adoring crowd that does not exist.

"Any day now, Nine."

I open my eyes and step forward. I unfurl the flag, using it to tether myself to the pole, making sure the knot is super-tight. I reach up, grab the pole and start to pull my weight higher. I grunt with every movement, remembering my tennis instructor when I was little telling me this would add extra force to my swing. It is not a ladylike sound. I place my feet against the cool metal, feeling my bare soles grip, then reach one arm up, followed by the other. I reposition my feet accordingly, then repeat the process again and again.

Finally I glance down. I'm about halfway. I take a deep breath and, remembering Jackie telling me once to engage my core, focus on one small movement at a time, maintain three points of contact.

My arms ache, but it feels good, like my muscles are working.

Now I'm three-quarters of the way there, and there's chatter on the ground again. Even from here I can tell the tone has shifted, but I don't let that go to my head. I remember their lack of belief, let it burn in my chest and push me forward.

I reach the top and rip Sigma Alpha's flag from its string with one hand, releasing it so it flutters to the dusty ground.

Now for the hard part.

I wrap my legs around the pole and engage my thighs. With

my right hand I hold on literally for my life. With my left, I untie the flag that's tethering me to the pole. Luckily there's a carabiner at the end of the flag, so I'm able to attach it in one swift movement.

Then I grab the pole and slide down like a firefighter, which burns my thighs. The guys are clapping and screaming (some nice things and some obscenities) before I reach the bottom.

Setting both feet on the ground, I smile like it was no big deal. But inside I am *so* glad I did not die.

I step back from the pole and curtsy, hands holding an invisible skirt. I look up to greet my fans. Duncan is whooping and hollering, giving me a standing ovation. The others are still sitting, but I meet Jordan's eyes and he claps harder, then stands up slowly.

Marco runs up and hugs me, picking me up off the ground and spinning me around. "No one's ever actually done it!"

I laugh till I can't breathe, and he sets me down.

"Pledges, say hello to your new motherfucking top pledge!" Marcos says. "You're dismissed. See you bright and early tomorrow for houseclean."

"There's irony for you—the girl doesn't have to clean the house," a gruff voice says.

I turn around, but only see Duncan throwing me an apologetic thumbs-up. Whoever spoke has disappeared into the crowd.

So much for our moment of bonding. I was the weak pledge and they hated me, now I'm a threat, so it's time to hate me again.

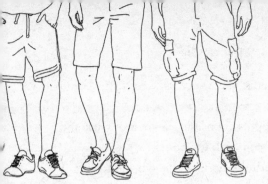

chapter twenty-six

MY FOOT CRUNCHES A PIECE OF PAPER AS I'M leaving to go study in the library that night. I lean down and pick up a small yellow Post-it note; someone must have slipped it under my door.

It takes two tries for me to read the words scrawled in black ink.

"But the greatest among you shall be your servant. Whoever exalts himself shall be humbled; and whoever humbles himself shall be exalted."

I would like to rise to the top, too, and I'm sure you want to stay there. Meet me under the guise of dusk (5:00 a.m.) in the courtyard to train to be the best.
—Bambi

I roll my eyes. *Dusk is sunset, not sunrise, you idiot.*

I shove the note in my pocket as I pull my door closed, turning the key in the lock. I really have no interest in "training" with him, but he seems like a nice kid. And this could be good material.

Hours later the library lights are bright, keyboards click and pages turn, although it's been dark for hours.

My phone vibrates audibly against the wooden desk. I glance around the room, embarrassed.

A girl with thick glasses looks up at me from her biology book before turning to lie sideways across her leather armchair, as if facing away from me will save her from my noise pollution.

I duck my head behind my MacBook.

The largest hall in the library is always the loudest, the arched ceilings sending even the smallest sound bouncing around the cavernous space. And the creaky, antique furniture makes it such an obstacle course of noise that I often find myself more stressed out by shushing strangers than about keeping up my GPA.

I brave it anyway for the arching windows looking out over the palm-tree-lined quad and the shelves of old books with cracked spines and thick pages that smell earthy and natural. Not that I'd sniff them, what with all the judgmental grad students around.

My phone buzzes again, and three people clear their throats. I grab it before they start their own version of the Salem witch trials.

"Connor (2)," the alert says. I slide my thumb to unlock the phone.

C: hey

C: what u up 2?

Studying, I type back. I'm about to set my phone back down on the table when it vibrates in my hand.

C: aw ☹

C: no fun

C: come hang

I glance at the time. Twelve thirty. I shake my head, trying to banish the part of me that wants to say yes. I'm basically done with this assignment, and it isn't even due until three tomorrow, and he hasn't texted me all week…but no.

Me: sorry! I have to be up early

C: lame

His typing text bubble pops up and then disappears. My heart sinks with it. Stupid Bambi. This frat boot camp he's dreamed up had better be good.

———

The next morning I cover my yawn as I stumble down the stairs and out to the courtyard. Bambi's already there, setting up a folding table. "Why so early?" I ask him.

He looks up at me. "Do you want people to know we are doing this?"

I tilt my head and consider this. "All right. But five o'clock?"

"Have you ever seen this house empty at another hour? Just late enough that people aren't still partying, but an hour before the athletes go to practice."

"Did you, like, track this or something?"

I'm being sarcastic, but he nods vigorously. "Of course." He pulls a stack of red cups out of his backpack.

"Do you...get up this early every day?"

He shrugs. "Not *every* day. Sometimes I sleep through my alarm. But I like time to just be myself, you know, and not have to worry about an upperclassman lobbing a beer can at me."

"This is where you live, Bambi. That time should be always." But even as I say the words, I know I'm being hypocritical.

"It's fine. Sure, if I was in a dorm I could play 'World of Warcraft' or watch anime during the day instead of at the crack of dawn. But DTC is my best shot at getting into the Warren Finance Club, considering I'm only in Econ I right now. And I need to get in if I ever want to work on Wall Street like my dad."

I try to picture Bambi hopping out of a cab in a thousand-dollar suit, yakking into a phone about stock prices and bull markets.

"That's not a bad plan." I smile weakly.

"Yeah, but it won't work if I end up bitch pledge." He finishes arranging the cups into a pyramid. "Okay, let's start, then."

I stand at attention, suddenly more willing to go along with his game.

"I was thinking water pong," he says as he pours an inch or so of Dasani into each cup. "Since it's so early."

"Really? It's five o'clock somewhere. Hell, it's technically five o'clock here."

"Ha-ha." He makes a face at me. "You're so funny."

"I really am." I smile and toss a Ping-Pong ball at the cups. It bounces off the rim of one and onto the courtyard floor.

"See, you've got the angle all wrong." He runs over to his backpack. "I've read up on this." He pulls out a notebook. "And it's all about the physics, how much arc you have in your throw."

I just nod. *This is going to be an interesting morning.*

After a few extremely meticulous games of water pong and an in-depth analysis of flip cup, we move on to shotgunning.

"Now we only have approximately twenty minutes until we need to clean up so no actives see us, but I think it's really important we master this one. It's a fundamental, you know?" He pauses.

I nod, realizing he was waiting for my reaction.

"So there weren't many articles about it, but I did find a really good YouTube video, so I thought we could watch that and practice."

Bambi produces a six-pack of sparkling water from his backpack and then sets his laptop on the table.

He leans over and starts typing.

"You know what, Bambi, I think you're actually gonna make quite the analyst someday."

He pops up, smiling goofily. "You really think so?"

"Yeah." I clear my throat. "I do. Get ready to lose now, though."

After the third round (I won two) we take a break, the carbonation rumbling in our stomachs.

We sit on the courtyard floor, surprisingly bare of weeds, despite the fact that no one does any gardening. I guess the alcohol spilled on it every night smothers them. The sun is just beginning to warm the stones.

"Who was that girl you were with at the party?" he says, breaking the silence.

"Who, Alex?"

He stares blankly.

"The blonde?"

"Yeah, yeah." He nods, his eyes sparkling.

"Yep, that's Alex."

"Does she—does she, uh, have a, is she single?"

"She actually just broke up with her girlfriend."

He turns back to me, eyes huge. "You mean she's a lesbian?"

I exhale. "She's bi."

"Oh my God." He looks around, like he's wondering who else was hearing this, but obviously we're alone. "Do you think she'd have a three—"

"Bambi, no." I point my finger sternly. "Do you really think that's what bi girls wanna hear every time they try to share that part of their identity with someone? Strangers requesting threesomes?"

He ducks his head. "I guess not."

"All right. So just don't do it again."

"Okay." His voice is timid.

"Now let's look up some kegstand techniques, and I'll explain how sexuality is a spectrum."

chapter twenty-seven

"THROUGHOUT HISTORY, SEXUAL OBJECTIFICATION has been one of the key tools men have used to suppress women. Women were bought and sold through prostitution, but also through marriage where pairings were not about love, but about the exchange of virginity for financial security." My professor, a middle-aged woman, flips through her notes.

It's Thursday morning, and I'm sitting next to Alex in Gender and Sexuality. My head is pounding, thanks to a long and eventful Wine Wednesday at Sigma Alpha, followed by staying up half the night fooling around on Connor's futon.

I dig through my bag and find a bottle of Advil, but it's missing the cap and is empty, of course.

"Do you have any ibuprofen?" I whisper.

Alex stops taking notes and shakes her head, mouthing, "Sorry."

I go back to listening to the professor. "I'm sure none of you have ever viewed pornography, as it is so hard to access in the age of the internet."

There's scattered laughter throughout the room. Unfortunately for Professor McKinley, an auditorium class at 9:00 a.m. is a much less receptive audience than the Laugh Factory on a Saturday night.

"But if you had viewed it, you might have noticed that the images are often of dominance and near violence. Sex under the patriarchy is not about sensuality or romance, but about degrading and dominating women."

I grope around the bottom of my backpack until I find two only slightly lint-covered pills.

Thank God. I down the Advil and a fair amount of water and already feel a bit better.

"As you already know from the reading, Andrea Dworkin and Catharine MacKinnon viewed male sexual dominance as the root of all female oppression. Many second-wave scholars have suggested remedies from this poison. Roxanne Dunbar-Ortiz promoted celibacy, while others advocated political lesbianism, suggesting that even heterosexual women engage only in same-sex relationships or remain celibate."

Next to me, Alex's hand shoots up.

I look around, searching for the fire. This is a two-hundred-plus-person lecture class, and no question was posed. Which means you sit there and take notes or play on your phone, but you definitely do not interrupt the teacher.

Professor McKinley looks as surprised as I am. "Um...yes? Miss in the white blouse."

Alex stands up. Her white tank top—commonly known as (and if this doesn't convince you that the course I'm taking should be a graduation requirement, I don't know what will) a "wife beater"—shows off most of her tattoos.

"What about sex positivity?"

"Excuse me?"

"What about sex-positive feminism? The notion that men

can enjoy sex without guilt, so women should, too? The idea of removing shame from sexuality so that a woman can make the choice to have sex with one hundred different people or remain celibate, and be afforded the same respect as a man."

"I really do not have time to diverge into this. Office hours are on Mondays, and I have material to get through. But the fact is, sexual liberation often distracts from real feminist issues."

"The right to exercise ownership of my own body is a fundamental feminist issue. It's a fundamental human rights issue."

"Sex-positive so-called feminism is a way to structure your feminism in a way that pleases men, and that is not feminism at all. Those of us who follow in the footsteps of the suffragists have no time for Beyoncé feminists who took up the movement when it became trendy, who live in liberal cities where sex makes you popular and crying feminism makes your pleasure politically popular, too."

My jaw drops.

Alex keeps her face blank. But I can see that she has a death grip on her pen.

I want her to tell this woman that we went to schools where sex ed consisted of "don't do it—it's a sin."

How neither of us knew what a period was until it happened and we thought we were dying because God help you if you used the word *vagina* in a health class.

How I was told never to wear short skirts unless I wanted to attract the wrong kind of attention, like the pervert dads looking at the thirteen-year-old's legs at a birthday party weren't the problem.

How we were told that losing our virginity meant "giving him all you had" and that "no one buys the cow when they can get the milk for free," so if you had sex, you weren't deserving of love. *Keep your legs closed because your worth is your virginity.*

How I didn't even know the word *clitoris* until I was seventeen and in biology class, and Alex didn't know female orgasm was possible until she had one.

That's some patriarchy bullshit if I ever heard it.

Alex begins to speak again but the professor holds up her hand to stop her before she can get a word out.

"You can leave my class now," she says to her.

Alex silently picks up her messenger bag and moves swiftly up the stairs. I grab my backpack and follow.

"What bullshit!" she says when we're barely in the hallway. The door slams behind me.

"Arghhhh!" She throws her bag across the hallway.

I walk over and pick it up, looking inside to check for the shattered remains of a laptop, but luckily there are only some papers and books.

"Here you go." I hand it back to her.

She's slumped over on the floor, her face red. Looking up at me, she blows her bleached hair out of her face.

"Wanna go get coffee?" I reach for her hand.

"A better use of my time than this shit." She lets me help her up.

We sit on the grassy lawn in front of the main quad, sipping coffee and sunning ourselves, our book bags as pillows, still a half hour left till class gets out.

"It's just annoying, because this isn't some random asshole. This is the person who's, like, supposed to be our voice in academia."

"Yeah," I say.

"It's just classic second wave versus third wave."

I nod and sip my coffee.

"If I enjoy giving my boyfriend a blow job, isn't it feminist to do that despite what men in power may think of me?"

"You should write a book. *How to Give a Feminist Blow Job.*"

She nods thoughtfully. "I really should."

I think of all the negative comments I hear around the house from the guys about girls who probably think they're just expressing their sexual agency.

I turn to Alex. "But how do you tell the difference between the ones who respect your sexual agency and want to have fun, too, and those who'll tell their friends the next morning that you're a slut? The ones who'll treat you like trash after? Because even if I shouldn't care what men think of me, it doesn't help when the one I hooked up with calls me a slut."

"Well, first of all, you wanna avoid frat houses."

I roll my eyes, but I can't argue with that.

She sighs. "I feel like it's because they assume we don't really want it. They can't picture a woman having sex because she wants to, because the way they see it, they're the hunters and we're the hunted. So they assume if we get with them it's cuz what we really want is a relationship. And if *they* don't want that, they think they have to be extra shitty to us so we know that door is closed. Or they're just straight-up assholes."

"Ugh, I hate when they assume we want a relationship." I stir my iced coffee. "We're smart fucking feminist women. Don't tie me to the husband-search narrative just because I don't want to be demeaned."

She sits up and shields her eyes from the sun. "Well, there's always the potential for a hookup to end in hurt, because one person might just be into it more than the other one, even if respect is totally there."

I nod.

"But that's personal, emotional," she says. "There's also some ingrained shit. Men even talk about their wives, the loves of their lives, like they're some kind of burden, the old ball and chain, when they're bro-ing out with the guys. So when it comes to a woman they have casual sex with, are they gonna say, 'Oh, she's not my girlfriend—she's this chill girl I'm only physical with,' or are they gonna say, 'She's this slut who blew me'?"

"God." I shake my head.

"But I think that means we have a tough road to travel to create change," she says. "Men have taken control of our sexuality for so long. Turned us into sexual objects, then told us to hate sex except for when it's with them, as if our only purpose is to give them our bodies, but then we're worthless once we do."

"So there's no way to be sexual and please the patriarchy?"

"Basically."

"So what do we do?"

A smirk creeps onto her face. "Well, I think we do whatever the hell we want. I mean, it's called women's liberation for a reason. What's the point of feminism if it doesn't mean we're free?"

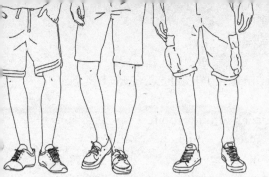

chapter twenty-eight

THERE'S SOMETHING WEIRD ABOUT A FRAT HOUSE after a party. An almost postapocalyptic quiet.

You'd think I'd be used to it, living in one and all. But it's different here, in a house that's not my own.

Much of the destruction remains, and people are passed out in odd positions all through the house. Somewhere a TV is on, some infomercial blaring away unwatched, but the foundation-shaking music is off. A calm after the cheap-beer-and-bad-rap storm.

At four in the morning, there are a few crazy souls still up at Sigma Alpha. I can hear their voices as they chat among the wreckage, but most people are tucked in bed trying to sleep off the Taaka, or...engaging in other activities.

On my walk back from the bathroom I step over an empty plastic handle and kick a few empty beer cans.

Luckily I don't see anyone on my voyage back to Connor's room, considering I'm wearing only one of his T-shirts, which, granted, does cover my ass, if barely, over my lacy bra and underwear.

"Hey," he says as I step back into his room. I can hear the early morning and the strain from the night before in his voice.

I close the door behind me. "Hey."

He smiles lazily and moves to the edge of the bed, wearing just his boxers. He reaches for me. "I've missed you."

I kiss him lightly. "I've been gone for less than five minutes."

"I know," he says between pecks. "But that doesn't mean—" kiss "—I didn't miss you."

I laugh against his lips, and he lifts me up by my waist, pulling me onto the bed with him.

He sits on the edge of the bed, and I sit on his lap, one leg on either side of him. We kiss slowly, deeply.

His hands tangle in my hair, and his lips are soft on mine. Kissing him is like good red wine, slow, dark and heavy. And a little bit sweet.

He lifts the hem of the shirt, and I raise my arms so he can slip it off. He turns and lays me down on the bed. He kneels above me, and for a second his eyes scan my body.

And then he's on top of me, kissing my lips and then my neck.

"Do you want to?" he whispers in my ear.

"Want to what?" My voice is tense.

"You know." His fingers trace the edges of my underwear.

I press my hand against his chest and slip out from under him.

He looks at me with pouting eyes.

If our relationship hasn't advanced to the point that we can say the word *sex*, I doubt it's a good decision to actually have it.

I shake my head. "I don't feel ready."

He places his hand on my hip, trying to pull me into him.

My heart picks up. The sultry mood has dissipated, and I just want to go back to earlier, to the other nights, when he seemed perfectly fine just being around me.

"Cassie, c'mon—we've hooked up, like, five times now."

"Four," I correct. Not that it matters.

"But still…"

"I don't want to." My voice is higher than it was thirty seconds ago. "Not tonight."

"It's killing me, Cass, seeing you like this. You can't do this to a guy."

I wrinkle my nose. "Okay, if it's so *painful* for you to just kiss me and see me half-naked, we can stop doing that, too."

"For God's sake." He exhales, impatient. "I'm on the baseball team. I'm in Sigma Alpha."

Oh my God. I roll my eyes and carefully pick up his hand. Something changes in his eyes. "Fine. Then leave."

"What?"

"I need to get some sleep, so if you're not going to make it worth it for me, then you might as well get out."

"Make it *worth it* for you?"

"Yeah. For God's sake, Cassie, this isn't high school."

I flinch. I scramble off the bed and search for my clothes. I find my dress crumpled on the floor and pull it on, my hands shaking.

"Well, will you at least walk me home? It's four in the morning."

"I'm really tired." He's still sitting up on the bed, his eyes locked on me.

"That's fine. I can call someone." There is no life in my voice.

I can't find my other shoe. *Where the fuck is my other shoe?*

"Are you really gonna leave at four in the morning?" He grabs my wrist.

I turn to look him in the eyes. "You just said—"

His other hand is on my leg, pushing up the hem of my dress, and I understand what he means.

I rip my hand away from his grip and decide to just leave my other shoe.

"You're such a bitch, Cassie. You fucking prude," he says as I cross the room.

I slam the door on my way out.

I manage not to cry until I'm outside. Then mascara-darkened tears roll down my cheeks and fall in little droplets to the concrete.

The two most common pieces of advice I got when going to college were to watch my drinks and never walk home alone at night. I've followed number one reasonably well and number two vigilantly. And now, with my mind still fuzzy from the tequila earlier, carrying one shoe and wearing a short dress, I'm not about to break that rule.

I pull out my cell phone. My vision blurry, I dial Alex. It rings, but she doesn't answer.

I try two more times, but am just greeted by her seventh grade voice saying, "Hi, you've reached Alex. Leave a message!" *No, no, no, this can't be happening.* I look around, but it's pitch-black. There are no lights along the lake.

I scroll through my contacts, until my thumb hovers over another name. He did tell us to call if we're ever in a sticky situation.

I shake my head as I click the button. I can't believe I'm fucking doing this.

It rings three times. *C'mon, c'mon, c'mon, c'mon…*

"Hello?" Peter sounds tired, like I woke him up. Which I probably did, at 4:00 a.m.

"Hey. I'm outside Sig A. Can you come get me?"

"Oh no. Cassie, did you try to pull something alone?" He's fully awake now.

"What?"

"Pee on their lawn? TP the house? The flag again? Oh my God, did you try to steal their weird shield thing? Are the police there?"

"What? No."

"Then why the fuck were you at Sig A?"

"I was with a boy."

"Oh."

I don't say anything.

"Are you crying?"

I nod, and then remember he can't see me. I clear my throat. "Um, yeah."

"What did he do?" His voice is weirdly calm, but with tension coursing through it just below the surface.

"It doesn't matter." My voice breaks and betrays me.

"That fuckin'—you know what, I'll be right there. Don't move."

Keeping my eyes on the dark path, I try to figure out how the hell I got here. How I thought I could beat them, and it would all just be fun and games.

A dark figure runs toward me through the shadows. It's been only about five minutes, so he must have truly sprinted from the house.

He's barely around the corner when three more figures appear behind him. Bambi, Marco and Duncan.

"They insisted," Peter says from a few feet away, only slightly out of breath.

When he's close enough, he grabs my shoulders, probably a little too hard. "Are you okay?"

His eyes bore into me.

I nod.

"Did he hurt you?"

I shake my head no. "Let's just go home. It's not a big deal. I'm just being a stupid girl."

Marco and Duncan run up.

Bambi is just behind them, struggling for breath. Doubled over, he looks up at me. "Cass, what's up?"

"Nothing." My eyes start to fill with tears. "Let's just go home. I was kicked out and didn't want to walk back alone."

"Kicked out? What, for being a DTC?" Bambi turns to the other guys. "Fuck that shit. The next time one of these second-tier assholes tries to get into one of our parties, I swear to God—"

"Oh my God, no. It wasn't because I'm DTC. It was because I was a prude, okay?"

"Some boy kicked you out of bed because you didn't want to fuck his scrawny Sig A ass?" Bambi says.

Peter looks at Bambi like he wants to say something but then shakes his head and turns back to me. "He called you that?"

I exhale. "Yeah."

"Which one is his room?"

"Let's just go back…"

"Cass, answer him," Duncan says. "That's fucked."

I wave my hand. "It's not a big—"

"Pledge, you are going to show me where this son of a bitch sleeps right now or you're gonna have so many shots tomorrow—"

My face heats up, and I try not to smile. "All right," I say. "Follow me."

The back door is still propped open with a plastic handle from the party earlier in the night, and we make our way through the house unnoticed.

When we get to Connor's room I point, and Peter nods.

He approaches quietly and raises his fist. He pounds on the door. "Wake the fuck up, shmeg!"

The door still seems to be vibrating when it swings open a few seconds later. Connor stands in the doorway with tousled hair and sleepy eyes, wearing an undershirt and boxers.

Bambi's right, he does look kind of scrawny after all, especially with Peter towering over him.

"Are you the fucker who was an asshole to my Cassie?"

"Who the fuck are you?" Connor looks from me to Peter. "Her boyfriend?"

"Ew, no. She's my frat brother, you shithead."

"Your what?" Connor's eyes dart to me.

I shrug.

"She's one of my goddamn pledges, asshole." Peter grabs him by his collar, pulling him forward until their faces are just inches from each other. "I got the motherfucking football team and the—"

"Frisbee!" Bambi interjects, stepping between Connor and me. I try not to laugh at his valiant attempt to defend my honor.

"The motherfucking Ultimate Frisbee team and the goddamn United States Army stand behind this girl," Peter says. "Remember that the next time you're trying to tell her she needs to fuck you and your four-inch fucking dick just to stay in your goddamn house, you shitty excuse for a man."

He pushes Connor against the door frame. "If it wouldn't cost me my scholarship, I would beat your tiny West Coast beach boy ass into a pulp of quinoa and motherfucking kale." He lets him go. "And next time I will. So don't think about being a douche to any of the girls in DTC again! I mean— shit. Just—" He holds up one finger. "One, don't be a douche to any girls, and—" the second finger goes up "—two, don't mess with my frat."

Peter turns to me. "That should cover you in, like, at least two ways."

I nod.

"Okay, let's go."

He starts to walk away, then turns back and lunges toward Connor. He stops before he makes contact, but Connor flinches anyway, quickly scrambles into his room and closes the door.

"All right, let's roll." Peter nods to the rest of us.

We follow him back into the main room.

"Let's fuck up some of their shit on the way out," Duncan says.

"Good call." Peter picks up a full handle of Taaka from under a table and hurls it at a large silver shield on the wall.

It ricochets off with a dinging sound and falls to the floor, where it explodes, spreading the smell of nail polish remover through the room.

I'm reminded that below all the big brother, mama bear protectiveness, he's still a frat boy.

But for some reason that doesn't seem so bad anymore.

Bambi steps on a wine bag and probably does more damage to his jeans than anything else.

Duncan starts to knock over their beer pong tables.

"You guys, follow me," I say. I lead them into the kitchen and start knocking all the clean cups on the floor—if there's one thing rare and precious to a frat, it's their clean cups.

I swipe my arm over the table, and they clatter to the floor loudly. It feels so good. Adrenaline rushes to my head.

"What the fuck are you guys doing?" A Sigma Alpha is standing at the kitchen door.

We all look at each other.

"Run!" Peter says.

"Cassie," Duncan says, gesturing toward me and bending his knees.

I jump on him, piggyback-style, and we take off, out the door and down the hill, toward the path around the lake.

They start to sing the song from bid night, and I join in, screaming the words.

We whoop and holler as we make our way across the silent campus, victorious.

I wonder if this is what it's like to have biological brothers.

My heart is full, and for the first time, thousands of miles from where I was born, where I spent eighteen years, where my family and friends live, where I learned to walk and French kiss, I feel like I'm home.

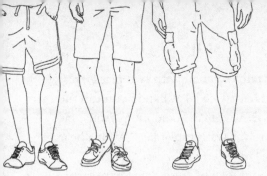

chapter twenty-nine

SLIPPING OFF MY HEADPHONES, I RUB MY TEMPLES.
My vision is blurry, and it feels like my skull is pressing on my brain. I've been watching videos of Stephanie's interviews for the last four hours.

My first report is due right as the semester ends, which means I have exactly five days to turn it in, while also, you know, being a freshman preparing for her first finals. It seemed like a great idea to have my work schedule mirror the school calendar back at the beginning of the semester, but I forgot to consider this part.

I stare at the blank screen, watching the thin black line of my cursor flash as the clock in the corner ticks on.

Fifty journal entries, five days, twenty hours and counting.

I think about the boys who carried me home singing just a few nights ago.

But they're also boys who keep tallies in the hallways of how many women they've fucked so far, who made a very public list ranking the hottest girls in the freshman class, who make jokes like, "What do you tell a woman with two black eyes? Nothing, you already told her twice," "What do you call the useless skin around a pussy? A woman," and my personal favorite, the so-direct-it-barely-passes-as-a-joke: "Wanna hear a joke? Women's rights."

But do you decry the sexist joke because it normalizes misogynistic attitudes, or do you brush off the joke, so it doesn't seem like you're an alarmist and going after the little things? Because plenty of men make crude comments but would never dream of harming a woman, right?

Because there are women being shot when they try to go to school or having acid thrown on them, women being beaten and raped just for being women. Do we delegitimize our ability to speak out against those things when we take the bait and make feminism about being mad about shaving our armpits or men in "make me a sandwich" T-shirts?

I mean, after half a year I can tell there's definitely something not right about the Greek system, especially for women and minorities.

But I can't tell what's uniquely Greek and what's simply societal.

Do I blame these boys for basically continuing what society has been feeding them their entire lives? Wouldn't that just be avoiding the problem? To blame them and then dust off our hands like that takes care of the problem?

When people talk about posters hung in the women's bathroom of DTC last year that read, "Why do women have periods? Because they deserve them," I am disgusted.

But I also know that Judeo-Christian teaching—which most of Western society is based on—says both that God punished Eve with the pain of childbirth and that women were to be shunned until they were "clean" again after menstruation.

They had to kill a dove to come back home after their period. Let's be honest—frat boys' bad jokes are nothing compared with bird murder.

And then there's the girl who heard a male student yell, "No means yes, yes means anal!" at the participants in a sexual assault rally last year.

Anyone who heard that would want to vomit, right? What kind of uniquely awful human would say something like that? Fraternities that say stuff like that must be scorned by the rest of society, right?

Nope. We elect presidents from them. A quick Google search of the phrase reveals that George W. Bush's Yale frat was using it as recently as a few years ago.

Uggghh. I slam my head down, and "ytbgbbv" appears on the screen.

Ah yes, exactly what I want to send to one of the top scholars in the world and the people paying for my college education.

I bite my lip.

What is there to do but state the facts? To simply present what I've found, what I've seen, what the interviewees have seen, accompanied by the data from other studies.

Like a reporter, I will show what happens without comment.

An anecdote, statistics on how that sort of thing is a trend, transition, another anecdote, stats, another anecdote. Repeat, repeat, repeat ad infinitum.

It feels a bit like a cop-out to not take a stance, but it's fine for the first segment of my study, right? It would be irresponsible to rush to judgment. Reporting the facts I gathered is all I can do at this point, really. Everything will become more conclusive after another semester.

Before I do this, I add one more entry to my journal, although I had liked having an even number.

Entry 51:

Some fraternity men illustrate a sense of entitlement when it comes to sex. Some seem to view the Greek system as a sort of vague, horrendous barter system, where they supply the alcohol and party site, and female guests repay them with sexual attention. They see the status coming from membership in the organization as reason to demand sexual favors from women who socialize at the house. Women who refuse to engage in this barter—barring those with the excuse of being already claimed by another man ("I can't because I have a boyfriend")—are seen as "bitches" and "teases" who don't hold up their part of what is seen by the men as an unwritten agreement.

At the same time, a number of fraternity men go out of their way to make sure the house is a safe place for women. They kick men out of parties who seem to be acting "creepy" toward female guests, offer to walk their female friends home from parties and, in at least one case, have threatened to fight a man who acted entitled to sex.

It's impossible not to wonder whether this is a matter of groupthink or personal morality. Putting both these groups under the same umbrella when it comes to the treatment of women, simply because both groups are members of fraternities, seems deeply flawed.

I hit Submit and start trying to make sense of everything I've done so far. I use my notes from the interviews to get a general idea of what people said, but then have to go back and look at old tapes so I don't misrepresent or misquote.

It takes hours to get a few hundred words done. I decide to sleep in the lab until I get things finished, four-hour intervals at a time, leaving only to go to class or back to the house to eat and shower.

After three days, twenty cups of coffee, half a disgusting-tasting energy drink I threw away, two sessions of crying and more than a few spontaneous dance breaks, I type the last sentence of the report.

My brain can barely process it. I'm done.

Well, with the first draft.

When my phone dings, I pick up my head and realize I'd fallen asleep.

I glance at the clock: three hours until delivery. I still need to proofread, at the very least, and Professor Price wants a hard copy.

Shit, shit, shit, shit, shit.

I quickly reread the whole thing.

Actually, it's not too bad.

I print it, read it again in hard copy, fix a few errors, print again, search for a stapler and glance at the clock.

Thirty minutes.

I sprint up the stairs and out into the early morning, my messenger bag smacking my butt with every step.

Professor Price's office is on the other side of campus, but I can make it if I run.

I get to her door and glance at my phone. Ten minutes to spare. I stare at her name plaque for a second, trying to catch my breath before I knock.

"Come in," she says from the other side of the door.

I have to exert way too much energy to open the heavy wooden door.

She smiles at me, and her skin gleams in the sparkling daylight coming through the large windows behind her. She adjusts her brightly colored blouse. She's like the sunshine to my storm cloud.

"Good morning, Cassandra."

I clear my throat and try to manufacture a smile. "Good morning. I, um, have my first report," I say. "The Stevenson people wanted you to read and approve it for sometime after the holidays."

She extends her hand, and I shuffle over to give the report to her. She slips on her glasses, which had been hanging on a chain around her neck. She nods and flips to the first page.

My stomach is in knots.

After a minute she looks up. "This seems really great, Cassie. You should be proud."

"Thanks." My voice sounds weak.

She looks up, and for a second her eyes scan me up and down.

I squirm, feeling dirty and greasy, unshowered in my wrinkled, two-day-old clothes.

"Cassandra, how many hours of sleep have you had this week?"

"I'm not sure."

"But in the last few days?"

"Um, probably like four or five hours a night."

She shakes her head. "Go home right now. I'll send you my thoughts as soon as I've had a chance to read this."

Tears fill my eyes, and I remember when I was in the fifth grade and cried in front of my teacher, then was mortified for the next five years. *Suck it up, Cassie—no one wants a repeat.*

"Okay." My voice breaks, and a Nobel winner pulls a tissue out of her purse and hugs me, and I'm not quite sure how my life got like this.

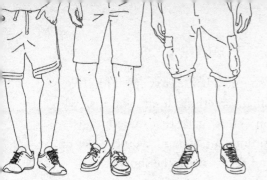

chapter thirty

THE DOOR CLOSES BEHIND ME, AND I SQUINT UP at the sky. It doesn't seem real, the sun shining through the palm trees. It's like looking at a postcard of this happy scene while I feel hollowed out and overcaffeinated. Nauseous yet hungry.

I look down at my hands, watching as I squeeze them into fists and open them back up, slowly, again and again. My old therapist used to recommend movements that caused release, to tighten and then relax your muscles. Hoping it will cause my brain to do the same. I'm not sure if it's easing my tension or making it worse.

I try to dispel this feeling of nervousness, of anxiety, but it's hard to do when it's so amorphous. You can be nervous about a test or job, and though it bothers you, at least you know that in a week or a year it will be decided either way. It's easy to logic your way out of rational stress. I'm worried about this test, but if I don't ace it, I just have to do better on the paper. But when the stress doesn't have a rational source, when it's simply anxiety about life, it's so much harder to cope with. How do you shake the feeling that something inside you is slowly killing you, when you don't know what that something is?

This used to happen junior year, when I would wake up feeling like I was dying and throw up in the shower.

When I would check all my water bottles and coffee cups for mold every three sips.

That was about the SAT, just like this is about the project. Both are just the seed that makes me worry about what I'm doing with my life.

And now I feel paralyzed because I can't be perfect.

So worried about doing the wrong thing that I do nothing.

That's why, in my totally untrained and not at all qualified mind, I think anxiety and depression are so commonly tied.

When everything is rushing past too fast, when it's so scary and there's so much to do…

Why not just lie down, close your eyes and try to sleep away your problems?

And maybe that's all it is; maybe I'm just tired. Maybe this isn't junior year again, and it's just the lack of sleep and nothing more making me feel like this.

Maybe when I wake up tomorrow, the way this lie is eating away at me, the way I feel like my body will be ripped apart straight down the middle by my torn-up mind…maybe when I wake up tomorrow all of that will be gone.

I just need a nap, or another cup of coffee, or a shower, and I'll be all right.

Which is always the part that makes me more confused. How much is self-care, and how much is actually needing coffee to keep myself together?

Where's the line between getting enough sleep so my mind is healthy and giving in to the desire to sleep my life away?

I squeeze my eyes closed and reopen them. Another one of the moves my therapist talked about.

It works about as well as when you smile and hope it makes you happy.

I exhale and start to make my way across the quad, empty at 8:00 a.m. in a world where life begins at ten in the morning as people rub their eyes and crawl out of their twin beds.

They say this campus is like a bubble because people get so caught up in this tiny world.

And I feel like I may suffocate inside it.

It's not until I reach the door that I realize I don't have my key card. As I dump out the entire contents of my bag, I think I may start sobbing. I'll just have to sit here until someone comes along to find me crying on the steps of my frat.

But then I remember the back door.

After shoving everything back into my bag, I walk around to the back, where luckily the door is propped open. The screen door slams as I stumble into the kitchen.

I set my messenger bag down on the island with a thud.

"Walk of shame?"

I spin around. I hadn't even realized anyone else was here. Jordan is standing near the cereal cabinet, wearing a worn T-shirt with the sleeves cut off and tight workout shorts. My eyes linger on his really quite beautiful arms and—

Nope, nope, nope, look away, Cassie—this is a bad idea.

"What?" I make a concerted effort to meet his eyes, which also aren't too bad a view.

"Those are the same clothes you were wearing at dinner last night."

I look down. He's right, of course. I roll my eyes. "Saddest walk of shame ever."

"Long night?"

I laugh, and it barely floats across the room. Slumping onto one of the stools by the counter, I take off my glasses, rubbing my eyes.

"Long night, long week." I rest my head in my hands.

"Final papers?"

I nod. *You literally don't know the half of it*, I think.

He tosses his gym bag onto the stool next to me. "Well, I just got back from practice and don't have class for another hour, if you'd like to have breakfast and talk about it."

I look up, and even given my blurry vision, his smile is cute.

"I mean, if you're going the nap route, I don't want to keep you, but if you want caffeine, I can make coffee." He grabs the pot in a sweeping motion, and a bunch of cups clatter to the ground. "Oh God," he says under his breath as he scrambles to pick them up.

I slip my glasses back on and smile. "Sure."

"Okay, first coffee, and then tell me about what has you doing the walk of shame."

"It's not really—"

"Okay, okay." He holds up his hands innocently, coffeepot still in his right. "But you can't blame me for thinking that."

He fumbles with the filters and then pours in what's probably way too much coffee.

"What's that supposed to mean?"

He turns around. "Oh, c'mon, there must be so many guys after you. Didn't they just beat up that Sig A that was being an asshat? Terrible taste in guys, by the way—and I'm not just saying that because of his frat."

I laugh. He pulls out a frying pan and stares at it. He turns it around and examines the back, as if there might be instructions or something.

"So yeah." He turns on the burner and flinches slightly when it lights. "It's not a ridiculous suggestion. I mean, that story alone proves there's at least one person here you're sleeping with."

"Actually not. That, uh, that would be why he got mad the other night."

He looks up. "Are you shitting me?"

"Uh, no. Believe it or not I *am* an eighteen-year-old virgin. We do exist."

"No." He shakes his head. "I mean, *that's* what he was mad about?"

I nod.

"Shit, Cassie, I'm sorry." He pours two cups of coffee, hands me one and then pulls a carton of eggs from the industrial-size fridge.

"Yeah, I mean, it happens."

"Well, if you ever want to talk or, like, for me to beat the shit out of him—"

"Fire!" I stand up and yell. A dish towel too close to the burner has erupted into flames. The smoke detector begins to blare.

He spins around and looks rapidly from the fire to me and back to the fire. "Shit."

He grabs the pot and dumps the coffee over the flames, which sizzle and then fade.

His shoulders fall, and he turns around to face me. When our eyes meet, we both burst out laughing.

"That was impressive." I raise my cup to take a sip, smiling.

He shrugs. "How about cereal?"

I nod quickly. "Yeah, that's probably a better idea."

He pours the Lucky Charms carefully and then sets the bowl in front of me. "Madame."

I smile. "Thank you."

He grabs the milk from the fridge and presents it like a bottle of fine wine. "Alta Dena's finest skim."

I inspect it. "That'll do."

He nods and unscrews the top, pouring the milk into my sugary cereal with a show of ceremony, holding it high above the bowl.

Milk splatters, and I let out a squeal that turns into another laugh.

"The finishing touch..." Jordan yanks open a drawer and slides a spoon across the counter to me.

"Thank you, sir."

I take a bite, and I must say, it may be the best cereal I've ever had.

"You know, I've never made a girl breakfast before."

I cough as I try to swallow. "Huh. I would've pegged you as the type to have a lot of girls coming in and out of the house."

I mean, I've seen them, I add silently.

"Well, I mean..." He puts the milk away and turns back to me. "I've hooked up with girls, but I guess I've just never had any of them stay for breakfast—or the night, really."

"So what you're saying," I grumble through a mouth full of cereal, "is that you're usually an asshole."

He laughs. "I guess so."

I raise my eyebrows. Part of me wants to ream him out, rant about the sexual politics of college hookup culture, about objectification and third-wave feminism.

I don't do it.

"Well," I say as pick up another spoonful, "I, for one, am happy that you changed your ways today, because this is delicious."

He laughs and settles onto the stool next to me with his own cup of coffee. I look over at him, trying not to smile so much so I can sip my coffee. And something about it just feels right.

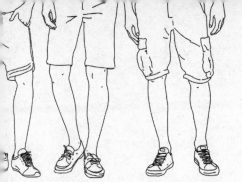

chapter thirty-one

SO THERE'S THIS ACRONYM. I'M NOT SURE WHERE it started, but somehow it's the only thing all college students seem to know, besides, let's say, the price of Natty and how messed up the military-industrial complex is.

And that acronym is FOMO.

Fear of missing out.

It plagues us all. It's the devil on our shoulders, in contrast to the angel that says we should just go to class, study, work out and sleep.

And it's the reason that after the most exhausting week of my life, after sleeping through the day despite the incredibly strong coffee and missing sociology (we'd already turned in our papers online—what could they possibly be doing today?) I decided to go get drunk. I've spent too many days writing about life in this house, goddammit; I want to live it.

I wake up at eight, eat a quick dinner of cereal and have my first beer in the shower. As I'm doing my makeup, I text Jackie.

Me: I have a problem

Jackie: Oh no!

Jackie: what's up?

Me: I think I may like a boy

Jackie: lol why is that a problem...

Me: Because he's in my frat

Jackie: omg WHO?!?!

I roll my eyes, probably not a good call since I'd just put on liquid eyeliner that's probably now duplicated on the creases of my eyelids, creating what probably looks like a second set of thinner, darker eyebrows below my original ones.

Me: It doesn't matter. It can't happen anyway

Jackie: oh shut up. Whooooo?!!!

Jackie: I won't tell anyone. I promise.

Me: ugh, okay, Jordan. But don't u think it would be a shit show? even IF he did like me, which he probably doesn't, it would create a whole mess, he's in my frat ffs

The frat I'm spying on, I add in my head.

Jackie: omg!!! yay!!! He's sooo cute!

Jackie: and you guys could double date with me and Duncan!!

She gives no regard to the Huge Problem that made up the majority of my text. I shake my head and lock my phone, heading downstairs just as people start filing in for the progressive, a sort of mixer where different groups progress through mini-parties throughout the house.

We break into groups of four, split between us and the girls from the sorority visiting tonight, and I look for Jordan despite myself.

But he's already by the door, with a tanned blonde on his arm. Kappa Alpha Delta Barbie, comes with her own bottle of rosé and monogrammed halter top.

I swallow whatever weird feeling it is that's risen inside me and turn around, almost bumping into Duncan.

"Cassie!" He smiles goofily and pulls me into a big hug. He already reeks of beer. "You're in my group."

I laugh. "Okay."

Also in our group is a junior DTC, who just nods to me, and a brunette on his arm, who rolls her eyes.

Which is fine.

Which is expected, honestly.

The theme is PAC 13—the football conference Warren is in. The first room we enter is Arizona. There's red tissue paper over the lights and the window air-conditioning unit is off. "Because the desert or whatever," the upperclassmen running the station informs me.

Someone hands us iced tea mixed with tequila and margarita mix, which is surprisingly good.

The next room is Arizona State, where we do kegstands, "Because ASU partaaaays."

My cell buzzes, and I'm about to check it when we're ushered to the Cal Berkeley room. I slip the phone back into my pocket, the text unread. I'll deal with it later.

Here we're assigned to make "fratty protest signs." My group comes up with "Ass or Boobs? Why must we choose?"

Then we all read our signs aloud.

"Lower the drinking age now!"

"Legalize coke!"

And the pretty edgy, so much so that I'm pretty impressed with the KAD who came up with it, "Repeal Title IX."

Shots of Jägermeister are allotted accordingly.

The University of Colorado, Boulder, is just a room with half an ounce of pot and a bong on the table. Creative.

The evil party masterminds redeem themselves with the next station: our rival, the University of Southern California, USC, or, as it's often referred to around campus, the University of Spoiled Children or U$C.

We're divided into teams of two and have to race bikinied Barbie dolls in their convertible Corvettes down a hill (a table tilted by a number of $500 textbooks under two of the legs).

If your car wins, you get an "acceptance letter"—a shot of Grey Goose. If you lose, you have to take a pull of Taaka with a Post-it taped to the bottle that says, "Financial aid kid."

Well, that's certainly making it into my next journal entry.

I'm starting to feel the booze as we make our way to Stanford, where we have to race through simple learning-to-code games, taking a shot if the person across from you finishes a level before you.

It turns out that the brunette is a Computer Science major, so I am well on my way to wasted by the time we finish that station. Some of these sorority girls may be more than I pegged them for.

I stumble my way to the kitchen—Utah—where they give

us Irish coffee, booze mixed with caffeine apparently being "the ultimate Mormon sin."

With great concentration I grab an empty cup and walk over to the sink. I take a deep breath and center myself before turning on the faucet.

I sip the water and try to refocus, knowing I'm going to need to remember all this bullshit later.

My phone vibrates again, but I am decidedly waaay past the point of coherently texting. I leave it in my pocket.

Apparently they had no ideas for Oregon and Washington, because after this we finish at the main room, which is Warren themed.

The theme is a dance party "because we go hardest," as a junior explains to me.

Someone shuts off the lights and turns on the music, and we dance on the tables, screaming the words to pop songs that depict women as objects, as the liquor starts to catch up with me more and more.

As more groups finish the progressive, the crowd grows and the windows start to steam up, and someone props open the back door.

"Here come the geeds!" Duncan yells over the music, and I just laugh and hiccup because I'm too bubbly and loopy to object.

People start to slip in, and everything gets dizzy, happy and sweaty.

Dancing there in the flashing lights, I feel alive. Part of my mind knows it's bad, considering how I felt this morning, to finally—only?—feel alive drunk. But someone offers me a handle, and I drown that thought in Taaka.

I should've realized how screwed up I was when the Taaka didn't go down so bad. A lot more people show up, and somewhere along the way I start blacking in and out.

Images swirl in front of me, lights and colors and pretty eyes and smiles.

Then it's the tile of a bathroom floor. I giggle to myself as I pee and look down at my shoes, which are so red, and the floor, which is so white, but they make pink between.

I close one eye, two shoes. I open it, four.

Flash and I'm pushing through the crowd, using strangers to stay upright.

Flash and I see him.

Connor.

And he's smiling at some blonde girl.

Kissing some blonde girl.

I spin around, so he won't see me crying when he pulls away.

I push through people.

And I run.

I don't even know why I am so upset. I mean after everything that's happened I know he's the scum of the earth. It's not that I care that he's kissing someone else; I just *hate* seeing him. Especially seeing him looking so goddamn happy. It's not fair that he can be so terrible to me and then just go on to be awful to another undeserving girl. I lock myself in the bathroom and pull out my phone to call Alex. Because that's what I've always done when boys have made me cry.

I have four texts from her, but the letters keep turning into alphabet soup.

I click the phone icon next to her name.

"Thank God, I've been worried." She's talking a mile a minute, and my alcohol-soaked brain cannot keep up. "I've texted you, like, a million times. Traffic's a bitch, so I thought that might be it, but it's been like an hour and a half."

Huh? "Huh?"

"Where the hell are you, Cassie?"

I hiccup. "The house."

"What?"

"Delta Tau—" hiccup "—Chi."

"Cass, do you know where *I* am right now?"

Whoops, I might be in trouble. "Your house?" My voice gets high at the end, and I sound like a small child.

"No, Cassie, I'm in San Francisco, at the Art House in the Haight-Ashbury. Do you even know why you should be here, Cassie?"

Fuck. Alex's art show, *of course.* I'd promised weeks ago I'd be there. *"Wouldn't miss it for the world."* But I would for a stupid progressive, apparently.

"Oh my God, Alex, I'm so sorry. I've been so busy with project stuff, I just forgot." It's a pitiful excuse, but it's all I've got.

"Oh yeah, it sounds like you're working *very* hard right now. Does Captain Morgan get a research credit, or is Jose Cuervo your coauthor?"

"Don't be a bitch, Alex—you know this is my job."

"Oh, is part of your job being awful to everyone who's ever cared about you? You spend all day judging the fuck out of them in your little reports and then every night being one of them. Pick one or the other, Cass, but don't expect me to be best friends with a hypocrite."

"That's not—"

"Look, I know you have to live in a frat house to get free college, boo hoo, but no one said you had to become a fratboy asshole."

"That's unfair, Alex. I'm being a feminist. If they get to get drunk and hook up with girls, why are you mad at me for doing the same thing?"

"Sinking to their fucking level isn't exactly the type of equality I've been dreaming of."

I open my mouth to say something, but dead silence buzzes in my ear.

She hung up on me.

And that's enough to push me over the edge. I make my way out of the bathroom, stumbling through the swimming lights, people crowding into me, closing in on me.

Sobbing, I stumble upstairs and collapse at the top. I'm hyperventilating and try to focus on my breath, but it escapes my control. A giggling couple steps over me on their way to someone's room.

When I've had panic attacks in the past, I've used a strategy called grounding. You touch, feel and smell things to establish that they're real and calm yourself down.

But all my senses are drowning in alcohol, and grounding seems next to impossible.

Suddenly a familiar face swims in front of me.

"Cassie?"

"Duncan." I smile faintly. I blink, and suddenly Jackie is peeking out from behind him, looking concerned, as well. "And whoa, Jackie."

"Shit, Cass," Duncan says. I smile and wipe away my tears, hiccuping as my breathing starts to return to normal.

He exhales. "Um, shit. Okay, here." He picks me up and throws me over his shoulder, sack-of-potatoes-style, as I used to call it when I was little.

"Here," I hear Jackie say softly. She pulls down my skirt, so my butt isn't exposed to the world. I hadn't even realized it was bunched up.

Duncan starts to walk.

Whee, I'm upside down. I giggle.

He sets me down inside an upstairs bathroom. Pointing to the toilet, he says, "Cassie, the toilet is right there." Like, *duh.* Then he makes me a little pillow out of somebody's towel.

I'm not a dog, I think. The thought makes me giggle again.

Jackie sits down beside me, combing my hair back and making little soothing sounds.

Duncan grabs me by the shoulders. "Stay here, okay?" He looks into my eyes, very serious.

I shrug.

He turns to Jackie, asking if she'll be okay for a few minutes, and is gone as soon as she answers. She starts talking to me, but my head is spinning too much to understand. I just stare at the tile instead of looking at her, trying to get my eyes to focus.

Why did they bring me to a bathroom?

Right after I think this, my stomach turns and I throw up. I'm only halfway successful in getting it in the toilet.

Oh.

That's why.

The weird thing about being drunk is throwing up seems so much less gross than when you're sober. Like, "whoopsy daisy, that just happened—I guess that's fine." I should get drunk the next time I get the stomach flu just to take the edge off.

The door opens, and Duncan comes back into the room, along with Marco.

"I threw up," I say by way of introduction.

Marco laughs. "I can see that."

"Jackie, this is our social chair, Marco."

"Marco's an ass guy," I add.

"What?" Duncan asks.

Behind me, Jackie laughs.

"You remember that—" I say to Marco, then hiccup, and my hand flies to my mouth. "Sorry. You remember, though, *that's how we met*." I say the last part in a singsong way, like we're a couple and not frat brothers.

He rolls his eyes. "Of course I remember."

"Hey, Marco?"

"What, Cassie?"

"Have you ever done body shots?" I ask like he asked me that first day we met. I throw my head back, cackling.

He shakes his head. "Will I ever live that down?"

"Nope!" Then I turn back to the toilet, thinking I'm going to throw up again.

I'm right.

I hear Marco dispensing orders.

For Duncan and Jackie to fetch water and food, for me to take deep breaths.

Breathe in, breathe out. Breathe in, breathe out.

"How ya doing, Cass?" Jackie says when the door opens again.

I turn to see her and Duncan hand the food and water to Marco.

"You guys are sooooo cute," I say, with way too much emotion in my voice. "I love you both, and you should go have a fun time together, not be here." I hiccup yet again. "I'm good. I've got Marco."

Marco laughs and turns to say something to them, too quiet for me to hear. They give me pitying smiles and sad waves as they slip out of the bathroom.

Between sips of water and bites of saltines, I repeat a chorus of "I'm such an idiot," "he's such a fuckboi" and "Alex is going to hate me."

After a while I start to feel better. Like a wrung-out towel, but at least not sick.

I lie down on the dirty floor. The cool tile feels nice.

Marco lies down, too. "You know what you gotta do, Cass."

"Huh?"

"Gotta focus on your guys."

"What do you mean?"

"If you're always focused on sex and partying, you devalue yourself."

"That's—"

"Hey, I'm not saying don't get drunk or get laid. But that Sigma Alpha, he's a tool. You should be out there having the time of your life with this Alex dude or with us, not giving a shit about people like him. If you go out and spend the whole night looking to get shit-faced or for someone to get freaky with, you're gonna be bummed and you won't be fun to hang out with. I mean, I did it in high school, and it sucked."

"Huh?"

"You party to have fun with your friends. They're the most important thing. Which means if they need you to stay sober to drive them to their flight later, or go to a lame wine tasting the girl they like is throwing instead of a party or—" he pats me on the head "—help them because they're getting sick in the other room, you gotta put them first. If you ditch your friends for a party, what's the point?"

"Mmm," I say.

He sits up. "Drink some more water."

I sit up and do as he said.

"You're not alone in messing that part up. I mean, the freshmen guys, they don't get it yet, either. They join frats so girls will get with them, but, like, what a pussy move. I don't need to be in a frat to get with girls. Frats are for the brotherhood. But don't worry—we'll whip them into shape."

I kill the rest of the water. "Some people think they're assholes because they're in a frat."

"Maybe Sigma Alpha, but not here."

"But, Marco?"

"What?"

"There are some assholes here, too."

"You mean Bass?"

"Yeah."

"Well, yeah. He's kind of a dick."

"No one tells him that."

He shrugs.

"You should," I say.

"Hey, right now I'm not taking orders from someone who's just puked up her guts, okay? We can discuss this tomorrow."

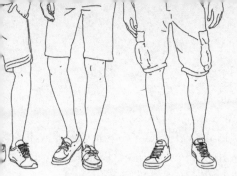

chapter thirty-two

"CASSIE?" THE BATHROOM DOOR SWINGS OPEN, and Jordan is standing there looking really, genuinely concerned. "I, uh, heard you were sick."

Oh my God. This is literally the last scenario I want him to see me in. I look down at my wrinkled clothes and think about how clownlike my makeup must seem. At least I didn't get any of the vomit on myself.

At least I didn't get any of the vomit on myself? How have things come to this?

"I'm fine," I say, but my voice betrays me.

"She just drank a little too much." Marco looks from me to Jordan and back. He pulls out his phone. "Well, look at that, Bambi is freaking out about door duty again. I got to go. J, you got this?"

He doesn't wait for an answer, practically sprinting out.

Jordan takes a seat beside me, leaning against the wall.

"You should go back to the party," I say.

He shakes his head. "I want to stay here with you."

"I don't need you."

"I know. I just want to stay."

I roll my eyes.

"No, seriously, I mean, look at this. We've got water, and what is this?" He picks up the box of saltines. Examining it, he raises his eyebrows. "Whole grain, that's pretty badass."

I laugh.

"I mean, why would I leave when the real party is in here?"

I smile weakly.

He slips his arm around me. My heart picks up, but it's meant as just a friendly, brotherly gesture. Right?

"I fucked up." My voice catches, and the tears spill over.

He pulls me into him and I'm enveloped in his arms. My cheek pressed against his chest, my tears soaking his shirt. He smells good, intoxicatingly so.

"What happened?" His voice is softer than I've ever heard it. The overly positive student government politician, golden boy, cruise director bravado is gone. He's just real.

I shake my head. "I can't explain it. I just don't know who I am anymore."

He makes a kind of humming noise in the affirmative and pushes my hair away from my face.

After a minute he says, "I think being away from home, at first it feels like camp or vacation. Everything at school is so new and exciting, and everything at home seems so dated and toxic, and meant for someone younger than you. And then you realize you're changing faster than you can process, and that you'll sleep in a dorm room more nights of the year than you'll be in your own bed. And it feels like this is a dream, or maybe that was, and nothing seems real. But then you think everyone does this, so why am I being such a pussy? I know I'm lucky to be at college, but sometimes, especially when

I'm drunk, if something reminds me of home, I can kind of spiral. It's terrifying."

He pauses. I sniffle. The bathroom is quiet, just the sound of a leaky faucet and the low hum of the music, which must be deafening downstairs.

I don't know what to say, and then he starts talking again.

"I'll hear some song that my mom likes, or smell the perfume she's been wearing since I was, like, a baby...it's like I can almost feel how it was back then, you know, when I was just playing outside and worrying about how many days were left in summer or when the ice-cream truck would come around again or if my dad would be home early enough to play catch... And it feels like I might throw up, because that whole part of my life is gone, and I just want to go home and sit on my couch and watch *American Idol* with my parents again."

He pauses. I look up. He bites his lip.

"But my dad lives across town now, and in the basement before that, when they only spoke to divide up chores or fight. And I love them, you know. But it was suffocating living there. Like, it's not just that I've grown up and left. What I thought home was...that's gone, too, and how do you know what's a toxic place you need to leave and what's just people being people?"

He clears his throat. "And I miss it so much, but what hurts more than missing it is when I catch myself being glad I'm gone. But then I think, in four years I leave here, and what if I'm glad to say goodbye then, too, and what if I have no one?"

We're both silent again. It's just us breathing and the sound of the bass from downstairs.

"Was that supposed to cheer me up?"

I look up at him, and for a second, he smiles, really smiles.

"No." His laugh sounds kind of forced. "I just...get it. I don't know what to tell you, except maybe, even though I don't really know the details of what's going on with you, I kind of get it." He pulls on a string hanging off the frayed towel that had been my pillow. "Plus, I always feel weird talking about this stuff, and I'm fairly sure you won't remember this conversation tomorrow."

"Hey!" I feign offense.

He shrugs, a smile playing across his lips.

I lean my head on his shoulder and feel a shaky kind of better. Good right now, but like at any moment laughter may turn back to crying.

"C'mon, let's get you into bed." He takes my hand and leads me to my room. Before I climb into bed, I take off my earrings but leave on my dress. So much for my nightly skincare routine or, for God's sake, brushing my teeth. I'll assess the damage tomorrow.

Jordan tucks me in, wrapping the big comforter around me. He takes his task seriously, his brow furrowing. I giggle, the salty taste of tears in my mouth.

I extract one hand to wipe my face. "Thanks."

"No problem, Cass." He pushes back a strand of my hair, wet with tears.

He turns to go, shutting off my light. The outline of him is reaching for the door when I blurt out, "Wait!"

"Hmm?"

"Can you—um, can you not leave?"

"Sure." I can't see his face in the dark, but he exhales loudly as the outline of his body moves toward me. I know I'm a burden, but I don't care. I just need someone right now, even if that means I have to show weakness. I *am* weak right now. Hiding it is the least of my concerns.

I scooch over, and he climbs into the bed, lying on top of the blankets.

Wow. Tall boys take up so much more space than you think.

I don't know if it's acceptable to touch him, but it's hard to avoid, so I end up with my back pressed up against the wall.

It feels so good to have him here, though. To feel his energy, the heat radiating off him and through the blankets to me. Or at least the energy I imagine I can feel.

He clears his throat. "Um, Cassie?"

"Yeah?" I glance at him. He's looking at the ceiling. I turn quickly back to staring at it, too.

"Do you mind if I get under the covers?"

"Oh, yeah, that's fine. Of course."

He hops off the bed, pulls back the covers and pauses, the comforter still in his hand.

"Um is it okay—if you say no that's fine—is it okay, if, I, uh, take off my pants?"

What?

"Um, sure, yeah."

"I mean, I won't if you don't want me to, I don't want you to be uncomfortable, but these jeans are kind of—"

"No, no, it's fine."

"Okay, thanks."

He slips off his shirt—he hadn't mentioned that, and *oh my*—and then goes to unbutton his jeans. I avert my eyes. *That's the polite thing to do, right?*

I feel him shift closer, and I can't help it, I turn my head and take in his body, barely lit by the moonlight from the window.

My eyes run over his perfect abs that melt into these little triangle things above his hips that almost seem to be pointing downward...

God, I hope it's too dark for him to see my face, because my cheeks must be crimson.

He slides into the bed, and his arm brushes mine, his skin warm. I inch over tentatively and rest my head on his shoulder. He slips his arm around me, and my eyes flutter closed.

A little bubble of warmth forms in my chest and spreads through me, thawing my body when I didn't even know I was cold.

Everything seems kind of heavy, and I slip into darkness...

My eyelids flutter open, and for a second I'm not sure where I am. I'm just overwhelmed by the light from the window that was left open.

I blink and process the strong arms around me.

I—I'm spooning with...someone. What the hell did I do last—

I whip my head around. Oh my God, I'm spooning with *Jordan*.

The events of the night before start to come back in flashes, and I exhale, relieved. Nothing happened.

Still, I am very aware of his arms around me and my loose dress, which I can tell slid up as I slept to reveal my barely there lacy thong, and with that plus his boxers, I'm hyper-aware of how much our skin is touching.

And for a second, I'm almost...disappointed that nothing happened.

I sit up, my head ringing with the motion. No, that's crazy. If that *were* to happen, I wouldn't want it to be under those sorts of circumstances. I mean, not that it *would* happen. *Oh my God, Cassie, he's in your frat.*

Shaking my head, I carefully crawl across him to extract myself, trying not to wake him up. He groans and cuddles the blanket bunched up in my place but doesn't open his eyes.

I go shower, and when I return the bed is empty.

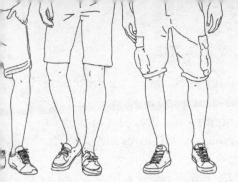

chapter thirty-three

"I'M REALLY, REALLY SORRY."

Alex chews on the cap of a silver Sharpie and stares back at me. We're upstairs in Dionysus, and she's wearing a simple, flowy white dress that juxtaposes perfectly with her grungy hair, tattoos and smeared black eyeliner.

Hungover Sunday Morning Chic.

I'm in yoga pants, a sports bra and a tank, even though there's no way I could work out right now if my life depended on it.

"I want to say, 'It's okay,' but it's not."

"I know."

She continues to examine me.

"I'm still sorry," I say.

She exhales. "God, Cassie, do you have any idea what you're doing?" The question is half sympathetic, half angry.

I shake my head. "No." My voice catches. I clear my throat.

She bites her lip. "Well, are you gonna help me paint this wall or not?"

Not exactly profound forgiveness, but it's not nothing. I know I'll have to keep apologizing and proving myself to rebuild our friendship. But nothing has been irrevocably broken. As much as she hates me, she still loves me. And that's the important part right now.

And I *will* get better. Not just at being a friend, but as a person. Because I'm mad at me, too.

"Should I do black paint or Sharpie the quotes?" I ask.

Half the far wall is painted black, ending in a half-done jigsaw. The room is not hers, of course, as Dionysus has a communal sleeping porch, but they voted to let her have this wall for her artwork.

She laughs. "You definitely don't get to do the quotes. Get back on my good side and we'll talk."

I pick up a roller and the black paint, and work carefully.

She kneels on the already done side with her pen and writes her favorite quotes, some in flowing calligraphy, others printed, and some in this tortured-looking scrawl.

It is a far, far better thing that I do now, than I have ever done; it is a far, far better rest that I go to than I have ever known.

Let me live, love and say it well in good sentences.

Did you hear about the rose that grew from concrete?

Only Alex would put Dickens, Plath and Tupac next to each other.

She continues to create art; I continue to create stripes of darkness.

After an hour she goes downstairs to make tea, then returns with two cups and an armful of blankets. We wrap ourselves in the warm coziness and sip the green tea that has promised it will counteract the toxins of the night before.

The almost painted wall and words of so many amazing artists hang above us.

We probably inhale too much of the paint fumes, but let's

be real, that's the least dangerous thing you may get exposed to secondhand at Dionysus.

I hug my mug to my chest and let the liquid warm my hands.

"So tell me about this boy."

I take a sip of my tea. "The one who made me cry?"

"No. The one who texted me from your phone last night to say that he was taking care of you and that you were going to be fine."

Jordan did that?

I raise my eyebrows.

She shrugs. "I was worried. He must have seen my texts."

I pull out my phone. Sure enough, in response to an assortment of concerned texts from Alex after our fight—including the gem "Still pissed but you're not dead in a ditch, right?"—Jordan replied that she shouldn't worry.

"There's nothing to tell." I click my phone off and shove it back in my pocket.

"I don't believe that. What boy, what *Delta*, is that sensitive?"

"He was just being a good person."

"Yeah, but if those fuckbois are being decent human beings, something's up." She laughs. "He liiiikes you."

I elbow her.

"Ow, you're gonna spill my tea!"

I roll my eyes. "I guess he did go a little bit beyond the call of like, making sure I didn't die," I say. I run my thumb along the rim of my mug. "He kind of slept over."

"Like in your bed?"

"Yeah."

"Oh my God, Cassie." She pops up, spilling tea on the blanket. She looks down at it. "Fuck. Whatever." She looks back up. "Oh my God, why did you not open with that? Details, details!"

"There's nothing to say—nothing happened, dude."

She squints her eyes. "So, like, you didn't screw?"

"No, Alex, I did not lose my virginity last night."

"Right, right." She shakes her head. "I always forget you haven't fucked. But you know what I mean. You didn't even *kiss* or anything?"

"No."

"Hmm." She purses her lips. "Did you cuddle?" She raises her eyebrows.

"No—I mean, yes, but it wasn't like that."

She squeals and jumps again. "Oh my God! That's so cute. I love it!"

I sip my tea.

"And really, in a way that's kind of like a bigger deal," she says. "Very sensitive of him to want to sleep with you but only *sleep* with you. Not at all Delta Tau, but that's kind of fabulous."

"I don't know. I mean, he definitely hooks up with a lot of girls, and none of them sleep over, so maybe he just doesn't see me that way. He probably just felt bad for me. Tears are not very sexy, A."

She shakes her head. "No. I think he just thinks you're different from other girls, which, don't get me wrong, is the sign of some underlying issues with his view of women in general, but it's also kind of cute."

We sip our tea.

"Also, what does that mean for the project?" she asks.

"I don't know. They never said anything about dating the guys, and I never really thought about it. I kind of thought I would just hate them."

She laughs. "Honestly, they were probably rooting for it secretly. What sells research more than a little sex?"

I almost choke on my tea. "This will not be funny when I lose my scholarship."

"Eh, you won't lose your scholarship. Have a little fun. You deserve it."

We spend most of the day on the floor. Talking about our parents back home and divorce, friends who are trailer hopping and going to rehab, or who don't have the money for rehab and are sleeping around for drugs or sleeping around for food.

And then we talk about classes with Nobel laureates and frat parties and football games.

"Can I write something?" I ask as we stand up to leave.

"Sure." She hands me a Sharpie.

Feminist: a person who believes in the social, political and economic equality of the sexes. "Nice."

"Thanks."

"Beyoncé?"

I laugh. "Chimamanda Ngozi Adichie. You know her book, *We Should All Be Feminists*? I lent it to you like a year ago."

"Right. Knew that."

"Of course."

My phone beeps, and I glance down.

"Shit, this is an email from the Stevenson people. I've got to go." I cap the Sharpie, hand it to her and am out the door and pounding down the stairs by the time the email opens.

It's a reply to an email Professor Price sent to me with her notes about the project she cc'd the Fund on. A very professional message where she outlines the research, gives her endorsement and adds her notes and suggestions moving forward.

My project coordinator responded like this:

From: mmacey@stevenson.org
To: cassandradavis@warren.edu
Subject: Project Notes

Hey there,
So I haven't finished reading it yet but so far it's good but kind of a little too...science-y. If you know what I mean? Like we want something that really pops: lists, catchy headlines...maybe gifs? I don't know. This seems good for the first semester, but next time let's try to make it more fun!
Thanks!
Madison Macey
Region Five Project Coordinator
Stevenson Fund

I have to read it twice, and I still can't believe my eyes. How can academic research be "too scientific"? Excuse me, I mean "science-y."

Like seriously, I do all this research and they want clickbait?

"Um, excuse me." A girl with glasses and a purple stripe in her hair pushes past me.

"Oh, sorry." I'd forgotten I was still in the doorway.

I step forward, eyes still on my phone.

I mean really, these are human issues. They are nuanced, they don't tie up in a bow. It's hard enough to be lying to the boys to run an academic study I'm proud of, but how can I justify a...a hack job?

I shove my phone back in my bag and take off toward home.

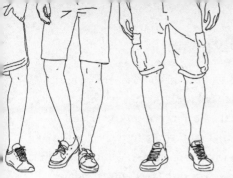

chapter thirty-four

SOMEONE'S ZIPPER CLICKS AGAINST THE INSIDE OF the dryer. I look up, easily pulled away from the notes in front of me.

I'm sitting in the laundry room on Sunday night, studying for my only remaining final. I've already turned in my papers for my other classes. The first a piece on feminism, intersectionality and media called "The Taylor Swift Effect." The idea was to examine whether the trendiness and popularity of feminism will create real and lasting activism or just more social media likes and no real change, as well as how having celebrity quasi-spokespeople for feminism affects what people think a feminist looks, acts and thinks like. My rhetoric paper was a blur, fifteen pages written in three days about JFK. With grade inflation, I'll pull off a C, at least.

And obviously I turned in the first half of my project.

So now all that stands between me and the snow, turkeys, plastic yard Santas, cookies, absence of homework and, most likely, family drama of winter break is my sociology exam. It's worth 30 percent of my grade, but I have a 97 percent as things stand, even with the few weeks I took the quizzes hungover or still drunk from Rush events. So I'm not too worried.

Actually, that's not all that stands in my way. I still have to pack all my shit for a monthlong break. Which of course means catching up on *three weeks* of backed-up laundry.

A dryer beeps, and I try to refocus on reading through my notes. I flip through my flash cards again, interrupted every thirty seconds by that freakin' beep.

"Cassie."

"What?" I look up. Jordan stands in the doorway, a blue military-style duffel, the classic manly-man-I-don't-do-laundry way to carry your dirty clothes, slung over his shoulder.

"I mean, hey." I sit up straighter. "Sorry, I, uh, I'm just mad at the beeps." He gives me an odd look but doesn't say anything. As he sets his bag on the other side of the table, his eyes don't leave me.

I look down at my hands and my note cards. It's the first time I've seen him since our night of…nothing, it was nothing.

"Uh." I look up. "Thanks, for, um, last night and everything."

He looks down at his bag, tugging on the drawstring. "Don't mention it." He starts to pull out T-shirts, gray, blue and black, then shoves them into the washer with great purpose.

I turn back to my notes.

"You hungover today?"

What? "Oh, only a little."

He smirks. "I'm jealous. I know when I first started drinking, I could black out and pop up the next morning and head to practice. Now I'm like an old man—too much Taaka and I'm bedridden for days."

I laugh lightly. "I don't think old men drink Taaka."

"True."

Something beeps again and luckily this time it's the washer *my* clothes are in. I walk over and start to quickly throw them in a dryer, my mind still running through sociology terms.

I pause suddenly, staring down at the bright pink lace in my hand.

Fuck.

My underwear can't go in the dryer, otherwise it will fall apart. It needs to be hung up to dry, but now Jordan's here and...

I glance around the room. There's a metal contraption on the other side of the room that's meant for this, and it's empty. That's pretty typical, except for when there's a career fair or formal, and it gets hidden under a rainbow of button-downs.

I've used it for my delicates before. But I also usually do my laundry at odd hours to avoid this kind of situation.

But with finals and the project and still showing up to frat events, I hadn't had the time, and I need these things to dry before I can pack them, so...

I stand up straight and will myself not to blush as I cross the room and carefully, professionally hang the thong.

He whistles.

I turn around and flip him off, although the effect is probably diminished by my bright red cheeks.

"What?" He holds up his hands innocently.

"Don't be a perv."

"I can't appreciate high fashion?"

I roll my eyes and walk back to the washer. I continue to unload it, praying I have a dress or something that can't go in the dryer so my panties won't be alone.

Unfortunately, this load contains only two more lacy panties and three bras.

"It's like a Christmas tree of lingerie." He stands next to

me as I hang the last bra, examining the display, head tilted to the side and hand on his chin.

I playfully hit him. "Focus on your own shit. There's so much to do before we leave."

"Not for me."

I scoff. "Oh, I'm Jordan, I have my shit sooo together, blah, blah, blah."

He sticks his tongue out at me, and I do the same in response.

Because Warren students come from so many places, even other countries, we have a weird schedule where we get off from Thanksgiving to January 2, so people don't have to travel twice. Unfortunately, that also means packing for four and a half weeks before we leave.

Sliding up to sit on the table, he says, "I'm actually not going home."

"What? Why, because of soccer?"

"Yes and no." He swings his foot against the leg of the table. "They give us a week off for Thanksgiving and then again for Christmas."

"Oh, that's not too bad. You'd have a day of traveling each time, but that's worth it for time at home, right?"

"Yeah, if you can afford it."

I look up. Even by Warren standards, the Greek community is a bit of a rich kids' club. The 1 percent of the .001 percent. Most of the kids in DTC live on Park Avenue or in Beverly Hills mansions, not...

"Where are you from again?"

"West Virginia."

I nod. "Yeah, that's far."

"Yep."

I lean against the washer and bite my lip. I think of the way financial aid is referred to around the house, the way people spend fortunes on speakers they'll spill beer on and sports cars they'll crash. I guess I'm not the only one who doesn't quite fit in here.

"So what are you gonna do?"

"Huh?"

"During break?"

"Haven't thought about it too much. Probably sleep. I've been missing that a lot lately."

I nod.

"Play soccer, work out, read. I like to read when I have free time. Last summer I did *The Iliad* and—"

"The Iliad?"

He nods.

"Oh, c'mon," I scoff. "People don't read that shit for fun. No use in trying to impress me."

He shrugs. "I'm serious. I like challenging books. I mean, I like thrillers, too, but when I have a lot of free time, I could get down to some Ayn Rand."

"Really?"

He raises his eyebrows. "I'm surprised something that simple would impress a girl like you."

"What do you mean?"

"You're brilliant, and what? You're impressed the jock can read."

Brilliant? "No, that's not what I—"

"I mean, if you really want to be impressed…" He hops down from the table. "I know a lot of big words. *Ethnocentrism, heteronormativity.*" He walks toward me. "*Ethnomethodology*— those are from our class." He leans against the dryer. "See? Impressive. For an athlete, at least."

"I didn't mean—"

"I know what you meant, Cassie." A smirk spreads across

his face, and he leans forward. "*Antidisestablishmentarianism.* Have you ever even heard a word that big?"

"Oh, shut up. You are such a dork!" I swat his arm.

He grabs my hand, holding on to my wrist. "You're seriously going to have to stop hitting me or I'll report you to Sebastian."

"You wouldn't dare." I make my best tough-guy face.

"Try me."

He continues to hold on and stares at me for a second too long.

"Cassie..." His voice is serious.

"What?"

"I need you to move. You're standing in front of my clothes."

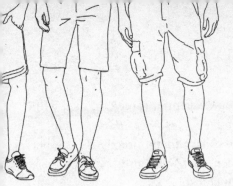

chapter thirty-five

MONDAY MORNING I START OFF WITH TWO CUPS of coffee while I flip through my note cards. As soon as I finish, I check the clock on my phone.

I still have time for one more cup before I have to leave for my exam.

I laugh as I pour another cup, black, and think wistfully of the days when my mom would shake her head in disdain when I ordered a small with extra cream and sugar at Dunkin' Donuts.

It's going to be quite a shock heading home.

Returning from the kitchen, I set my mug back down alongside my notes as four boys I know vaguely walk into the room, arguing about something.

So much for studying. I pile up my note cards. It's fine; I'm more than prepared for this thing already.

"So you just didn't sleep with her?" The boys sit down at the other end of the table.

"Yeah, dude, I don't want that getting on me, all that blood and shit."

"I guess but—"

"Plus there's an egg, right? What if it came out, like, while we were having sex?"

I sip my coffee and turn to face them directly. This is better than anything that's been on TV recently.

"Dude, she's not like…a chicken."

"Yeah, but I mean, that's pretty much what she's doing, right? Laying an egg? Did you ever think about that?"

I almost choke on my coffee. I cannot emphasize enough that these are adult men, who attend one of the best universities in the United States of America, and they think human women *lay eggs*.

His friends seem to consider this for a moment.

"I never thought about it that way," one of them says.

"Periods are so weird," another one adds.

"I've just always wondered how they can pee, what with the tampons up in there and whatnot."

"Dude, you are so stupid—it's a different place from where the pee comes out."

Okay, this has gone on long enough.

"Hey, um, excuse me." I raise my hand slightly. "I'm sorry to interrupt. I'm Cassie—I'm a pledge here."

They nod.

"Title IX," one of them says. It doesn't even seem like he's trying to insult me, just that his only frame of reference is my pledge name.

"Yeah, right, whatever. So, I didn't mean to eavesdrop or anything, but I, uh, think I may be able to shed some light on the…debate you're having."

"Really?"

No effing duh. I am a postpubescent woman, and believe it or not, I know more about this than you.

I rub my eyes. God, where do I start? "So it's like…when

a woman has her period…no, let's start with basic anatomy. Have you guys ever seen a diagram of—"

My phone goes off. A calendar alert: LEAVE FOR FINAL NOW. DO IT. IF YOU ARE STILL ASLEEP, I AM TIME TRAVELING TO PUNCH YOU IN THE FACE.

I like to get creative with my event names.

"Shit, you know what? I'll explain later. I have to go to a final. Will you all be around later today?"

They nod.

"Okay, meet me in the lounge at, like, three. I'll teach you everything you need to know. But just don't…share these thoughts with anyone until I get back."

I grab my bag and rush out.

Oh my God, they are *Warren students*. How do they know so little?

The exam goes fine, as expected. I finish with an hour left.

They aren't kidding when they say the hardest part of going to an elite university is getting in.

As I step outside to sunshine and freedom, my phone buzzes. I have multiple texts from Ben Worthington.

Ben Worthington? If he's in my contacts it's because I've put him there, but I can't place the name, although it does sound vaguely familiar.

Oh my God, it's Bambi.

I open the messages.

B: Hey… I heard you were going to talk about lady stuff

Then, three minutes later…

B: And I've kind of never been with a girl before

Then, ten minutes after that…

B: So I was wondering if I could come

B: And if you would, you know, talk about the basics a little

And then a minute after that...

B: BUT OMG DON'T TELL ANYONE I'M A VIRGIN!! ESP IN THE HOUSE

This is out of hand. I shove my phone back into my messenger bag. Bambi wasn't even in the kitchen this morning. How many people have heard about this?

I'm not about to teach sex ed in a frat house.

Except...

What if I teach a formal sex ed program in a frat house? Is that gimmicky enough for you, Macey?

I pull my phone back out and click on my email.

From: cassandradavis@warren.edu
To: dopest-house-on-campus@lists.warren.edu
Subject: Who? Who-ha
Greetings fellow pledge bitches and respected actives,

Ever wondered what the heck a period is?

G spot harder to find than a parking spot near main quad?

Baffled by ovulation?

Recently discovered that women can orgasm and wanting to make that happen?

Do you ever encounter women in your life, or think, hey, maybe I should know something about the health and body of half the human population?

You are in luck!

Due to a number of requests I will be teaching sex ed in the lounge this afternoon @ 3 (but let's be real—I'll be late and it will be 3:15)

   See you there

Xoxo,

Cassie, aka Title IX

PS: There may also be doughnuts if I have time to pick them up.

After the final, I head over to the building Professor Price works in and find an assistant with thick-rimmed glasses and a pencil skirt, which she probably wears to distinguish her from the students, who are about her age but all seem to be wearing sweatpants.

I tell her I work for Price and I'm teaching sex ed at DTC this afternoon (both true separately, although I *am* massaging the truth a bit by saying them in that order).

Her eyes grow huge at the sound of Price's name, and she scrambles away, saying she has just what I need.

She hooks me up with some poster-size anatomical diagrams and some plastic models.

"Wait, take these, too." She adds a giant box of individually wrapped condoms to the pile in my arms.

"It's great you're doing this. They really need it," she says.

I nod and thank her, taking the supplies.

She waves as I close the door behind me with my hip. I smile faintly, fulfilling my role as patron saint of educated frat boys.

I head to the doughnut store and then back to the house, garnering more than a few stares with my giant vagina posters.

The common room is already pretty full when I open the door.

I make my way toward the front of the room, trying not to drop the plastic vulva as I weave between frat boys.

The couches are full, and a lot of the floor space has been taken up, too. A few guys loiter in the far doorways, like they're accidentally here.

Some look timid, like Bambi, who's sitting on the arm of a couch, avoiding eye contact with me.

Some have a "sue me" kind of look, secure enough to be here and not feel bad.

But the worst are the ones acting like they came here as a joke. They need the info but are terrified anyone thinks they don't, at eighteen or nineteen, know everything there is to know about sex.

"Will you be stripping, Cassie?" one of them asks.

I ignore them and set down my teaching materials.

"Do you need volunteers to demonstrate?" someone yells, and a bunch of them laugh together.

I turn around and just stare at them. Most of the trouble-makers are sitting on the floor in front of the couches. And most of them are in my pledge class, although Sebastian is there, too. *Fabulous.* He's not making comments, but he has a smirk on his spoiled little face.

This could go south fast.

I scan the room. "I'll be right back."

I practically run upstairs and start knocking vigorously on Duncan's door.

After a minute he answers, shirtless and in basketball shorts. The room is dark, and there's still sleep in his eyes.

"Hey, Cass." He yawns. "'Sup?"

"Are you busy?" I ask, although the answer is obvious.

He scrubs his hand over his face. "Nah, I, uh, got back from practice and was taking a nap."

"I need your help with something." I cringe, feeling bad at taking away some of his precious time to sleep. He looks so tired, but I really do need him.

"No problem. Just give me a second." He closes the door and after a minute reemerges, this time wearing a black T-shirt and looking slightly—though only slightly—more awake.

We make it downstairs to find that the little assholes have opened the box of condoms and helped themselves already. I tell myself at least they're using them.

"Oh, it looks like she already has a volunteer," someone says.

I want to flip him off, but that would set a bad tone.

I clear my throat. "All right."

My voice can barely be heard above the rowdiness.

"All right," I yell. The noise in the room turns to a murmur. "Let's begin."

"Can't wait to finish!" a member of the peanut gallery contributes.

I side-eye them and then turn back to the rest of the room.

"Okay, here's the deal. Duncan is my bouncer." I gesture toward him, and he crosses his large arms in front of his chest. He makes what I guess is supposed to be an intimidating face, but he still looks more like a teddy than a grizzly. Doesn't matter. His size does the trick.

"If you make a comment or a joke that makes people—including me—uncomfortable, he kicks you out."

I smile mechanically. They all shut up, and some even squirm. God, this feels good.

"Okay, we're gonna start with a little survey." I look challengingly around the room. "So who thinks they know about sex?"

Most of them raise their hands. Bambi's eyes dart side to side before he raises his. There are a few snickers, but nothing that requires Duncan's assistance.

I nod. "Who learned about sex at school?"

About half the hands go up this time.

Okay…

"Who learned about sex from porn?"

Three hands go up. People shift in their seats to look at who responded. Those faces turn red. *Hmm…*

"Everyone close your eyes." They do. "Who learned about sex from porn?"

There is a slight rustle in the room as practically every hand goes up.

Okay, that's more like what I expected.

"'Kay, hands down. All right, so the bad news is most porn is more reflective of fantasy than reality. And even worse, it's reflective of stereotypical fantasy, like male dominance of innocent and naive women, that really doesn't reflect the reality of sex. And it leads to a skewed view of what safe, consensual sex is like.

"It rarely to never caters to the desires of women, and the bodies featured in it are almost impossible to achieve without surgery. And that goes for the men as well as the women.

"But the good news is, real sex doesn't require impossible bodies or crazy scenarios to be fantastic. And women actually get to enjoy it, not just show off their less-than-great acting skills.

"The problem is, since most of us get our education more from people who are paid to be over the top than from objectively accurate places, sometimes great and, even more importantly, healthy sex is way too rare."

I wait a moment to let that sink in.

"Okay, so let's start with some simple anatomy."

I go through the basics. Explaining that period blood is just blood, and that women do not "lay eggs." I explain how women pee, and the basics of tampons and pads.

At one point a large football player pulls a small pad of paper from his backpack and starts to take notes. I have to keep from laughing.

I explain affirmative consent and the Kinsey scale, the theory that sexual orientation is really a spectrum. As a consequence, I end up answering a lot of genuine, if not a little too concerned, questions about if this means everyone is a little bit gay.

I explain ovulation, and then play a review quiz-show-style game called "Can she get pregnant if...?"

I read off note cards. "She's on her period?"

"Yes!" someone on the farthest couch yells.

"Correct." I throw a condom in his general direction.

"If she's on the pill?"

"Yes!"

I throw another one, and people lunge to get it.

I want to laugh. *Like, dude, it's a condom.* These idiots will get competitive about anything. "If taken correctly, the pill is ninety-nine percent effective, but given the way women usually take it, that drops to ninety-one percent. So use one of these."

I flip the cards. "If you pull out?"

"Precum!" someone yells.

"I was just looking for a simple yes." I use my best game show host voice. "But that *is* correct."

When the game is over I pass around the box. "If you didn't answer those questions correctly, you need these even more."

Then I take questions from them.

"What's your favorite position?" the kid sitting next to Sebastian asks. He's in my pledge class but hasn't said a word to me this whole semester.

I look at Duncan and point. The kid is probably average size, but Duncan throws him over his shoulder like a rag doll and carries him out with ease. Sebastian follows them out, huffing and puffing.

The football player with the notepad raises his hand. "What about the tube things?"

"Fallopian tubes?"

He nods.

"Honestly, you really don't need to worry about them. I know that most sex ed programs talk about them, even if they don't talk about much else, but I assure you, I'm a girl and I don't really ever need to think about them. So if you're not becoming a doctor, you probably don't need to, either. Next?"

"How can I have sex with a virgin and not hurt her?"

"She really shouldn't bleed too much or be in severe pain. But also don't take it personally if the first time's not great for her, because it's a little nerve-racking and uncomfortable." I say this with confidence, trusting all I have read, although I wouldn't know personally.

I hand out more condoms, and links to websites like the Centers for Disease Control and Planned Parenthood.

And I walk away kind of proud, with surprisingly little material for my report, but feeling like I may have just taught some people some really important things.

And I'm not sure if I should be happy about that or not.

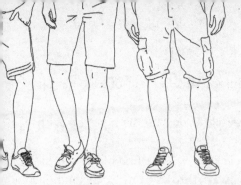

chapter thirty-six

"FINALS ARE OVER. LET'S PARTAAAAY!" DUNCAN shows up to my door at exactly five o'clock of our last night on campus. "If classy grown-ups don't have to wait past that why do we?"

I laugh but stick to straight lemonade, while he mixes his Minute Maid with Smirnoff.

"Want me to play the good stuff?" I ask, syncing my speakers to my phone's Bluetooth.

"What else?" Duncan smiles.

So we blast boy band music, a mix of '90s throwbacks and modern. Sebastian keeps emerging from his room to glare at us, clearly frustrated by the suspension of punishment shots Peter established during finals week.

Every few minutes Duncan yells out something like, "Fuck school!" or "I wanna black out so hard tonight I forget everything I just crammed!"

I just nod along and match him at a one-to-five ratio.

He passes out in the hallway outside my room before the

rest of the house starts drinking. It takes four of us to get him into his bed.

He snores away, and the party downstairs rages on without him.

By eleven the house is packed for "The End of the World," a huge open party DTC always throws to mark the end of a semester.

They've—I mean *we've*—gone all out this time, bringing in a DJ from San Francisco and everything.

Alex shows up pretty early, and I have the most fun I've had in a long time, dancing with her and my "brothers."

I don't see Jordan anywhere, even though he did mention he'd be going when I talked to him earlier. Not that I'm not having fun with everyone else. I just have a feeling my night would be even better if he was here beside me, as well.

I shake the thought away and refocus on the beat and the lights and the pulse of the room.

And I smile.

Alex and I are both quite drunk and quite sweaty when we stumble into the bathroom, the bright light a shock that makes us giggle even though there's nothing actually funny about it.

The door swings closed so the music is muffled.

"Dude, aren't your feet killing you?" she asks.

"Yeah, kind of a lot," I say, balancing on one foot.

The black stiletto-heeled boots had seemed so perfect earlier with my dark jeans and paired with a sheer black tank.

Adding the winged eyeliner, I'd felt badass and sexy. Like Catwoman, and, granted, my first thought being "like Catwoman" probably takes away from the badass-ness, but I digress.

Anyway, I feel cool. Well, I did five hours ago.

Now I just feel very sore.

"Why don't you go change?"

Oh my God, what a good idea. "Oh my God, what a good idea!"

She shrugs. "I try."

"Why didn't I think of that? You know, sometimes it's like I forget I live here." I shake my head and start to unzip the boots.

Alex fixes her melting makeup in the grimy mirror.

"Do you want to come up with me, or are you chillin'?"

"I'm chillin'." She turns back to me. "I'll meet you out there." She pats my shoulder as she heads past me out the bathroom door.

I walk across the tile floor shoeless, a decision I may regret when I'm sober, and head upstairs.

I stand in the doorway of my room and quickly pull on sneakers. I toss my heels in the vague direction of my already packed suitcase.

Remember to set an alarm! Wake up at seven! You cannot miss your flight! I try to push through the vodka and hope I'll remember...

As I'm closing the door behind me, I realize I'm not alone in the hallway.

Leaning against the wall, bourbon on his breath and in his eyes, is Sebastian. He looks me up and down before pushing himself off the wall and stumbling a few steps forward.

"Sorry I missed the end of your little presentation the other day." He smiles a smile that would be charming if I didn't know him. "Maybe I can get a private lesson."

I laugh, forced but polite, and eye the stairs behind him.

"Might earn you some extra pledge points..." If the word *sleazy* could anthropomorphize it would become Bass in this moment.

"No thanks," I say through a poisonous smile. "I plan to make top pledge my own way."

"C'mon…" He lurches forward. "Why do you think you're here, Cassie?" He grabs my hips, slipping a hand under the waistband of my jeans.

I stumble backward, fire burning in my chest. I want to punch him, but I just extract his hand and push it away.

I'm looking into his eyes fiercely, but in the back of my mind I'm trying to figure out if anyone will hear me over the music if I scream.

He doesn't fight me, though. Just shrugs and watches me.

I don't feel much better.

Stepping around him, I walk quickly down the hall.

"It's too bad you don't have sex!" he yells after me. I spin around. "You're missing out. It's the best drug there is."

I stare at him silently for a second. As much as I've disliked him since I arrived here, there's something haunting about that statement, which he makes so flippantly.

With no one to love, no one to care about or to care about you, what is there to do but drown yourself in excess?

Here is this broken boy who fucks to feel high for a second. Who I thought didn't feel but now know must carry around the kind of loneliness that carves out your insides.

I don't feel bad for him, and I never will. But standing here, he's just a person in pain.

And because of that, I can't hate him.

Then he opens his mouth to speak again, and it becomes so easy for my old antipathy to come rushing back. "No one likes a prude, Nine."

Unbelievable.

He's like a Disney villain. I almost expect him to twist the end of his imaginary mustache.

"You're drunk, Bass. You should go back in your room and sleep it off before you say something you'll really regret."

I turn away and shiver, a creepy feeling running down my

spine. Because I've seen drunk frat boys. They break things and throw up on your shoes and laugh too loud and sometimes they lay it on too heavy with the cheesy pickup lines.

But they don't look at you like a lion looks at a gazelle. I don't think it was the whiskey that made him say that.

"Cassie!" Jordan yells my name as soon as I hit the bottom stair. He runs up to me, bright and loose with life and booze. "I've been looking for you. C'mon, I have an idea."

He grabs my hand and pulls me down the hall toward the main room. "The DJ just went on a smoke break." He turns around to look at me, mischief in his eyes. "And all his equipment is unguarded."

I raise my eyebrows. "Are you suggesting…?"

He smiles. "C'mon, before the actives can stop us."

In the main room the music is lower now as a premade playlist runs, and the crowd is reacting accordingly. Some people are chatting and leaning against the walls, sipping drinks. No one is dancing.

"Excuse me, excuse me, talent coming through." Jordan pushes through the bored students practically at a run, pulling me along, laughing, behind him.

He hops onto the stage effortlessly and then reaches down to pull me up.

The DJ has a ton of speakers and lights, and a set of fancy turntables. There is also a Mac with Spotify open that seems to be the real brains of the operation.

Jordan grabs the studio-style headphones and wraps them around his neck. He turns to me. "Gotta look the part."

I nod. "Of course."

He turns to the screen for a second, his fingers poised over the keyboard. He glances back at me. "What do I play?"

"I don't know. Why didn't you think of that before?"

"I only had this much of the plan."

I shake my head. "Move." I push him out of the way with my hips.

I quickly search some EDM Alex likes, the pop-friendly, dance-y kind. I crank the dial to the right and click on the flashing lights.

"This is good!" Jordan yells over the bass. "What are you playing next?"

"I have no idea!"

I search frantically and settle on a throwback I'm sure everyone will know the words to.

At the sound of the opening bars, people cheer. It's such a rush, this kind of power. It's like I have control over this mass of people, of their mood and how they move.

I feel like I'm on top of the world.

The lights flash through the dark and illuminate some of their faces, starry eyes gazing up at us.

We dance, and they do, too, screaming the words back at us.

"I've never felt like this before!" I yell to Jordan.

"What?" His voice barely carries over the music.

"I said—"

I didn't know I could feel more alive, but I turn and there he is just inches from me, and we're sweaty and the light is flashing, and his lips look so soft and his eyes so bright, and I swear I can feel his heart beating in sync with the music and mine.

When they say something takes your breath away, I thought they meant it figuratively. But there seems to be no air to breathe in the space between us. Strangely, I'm okay with that; in fact, all I want to do is dive deeper into this feeling.

But the song is heading into the last chorus, and I snap out of my trance and back to the computer.

Not having time to think, I quickly cue up the cheesy but amazing "I Love College." Attempting to use an app I barely understand, I speed it up and crank the bass.

"This is great." I turn to Jordan. But he's not smiling back. "What?"

"Fuck, do you see that?" He slowly removes his headphones, not taking his eyes off something in the crowd.

I turn. Three actives are at the other end of the room. And they're *pissed*.

Shit. Well, we knew our minutes up here were numbered.

The dancing people make it hard for them to move through the crowd, but they're making impressive progress.

"Run, run, run, run, run." Jordan guides me forward, his hand on the small of my back sending electric shocks through my body.

He jumps off the stage and then helps me down, grabbing my waist.

With both arms he shoves through the crowd, garnering a few nasty looks. I keep my head down and slip through in his wake. Out of breath, we burst into the kitchen.

The bright lights are unsettling. Through the little window in the door, I see two actives arriving on the stage, along with the disgruntled DJ.

I laugh, and it turns into a kind of giddy squeal.

"That was amazing!" he says.

"I know!" I spin around, and my mind is singing.

He's inches from me, and we're both breathing heavily, almost in sync.

Our eyes lock, a question flickering between us.

I don't blush or giggle or turn away. I bite my lip and stare back, breathing in the heaviness, the heat between us.

When he leans in, I don't back away. His lips brush mine, and he kisses me, tentatively at first. And then his lips are crushing mine and his hands are in my hair. And I want to wrap my legs around him, for him to press me against a wall, or pick me up and carry me upstairs so we can sprawl out on his bed.

But the kitchen door opens, slamming against the wall.

We burst apart.

A drunk girl I've never seen before stares at us. "Oh, sorry... I was just looking for cups."

"You're fine." I smile at her.

Jordan looks at me like a deer in headlights.

She opens a bunch of cabinets, none of which are where we keep the cups, but I'm too distracted to help her.

I turn back to Jordan, waiting for him to say something. Anything.

"I—I gotta—" He turns and runs back into the party.

"Hey, were you guys the ones on the stage?"

"Uh-huh." I nod.

"That was soooo cool. I love that one song you played."

"Um, thank you."

"Ugh, I hate frats. There are never cups." She storms out, and just like that, I'm alone with the pots and pans, stunned.

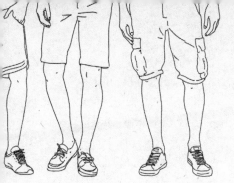

chapter thirty-seven

From: peterford@warren.edu
To: dopest-house-on-campus@lists.warren.edu
Subject: Keep it in your pants
Hey guys,
This is just a reminder to all pledges that dating (or any kind of funny business) within the house is forbidden under the bylaws as of this year. It could cost you your bid, and if you're an active, it could mean compelled disaffiliation.

I hope you all have a great break.

See you when we get back.
Peter Ford
US Army ROTC Candidate
President of Delta Tau Chi Fraternity
B.A. Candidate in the McKinley School of Political Science

I STAND IN THE DOMESTIC TERMINAL OF THE Indianapolis airport and laugh. I just stare at my phone and laugh out loud like the crazy person I probably am.

I take a screenshot of the email and send it to Jackie.

Me: I told u this would be nothing but trouble. One kiss and already an official scolding

Jackie: YOU KISSED?!

A mother with a kid in a stroller and a three-year-old boy clinging to her giant winter coat pushes past me, huffing, and I realize I'm blocking the jet bridge from our plane to the rest of the airport.

"Oh shit, sorry."

The mother glares at me, and it occurs to me that my apology may have been negated by the new word I just taught her son.

Not on a college campus anymore, Cassie. Not on a college campus.

I grab my carry-on and step to the side, much to the chagrin of a bustling businessman behind me.

A strand of hair falls in front of my eyes, and I push it back hurriedly. I return to the email and scroll down, looking for the remaining half of the message, the part saying, "Just kidding—we're pranking Cassie." The half that doesn't exist.

This morning I had spent far too long staring at Jordan's door, bags in my hands and so many words that I couldn't say on my lips.

Because what *could* I say?

He *ran away.*

I could not imagine a worse reaction to a kiss than that. Except for, maybe, I guess the equivalent of a cease-and-desist letter I just received.

Clicking the lock button on my phone, I shake my head and laugh again, even though none of this is funny at all.

How had anyone in the house even seen the kiss, let alone

assembled an angry mob quickly enough to get an undoubtedly hungover Peter to send a house-wide email?

Unless, oh my God, unless Jordan had asked for that email.

I make my way onto the moving sidewalk, reminiscing
about the amazing kiss and all that didn't happen after, such
a high and then such a crash.

At baggage claim I lug my giant suitcase from the conveyor
belt and then waddle my way toward the automatic door.

The cold hits me like a wall as soon as I step outside.

Oh. My. God.

The wind burns my face and slices through my many lay-
ers. I want to fold my arms over my chest, but I have to deal
with all these damn bags. I feel like crying, but I think my
tear ducts are frozen.

I glance around at the people in lightweight jackets and even
sweatshirts, smoking or yapping into their phones, their breath
visible. They don't look pleased with the weather, but I'm the
only one who seems to have caught instant hypothermia.

I can't believe I've lived here for eighteen years and after
three months in California I've apparently gone soft. I shiver
my way toward the curb. My teeth actually chatter.

I weave between the buses and taxis and one very suave
limo to where the regular cars are circling.

Drivers honk and lean out their windows to yell at the
neon-vested, earmuffed parking attendants, who whistle and
yell back, clouds of white escaping from their mouths with
every breath.

Through the madness I spot my mom in a silver minivan.
She triggers the automatic sliding door, and I use my whole
body to launch my suitcase into the car. My dad usually helps
me with this part.

"You gotta move, lady—no stopping!" a parking atten-
dant yells.

Scowling, I turn around to give him a look before I throw the duffel bag and my backpack in, as well.

I close the door and run for the passenger seat.

"Whoo, that was crazy," I say as I climb in.

I turn to my mother, who's smiling at me with glassy eyes like I'm one of her beloved Hallmark movies come to life.

"Hey, Care Bear."

"Hey, Mom."

We do this weird side hug over the steering wheel, but people start to honk, so it's short-lived.

"Where's Dad?" I ask as we pull away from the curb.

She bites her lip. I adjust the radio and turn up the heat. Maybe she was too focused on escaping the madness of the airport to hear me.

Once we're on the expressway I ask again.

"Your father is…a little unhappy with you." She keeps her eyes on the road, dusted with the flurries falling from the sky. The wipers fly back and forth across the windshield. "You know he wasn't so happy with you going to school in California. Everyone we know who's moved there has been so brainwashed by those hippie liberals, and now, moving in with a bunch of boys…" She exhales. "He almost wanted to cancel your visit or for you to stay with Aunt Helen."

"What—"

She holds up her hand. "He's come around. I've seen to that. But go easy on him."

"This is unbelievable." Outside, heavier snow swirls to the dirty streets, turning everything gray. I lean against the window and bury myself in my phone.

I'm scrolling through Twitter when an alert pops up.

Jordan Louis: iMessage.

What?

I click on it.

J: Hey

I don't know what to say, so I opt for saying pretty much nothing, letting him determine where this conversation is going.

C: Hey

J: How was your night yesterday?

How was my night? My crush of the last three months and best frat friend kissed me and ran away. *How do you think it was?*

C: Not bad

And then after a second, because I worry this will end the conversation and I'm weak, so, so weak…

C: Hbu?

The little response bubble pops up and sets butterflies off in my stomach.

J: Okay

Well, maybe it would've been more than okay if you'd hung around the kitchen a little longer…

J: Are you home now?

C: Yeah

The response bubble pops up, then fades away. It's ridiculous how dependent I feel on this little image on a screen.

After thirty seconds or so, I lock my phone and slip it back into my pocket, then listen to a static-filled rendition of the top forty for the rest of the way home.

When we open the door to the cramped house, my father is sitting on the couch watching TV. He turns to look at me, then goes back to the game. No, wait, the game hasn't started yet. It's just talking heads predicting who might win.

Lovely.

"Hello, Father." I smile through the poison in my mouth and carry my stuff to my room, kicking the duffel bag down the hall so I won't have to make two trips.

I flop down on my bed and stare at my ceiling fan, at the old posters fading on my walls.

Day one of thirty.

My phone buzzes, and I pop up.

Jordan: The house is really quiet w/ out everyone else

I start to type but his bubble is still there, and he beats me.

J: How long till you're back again?

I smile down at my phone.

C: Like a month :/

J: Fuck

J: That's a long time

C: lol ik

His bubble disappears and reappears a few times. He's deciding what to say.

J: How do you think you did on soc?

C: idk I feel good about it. hbu?

J: Same

I'm not sure how to reply, and his bubble is nowhere to be found. Is this the end of the conversation or...? I watch my screen fade to black.

After a minute, a text lights it up.

J: Too bad we won't have a class together this semester

C: Yeah

There's a pause. I wonder if I should say something more. *Is it rude to give a one-word answer? Is it overeager to text him two times in a row?*

J: Cassie, I have a very important question for you

I bite my lip and carefully type back, my heartbeat picking up.

C: what?

J: what should I watch on Netflix?

C: lol

C: idk

J: seriously I am so bored. We are at Snoozecon 10

C: wow, that is serious. I don't know. Lost is supposed to be good?

J: Lost it is

J: Do you want to watch with me?

So we start watching TV together and live texting our reactions. It's quite the challenge, actually, because I want to be able to understand the jokes and references he makes and respond with something just as witty, but I often find myself daydreaming about the boy instead of watching the screen.

———

By my third day home my mom seems to have had enough of my hermit lifestyle.

"Hey, sweetie, what's your plan for today?" she asks at breakfast.

Well, I mean it's kind of breakfast. I'm eating Lucky Charms, but the clock above the stove reads one. Jordan and I made it through the end of season two at 3:00 a.m.

"I don't know, probably just hang out," I say through a mouthful of cereal.

She stares at me, wringing the dish towel in her hands. She knows I mean I plan to hole up in my room all day, laughing at the computer screen.

But really, it's cold outside and what else is there to do? Alex isn't in Indy yet. I'm thousands of miles from my friends and everything I like to do. And honestly, I think after such an intense semester of working and playing hard, the only thing left I want to do—the only sane thing, really—is to rest hard. Reach new levels of Netflixing. Ascend to the highest evolution of couch potato.

After all, I've always been an overachiever.

"Maybe it'd be good to get out of the house today. See if one of your friends wants to do something."

But that would require real pants. I look down at my trusty sweats that say "Warren" in large letters across the ass, which is ironic, because they're so baggy my butt is indistinguishable in them.

"Maybe." I smile up at her.

Placing my bowl in the sink, I consider how sad it is that my mom is suggesting, although gently, that I get a life.

I text Jay.

C: Hey! Do you wanna hang out today?

J: Sorry chick-a-d. Still in Florida to hang with the grandparents for the next two weeks.

C: fun! Let's hang when you get back

J: I have plans w/ people from school some of the days

J: but sure!

I send back a thumbs-up emoji before dialing Alex.

"Hey, girl!" she yells over the sound of wind rushing by and traffic blaring. I have to hold the phone a little away from my ear.

"Hey, how's Chicago?"

Alex booked her flight home via O'Hare when her long-distance, nonexclusive, I'm-not-sure-what from high school called to announce he'd be playing a few nights at the House of Blues.

Before you wonder how a kid from her high school is playing such a cool venue, don't. She met him when he pulled her out of the crowd and invited her backstage at his Indy show a few years ago.

As happens to normal people.

"Oh my God, it's fabulous! The shows have been great, and then afterward they buy tables all over the city. And the sex, oh my God, Cassie, the sex. I—" She breaks off, and I hear her yell at some passerby. "Well, excuse you, it's not my fault you have your kid on the Mag Mile. I'm nineteen years old. I'm allowed to talk about dick if I want." Back to me with barely a pause to breathe. "Ugh, I hate people! Sorry, Cassie, what was I saying?"

I shake my head and stare at my empty windowsill. "The sex..."

"Is fantastic! I mean, I couldn't be exclusive with Joey even if we lived in the same place, because you just know he wouldn't stick around when the party stopped. But when I'm with him..." She moans in mock ecstasy.

I laugh. "When will you be back? I miss you."

"Not sure. I'll probably take the bus back in two days or so."

"Cool. Let's hang out then."

"For sure! Listen, Cass, I'm at the hotel and I have to get in an elevator, but I'll talk to you soon."

"Oh, all—"

The phone clicks off before I can finish. I wish I'd had time to tell her about...well, about the texts I've been sending back and forth with a boy. Doesn't seem like much when you compare it with sex with a rock star, though.

I return to my cave of television, thinking vaguely that I may shower later.

This is how my break goes. Which is honestly fine. I prefer the stillness to whatever may happen when this balancing act with my family gives way.

My dad has continued to ignore me, which is kind of hilarious, because you know at some point I'll have the salt and he'll want it but his principles won't even allow him to say, "Please pass the salt" without, in his mind, basically endorsing my wanton lifestyle.

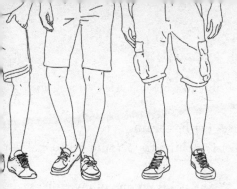

chapter thirty-eight

"HEY, I THINK I'M GONNA GO OUT WITH ALEX LATER."
I look up from my phone and the "I'm back bitchezzzz" text
I'd received earlier in the morning.

My mother sets down her iron and purses her lips. She's
never been a huge fan of Alex, for some fair reasons (drinking
and smoking in our house, and saying "Oh my God I'm so
sorry. I should've offered—did you want one?" when she was
caught) but also for some unfair ones. Mom would never say
it in so many words, but I could tell by the way her voice lin-
gered on the vowels when she said *Paradise Springs*, the trailer
park Alex grew up in, that she felt her middle-class daughter
should not be fraternizing with the lower middle class.

"Where will you be going?"
I lean against the kitchen doorway.
Honestly, we'll probably be going to the college bars, or, if
our luck runs out, the slightly creepier ones where they won't
card us and middle-aged men will send us drinks.

"Not sure yet. We'll probably just meet at Alex's house and figure it out from there."

"Her 'house'?" She purses her lips again.

"Yep." I blink at her, like I'm oblivious. Daring her to explain.

"I'm not sure about this." She holds up one of my father's dress shirts, examining her work.

I really hadn't meant it as a question as much as an "FYI, this is where I'll be, so if you're alarmed by my suddenly empty bed, don't call the cops," but clearly Mom still thinks I'm her little girl.

"Okay..."

"I'll have to see what your father thinks."

I snort before I can stop myself. *He's not even speaking to me, but yeah, let's get his opinion on the matter.*

"What was that?"

I stand up straight. "Nothing."

"Why don't you invite her for dinner here instead?"

Yeah, great idea, Mom. Why don't we invite someone into our tense, silent meals? That's just what this toxic household needs: a guest.

But her eyes are sad, and it occurs to me that this situation may be even harder on her than it is on me. "Sure."

So I invite her to dinner.

My mom makes meat loaf and green beans. Alex wears leather pants.

We all pack into the cramped kitchen, walking around one another as we choose chairs, the shuffling sound of our feet against the linoleum loud when the rest of the room is silent.

My father still ignores me, but at least he'd thrown out a nice, "Hello, Alexandra," when he opened the door.

So he *can* speak.

My mom stares at the pink stripe running through Alex's hair and straightens the apron she wears over her dress.

She asks us about school, and Alex talks about her work with different charities on campus while my mom nods.

Then Mom turns to me. "So, Care Bear, is there a boy?"

My father makes an unintelligible sound.

"No, Mom."

"Humph." Her lips, done in a sensible light pink shade, tighten.

I chew my green beans and pray for this to end.

"I don't know how I feel about this fraternity stuff, Cassie," she says. "Who wants to date a girl who's been so...passed around?"

"Mom." So we're really doing this. Now. I don't know whether to be glad or horrified that Alex is here.

Her voice gets high. "I'm just saying—"

"You're being ridiculous!"

"She's being ridiculous?" My father scoffs. "I'll tell you what's ridiculous. My daughter is living with a bunch of boys like a cheap hooker."

Alex's eyes go as wide as saucers.

My mother takes my hand and looks at me pleadingly. "Come back, Cass. The school here will still let you in, and the Andersons' son goes there. He was on the football team, you know, very handsome."

I laugh, but it's not funny. "Mom, you know I can't do that."

"Cassie, *please*, just—"

"No." My voice sounds harsher than I meant it to. But it kind of feels good, too. Strong. I pull my hand away. "You want me to move into a shoe box down the road with a husband and pop out kids. It's like that's all that will make you proud. I'm out there in California doing amazing things. I work for a Nobel Prize winner. Mom, do you realize how amazing that is? Why can't you be proud of that?"

She just blinks at me with her Mary Kay made-up eyes.

"You know, I may not be able to give you that dream of coming home and living down the street with a bunch of kids, but keep this up and one of these days I won't come home at all. Wouldn't you rather love me on the other side of the country, where I'm doing what I love, than miserable and trapped here, or—or gone from your lives and never coming back?"

Tears sting my eyes. Her face is blank, and I can't tell if she's in shock or just doesn't care. I stand up abruptly, my chair practically tipping over. "You know what? Don't even worry about deciding. This will be my last break coming back here."

"Yeah?" My father's face grows red. "Well, why don't you start now?"

"What?"

He slams down his Budweiser. "Get out of my house!"

I throw my napkin on the table "Gladly."

"Cassie!" my mom calls after me.

I grab my purse off the counter. "I'll stay at Alex's tonight and call you in the morning, Mom."

I burst out into the cold and immediately hear someone behind me. I turn around to see Alex, the storm door ricocheting off the frame behind her, pounding down the stairs.

"What the hell was that?"

"I know, right? Sometimes I hate them so—"

"Not them. *You.*"

"What?"

"You can't tell your parents you won't ever visit them again."

What? "Are you kidding me? Did you hear what they said?"

"Yeah, and I get it. But this place also made you who you are."

"Yeah, this is the place that fucked me up. God, don't tell

me growing up here didn't fuck you up, too." Alex had it much worse than me, and we both know it.

She runs a hand through her short hair, which is flying up almost vertically in the wind.

"Yeah, but I'd prefer to be fucked up and here than not here at all. And my parents, even when they suck, they gave me that. Can't you see that?"

I flinch. "See what? Fine, we're better people because we dealt with all this shit and managed to make it out, but why the hell would that make me want to come back? I just, I'm done with this okay. My life at school is what I want."

She looks back at the house and then at me. "There's a difference between wanting something better and thinking you're too good for the people who can't have it."

I cross my arms protectively over my chest. "Maybe I want better people, too."

"*Jesus*, Cassie. Who the hell are you? Can't have non–Ivy League friends now? Who are these people you think are so evolved? Those frat boys? You know they aren't any better than your dad, right?"

"That's—"

"Don't want to be left in the trailer while your husband works in the factory, Cass? So now you can find a man who'll leave you in the penthouse while he clocks in on Wall Street. Congrats. A great improvement you've made."

I just gape.

She swears as she rustles through her purse and struggles to pull out a cigarette. She lights it with shaking hands.

"I don't know what to say." My words have lost their edge.

She doesn't turn, just stares out at the road, at the snow falling like ashes down on the street I grew up on. The one I biked down, pretending if I pedaled fast enough I might fly away like E.T., the one we stared down on from the roof, hoping for bigger and better places someday.

"I have no idea what I want, okay?" My voice breaks. I clear my throat. "I just know I'm not going to find it here."

I watch her as she smokes in the light from the moon and the streetlamps, shivering in the Midwest wind. She smokes the cigarette down to the end and then flicks it to the concrete, squashing the last embers with her worn-out combat boot.

"Ready?" she asks.

"Yeah." What choice do I have?

The walk to Paradise Springs is far, but not too far. She calls out when we come through the door. Her father is nowhere to be found, driving his truck down south again. Her mother is fast asleep in the bedroom.

I tiptoe inside.

"Don't worry about it. She's so drugged out, you won't wake her."

Alex clicks on the little TV, and we huddle together on the small couch, under three blankets because the heater is shit.

We talk about everything but what's important and watch stupid TV. When she turns the light out, I cry against her shoulder, but she doesn't ask why, just strokes my hair.

And for a minute I miss school. I miss that stupid frat house, where even though I'm lying and playing a part at least most people like the pretend me and no one kicks me out.

When I ring the bell the next morning, my mom unlocks the door. Which is good, I guess.

It's probably better that I just came home instead of calling, since I think it is harder this way for them to tell me to stay gone. Instead I'm grounded for the rest of break, which isn't much of a change.

My dad yells again, and my mom cries, and I nod silently before making my way to my room and Netflix.

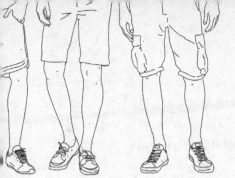

chapter thirty-nine

JORDAN HASN'T TEXTED ME BACK IN TWELVE HOURS.
Twelve hours. All day. Literally half a rotation of the earth.

I know I sound crazy, so just let me back up. What started as casual conversation and live texting *Lost* carried over from one day to the next and then the next. More things came up in conversation, more twists about what was happening on the island were revealed, and then it just became an expected part of my morning, to grab my phone off the charger and see a text from him, saying good morning or continuing the conversation from the night before.

I found myself staying up late, willing myself to keep my eyes open to see what might materialize from his little type bubble.

And then I'd be smiling at my phone like an idiot and rolling around my bed giggling at nothing but words on a screen.

We would narrate our days and talk about our likes and dislikes. (We have a common love for Corona with lime, especially in the shower, as well as upbeat EDM music with sneakily deep lyrics. We both find baseball boring and horror movies to be like paying for torture. But he hates chocolate ice cream, finding it "too rich"—which is insane.) We never talked about what we were or what our correspondence meant. It was just a really good conversation that kept pouring over into the next day.

And it just hasn't stopped.

Until now. He hasn't texted me all day. *All day.* I've checked my phone, like, five million times. Easily.

I read our old texts to see where I royally messed up, but I seem perfectly charming. And look at that, at most an hour or two between replies.

God, I am going so crazy.

But really, in his last text to me he said, "Let's Skype tomorrow."

Skype. That's, like, real. People do that with their moms and best friends and boyfriends. You don't Skype the kind of people who you don't text back. What kind of *Jekyll and Hyde* shit is this?

Ugh. I flop onto my bed. My phone dings. Just an email, though. My Warren account, so I'm probably being reminded about some sort of deadline. I open it, barely able to muster interest.

From: Jordanlouis@warren.edu
To: cassandradavis@warren.edu
Subject: Critical Thirst
Heyyyyyyy
So yeah. my phone broke. But I'd still like to Skype later if you want to. Let me know.
Jordan "please think this is cute not desperate" Louis

I read it three times, smiling to myself before I type my reply.

To: jordanlouis@warren.edu
From: cassandradavis@warrren.edu
Subject: Re: Critical Thirst
To Whom It May Concern:
As this is an email, I thought I would be formal:
    Sounds good. Gotta run some errands and shower but could
@ 10 my time.
Sincerely,
Cassie
PS: I like your middle name

From: jordanlouis@warren.edu
To: cassandradavis@warren.edu
Subject: Re: Critical Thirst
Ms. Davis,
Do take your time. I look forward to speaking with you.
Yours very truly,
Jordan Louis

I practically run to the shower, letting the warm water soothe my nervousness as I wash away far too many days of Netflix in pj's and not touching a bar of soap. I shave for the first time in a week, even though my legs will not likely be visible.

Standing in my towel, I examine my reflection in the mirror, which is quickly clouding with steam.

I wonder if I look different from when I left here. I definitely dress differently: older, more daring. But I still look like me, right?

I wipe the mirror with my towel. It's hard to notice change

when you see your reflection every day. I wonder how I would feel if I could have a side-by-side image of me now and the night I left. Would all my inner changes show on the outside?

Shaking the thought from my head, I check the time. *Okay. Focus, Cassie, focus.* Twenty minutes until your Skype…not date but, whatever. Twenty minutes until your Skype What-ever.

I bite my lip. One day I'm gonna look back and be ashamed of myself, but I'm putting on makeup. I'm putting on makeup to sit in my room and talk to a boy online. After all, I'm only human.

"Hey!"

The call finally connects, and he appears on the screen, his beautiful brown eyes sparkling.

"God, it's so good to see your face," he says.

I smile and glance down at the keyboard. "You, too."

"And look, it's the house." He picks up his laptop and spins around. "It misses you."

"Aw, that's swee—*oh my God*, your room is so messy."

Mountains of clothes cover the floor, along with empty water bottles, plastic handles and red cups. And beer cans, so many beer cans.

"What? Oh, yeah." He shrugs, setting his computer back down. "I'm not very neat."

"Jordan, I can't see, like, your *floor*."

"Its maaaddness!" He shakes the camera.

I laugh.

"How do you even know what's clean and what's dirty?"

"Smell test, dude." I can hear the *duh* in his voice.

"What's the smell test?" Part of me already knows, but I need to make sure it's as bad as I think it is. I immediately regret asking.

He picks up a shirt and sniffs it. He raises his eyebrows.

"Clean." He throws it back on the floor and grabs a gray T-shirt. "Basically clean." He sniffs another and shakes his head. "Not clean, not clean."

Boys are so gross. "I can't believe I live among you freaks."

He laughs. "No wonder they gave you your own room."

We talk for hours, and I pray my parents don't overhear. Although, I guess I'm only talking to a friend, so what is there to be worried about?

I yawn, but I turn away to try to hide it.

"I should go to sleep soon. I have to be at practice early," he says. "We've been talking for—shit, three hours. Is that right?"

I check my phone and laugh. "Oh my God, yeah."

"Damn. And with the time change, it's so late there. I'm sorry."

"I'm fine." But I yawn again, giving myself away. "I'm kind of a night owl." Which is true, I'm not staying up just to talk to him. Although I probably would.

"God, I used to love staying up late. But I can't with soccer, you know?" He picks up the computer and starts to walk.

"Where are you going?"

"I have to brush my teeth, but I thought you could come along."

"Okay." I laugh. "I feel like R2-D2 or something."

"What?" He furrows his eyebrows.

"Oh no, c'mon, Louis. Do not let me down like this. You *have* seen *Star Wars*, right?"

"Um…" He glances away from the camera.

"You have to be one of three people on this earth who haven't seen *Star Wars*. How is that possible?"

"I don't know. I just haven't—"

"That's it. Forget *Lost*, we're starting a George Lucas marathon tomorrow."

"George who? Why don't we just watch *Star Wars*?"

"Oh my God," I say with my head in my hands. *Deep breaths, Cassie. Patience, patience.* "You have so much to learn."

"Hold on." He sets me down on the floor and steps toward the sink, giving me quite the view of the lower half of his body, clad only in boxers.

"You'll have to be my official *Star Trek* tutor," he says from somewhere out of frame.

"Mmm-hmm," I say. I mean to correct him, but I'm distracted by the sight of him in just boxers as he reenters the frame.

Wow, brush those teeth.

When he's done, he picks up the computer and smiles at me. "Okay, cool. Why is your face so red?"

I cover my cheeks. "No reason."

He carries the computer back, and my view changes from tile to the carpet of the hallway.

"Hey, look, your room!"

He turns the laptop so I can see my door, then a sliver of Sebastian's as he turns it back. Just a reminder of how much trouble I could get in if any of my fantasies from a few minutes ago were to come true.

"Can't wait for you to be back," he says as he sets me on the desk.

"Me, too."

"I'll talk to you tomorrow."

"Okay." I look into his eyes, even though he's thousands of miles away. Everything I want to say but can't is hanging in the air.

"'Night."

"'Night."

The window goes black and closes with a quick beep. My screen saver, a beach as far away as Jordan, replaces his face.

I click on the calendar icon.

Less than five days until I see him in person and…and I don't know exactly. I go to bed, dreaming of Jordan and what can't be.

———

Contrary to what I've been taught to expect from numerous December film releases, the holidays pass and there's no major emotional breakthrough in my family. The Hallmark Channel would be baffled to witness our silence over goose and champagne, no spirit moving either party to make amends.

In fact, the closest I get to a "God bless us, everyone" moment is at the departure drop-off area at Indianapolis International Airport. Not exactly a feel-good movie set, but I take what I can get.

"Listen," my mother says.

I turn, the door half open, the wind cutting through my coat.

"What you're doing…it might not be what I'd choose." She exhales with her whole body. "And it's certainly not what your father wants. But I love you anyway. And I *am* proud. You're…you're very brave."

"Thanks, Mom. Really. That means a lot." I lean across the console and kiss her on the cheek.

I climb out of the car and watch her drive away, giving me a small wave before one of the airport staff whistles at her and she has to speed forward, disappearing.

I just stand there, in the cold, for a second before heading inside.

Wondering if I will ever get used to the feeling of airports and leaving.

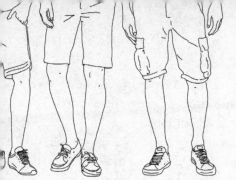

chapter forty

"PLEDGING'S OVER, BITCHESSS!" DUNCAN IS ALREADY celebrating when I drag my suitcases through the door.

With a semester of setting up for parties and shot lists behind us, and some of my fellow pledges' academic probations smoothed over by calls from daddy offering multifigure donations, it's almost time for us to be initiated as full members of the Delta Tau Chi Order.

"*Cass!*" Duncan pulls me into a hug, and my feet completely leave the ground. "Let me get that," he says as he sets me down.

He picks up my biggest suitcase like it's inflated with air and not stuffed with half of everything I own.

We make our way up the stairs, and he recounts his short visit home to see his mom, "my favorite person in the world, and her cooking… OMG, Cass, you would die" and his weeks of practice and team bonding.

We reach the top of the stairs, and he sets my bag down in my room.

"Damn." He crosses his arms in front of his chest. "We made it. Hell is over, now it's time for everyone to party."

"Mind if I sit here?" Peter asks at lunch.

Less than half the house is already back, so there are tons of seats, including near other seniors. Our table is mostly freshmen.

"Sure." Bambi slides down, leaving space between him and me on the bench.

Peter sits down with a mountain of food.

"Hi," I say.

He nods. "Are y'all excited for initiation?" Peter asks.

Everyone mumbles something in the affirmative, afraid this may be a trick question that will cost them their bid in the eleventh hour.

"How about you, Cassie?" He stares at me as he reaches for his drink.

"Um, yeah, for sure. A bit nervous, though."

"Yeah, I would be nervous, too, if I were you."

Um…

I push my food around my plate and chew over the words I finally risk saying. "Like me especially…?"

"Yeah, you especially." He looks at me like I should know what he is talking about. "I mean, nationals approved you getting a bid, but we still have to vote on whether the use of male pronouns in the bylaws means you can't be initiated."

What?

I cough, trying not to spit water all over the table. "Um, no one told me about that."

"Really?"

Yeah. I think I'd remember that. "Mmm-hmm."

"Well…" He cuts his food. "I'm just saying. Keep your head down." He takes a bite, but that doesn't stop him from talking. "You upset someone, you might not be living here next week."

So the upperclassmen get to vote on my fate. *Fabulous*. And with the president vaguely threatening me before the vote begins, my chances are looking just peachy.

The kitchen door swings open, slamming into the wall and interrupting my thoughts.

"Game tonight," Marco says, charging through the room, throwing tickets down on the tables.

"Weren't both football and basketball last semester?" I ask. I didn't go to the games, but I remember the emails about tailgates and student sections.

"It's tennis," Bambi says as he examines one of the tickets. "He means match."

"Two of our brothers are on the team," Peter says. "The soccer guys had the idea to try to bring out support for the less attended sports."

I try to mask my reaction to the soccer guys. Or, really, my reaction to one particular soccer guy. The team had an out-of-town scrimmage this weekend and haven't gotten back yet. I'm trying not to let myself think about him, at least until I see him and figure out, well, what exactly there is to think about.

"Marco's trying to make a whole event out of it," Bambi continues. "Putting it in the social calendar, inviting KAD and everything."

Great. KAD.

Kappa Alpha Delta.

The "top sorority," according to Greek Rank dot com and Total Frat Move dot com.

Known on campus as the home of walking, talking, almost-thinking Barbie dolls, not to mention my great friend and ex-roommate Leighton.

Just the setting I want to be in when I see Jordan again.

All afternoon, I debate whether or not I should go. I put on makeup and my cutest Warren T-shirt. I pace my room and check my phone obsessively. No texts from Jordan, probably because he's still on a plane.

I watch them leave, hauling beer and chanting, from my window. Five minutes later, I grab my keys and head toward the stadium.

Warren is one of the few schools in the country that invests almost equally in all its sports. They've built a beautiful tennis stadium with five courts and the names of alumni Olympians engraved before the grand entrance. Filling such a stadium is another matter, though.

I hear cheers from inside as I wait behind a woman in a big white hat to get my ticket scanned. My vision wanders from the entrance.

Next to the stadium is a beautiful oak tree. The kind where the branches split apart after a few feet, creating a flat ledge perfect for a tree house. Or, in this case, for perching a thirty-rack of Natty Light.

Oh my God.

"Enjoy the match." The red-vested ticket guy smiles at me.

I walk past him, speechless, still thinking of that thirty-rack that they've stowed so shamelessly. I make my way to the top of the stands. Below, there are two simultaneous matches going on, but the stands are less than half full. Up here the seats are littered with parents towing kids with Palo Alto grade school sweatshirts and iPads, and old people, the men in khakis and polos, the women in sundresses and hats like they're at the Kentucky Derby.

And then there are my people. Reclining in their seats, their feet up on the row in front of them. Half of them shirtless, AWRREN spelled out, or I guess, misspelled out, in smeared body paint on their chests.

Mixed in with the guys, sitting in clusters of three and four, are the sisters of Kappa Alpha Delta, all wearing crop tops and short skirts in a variety of colors.

I walk to the end of the aisle and down a few rows.

"Hey," I say to Duncan.

"Hi!" He looks up at me, eyes bright. "Saved you a seat." He moves his sweatshirt off the chair next to him.

"Oh, um…" I scan the group around us, looking for a certain smile, a certain pair of brown eyes. "Thanks," I say as I collapse into the chair.

But he's already turned back to the game. Match. "Aw, c'mon, ref!" He gestures so aggressively, I flinch, worried I'll be knocked over. "Bullshit! Flag!"

I turn to him. "Are there flags in tennis?"

He shrugs. "No idea. Never watched it before."

"Ah." I nod. "Hey, outside—"

"Beer tree?"

"Yeah, is that—"

"Yep. Ours." He chuckles. "It certainly isn't the Golden Girls'." He nods to a group of old, pastel-clad women a few rows down. "Want one?"

"Sure," I say.

I expect him to reach in a pocket, or ask one of the guys to run outside and grab a few more, but he just turns to the seat on the other side of him. "Bambi, beer."

Bambi nods and turns around so that Duncan can reach into the hood of his sweatshirt. He pulls out a silver can and hands it to me.

I laugh and pop the top.

———

One of the matches ends and new players take the court. One of them looks vaguely familiar.

One of the upperclassmen stands up and yells, "That's Dave!"

"Dave, Dave, Dave, Dave, Dave!" they all chant.

The boy looks up and smiles.

Dave's opponent, a scrawny blond with a menacing look on his face, who can only be described as a white-polo-wearing Draco Malfoy, is less amused.

Dave and Malfoy shake hands over the net, the latter avoiding eye contact, before moving to their respective sides.

Malfoy bounces the ball on the ground twice before shifting into his serving stance, at which point our entire section starts yelling uncontrollably and banging on the plastic seats, like you might do at a basketball game to distract the opponent during a free throw.

The ball goes screaming out of bounds.

The ref moves to the edge of the court closest to our section and calls up to us, "Men, I'm going to have to ask you not to yell during a serve."

"Yes, sir, of course," Peter yells back down to the ref. He adds his politician wave.

Dave serves, and Malfoy volleys it back with a loud "Huh!"

Duncan's eyes light up. He leans forward and says something to the shirtless pals. Dave scores a point, and everyone goes mad.

This time everyone is respectfully quiet for Malfoy's serve. It lands inbounds, and Dave volleys it back smoothly. Malfoy sends it back, with his signature, "Huh!"

As Dave sprints toward the ball, every member of the California Beta chapter of Delta Tau Chi, barring myself and an upperclassman with a *W* on his chest who seems to have passed out, stands up and yells, "Huh!"

Malfoy's eyes go immediately to the stands as the ball bounces twice before rolling past him.

He turns to the referee, who just shrugs.

"You guys are unbelievable," I say.

Duncan beams.

I find myself smiling and laughing, and almost forget about Jordan. And that's when I see him. Standing in the aisle at the other end of the row, his eyes searching our group.

He has a day or two's worth of scruff on his face. Just a shadow, sexy in a Dr. McDreamy way. His eyes are red-rimmed, and his white button-down is disheveled.

But damn, he's hot.

He's close enough to speak to, but far enough that everyone else will hear, too.

Through the crowd our eyes meet, and I want to walk over, to talk to him, to say something, anything. But what can I say?

"Jordan, oh my God! I missed you so much over break!"

Well, I guess I could have said that. One of the sorority girls, a bottle blonde wearing a blue halter top, practically jumps out of her seat halfway between us and throws two fake-tanned arms around him. He stumbles backward, breaking eye contact with me.

My stomach plummets.

And it's funny in the kind of way that makes me want to cry. Because of course he wasn't really looking at me; he was looking at her.

It was all in my head, this idea that there's something besides friendship between us. And that returning to school meant we could figure out exactly what that is.

He wanted me when he was alone on campus and bored, willing to talk to the girl with the embarrassing crush on him.

But with everyone back on campus, with a different gaggle of sorority girls parading themselves in front of him every night, with all the girls who swoon at the words *varsity sport*, why the hell would he pick me?

In seconds he's overwhelmed with people welcoming him, hugging him, pulling him into a seat and asking him questions.

He looks over his shoulder and waves to me weakly, mouthing something I can't make out. Or at least, I think he's waving at me, but maybe that's just what I want to see.

"Hey! Cassie!"

"What?" I turn to Duncan, eyes wide.

"I said, did you see that play, the way Dave dove?"

"Uh, no." I shake my head. "Sorry, I was…"

Blue-halter-top girl tilts her head as she laughs at something Jordan says, smiling her stupid toothpaste-commercial smile.

"You're being so weird. You okay?"

"I, uh, yeah, I'm fine." I set my beer in a cup holder. "Excuse me for a second."

I head up the aisle, past the food vendors and families lined up for overpriced hot dogs, trying not to look in Jordan's direction. I barely make it to the bathroom before the first tear slides down my face. Grabbing toilet paper from the nearest stall, I dab my eyes, then check my makeup in the mirror.

What the fuck am I doing, crying about a guy I could never have anyway? A guy who could get me kicked out of the frat, ruin my project before I've even been here a year.

The door swings open, and a group of girls comes giggling in. Two of them, a pale redhead and a dark-skinned girl, shuffle around me to stare at themselves in the mirror.

But the blonde stops in her tracks.

"Oh my God, Cassie!" Leighton flashes me a warm and possibly not fake smile and pulls me into a hug.

"Hey there." I extract myself carefully.

"Lizzie, Aisha, this is Cassie. She used to be my roommate."

They wave and smile.

"Nice to meet you." I struggle to sound interested.

"I've missed you!" Leighton's ponytail bounces. "We never see you at any of our events."

"Yeah, well, sororities aren't really my speed."

"What do you mean?"

"It's just a lot of…" I raise my eyebrows. "You know, like the whole wear-pink-and-monograms-and-search-for-a-husband-to-pop-out-kids thing."

One of the girls doing her makeup turns around and gapes at me, lipstick halfway to her mouth.

I eye the door over Leighton's shoulder.

"Is that really what you think we're all about?" Leighton asks.

Yes. "No. Well, I mean…"

"God, and you call yourself a feminist."

Yeah, I do, and that's why I'm not in a sorority. "Leighton, you were the one who thought feminism was 'not a good look.'"

"That was the first week of school, Cassie. I'm not allowed to learn something in college?"

I step back. "I guess. It's just—"

"*Seriously.* It's a group of women who support each other."

That's rich. I close my eyes and bring my hand to my forehead. "Oh, please, it's a group of women who support each other in blowing frat boys and drinking wine coolers. No, I take that back, they blow frat boys and drink wine coolers, and then judge their sisters for doing the same thing."

Now all eyes are on me.

"We promote female friendship and create a career network for women after they graduate." Leighton tallies the points on her manicured fingers. "Not to mention that we were started by women who felt it was unjust that they couldn't be part of men's secret societies, aka *fraternities*." She says the last word like it's a swear.

"And yeah, I like to wear pink. And yeah, I want to bake

cookies. And maybe I don't want to manage a hedge fund—maybe I *want* to raise kids. But I want those things because *I* want those things, Cassandra, not because I was told I had to by society or whatever. These are my friends." She gestures to the two other girls. "I like to do this stuff with them. And I think us doing this stuff, despite people like you thinking that a group of women and their interests must be inherently vapid and shallow, is kind of the most feminist thing we could be doing."

She turns to her friends. "Wanna go back?"

Lizzie nods.

"Yeah," Aisha says. She drops her lipstick back into her purse and turns around. "Actually, no. I have something to say, as well." She sighs. "I am sooo sick of you and your white feminism bullshit. You've become synonymous with the women's movement on campus. Because, poor baby, it's so hard for a girl to join a frat. But do you know what happens to black girls that try to join Greek Life? There are houses on university campuses in the South with portraits of Robert E. Lee over the fireplace and cannons pointed north. Even here, there are girls at Rush who say, 'Yeah she was great, but she's black.' In *front* of me, they say that. We're still trying to break through to sororities, and you have to play oppressed by joining a frat?" She sneers. "Fuck off. There are plenty of barriers all sorts of women face just trying to live, not while putting themselves in such an artificial situation. Why the hell aren't you talking about them instead of pulling this shit?" She pauses, but I have no answer. "You can do all the beer bongs and plastic bottle shots you want, but you are not *my* feminist hero." She turns and walks out, her friends following closely.

The door swings shut behind them, and I'm left alone in the bathroom. Astonished. I'm not mad…well, definitely not at them, maybe a little at myself. Okay, maybe a lot at myself.

They were just so *right*. And now I'm so confused. I've been calling myself a crusader for women while viewing groups of them as one fake-blonde, *Bachelorette*-watching horde. What the hell is wrong with me?

I leave the bathroom but turn away from the crowd and instead head toward the exit sign. I practically sprint back to the house, Aisha's and Leighton's words running through my head all the way.

I click the lock on my door, run to my desk and pull out my computer.

C'mon, c'mon. I tap my foot as I wait for the Stevenson website to load. I sign in and start a new entry.

Entry 54:
In defense of sororities…

I type furiously, trying to get down everything that happened today, everything that I've seen over the last few months.

Ten pages later, I go downstairs to grab some food. I'm headed back to my room, when the front door swings open.

Jordan walks through, looking over his shoulder and laughing at something Duncan's saying. Then he sees me and stops, the laughter falling from his face. Duncan stumbles into him, but Jordan doesn't seem to notice.

I turn away and head up the stairs without a word.

"Cassie."

I don't turn around.

"Cassie!"

As I reach the landing, I risk a quick look and see him taking the stairs two at a time. Sighing, I turn and wait.

He grabs the railing to avoid running into me. "I've been looking for you. You left early."

"Yeah." I bite my lip and look beyond him to the photographs of classes past that line the staircase. "Uh, something came up."

"Oh." Then, "I've missed you."

Like you miss a friend? Like you miss your little sister Or…? I don't ask, of course.

"I missed you, too." My voice sounds jittery, nervous. I clear my throat. "What's up?"

He furrows his brow. "Nothing, really."

"I mean, you said you were looking for me. I thought you wanted to say something."

"Oh." He smiles. "I wanted to do this."

He steps forward, and before I can even process what's happening, his lips are on mine and he's kissing me again.

I push him away. "What, are you crazy?" I whisper-yell. "Didn't you read the email? Someone might see!"

"No one's here."

I look around. He's right.

"Oh." This time *I* kiss *him*. His lips are soft, and this kiss is slower, more sensual. But a thought tugs at the back of my mind. I step back.

"Wait, I'm sorry, but I can't. I just don't understand. Before Christmas, you—you *ran away*."

"Yeah, uh, sorry. I kinda panicked. I'd been crushing on you all year, and you looked so shocked and I—I don't know. I didn't know what to do."

"Oh."

He leans in again, but I hold up my hand.

"Okay, but wait, wait. I'm still confused."

"Why?"

"If you had a crush on me, too, why didn't you make a move anytime last quarter?"

"Crush on you, *too*? As in—"

"Answer the question, Louis."

"Okay, okay." He smiles. "I… I don't know. I guess I was just nervous to do it. But, hey, I could ask you the same question. Aren't you supposed to be this great crusader, going places women haven't before? And you still think the guy has to make the first move?" He shakes his head in mock disappointment. I laugh and pull him into me.

His lips are soft against mine, and his hands explore my body, sliding over every curve and then pulling me into him. My own hands on his back, I pull him even closer, his hips to mine.

We break apart, our foreheads leaning against each other.

"Let's get out of here," I hear myself say between heavy breaths before I can even think.

"I don't care where we go—I just want to keep kissing you." He pecks me quickly on the lips.

Footsteps echo along the hall above us.

"Okay, that's sweet and all, but can you move? Because I really don't want to get caught."

He nods. I push him playfully, and we laugh as we scurry up the stairs.

We almost run right into Bass as he heads down. "What are you pledges doing?"

"Just going to bed," Jordan says. "Not together, we, uh, live next to each other."

I look at him, trying to communicate with my eyes that if he says another word I will scream.

"You're going to sleep?" Sebastian pulls back his sleeve to examine an expensive watch. "At seven?"

"Well, you know…" Jordan extends a hand to lean on the wall but misjudges the distance and stumbles forward. "Jet lag."

"Mmm-hmm." Sebastian studies us suspiciously.

I smile innocently. "Well, see you in the morning, Bass. Bye!"

I practically run the rest of the way up the stairs.

"What the hell was that?" I say as soon as the door to my room is closed.

"I'm really bad at lying."

"Ya think?"

He shrugs.

"Ugh." I press my hand to my forehead. "Well, now you can't stay here."

"Why?"

"Because you have roommates. Bass could threaten any of them to make them talk and probably will, because he's obviously on our trail."

"Okay, that's fair." He reaches toward me and takes my hand. "I'll leave. But, Cassie?"

"Huh?"

"Can I kiss you one more time first?"

I smile and nod. He tugs my wrist, and I fall into him. His hand brushing under my jaw, he lifts my face to his and his lips meet mine.

And I know what he means. I don't want this moment to end, either.

"Now I'll leave."

He kisses me again.

"Okay, now."

He smiles and disappears out the door, and I'm left to replay the moment again and again.

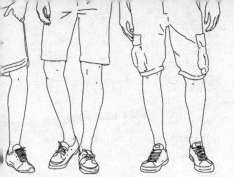

chapter forty-one

THE NIGHT BEFORE INITIATION, EVERYONE IS SITTING
out on the porch, relaxing with a beer as the sun sets. Still having heard nothing about the verdict on my membership, I feel uneasy hanging out with those who may vote to kick me out. But also, if this is my last night in the house, I don't want to spend it locked in my room.

Some of the guys are engaged in an intense round of Snappa, a drinking game I've never played before that involves tossing a die across a table with the person across from you having to drink if you make it between two cups but don't hit the ceiling, or throw it too low, or say the word *five*, or move your own cup out of its precisely measured spot.

I'm not really sure how you win, maybe when the other person gets drunk and falls out of his chair.

"Cassie, you playing?" Duncan yells across the porch.

"Oh, no, I've never—"

"Sorry, Bambi. I'm gonna have to be partners with Cassie."

I head in their direction.

"I mean, look at her, not gonna take no for an answer."

I shrug. "You know me. Such a bully."

Bambi laughs as he stands up, offering me his chair.

"Dream team right here!" Duncan yells as Bambi walks off.

"I don't know how to play," I whisper.

"It's fine—you can't be as bad as Bambi," he whispers back as he fills the cups in front of us with Natty.

Yum.

"Looking for some competition?" I turn to see Jordan at the other end of the table, along with a tall, good-looking Indian dude.

"Sure," Duncan answers.

"Cassie, do you know Sai?"

"I think we met at the Rush Retreat," Sai says.

They sit down, and Duncan slides the die across the table to them.

Jordan is across from me. "Are you sure you will be able to handle this, Cass?"

I roll my eyes and open my mouth to say something sassy, but before I can he throws the die high into the air. It ricochets of the edge of my cup and onto the porch.

Ha, he didn't sink it.

"Cassie!" Duncan looks at me like I'm crazy.

"What?"

"You didn't even try!"

"Try to what?"

"Catch the die!"

"Oh." I walk over to pick it up. "I didn't know I was supposed to."

He holds his head in his hands. "Oh God, not another one."

On the other side of the table Jordan is doubled over laughing. "That's…a point…for…us." He can barely get the words out between laughs.

"You're really not exemplifying good sportsmanship." I throw the die, which bounces once off the table before Jordan catches it with one hand.

He shrugs. "What can I say? I'm a competitive guy."

He tosses the die again, and this time Duncan catches it.

"I broke my arm during pool basketball once," Jordan says.

"Oh my God," I gasp. "That's insane."

"That's my shit. It motivates me. Hate to lose."

I throw the die, and he catches it without so much as blinking.

"When I was little, I would freak out and, like, flip board games if I was losing," Jordan says.

He sinks the die into the cup in front of me, and I have to drink. To say the beer tastes like water would be too kind; water doesn't make you cringe.

"They had to cancel family game night because I'd cry."

I laugh, and beer almost comes out my nose. "Oh my God, you are ridiculous." I set the cup down.

"I'm still like that."

Sai catches the die this time.

"Not the crying, of course. But the competitiveness."

"Doesn't that get exhausting?"

"Nah, I just try to pick the things I care about and not lose those." He looks at me. "And when I really want something, I typically get it."

He stares at me for a second too long, or maybe I'm just imagining it.

"Okay, enough of your life story," Sai says. "Can you play the game?"

"Oh, sorry." He throws the die and sinks it in my cup again. "Cheers, Cassie."

I brace myself and drink.

God, he really is an all-American boy, isn't he? Well dressed and athletic, he's like a Ken doll. While I'm over here in sweat-pants, happy if I work out once a month.

He's way too good for me.

He's the type who will be happy going to work and going to the gym and climbing ladders and reading self-help books and trying that new all-natural diet and making home im-provements and taking it a day at a time. While I can't decide if I want to never again get out of bed, or get up and go, go, go and never come back.

He has a beautiful heart full and sweet, and mine is wild but woven in barbed wire. And yet for some reason he seems to find my particular brand of fucked-up-ness fascinating. But I'm sure at some point he'll realize he belongs with All-American Bar-bie, who doesn't wake up sad sometimes for no reason or drink too much, who has perfect blond hair and a skinny body from the marathons she runs, and parents who love her.

Is it bad that I just want to bask in his goodness for a while before I free him of the hurt I know I'll end up causing him, or he'll end up causing me?

Is it fair to be with him at all, knowing this whole thing is built on lies? Knowing he has no idea that I'm using him and all his best friends to selfishly claw my way to the life I want?

Of course it isn't fair. But here I am, smiling at him and challenging him to another game.

Jordan and Sai remain undefeated. And after the second game, every little thing becomes so much funnier and I feel bubbly.

As the last few games end, someone lights a bonfire.

"Are we making s'mores?" I ask Duncan.

Jordan laughs at me. "Oh, Cassie, you're so innocent some-times."

I flip him off.

"I wish we were," Duncan says.

It turns out the bonfire is really just meant to cover up another kind of smoke, but I mean, c'mon, who wouldn't want s'mores when you have the munchies?

People sit in a circle and pass around a joint. Since I don't smoke, I decide to have a Corona, hoping it will keep me at the same level as everyone else but knowing it won't.

"Are the games over?" Bambi asks when I enter the kitchen.

"Yeah." I close the fridge with a clunk.

The nice beers are marked with a Post-it saying: "Upperclassmen only. No pledges. We are serious, guys." But everyone will probably be too crossed to notice.

"Finally!" Bambi follows me outside, practically skipping.

We drag two chairs over toward Duncan. Bambi sits with his back to him but clearly would still rather be with us than the upperclassmen on the far side of the circle, who are involved in an in-depth debate about the cost versus benefit of buying a bong.

Jordan is across the circle from us, lying in a lounge chair with his eyes closed. He looks so peaceful in the firelight.

"Cassie?" Duncan says.

"Hmm?"

"Have you ever been in love?"

"What, why?" I look away from Jordan quickly.

"Oh God," Bambi says. "Are you still all about that climber girl? You've had, what? Like three dates? Duncan, just because she has a nice ass does not mean you love her."

"You know what? Maybe I'm just trying to have a hypothetical, intellectual conversation with one of my best friends. And, for the record, her *name* is Jackie, and she also happens to have a nice smile." He turns back to me. "Sorry about that *rude* interruption."

"I don't know." I peel the corner of the Corona label back with my thumb and think back to high school, to the boys I thought I "loved." The ones I would stare at in class, dream about at midnight, staring at the ceiling and listening to Taylor Swift, the ones I would cry about in rec center bathrooms at dances when they kissed someone else.

"Yeah, me neither." Duncan sighs.

"But I feel like that's what everyone says at this age," I say. "'I don't know.' Because we've all thought we had it at least once and lost it, so we don't know if that was love and now it's gone or if we just *thought* that was love, and maybe people only ever just think that, and what if it doesn't exist at all?"

"Cheerful." Bambi coughs on the smoke.

He passes me the joint, but I shake my head and pass it on to Duncan.

"I don't know." Jordan sits up. I didn't even know he was listening. "I don't think that's necessarily... I don't know. I think the problem is, we expect happily-ever-after-forever-and-ever-amen-until-death-do-us-part, but, like, what are the odds of that happening with the first person you fall for? Hell, what are the odds of that happening with the person you marry?"

"Fifty-fifty, actually," Bambi replies.

Jordan cuts his eyes at him. "I'm just saying." He reaches for the joint when it makes it around the circle. "Shit, does someone have a lighter? Love. It's a beautiful and awful thing we do to ourselves."

Someone hands him a Zippo. "Thanks, man." He relights the joint and takes a drag before continuing. "We know no relationship can last forever, but we convince ourselves it will. And then it ends."

He pauses to light the joint again, the fire from the lighter illuminating every beautiful detail of his face.

"And you know, the heartbreak isn't the worst part for me. Like you think it is, but those extreme highs and lows are what make you feel alive. The worst part for me is always right before it ends, when you're bored and suffocating and not sure if you were ever in love or just craved the idea of it so much that you put up with something half as good as what you thought it would be. It's not when you lose the person you thought you couldn't live without—it's when you lose them and survive, and you realize you can live without any of these people, that if you disappeared tomorrow they'd be sad, but they'd move on, and this is a pretty goddamn lonely life."

"That's bullshit," Duncan says. "You've never had a moment where someone made you glad to be alive?"

"Yeah, but not forever," I say.

"I guess that's kind of the point," Jordan says. "I think it's about moments. Moments of turning the ordinary into something more. Like when you find a five-dollar scarf under your bed that smells like them, and for ten seconds you just kneel on the floor breathing it in, because in that moment that cheap thing from Chinatown is like the axis the world turns around. And, yeah, later you may be on your own or with someone else, and they may be with someone new, too. But there are seven billion people in the world, and you collided with that one person for at least a little while, and they made synapses fire in your brain in a way they never would have otherwise, and that's remarkable. They left their mark on you, and just because they aren't around forever, that doesn't mean it wasn't super-fuckin'-cool when you were together. Love ending doesn't mean love never was. It just means that, like everything else on this earth, it's finite."

I stare at him from across the circle.

"Damn, Jordan," Duncan says. "How long have you been waiting to say that?"

Jordan shrugs and passes the joint.

"But how do you ever know?" Duncan asks.

"It's when you meet the person who makes you realize that everything before was kiddie pools and this is an ocean," Sai says.

"Wow," I say.

"Yeah, until she cheats on you." He shifts in his seat. "God, where's the weed? Puff, puff, pass. Were you raised in a barn?" he asks the guy next to him.

Thoughts of love and loss and lies and forever ricochet around in my head for the rest of the night, even as I'm heading upstairs to go to sleep.

"Cassie," a voice says just as I'm about to reach the top step.

Jordan grabs my arm, and when I spin around we're only inches apart.

"I can't stop thinking about you," he says. "And I want more than texts and stolen kisses."

I glance at Sebastian's door, but it's closed, with no light coming from the crack at the bottom.

"I want you," Jordan says as he pulls me into the most amazing kiss. "May I come in?" His voice is low and breathy.

I nod as I fumble with the lock, barely taking my eyes off him.

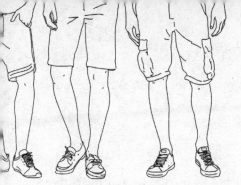

chapter forty-two

I WAKE UP HALF-NAKED TO SOMEONE POUNDING on my door.

"Shit, shit, shit." I turn to Jordan, who's still asleep, one armed draped around me and his face still in his so-cute-it's-stupid smile.

"Wake up," I whisper.

"Hmm?" He raises his head slowly.

I scramble to find where I threw his clothes the night before. We hadn't slept together; he'd been very respectful and gentlemanly about that, but what we did do was...well, a lady doesn't talk, but I'm not really much of a lady and... daaaammn.

He's sitting on the edge of the bed by the time I find his shirt and pants. I shove the clothes into his arms.

"Someone's here—get in the closet." He jumps up and climbs into the wardrobe, closing that door just as the room one opens.

"One second!" I jump into bed and pull the covers up to my chin.

"Cass!" Duncan barrels into the room. "They voted that you get to be initiated!"

"That's great!"

He suddenly notices that I've buried myself in blankets. "What are you doing? Are you okay?"

"Yeah, I'm just, uh, not wearing any clothes."

"Oh." He furrows his brow. "Oh my God, is there someone—"

"No, no, just me." I force a smile.

"Oh. *Oh*." His eyes go wide. "Well, um, I guess it would be antifeminist of me to judge, cuz, like, I do it, too, but..."

Oh. My. God. My face must be crimson. "Okayyy...well, bye then."

He leaves, and the closet door starts to open slowly.

"You can come out now."

Jordan steps out, covering his mouth as he tries not to crack up. "That was—" He can't even finish his sentence as he doubles over with laughter.

"Don't you dare!"

"There are so many jokes, I can't pick one." He gasps for breath between laughs. "That was great. That makes this whole sneaking-around shit worth it."

I make a face at him. He leans forward and kisses me on the cheek.

He pulls his clothes on quickly and then pecks me quickly on the lips. "See you at initiation."

He checks to make sure no one's there, then heads out into the hallway, but he peeks back around the door before he goes. "Hey, Cassie, try to finish quickly so you're not late, okay?"

"Ha-ha. You're funny."

He winks and disappears.

At exactly twelve all the pledges gather in the main room, but the actives are nowhere to be found. People lean against the wall, sit on the furniture, check their watches. Few people are really talking, and those who do just whisper nervously.

No one is exactly sure what we'll be required to do.

"All right, pledges, let's get started!" Marco shouts as he bursts into the room. He's wearing a long black robe, like he's a Jedi or something. "I'll call you into the ceremony room one by one."

People start to murmur at the word *ceremony*. Most things that involve words like *tradition*, *ceremony* and *rite of passage* have not been pleasant so far.

"Absolute silence in the pledge pen will be required."

Everyone shuts up.

"Okay. Ben 'Bambi' Worthington."

Bambi steps forward tentatively.

"We don't have all day! God, don't make me give you a shot with two fucking minutes left."

Bambi shuffles forward, almost tripping over his own feet.

"There's no way he sheds that nickname after this," Duncan murmurs after they disappear behind the doors. "It's too perfect."

Every five minutes or so Marco reappears to summon another pledge.

Until…

"Cassandra 'Title IX' Davis."

My heart slamming against my chest, I step forward and follow him into the darkened living room. Black curtains cover the walls and windows. The actives are standing on tables in a circle, all of them wearing black robes and holding flashlights up to their faces.

Oh my God. I'm about to join the dark side.

Darth Vader, I mean, Peter, steps forward.

"Pledge, state your name."

"Title IX?"

Even in the dark, I can tell he's trying not to laugh. "State your given name."

"Cassandra Davis."

"Pledge Cassandra Davis."

"Yes?"

"Please kneel."

Some of the hooded figures snicker. I roll my eyes but get on my knees anyway.

"Do you promise to lend your loyalty and friendship and brotherhood, I mean sisterhood, let's go with siblinghood, to the order of the Delta Tau Chi for the remainder of your life?"

"I do."

"And to take the secrets of this ritual and the brotherhood to the grave?"

I take a deep breath, thinking of all the transcripts locked in my desk upstairs. "I do."

"To uphold the virtues of Delta Tau Chi—valor, honesty and loyalty?"

I bite my lip. "I do."

"Stand."

I do.

He runs through the secret password and handshake so quickly that I remember nothing.

"Now, to prove your allegiance, you must drink the blood of former members."

He presents a large plastic bag, but unless Franzia used to run through Deltas' veins, I'm guessing this part of the ritual is a bit off script.

"Just slap the bag," he whispers.

He holds the sack of wine up while I chug and the rest of the actives count. "One, two, three, four, five, six, seven, seven, seven, seven, seven, seven."

I start to cough, and the wine burns in my throat and up my nose.

"Welcome to Delta Tau Chi, Sister Cassandra."

"Valor, honesty, loyalty, brotherhood," the hooded figures chant.

Marco grabs my wrist and leads me through the door to the kitchen, where the rest of the new initiates are waiting. The bright light burns my eyes.

"That's it?" I ask.

"I guess so," someone says.

"I hope so," Bambi says.

"I thought we were gonna have to kill a goat."

"I heard we were going to have to swallow a goldfish whole."

Finally Duncan comes through the door, the last pledge.

"Now what?" I whisper to Bambi.

"A'right, let's party!" Peter shouts as he joins us, throwing his black robe at Bambi.

The rest of the actives follow, also shedding their cloaks to reveal tanks and pastel shorts. The true frat uniform.

Bass and Marco start to hand people red cups. When I get mine, I take a small sip. Champagne, nice. I mean, cheap-ass, sugary champagne, but still…

"All right, men." Peter climbs onto the coffee table. "And Cassie. You are now members of the best fraternity in the world. If there was ever a time to black out or back out, it is right fuckin' now!"

People scream and yell and chant and make all sorts of animalistic noises.

"All right, all right," Peter says, and the chaos dulls to a low roar. "Everyone raise their glasses. To honesty and loyalty."

"To honesty and loyalty!" everyone else echoes.

And I swear, as we drink Peter's eyes lock on me.

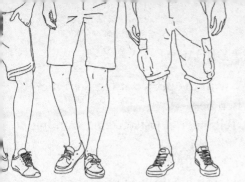

chapter forty-three

"I MUST SAY, CASSIE, WE'RE VERY EXCITED ABOUT THE project."

"Well, thank you. I've worked very hard on it."

I try my best to swallow all my nervousness and sound grateful and professional. Despite my insistence that we should keep everything confidential until the project is done, Madison pitched it to a select group of journalists—strictly embargoed, of course—on Monday. Which is why I'm out here hiding behind the trees by the lake at seven in the morning on a Wednesday, mud soaking into my shoes while I try to sound like I'm awake enough to follow what Karen, a New York journalist, is saying.

"I know you're probably mulling over a lot of offers for the exclusive. But we are *the place* for feminist news on the internet, as I'm sure you know, and I will make sure your story is right at home."

"That's really great," I say. "Thank you so much for your

interest. I'll have to speak with the people at the Stevenson Fund and my faculty adviser, be—"

"Oh, right! Eva Price. Tell me, is it just amazing working with her?"

"It is. It really is, Karen."

In all honesty, I've barely seen her this semester, and we're weeks in. But that's expected when she's off saving the world.

"You're so lucky."

"I really am."

Mostly. I hate that I have to hide out here like some kind of criminal, some traitor.

But I guess that's exactly what I'll seem like to the guys if they ever find out. I mean, *when* they find out.

"I'll keep in touch, Karen. Nice talking to you, bye." I tap the red button and push back my hair, which is sticking to my sweaty face. *Lovely.*

It's unusually hot today, but luckily I'm up three hours earlier than I need to be and have time to shower before class.

Ten minutes later I'm heading down the hall, pink robe cinched around my waist, towel and shower caddy in hand, my flip-flops squeaking, when I stop dead in my tracks.

A few feet away, Jordan is standing in front of his door in nothing but a towel he's holding around his waist with one hand. I take in his smooth skin, strong arms…and those abs.

But it's when we lock eyes that really gets me.

A week of quiet burning glances stolen from across the room, of going crazy not being able to kiss or hold hands or even really touch around the rest of the guys, of text messages, sweet and dirty, sent under the table, of wishing we could be alone, comes rushing back.

"Hey." My cheeks must be fire red, but I don't giggle. None of this is really funny anymore.

"Hey." His voice is breathy and even lower than usual.

"You, uh, you going to shower?" I ask.

"Um, yeah. You?"

"Yep."

I guess this is pretty obvious, but I didn't know what else to say.

"I like your, um, robe," he says.

"Thanks," I say, very aware I'm not wearing anything under it. I wonder if he is, too.

My flip-flops slap against my feet as we walk down the hall. We reach the bathroom, and he opens the door.

"After you."

"Thanks."

The shower curtain makes a screeching sound as I pull it closed. Taking a deep breath, I stare at the white plastic for a second before slipping off my robe.

I reach around the curtain to hang the robe on a small metal hook as the water in the stall next to me bursts on.

I turn on my own.

"Soooo, how was your morning so far?" he asks over the sound of the water.

"It's been good." I clear my throat. My voice sounds un-usually high.

"That's good."

"Mmm." I lather soap on my body and I think of him. His hands on me. Slipping over every curve. Pulling my hair.

"I, um, I'm really liking my classes this semester," he says.

"Yeah?"

"Mmm-hmm."

"Cool."

"Yep."

"Okay, fuck this." His water cuts off, and within seconds he's slipping around my curtain.

I step forward out of the spray.

A smile playing on his lips, he tilts his head down, eyes soaking in my body, wet from the shower.

I bite my lip. Electricity runs through me just from the thought of his eyes on me.

"God," he breathes.

His eyes flicker back up to mine, shining.

We step toward each other at the same time, and he slips his hand behind my neck, fingers weaving through my wet hair as his lips brush mine. We stumble backward into the water. I wrap my arms around his neck and pull him toward me.

His hands slide down my body, and we crash into each other, bodies, arms and legs intertwined.

He traces kisses down my neck. A sigh escapes my lips.

His lips return to mine, this time urgent. He pushes me against the wall, and I moan against his lips, pulling him closer and closer.

I'm overwhelmed by sensations, from the heat of the water to the heat between us. My head spins; I'm high off the taste of his lips.

He lifts me up, and I wrap my legs around him.

The bathroom door opens with a bang. We both look up.

I look down at the curtain. There's a foot of space between the bottom and the floor.

I hold one finger to my mouth in a shushing gesture and then point to the gap.

Jordan nods and continues to hold me up by my butt, a position that's a lot more awkward when instead of kissing we're trying to keep completely still. I wrap my arms tighter around his neck.

"Dude, do you have a pink robe?"

Jordan clears his throat. "Yeah. I, uh, lost a bet and had to buy one."

"Okay, you do you, I guess. I was gonna take a dump, but I guess I'll come back later."

"Thanks, man."

The door slams again.

I laugh as Jordan sets me back on my feet.

"Sorry about that," he says.

"No, it's fine. Adds to the romance."

"Oh, yeah, thinking about Dave's bowel movements always gets me in the mood."

I laugh and then stretch up on my tiptoes to kiss him on the cheek. He wraps an arm around me.

I lean my head against his chest. "We should go somewhere."

"What?"

"SF or the beach or something. For the long weekend, just both say we are going home?" We had a Friday off in a few weeks.

He exhales. "Cassie, I'm sorry. I want to, *really* want to, but I just can't afford—"

"I'll pay for it."

"What?"

Since the scholarship covers the full cost of attendance and fraternity dues, the few thousand dollars I'd made from my last summer job had become disposable income. Plus they gave me five hundred dollars for books, and with buying online instead of from the bookstore, I was able to pocket half of that.

I nod. "Yeah, it's fine."

"I can't let you—"

I place my hand on his chest. "Listen, just let me get a hotel. I really do not want to lose my virginity in a frat house."

"You—you want to…?"

I nod.

"Are you sure?"

I smile. "Yeah."

"Because you know I'm totally chill with whatever we do, and we should only do...*it* when you want to, because—"

"Shh." I place my finger over his mouth. "I want to."

I know that too soon there will come a day when he finds out the truth and I lose him. And I know that life is complicated, and even without the secrets I'm hiding, there's no way we can promise each other forever. And that losing my virginity isn't going to be like a teen movie.

But him and me, in this moment: it's pretty perfect. I trust him, and I care so deeply about him. And I *want* to do this with him. Even if I'm not sure what the future holds, I can promise him right now. And that's more than enough.

He kisses me, and I actually feel weak in the knees. Luckily his arms are wrapped tightly around me.

I weave my fingers through his hair, and everything gets kind of heavy and slow, like the rest of the world is falling away.

We break apart. "But not in the house?" he whispers.

I smile against his lips. "Not in the house."

"Okay, I respect that." He kisses me again. "This is okay, though?"

I laugh. "This is okay."

The bathroom door swings open.

I jump up, and he holds me like a bride being carried over the threshold. Frozen, we listen to someone pee.

When the door closes again, he sets me down, both of us laughing.

"Yeah," he says. "Definitely not here."

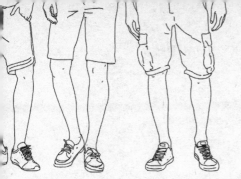

chapter forty-four

I'M SITTING AT BREAKFAST A WEEK OR SO BEFORE
our little trip when my phone buzzes with a text from Jordan.

J: Do you have a fancy dress?

I smile.

C: yes

J: cool. Bring it to SF

J: and heels

J: unless you don't roll that way

J: then your fanciest sneakers

C: lol I like heels

J: good shit

J: I'm gonna wine and dine you so hard

C: haha

C: you don't have to do that

J: I want to. Can't wait

And then he sends me a kissy face emoji, a little heart coming from the smiley face's lips.

And this is how I know I've got it bad: I do not find that little cartoon kiss cheesy or stupid or lame.

In fact, it warms my cold, sarcastic heart. Which is concerning, to say the least.

I'm smiling at my phone like an idiot when Peter sits down across from me.

"Going home to visit your parents this weekend?"

"Yep." I push the cereal around my bowl.

"You're gonna miss a lot of big parties."

"Yeah, that's why I emailed you that I couldn't help with anything."

"We can cover it. I'm just saying you'll miss out on the fun."

"Hey, it can't be as fun as spring snow in the Midwest and my parents fighting."

He looks down at his coffee. Then back at me. "Louis is going away, too."

"Really?" I sound like I'm more interested in the Lucky Charms I'm sorting through. Marshmallows first, of course.

"Yeah. Funny."

"It's a three day weekend. A lot of people go home." I smile up at him like I don't know what game he's playing.

He brings his mug to his lips, keeping his eyes on me. Waiting for me to break.

"Peter!" One of the juniors, Johnny Someone, runs into the room. "Have you seen the *Daily* this morning?"

My heart sinks. But no, I'm being crazy. It's still weeks if not months until my exposé will run, and even then it won't be in the student newspaper.

"No." He sets down his coffee. "Why?"

"It's not good." He shakes his head and sets his laptop on the table. "They have our emails."

Peter goes pale. "Exactly which emails?"

"Honestly, I've gotta think all of them, because this bitch seems to have handpicked the ones that make us look the worst."

He turns the screen around for Peter to see.

"Fuck!" Peter slams his hand on the table, exhales and runs his other hand through his hair. "I need to call Dean Robinson." He flies out of the kitchen and takes off down the hall.

Johnny follows close behind him.

I look around, but the room is empty save for Bambi, who's sleeping, his head on the table next to a heaping plate of just bacon and English muffins.

I turn the screen around. The article is still pulled up.

Accusations of misogyny have returned to Warren University's Delta Tau Chi house as a colorful email chain has been leaked online.

Crude descriptions of female students, invitations for underage drinking and illegal drug use, and other instances of debauchery are interspersed with correspondence about homework and internships, all sent with Warren email addresses. This has come as "quite the embarrassment" to the university, according to sources close to the administration.

The chapter has been a source of controversy ever since a party last spring in honor of International Women's Day that sparked outrage for decorations suggesting that women belong only in domestic and inferior roles. After a university investigation, the fraternity was placed on probation.

DTC seemed to be making an effort to change their culture early this year with the acceptance of the first female member to be initiated into a fraternity on the Warren campus or, reportedly, on any college campus.

But to some, even this move was seen as a sign of the problem, a stunt meant to put a Band-Aid over a multitude of past transgressions. It has been a divisive issue among women's groups on campus, some of which called the student in question, Cassandra Davis, "brave," while an anonymous gender studies major told us she was "simply a puppet of the patriarchy sent to tell us frat boys are a-okay."

Davis's email address is notably missing from the conversations leaked this week, although it should be noted that the emails in question are from the last five years and only a small sample is from this year, when she could have been included in the conversation.

The national office of Delta Tau Chi has no comment on the matter.

In a statement, Warren University called the reported behavior "inexcusable" and vowed "to look into the matter."

Below this was a link to thousands of pages of emails. I scan through them, my heart racing.

Many of them refer to parties, calling upon the brothers

to invite "sororisluts" but warning "no fat chicks." Others
announce their plans to "hate fuck that bitch" and then to
extract themselves from the situation: "told her I wasn't looking for a relationship…well, at least not with a shrew." They
praise each other for how "totally dope" their parties were,
and specify how many "drunken blow jobs" they deserved
for their efforts. There's a suggestion to use money raised at
a philanthropy event to buy a stripper pole, which was voted
down (but just barely).

It's everything I've documented in my journal entries and
so much more.

After a while I have to stop, nauseous from it all. I get up
and head to my room to lie down, thinking that maybe boys
who are nice to me but not to women generally aren't actually nice boys.

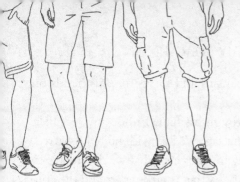

chapter forty-five

"CASSIE, DO YOU WANT TO SHARE AN UBER TO THE airport?" Jordan asks way too loudly.

"I'd love to." Even though I'm a much more experienced liar than he is, especially after the last year, my voice sounds a little overdone, as well.

No one even looks up from their lunch as we walk out the back door a little while later.

He helps me with my suitcase, and we slide into the car.

I reach over to pull down my seat belt, and when I turn back I'm met by Jordan's eyes.

I click the belt quickly and kiss him lightly on the lips.

"I can't believe we're doing this," he says.

"Me neither."

He slips his arm around my waist and pulls me closer.

"Both buckle," the driver says with a thick accent.

"Okay, okay." Jordan clicks himself into the middle seat, and in seconds his hands are back on me. Looking at me with a mischievous grin, he leans in and kisses me, his hands on my waist.

I weave my fingers through his hair. I undo my seat belt, and he pulls me half onto his lap. We kiss with no holds barred, giving in to every amazing instinct now that we don't have to keep our guard up in case Sebastian is lurking around the corner, just wanting and having and getting high off each other.

The driver clears his throat. "Unsafe for her to sit like that. Need to face forward."

My face crimson, I, uh, dismount, sit straight up in my seat and buckle myself back in, trying to avoid eye contact with the rearview mirror.

Jordan just laughs and laughs and laughs.

I swat his arm.

"Ow," he says, but the cheesy grin stays pasted on his face.

I watch out the window as we cruise down the highway. The mountains—maybe only hills, but mountains in my Midwestern-girl mind—rise on one side and the bay stretches out on the other. The water sparkles, a slightly different but equally vibrant blue from the sky, while white sailboats dot the horizon like crescent moons.

With great effort, I try to focus on the beauty of the view and not on the boy beside me. I reach out and take his hand despite myself.

"Oh my God," he suddenly says.

"What?" I turn to see him reading something on his phone.

"Shit. I guess we won't be missing such great parties after all."

"Why?"

"Email from Peter. The school's stepped up the probation rules. No guests in the house. No drinking in the common areas."

"Wow."

"Yeah."

And this is *before* my full report comes out.

I shake the thought out of my head and turn back to the window. This is my weekend off. I will not worry about frat stuff for the next seventy-two hours. I've earned at least that much time to just be with this boy.

We make our way down Embarcadero, passing piers numbered in ascending order, until finally we pull up to our hotel, an art deco building that towers into the sky.

A guy in a red uniform with a matching hat blows a whistle and waves our driver forward.

He pulls up to the entrance, stopping under a glittering awning stretching over stylish businesspeople and casually clad families as they hurry in and out of the building.

The bellhop pulls open my door.

"Thanks!" I say to the driver as we slide out of the car.

"Humph," he replies.

Bags in hand, we step inside the hotel and, it seems, into the past. The hotel is from the 1920s and is evocative of the era, but not in a cheesy, pinstripes-and-fringed-dresses kind of way, but in a way that makes me want to slip on a sleek dress and sip a dry martini while a jazz singer croons in the background.

The lobby has a grand, sweeping dark wood staircase on each side, and a glittering mosaic on the ceiling high above.

Among the clusters of dark furniture, bouquets bigger than I am sit on tables.

"Wow," Jordan says.

"I know," I say.

We cross the lobby and join the winding line to check in. Jordan slips his hand around my waist. I stretch up onto my tiptoes and kiss him on the cheek.

As soon as I'm back on my two feet, he kisses the top of my head, and I giggle. I know we are *those people*, but we never get to be like this, and, honestly, I just can't bring myself to give a damn.

"Next!"

He whispers something naughty in my ear, and I smile at him mischievously, even as my cheeks turn bright red.

He leans down and kisses me again, this time on the lips.

"Next!"

The guy behind us clears his throat. I look up.

"Shoot, that's us."

I hurry forward, dragging my bag behind me. "Sorry!"

The lady at the counter is not amused. "Name?"

"Davis."

She types into the computer for a minute and then, without looking up from the screen, reaches out a wrinkled but perfectly manicured hand.

I hand her my card, and she scans it swiftly.

Since the hotel hosts mainly business clients, it wasn't too expensive for the weekend.

"There's a two-hundred-dollar charge if there is any damage in the room." She hands back my card. "And we take noise complaints very seriously." She eyes Jordan, and I realize he's wearing his bid day T-shirt, which features a red, white and blue Solo cup and the phrase "Life, Liberty and the Pursuit of Frattiness."

I nod to tell her I'm taking her warnings seriously. Then, picking up the room keys and a map of San Francisco, I say a quiet thank-you and walk away.

We cross the lobby to the old-fashioned elevators lining the far wall.

"This is so cool." Jordan pushes the up button.

"I know!"

The elevator dings.

He kisses me all the way up, both of us unable to keep our

hands off each other as we walk down the hall, until I have to push him away so I can focus on opening the door to the room.

"What do you want to do?" I ask, sitting down on the crisp white-covered bed.

He checks his watch. "Well…we have dinner in, like, an hour."

"Oh!" I jump up. "I need to get ready."

"Already?"

"Yeah. I have to do makeup and hair and—just trust me."

He laughs and shakes his head. "Okay. I'll shower, then."

He leans down and kisses me before he leaves the room.

It makes me so happy I want to jump up and down and squeal with joy that we can do something as simple as kiss before leaving a room and there's no one here to tell us we can't.

I slip on a sparkling silver dress, dark and glittery, with thin straps and fabric that clings to my body. I step into strappy black heels and do my makeup dramatically, with winged eyeliner and nude lipstick.

I stare at myself in the gilded framed mirror. It's a grown-up look, and I feel a bit like a child playing dress-up.

Jordan and I are the same age, but I feel so young around him. So naive and inexperienced.

And even though he knows this is my first time, does he realize how little I know what I am doing? What if I'm shockingly bad?

I straighten my hair while Jordan showers. My mind wanders to him standing under the hot water, naked and shimmering wet.

Ow. I flinch. A red mark appears on my neck where I burned myself with the straightening iron. Great, I already have a hickey.

"Wow."

I spin around.

"You look amazing." Jordan's eyes sparkle.

As for him, he's wearing a charcoal suit over a perfect white shirt, with a thin black tie that's hanging a little crooked.

I walk over and straighten it, my hands lingering on his chest. "You don't look half-bad yourself."

———

We take a cab to the swanky steak house to save my poor feet.

An impossibly beautiful hostess in a sleek black dress greets us as we step into the restaurant. There's a sort of Old Hollywood glamour about the place, everything mahogany and leather, low lighting and dark wines.

The diners all wear cocktail dresses and suit coats, and clink champagne flutes over conversations about stocks and yachts and fancy lives, or at least I imagine that's what they're talking about. Some of the women may be in their early twenties, but for sure none of the men are under thirty.

"We're the youngest people here," I whisper as we follow the *Maxim* model to our table.

"I know." He takes my hand.

We're those annoying college kids who go to fancy restaurants. We'd scream *new money* if it wasn't for neither of us having any money at all.

The hostess leads us to a table in the back, tucked halfway around a corner. It's very intimate, very romantic.

She pulls a chair away from the table for me, and I sit down, the butter-soft leather luxurious against my bare legs.

Jordan sits to the right of me, and his hand brushes along my thigh under the tablecloth, which is so clean and bright it practically glows.

I glance at him, hoping he can see the effect it has on me, just being this close to him.

"Enjoy." The hostess sets down the menus and struts away, stilettos clicking.

I open the heavy leather menu.

Filet mignon…70.

And that's not even the most expensive choice. Oh, and if you want a side with your meat, then it will be fifteen more. Thirteen-fifty for a salad, even more if all you want is an iceberg wedge.

Not to mention the drinks, which are on a separate menu.

"God, they just rip people off." I look up at Jordan. "Let's try to get the most food for the least cost, beat them at their own game."

I'm smiling, way too dazzled by my own idea, but Jordan has gone pale. His hand is gone from my leg, both of them now gripping his menu.

"Cassie, you really don't have to—"

"Huh?"

"I feel bad."

"Why? We're both broke college students." I laugh and reach for his hand. "I'm really just excited to be here with you—alone, you looking hot in a suit. I'd be happy going to McDonald's."

He smiles. "You're a pretty cool girl—you know that, Cassie Davis?"

"Ahem." We tear our eyes away from each other to see our waiter, a skinny middle-aged man in a suit.

"Welcome. I'm Jeffery, and I'll be your server tonight."

He lists the specials and then asks, "What kind of water would you like?"

I look to Jordan. "Are there types of water?" I whisper.

"I can hear you." The waiter glances to a table a few feet away, where men in suits are drinking scotch and talking seriously. He exhales before turning back to us and quickly saying, "We have a variety of bottled waters, both still and sparkling. But I'm assuming you prefer tap."

I nod.

"All right." He calls over a busboy, who pours us water from a fancy vase and sets down a basket filled with ten different types of bread.

"We have an extensive wine list." Jeffrey hands us yet another menu. "Our director of wine is also here tonight and available to answer any questions about pairings you may have."

"Thank you, I think we need a second to look at this." Jordan picks up the wine list.

"Damn, that thing is like twenty pages."

"I know." He flips through it. "Is it unacceptable to ask the *director of wine* what the cheapest one on the list is?"

I fake a snooty accent. "Do you have anything in the boxed variety?"

"Exactly." He smiles. "But for real, do we get glasses or a bottle?"

"I don't know." I read over his shoulder. "Honestly, I don't even really like wine."

"Really?" He looks up. "I thought all girls like wine."

I wrinkle my nose. "One, *sexist*."

"Sorry." He shrugs and reaches for his water.

"Two, it reminds me too much of church."

He almost chokes on his water. "Complicated relationship with religion?" he asks between coughs.

"You could say that."

"Oh, great, here comes the return of the waiter."

"Probably wants to know if we want to switch our silverware out for gold."

Jordan stifles a laugh as Jeffery approaches the table. "Enjoying your water?"

"You know what? Hasn't killed me yet." I turn to Jordan. "Although I typically bathe in Dasani, maybe I will switch to this."

The waiter rolls his eyes. "Would you like anything else to drink?"

"Yes, I'll have a Manhattan," Jordan says.

"Me too." It seems like a grown-up drink to go with a grown-up night. Plus, I get a cherry! "Oh, and can we get more bread?" Jordan asks.

"Yeah, like, at least two more baskets," I add.

"Sure," he says through gritted teeth. He probably thinks our table will be more work than the rest and won't tip, because we're young. Jokes on him because I always do 18 percent or more. I'll just get my retribution by matching his sassy comments with my own.

"He didn't ID us!" I say as soon as Jeffrey is, hopefully, out of earshot.

"Yeah, well, who the hell comes here when they're eighteen?"

Jeffrey returns with two sunset-colored drinks.

"Would you like to tell me your order now?" he says, setting down our glasses.

"I'll have the garden salad." I snap my menu closed.

"And the Caesar for me." Jordan nods.

"Is that all?"

"Are the desserts on this menu?" I open it back up to look for myself.

"No."

"Then yeah, that's all for now."

Jeffrey seizes the menus from our hands and is gone in a flash.

"Oh, he is not happy with us," I say.

"Probably because of your water joke."

"Oh c'mon, he started it."

He laughs and reaches for his drink. "Can't wait to see the headlines tomorrow: Warren student brawls with waiter at Bay Area's finest steak house."

"Hey, as long as I win." I pick up my drink to toast.

Jordan does the same and says, "To…what was it? Loyalty, liberty and binge drinking?"

I laugh. "To valor, honesty, loyalty and brotherhood."

"Whatever." He shrugs. "It's all right. A bit clunky. Not terribly original." He wrinkles his nose. "How about…to us?"

I smile. "To us."

We clink glasses and sip.

"Wow," I say. "That is *not* Natty."

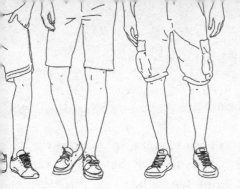

chapter forty-six

AFTER TIPPING 20 PERCENT ON OUR RECORD-settingly small bill, we set out into the city. The sky has gone dark, but the buildings are bright.

The wind off the bay blows back my hair, probably tangling it terribly. I shiver.

"Here." He slips off his jacket and slides it around me.

His hand brushes my shoulder, and I shiver again, this time not from the cold. "Thanks."

We walk around holding hands, past quiet storefronts and roaring bars. There's something so intimate about being in a big city with just one other person. There in the anonymity of a crowd, among people from all different places talking about their own lives in all different languages, in a way you have more privacy than you do out in the country alone. In the bustle and chaos of it all, you have found someone.

We're standing on the sidewalk, waiting for the walk sign, when I lean over and kiss him on the cheek. His five o'clock shadow scratches me lightly.

"What was that for?"

I shrug. "Just because I can."

He smiles.

People behind us start to push forward, so we cross the street. He tries to kiss me back as we walk but gets my ear instead. I laugh, and it's a twinkling sound I've never heard before.

Across from Ghirardelli Square there is a small park with a beach. We walk down to the water, the Golden Gate just visible in the fog.

"Wow," I say.

"I know."

I look around. We're the only people this far into the park. I bend down and undo the tiny buckles on my shoes.

"What are you doing?"

I step out of them and sigh in relief.

"This." I pick up my shoes and take off down the steps until my feet touch the sand.

I turn around to see Jordan still standing on the sidewalk.

"Well, c'mon, then!" I shout. The wind whips my hair back.

He rushes down the stairs as I keep walking until I'm ankle-deep in the water.

He stops on the beach to take off his shoes.

"Are you folding your socks?"

"Yes."

I laugh.

"These are my favorite ones." He sets them down carefully in his discarded shoes, rolls up his pants and wades into the water with me.

He steps forward and takes my hand, pulling me close, so my hand rests against his chest.

I never used to believe that you recognized life-changing moments while they were happening. It seemed like some sixth-sense bullshit, the type of thing women reading palms on the streets of San Francisco might talk about, not something I would experience.

One of my favorite scenes in literature is when Gatsby first kisses Daisy. He says no to a ladder to the heavens and kisses her instead. He ties his dreams to her, and in that way, limits them.

It's the fatal move. Asking one person to make your life complete. To save you. It's a dangerous game to play. But we tell the story again and again, because it's such a beautiful delusion, that there's a soul mate out there and finding him or her is all we have to worry about. But it *is* a delusion. So you resist it; you tell yourself that you have much grander ideas than dreams tied to one person. So you sit and discuss Gatsby's stupidity in high school English. You annotate and dissect in class. And you promise yourself that your sights are set on your dream, and that there is no person who will disrupt that. That there is no way you will settle for a normal, happy life and give up your dreams for a love that fades to average.

But then here you are, having run away from your life for a weekend with a boy you have no business falling in love with, about to watch your whole life change.

Or maybe that's just bullshit. Maybe you can't exactly know what your choice will mean. Sometimes all you know is that there's a beautiful, wonderful boy and you want to kiss him, so you do.

And when his lips touch mine, I know in my bones that this is a moment I will replay in my head for years to come, though whether as a sweet beginning or a what-might-have-been, I don't, can't, know. But F. Scott Fitzgerald was right. My dreams are tied to this boy now, and I'm either going to have to sever myself from him or watch those dreams wither away.

He rests his forehead against mine, and in the pale moon-light I can just barely see the outline of his smile.

"What do you want to do?" I whisper.

"I don't care—I'm just happy to be with you."

I kiss him on the cheek.

"We could go to a bar," he says. "Or check out Ghirardelli for a second dessert, or take a midnight boat ride…"

"Let's go back to the room," I say.

"Yeah?"

"Yeah."

We can't keep our hands off each other the whole way back to the hotel. But in the elevator, the nervousness starts to set in. Mostly I'm filled with exhilarating excitement, but I'm also a little bit scared.

"Give me a second," I say as we enter the room.

"Okay." He sits on the chair nearest the bed and undoes his tie.

I head to bathroom, trying to slyly pick up my duffel bag on the way.

Watching myself in the bathroom mirror and the unfortu-nate fluorescent lighting, I slip off my dress, revealing a simple black strapless bra and bikini-style panties.

I unzip my bag and dig through my clothes until my hand closes over plastic. Pulling out the package I'd ordered online a few weeks ago, I rip through the Victoria's Secret logo so the lacy fabric slips out.

Taking a deep breath, I set it down on the bathroom coun-ter and look at myself in the mirror. I slip off my bra and un-derwear, and shove them in my bag.

It takes me a second to figure out exactly how I'm supposed to put on the red corset, but then I manage fine.

Then comes the matching thong: fabric in the front, just a

single strip in the back. Ridiculous, but not really requiring an instruction manual.

Next come the black thigh-highs, which are easy enough, like socks, but they just keep going up.

But how do I attach the thigh-highs to the little plastic and metal clippie things hanging from the corset?

I reach for my phone to Google it, then remember it's on the dresser in the other room.

I try to pry one open and it closes on my finger. *Shit.*

Okay, got it open. Now I just have to slip it on the thigh-high and…yes! Perfect. One down, four to go, and then the other leg.

I take a deep breath and stand up.

The little ribbon pops off the thigh-high.

I'm going to write an angry email to Victoria tomorrow. Maybe that's her secret, how to work these goddamn contraptions.

Fuck, fuck fuck, fuck.

If I stay in here any longer, Jordan is gonna think I'm pooping.

"Jordan?" I open the door slowly.

"What's up?"

I step out tentatively. He's scrolling through his phone, sitting on the edge of his chair.

I look down at the ribbons swinging from my hips. I twist one of them around my finger.

"These things are supposed to clip onto the stockings, but I can't figure out…"

I look up. His eyes seem darker than usual, and yet more alive. Like slow-burning embers.

"Wow." The word barely escapes his lips. His phone falls to the carpet.

I smile and step toward him. When I reach him, I lean down to kiss him on the lips, slow and sensual.

"It's like a dream," he says when I pull away.
I can't help but agree.
He pulls me onto his lap, kissing me again.
The hell with those stupid ribbons.

chapter forty-seven

"HEY THERE," I SAY. I CAN FEEL THE SMILE IN MY VOICE.

The sheet is half twisted around us, where we lie naked in the bed.

Light shines through the half-open curtains. Outside the window the bay is sparkling and the city is coming to life.

"Mmm." He doesn't open his eyes, just pulls me closer and kisses me on the forehead.

I close my eyes again and rest my head on the little nook his shoulder forms.

Sometimes it's not big, dramatic moments. Sometimes it's just waking up and not knowing where you are or what time it is or anything at all, but seeing a face and feeling like you're home. Sometimes that's all it takes to know you're falling in love.

My phone rings, and I wake up for the second time. Jordan stays asleep, so I carefully untangle myself and climb out of bed. Stepping over the discarded corset and thong, I grab my phone off the charger.

Madison Macey's name is on the screen, but the phone stops ringing before I can hit the green button.

My missed messages and calls replace her on the screen. *Five* voice mails. How the hell did that happen?

I grab Jordan's undershirt off the floor and slip it over my head. Luckily it covers me up enough that I can step out onto the balcony, where I call her back, shutting the door quietly behind me.

"Cassie, where the hell have you been?"

I guess we're skipping *hello*, then. "Uh…asleep. It's only, like, ten."

"God, college kids."

"It's Saturday."

"Whatever. Anyway, I've been trying to call you to tell you *America Weekly* wants the story."

Oh my God! "That's—"

"For the final issue this month."

"This month? It's not done. We haven't even finished the second round of interviews. And then I have to write the report. Like, there is so much analysis to do, there's Professor Price to consult, peer reviews to submit and—"

"No, no, no. Cassie, stop talking."

My mouth snaps shut.

"They don't want an academic paper. They want to run your entries verbatim, diary-style. Just whatever you have so far will work."

"But that eliminates context, and there were times when I was wrong. They can't run it half-done. It won't be honest."

"It's more important that we run it when we have the most buzz, which is right now."

"But—"

"Cassie, these emails from your frat, they're all over the news. This is your opportunity to take the story wider, to a national audience. This will launch your career, Cassandra. Next week you could be on the *Today* show, so stop complaining."

"I'm not sure—"

There's a knock on the door behind me.

"You know what, I'll call you back." I hang up and press the lock button.

"Hey." I turn around as the door opens.

"What are you doing?" Jordan stands in the doorway, wrapped in a sheet.

"Just…thinking."

He furrows his brow. "You okay?"

"Yeah." My voice sounds frail. "Perfect." And it is *so* close to being the truth. If that call hadn't happened, if my reality was just him, a sheet barely covering his beautiful body, and me in his shirt, I'd have nothing in the world to worry about. But that call *did* happen, and it makes me sick to my stomach.

"Come back inside."

"I will in a minute." I lean over and peck him on the cheek, my phone still in my hand.

When I lean back he stares at me, concern in his eyes.

I force a smile.

"Okay, I'm gonna shower," he says.

I nod.

When the door closes again, I turn back to the city. Leaning over the railing, I stare out at the cars and debate calling Madison Macey back.

Then I decide maybe I can let myself stay in the dream just a little bit longer, so I turn my phone off and head back inside.

The bathroom door is slightly open, swirls of steam sneaking out. I walk over and open it farther.

I shed the T-shirt, letting it fall to the floor, and pull back the shower curtain.

"Hey." He smiles, then takes my hand to help me step over the edge of the tub.

He's so happy, in this pure, carefree, precious way. For him, there's no expiration date looming over us. There's just great sex and fun dates and sweet words and laughing until it hurts, waking up next to each other and days spent entirely in bed, snuggling, and adventures to more cities where we know no one and nothing except that we will go together, ad infinitum. I smile, so my face doesn't give away my sadness.

He kisses me slowly, sweetly. Like we have all the time in the world to just enjoy being with each other.

I kiss him back, and then slip under the water, so he doesn't see the tear slip down my cheek.

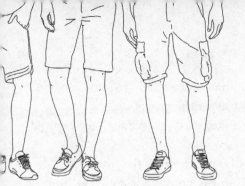

chapter forty-eight

THE REST OF THE WEEKEND IS SO GREAT. WE TAKE
a boat ride out to Alcatraz to see a modern art exhibit on
political prisoners, ride trolley cars down rolling hills, eat
sourdough bread by the water and chocolate sundaes from
Ghirardelli, walk through the Castro, where I buy a shot glass
that says, "Drink until He's Cute" just to mess with Jordan,
and to the Mission District, where we wait in line for an hour
to have the best tacos in America.

Oh, and we spend quite a bit of time rolling around the
king-size bed. We have such a good time that Jordan jokes
we may have to worry about that noise-complaints warning
after all.

I keep my phone off and in my bag, deciding I deserve to
just enjoy the weekend and planning, if Madison gets mad
again, to send an email saying I'd dropped it and had to wait
until after the holiday to get a new one.

We check out on Monday and head back to the house, me

in a cab, Jordan on the train an hour later. I'm expecting everyone to be pretty pissed about the probation.

But I wasn't expecting pretty much everyone to seem pissed at *me*.

"Hey, Bambi," I say as I walk through the front door.

He barely looks up from his book. "Cassie." He sounds tired at best, and mad at worst.

"That's it? I've been gone all weekend."

"Well, excuse me if I'm not pumped to see you." He snaps.

Jesus.

The two upperclassmen I pass on the stairs avoid my eyes and mumble something.

What the hell is going on?

There's a knock on my door as I unpack.

"Yeah?"

"What's going on, little lady?"

"Hey, Duncan!"

He pulls me into a big hug.

"How was your weekend?" I ask, returning to my dresser.

"Not good."

I assume this is in reaction to the probation decision.

"Yeah…listen," he goes on. "Peter wanted me to tell you, he wants to see you in his room."

I stop as I'm putting a couple of shirts in a drawer. "Did he say why?"

He avoids my eyes, picking at the chipping paint on my door frame. "I really shouldn't, Cass. He wants to be the one to talk to you."

"Yeah, um, okay." I drop the shirts on the bed. "I'll go now."

"Okay, come hang out after if you want."

I just nod.

As I go to the second floor, a million thoughts race through my head.

Does he know about Jordan?

Oh my God, does he know about the project?

My heart pounds against my chest as I pass the naked calendar. It seems so long since I first saw it at Rush.

Bracing myself, I knock on the door bearing the name plaque, "Mother Fuckin' President."

The door swings open, and for the second time in my life I walk into Peter's room to be interrogated, with what feels like my entire life hanging in the balance.

"Hey, Cassie, we need to talk about something."

"Okay…"

"You can sit down if you want."

I take a seat at the desk chair; he sits on the bed.

"So I know you've been gone all weekend, which is fine, but, um…" He runs a hand through his hair. "Sorry, I'm trying to figure out where to start. On Saturday the doorbell rang, which was weird, because obviously we all have keys and there were no guests allowed—you've heard about the new rules, right?"

I nod.

"So we sent a couple pledges to answer it, and when they do, this blonde girl collapses in their arms. They bring her inside, and Duncan recognizes her as your friend Alex."

It feels like all the blood drains from my brain. Like my heart is falling out of my body. I open my mouth, but nothing comes out.

"No, no, she's fine now."

I breathe again.

"But she was in bad shape when she showed up here. Alcohol, and maybe something else, so we had no choice but to call an ambulance. They took her to the hospital, where they pumped her stomach, and she's fine."

"Thank you. Thank you so much," I say.

He doesn't look proud. He's a hero who saved my best friend, shouldn't he look…happier about it?

"Cassie, substance use and guests, it looks like we had both. That's two strikes when we didn't have any left."

"Oh my God…"

"The housing board is voting at the end of the week, but with this, it doesn't look good. We're probably going to be disbanded."

I can't believe how much these words—these words that were my goal at the beginning of the year—make me want to cry.

"I wanted to talk to you first, because some people in the house are gonna blame you. But you need to know that it could've been any of us, any of our friends or girlfriends could've shown up needing help. But it's important you lay low. I'm trying to make sure if we go out, it's all as friends, not turning against each other. I know you would never purposely do anything to hurt the frat."

He's trying to protect me, even as his house goes down in part because of me. *Especially* because of me. If only he knew how wrong he was. That I was doing work that hurt the frat long before I even walked through the doors.

I nod, not trusting myself to speak.

"Hometown sweetheart?" he asks as I stand up to leave.

"What?"

He nods toward me. "The hickey."

My hand flies to my neck. "Oh, no. I burned myself with my straightening iron."

He laughs. "Relax, as long as it's not from someone in my house, I'm happy for you."

I smile feebly.

As soon as I'm back to my room, I power up my phone.

It lights up like a Christmas tree: texts and voice mails

from Alex, drunk and scared and alone, telling me she doesn't know where to go and is just going to come to the house. Then apologetic texts, letting me know she's okay and thanking the brothers.

Texts from a few brothers, including Peter, about the situation, and asking why the hell I haven't answered yet.

And then there are the three emails from Madison Macey, wanting to schedule a call soon.

I'll deal with her tomorrow. This is still a three-day weekend; I have an excuse.

And I've got bigger issues, one friend who was just hospitalized and one hundred who might be about to lose their home.

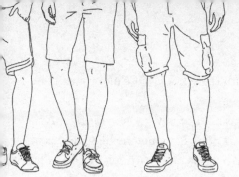

chapter forty-nine

"BUT YOU HAVE TO!"

"I don't *have* to do anything." Alex crosses her arms and turns away from me. I came here right away, and after checking in to make sure she was alive I suggested she tell the administration the boys were just taking care of her. I thought she would say of course, even say she'd already called and told them.

Which is why I was so taken aback by her *"No way in hell!"*

"They're going to lose their house."

"And I'm really sorry about that." She turns back to me. "But you know I can't tell the school."

"Why not? They already know you got fucked up and were taken to the hospital."

"They already know *a female undergrad* was transported from the house." She plops down into the beanbag chair. "Only the hospital knows my name, and they won't release it."

"Oh." I chew my lip for a second, considering this. "Okay,

so you get into trouble with the school, but c'mon, it can't be that big a deal."

"I'm on scholarship, Cassie. I literally go here for free. And that money's from Warren. I don't have anyone like Stevenson supporting me. If I get in trouble with the school, I'm fucked."

"They're not gonna take away your scholarship, that's— No, people get drunk all the time."

She exhales. "So they won't kick me out on the street. But will they approve my grant for my next show or a semester abroad?"

"Who cares? Dude, it was your fault. The house shouldn't take the fall for this."

"Yeah, because it's *this* that's bringing them down, not years of bullshit."

"But they're beginning to learn, Alex." I run my hands through my hair. "Most of them are really smart and thoughtful—they just didn't know before. And now, if we take away their house, they'll associate feminism with this moment when they were kicked out of their home for helping you. And you probably *will* be able to get funding for Paris still even if—"

"Nice, Cassie. You of all people telling me to risk my funding for them."

I step back, feeling like her words actually hit me.

"It doesn't matter what the hell *I* do," she says, "seeing as you're about to publish a takedown piece on them."

"It's not a takedown piece." I walk toward the window before spinning on my heel; the room is really too small for pacing. "It's—it's a story of progress, of how cultures can change, how knowing someone different from you—living with someone different from you—can help you become open-minded."

"That's a rose-colored way to look at it." She pushes herself off the beanbag chair.

"But you see my point. There's forward momentum, and that has to count for something."

She squats down in front of a small dresser she's painted baby blue. "I'm supposed to be quitting," she mumbles, yanking open a drawer, then pulling out a pack of Marlboro Reds and a white lighter.

"Bad luck, you know, the solid white lighter."

"I know." She flicks her thumb, and a flame shoots up. "But the way I think about it, the smoke's more likely to kill me." She taps the pack on the windowsill, pulls one out and lights up.

After the first drag, she turns back to me. The sun shines through her hair and illuminates the wall behind her, the silvery words shining. "I'm sorry."

"It's fine. You're kind of right. The story, no matter what, it's not gonna be good for them. I just… I feel trapped."

She flicks ash out the window. "Shit, dude."

"What if…" I breathe in. "I think…"

She raises her eyebrows, her eyes telling me to hurry up and spit it out.

"The thing is, so many people want the story, I have some control, right? So what if we turn this into a story like the admittedly cheesy one I just told about growth?" I'm talking quickly now, excited. The more I hear myself say it, this idea that's been bouncing around in my head, the more it sounds like reality. "But seriously, like them or not, I can't think of anything that would send them in a worse direction than just kicking them out, and we've seen—I've documented—that there's a better way. And I can talk to Dr. Price, because there's no way she'll let my entries run without a single peer review or any analysis of the last part of the data."

"Will the Stevenson people be down for that?" Her voice is higher.

"Do they have a choice? It's the truth."

"I guess so." She puts out her cigarette.

"Yes, this is good," I say. "I have a plan. It'll be fine." I don't even convince myself.

"Fine." She exhales the last of the smoke. "I'll think about going to the Dean of Alcohol and Whatever to tell the story. Not because I give a fuck about those frat boys, but because they helped me, and I have enough honor to take the fall for my own stupidity."

"Thank you!" She stumbles back when I hug her, then wraps her arms around me, too.

When I step back, she looks at me seriously. "But, dude, you better make sure it counts for something."

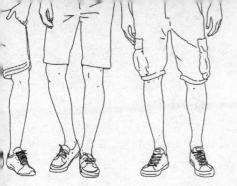

chapter fifty

I'M RUNNING THROUGH SOCIOLOGY TERMS IN MY
head and scanning email on my phone when I almost run
into someone.

"Oh, sorry." I look up to see a junior who's on the soccer
team with Jordan.

"It's chill." He steps around me. "Hey, wait, actually,
Cassie?"

I turn around. "What's up?"

"There's someone in the living room waiting for you, says
she's your aunt."

I have one aunt who lives in Indiana and collects china
dolls. She's never even been on a plane, let alone hopped over
to California to say hi.

"Okay, thanks. I'll go, uh, say hi."

As I step into the living room, I'm immediately greeted
by the opposite of Aunt Helen, Madison Macey, wearing a
Chanel suit and a ridiculous hat. She's sitting on the edge of
a couch, as if certain she'll catch a disease from it, and as far

away as she could be from the other occupants of the room, two seniors and Duncan playing *FIFA*.

"Cassie!"

"Aunt Mandy." I smile through gritted teeth. "What are you doing here?" It's all I can do not to spice up that sentence with a few expletives.

"Didn't your mother tell you? I wanted to visit you." She stands. "Come on—we're having a girls' day."

I glance toward the door. "I have class in ten minutes," I lie.

"I'm sure you can skip it. I haven't seen you in so long."

"Yeah, it's almost like it's the first time I've met you, *Aunt Mandy*."

She laughs and grabs me by my arm, her grip waaaay harder than it looks, and leads me toward the door.

"Great to meet you," she calls behind us.

The boys grunt something indistinguishable.

She's quiet until we arrive at a Starbucks off campus.

"I've been trying to reach you for two days."

I open my mouth to speak, but she holds up her hand so she can order a Venti nonfat vanilla something or other.

She turns to me, perfect eyebrows raised, while they swipe her platinum card for the three-dollar charge.

"My phone broke," I say.

"You're in the middle of the biggest negotiation of your little life." She stops as the barista hands her the cup. She rolls her eyes and spins it around to show me the word *Melanie* in large print. "Unbelievable."

We sit down, and she starts back in as if she'd never stopped. "So let's talk strategy."

"Huh?"

"We want to control exactly how this story breaks. Picture this…" She waves her hand. "The day the article runs, you hold a press conference on the lawn of the frat, with all the major news stations in attendance." She raises her eyebrows and takes a sip of her coffee.

"I don't know if that's a good… Madison, that's where I *live*. What am I supposed to do, just walk back inside afterward?"

"It's where you lived for the experiment. Cassie, it's over."

"Yeah, but maybe we could wait until the end of the school year. That way I can finish my first year in the house with my pledge class, move out for the summer and then deal with all this."

She tilts her head to the side, and her mouth forms a little o, like something has just occurred to her. "What do you care about ending the year with your pledge class? Don't tell me you've been Stockholmed?"

"No." I exhale. "I haven't lost my focus or anything, but I mean, this was always an undercover project that involved real people. A press conference in front of the house…it's not like someone was murdered there."

"But—"

"No." I look up at her. "This is supposed to be a nuanced project. There are real issues there, but there are also real teenagers, some of whom haven't done anything wrong and don't need to have their home plastered over every television in America."

"We're talking about *your project* being plastered over every television in America."

I tap my fingers on the table nervously. "What if we turn the project into some sort of program to educate fraternities about gender issues? You've read the entries. Most of these guys are just ignorant—they're not evil."

"Cassie, you know as well as I do, that sort of thing does not make money or create press for Stevenson. In fact, that would cost this project funds that you don't have. We've already invested so much in you. Now you need to produce what you promised us, what you proposed."

I run my hands through my hair and exhale. "Okay, what if you only go with print, and change the name of the frat. You already have to change the names of the people involved. After all, they didn't consent to the study."

"Cassie, you are the only girl in the world in a fraternity. People will know which one it is."

"Oh."

She sips her coffee.

I sigh. "I thought there was going to be a peer-reviewed academic paper."

She reaches out to take my hand in hers. "There will be, and there will be a brawl among the university presses over who gets to publish it, but only if we create enough buzz with the journal entries."

"But the entries alone are misleading. I don't want them to run without—"

"That's not the kind of call you get to make." She drops my hand and crosses her arms over her chest.

"What if I don't send them to you?"

She just stares at me like I'm an idiot.

"Oh…" It seems like the roof of the coffee shop is crashing down on me. "The online portals." For security reasons I wrote all my journal entries in a secure site. A secure site created by the Stevenson organization.

She nods. "We already have them, and so does *America Weekly*."

"And there's nothing I can do?"

She purses her lips. "I came here as a courtesy, because we'd like you to get on board. We don't need your permission."

"What if—what if I give up my scholarship?"

I can't believe the words, even as they come out of my mouth.

"It doesn't matter." She stands up. "This is what you signed up for. Read your own contract. You've spent a quarter of our money already, and we solely own all your work. We're moving forward, with or without you."

Without saying another word, I get up and head for the street. I barely notice the small bell ringing as I stumble out the door. I start walking, not really sure where I'm going. The sun is setting when I get to the main quad, turning the sandstone walkways a warm orange color.

A few tourists are lingering, left over from the groups that come in herds every day. A mother turns away from her camera to yell to her child in a language I don't understand, but the tone tells me she's saying it's time to go home.

The little boy slouches and pouts but waddles over. Her stern face softens as he approaches, and she places a hand on his head as they walk away.

A few students, backpacks on, make their way along the far side of the quad. They're talking, but I can't make out their words from this distance.

Rays of sunlight shoot between the columns that surround the quad and I squint my tired eyes. Sighing, I slide off my backpack and sink to the ground. I lie down, using my bag as a pillow, too tired and too worn down to care that people may stare, that I may end up in tourists' pictures or garner weird looks from someone who thinks they might recognize me from somewhere; maybe a class, maybe the news.

I reach into the pocket of my jeans, pull out my phone and dial. As the number rings, I listen to the sound of my breathing, trying to steady it.

"Cassie?" The surprise in her voice, despite caller ID, breaks the last remaining pieces of my heart. I guess that's what happens when you don't call your mother for an entire semester.

"Yeah," I say. "It's me." I hope she can hear the smile I somehow manage.

"How are you, sweetie?" There's noise in the background, the sounds of pots and pans, and a television, probably the soap operas she DVRs. At home dinnertime is already over, and she's probably watching TV while doing the dishes, while my father lounges with a beer in the den. My heart aches just picturing that stupid, tiny house in Indiana.

"I'm good," I lie.

The ensuing pause is long, and I picture words floating over the expanse of an already darkening country.

"You sound sick," she says. "Do you feel like you have a fever?"

"No." I sigh. "I, uh, I'm just tired."

She just makes a humming sound.

"Mom?"

"Mmm-hmm?"

"Can I ask you something?" I trace my fingers over the rough, sandy bricks below me, manicured perfectly to never allow a weed to emerge between them. "I have this, uh, class, and it's really important. If I do well, it could set up my entire career, because the professor offers internships. But to do well, I have to hurt people who've become my friends…some of the best friends I've made here."

I banish thoughts of the way Jordan's eyes sparkle when he laughs and Duncan's bear hugs.

"You see," I lie, "it's a journalism class, and I'm covering the football team. I found out that a lot of them used steroids for the first half of last season, and obviously that's wrong, but some of them have changed their minds, and some never did it in the first place, but they'll all be hurt by the scandal if I go with the story. I mean, it'll be huge, and my professor will hire me, but I'll have hurt my friends, and I'm not sure…" I exhale. This analogy sucks anyway.

"Well, Cass." My mother clears her throat. "I think you have to ask yourself, *if* you run the story, are you doing it because these people did something wrong and you have an obligation to expose it, or because it will help your career?"

"Can I say both?"

She laughs. "Yeah, but it won't help you very much with your decision."

I half smile. "I guess so."

We both go silent, and I wonder what else I can talk about. What do most kids say when they call their parents? Ask about the weather, news in the neighborhood, how pets are doing?

"I miss you, Mom," I say. "Sometimes I really just want to come home, sleep in my own bed. To hug you." My voice cracks. I can't believe I ache so badly for such a messed-up home.

I wipe a stray tear from my eye as she launches into a motherly chorus of missing me, too, and me always being her little girl and so on.

"Thanks, Mom." I bite my lip. "Listen… I gotta go." I shift my weight, the hard stone starting to make my body sore. "I have a…meeting soon."

"Oh, okay. Sorry I couldn't help you more, kiddo."

"No, Mom, you did help." I pause. "I'll call you again soon, okay?"

I stare at the lock screen for a while after the beeping that signals the end of the call.

The world is blue with dusk when I finally stand up, the weird, cold relief of having just finished crying lingering as I head back to the house.

chapter fifty-one

"AMERICA WEEKLY, PLEASE HOLD."

"No, no, no, no, *no!*" I yell into the phone, but the cheesy instrumental music doesn't care.

It's the fifth time I've called, after being repeatedly disconnected. I've been on hold on and off for three hours.

The music stops and a man answers. "Hello, Features Desk. This is Carl speaking."

Holy shit, a person.

"Ohmygod, hi, my name is Cassie Davis and I need to talk to features editor Stephen Bing."

"He's out for the rest of the day."

What? "No, he can't be. There's a story about me—no, more like a story I *wrote.* But I have to stop it, and I *need* to talk to him."

"I'm sorry. I don't know what to tell you. He's at the Supreme Court right now, and he doesn't have a phone with him."

"Oh my God, this can't be happening." I press my hand to my forehead.

"Wait, what'd you say your name was?"

"Cassandra Davis."

"You're the frat girl, right?"

People ask me this all the time, when a class is letting out, or when I'm in line at Campus Coffee. But it feels completely different coming from someone who works at one of the biggest magazines in the world.

"Uh, yeah."

"I've been working on your story all week. I think I can help you."

"Oh thank God."

There's a shuffling sound on the other end. "Let me just grab an open conference room, and then you can catch me up."

"Okay. Oh my God, thank you so much. You have no idea how much this means to me."

He laughs. "Okay, I'm all set, so why don't you first tell me why you want to stop yourself from getting the break of a lifetime."

"Okay, so the first one who was cool was Duncan…" I take a deep breath and explain how the project developed and so did my friendships with the guys. How everything I thought was black-and-white turned out to be gray the more I dug.

"And I just feel like, in feminist literature, there's this phrase where what's personal is political. That's kind of the basis of this project, that patriarchal ideas also affect our friendships and romantic relationships, and create issues that need to be addressed. But just because the personal is political, doesn't mean you can use the same tools to approach relationships that you use for dealing with political issues. When women can't vote and you fight for that right, you don't need to care what your opposition thinks of you, you can use whatever tatic you want as long as you get enough votes for the amendment.

"But when we talk about social equality, how bias plays a

role in friendships, we're talking about changing hearts and minds. Disbanding this frat won't get rid of the problems, which, yes, exist. It will just spread those people out and make them angry.

"We need to talk about nuance. We need to differentiate between seemingly mean comments made to me because friends of any sex give each other shit and always will, and comments that illustrate double standards and are a result of negative societal ideas. To see what's humor that pushes the envelope and what's bigotry disguised by a punch line. If we don't make that clear, those guys are just going to be pissed off because they think people are 'PC policing' them for the former, when we're really talking about the latter. And I just don't think the piece as it stands does that. I think it will do more harm than good. For the boys here and the entire Greek system, but also for feminism and women on college campuses."

I breathe.

"Damn. We should just run that in the magazine."

I laugh. "So you see what I mean?"

"Yeah, I really do. And you know, I was in a frat back in my day."

"Really?"

"Yup. Sig Nu."

"No way!"

"Yeah. And I've also been writing about gender issues for years and consider myself a card-holding feminist."

Huh.

"Okay," he goes on. "I'll tell you what. I'm gonna talk to Steve as soon as he gets back from Washington. Even all your great points aside, I think it's as simple as we can't run an article without the author's consent, and I don't care that, legally speaking, you gave up the rights. I mean, they're *your* journal entries, pretty much a diary, and nothing screams off the record more than a diary. Honestly, I wouldn't worry if I were you. I'll get back to you after I talk to Steve on Monday. But you can relax—it's taken care of."

"Thank you!"

I hang up and set my phone down on the desk, able to breathe again.

Almost immediately there's a knock at the door.

"Come in."

I look up as Jordan pushes the door open. "Peter wants everyone downstairs."

"That can't be good." I stand up, leaving my phone on the desk. I have no pockets, and I'll be back up in a few minutes. Hopefully not to pack.

"I don't know. He was smiling."

"Really?"

The whole chapter is crammed in the living room, and Peter's standing on the hearth, watching everyone file in with a ridiculous grin on his face.

"That everyone?" he asks as people shove over, and Jordan and I take a seat on the couch.

"Okay, men and whatever... Cassie, you get the idea. I have some fabulous news. Miss Alexandra McNeely, who some of you might have met when she graced us with her presence last Saturday, has volunteered to testify before the housing board as to what happened that night. And the housing board, for the first time ever, has agreed to hear testimony before they make a decision. Now, there are no guarantees, but when I spoke to the Greek adviser—who, as you all know, sits on the housing board—he said if her story checks out the way I told it to him, which of course it will, then our acts of Good Samaritan–ism will mean not just clearing these charges but taking us completely off probation."

A cheer erupts throughout the room.

"Now, everyone…" He waves his arms. "Back to your rooms to celebrate in a non-probation-breaking way!" He steps down off the hearth, laughing.

Jordan turns to me and says, "That's awesome!"

"Yep." I bite my lip, not sure if we should be so happy just yet.

"Cassie," Peter says as he saunters across the room toward me. "Your friend is really coming through for us, and we really appreciate it."

"I, um, I'll tell her that."

"Please do."

People don't heed the celebrating-in-their-rooms rule; they're already breaking out beers and getting ready to shotgun them right here in living room,

"To Alex!" they say, raising their beers.

"No, to Cassie!" Peter yells.

"To Cassie!"

"This is the kind of loyalty true Deltas are made of. Nice job, kid." Peter pats me on the shoulder.

I smile despite the poisonous taste in my mouth as he walks away.

"You saved us," Jordan says.

God, I hope so, I think.

Cheap champagne and cheaper beer flow freely, and someone turns on the music. A familiar melody floats through the air, the kind that swells in your chest, the kind that's contagiously happy.

The house doors are kept closed, and some underclassmen cover the windows with tinfoil.

Tonight will not be a party that gets out of hand. There will be no random people who sneak in or flirt their way onto the list. There will be no guests. Just family.

I float around the room, my smile stretched across my lips

but not making it to my eyes. I make jokes and suggest songs and dance with my friends. And I pretend there's not an anvil hanging above this happy room, an anvil only I can see. That I put there.

Someone taps my shoulder.

I turn around and find Jordan standing behind me. My false smile turns into a real one.

He leans closer. "What do you say we steal one of those bottles and go out on the lake?"

I raise my eyebrows. "Sounds perfect."

"Meet you outside in ten." He walks out through the kitchen.

I finish my beer and chat with Duncan for a minute before excusing myself to go to the bathroom and slipping out the main entrance.

I close the heavy door behind me and hear only a dull hum from the music. The tinfoil does its job well, and outside it's almost pitch-black. I make my way around the house, the grass cool against my ankles.

The backyard is empty, just a few overturned plastic chairs and beer cans left on tables or littered across the ground.

"Cassie!"

I jump. Jordan is peeking out from behind a tree.

"Oh God, you scared me."

"Sorry." He shrugs sheepishly as he steps into view. "I got you this." He holds out a bottle.

"Perfect."

We walk forward, and I lean over to kiss him on the cheek.

He takes my hand and helps me through the weeds and mud and down to the little dock.

We walk to the end of the pier, and I slip off my shoes before sitting down. I swing my feet into the cool water, dark in the moonlight. He takes longer to untie his shoes but eventually joins me, handing me the bottle of champagne.

"André?" I examine the four-dollar bottle.

He winks. "Only the best for you, love." He says the word causally, but it rings in my ears.

"Here, you can do the honors." He twists off the top and hands it back so I can take the first sip.

"Thank you." The champagne is probably too sweet and probably too warm, but in this moment it seems pretty perfect. I hand the bottle back to him.

After he drinks he says, "You know what? I think I like our little party better than the one in there."

I swipe the bottle back. "Me, too."

"Not to say I don't love the brothers."

"Oh, me, too."

"And, I mean, bros before hoes, of course." He smiles.

"Hey!" I shove him lightly.

"Oh, calm down—you know I'm kidding." He takes the hand I pushed him with, weaving his fingers through mine.

I roll my eyes.

"Really, though." He sets the bottle down on the pier next to him. "You're the most important person in my life, Cassie."

I remind myself to breathe.

He brushes a stray hair behind my ear, his eyes fixed on mine. "You're the only one I feel like I can really talk to, who knows about my life here and at home. And you always know what to say to help me deal with things—you're so smart like that. You're…you're like my best friend. And I think I might be falling for you."

A million thoughts race through my mind. What I want to say, what I feel. What I *should* say, knowing how much I've lied to him, knowing that all of this is hanging in a balance he doesn't know exists.

So I don't say anything. I just lean forward and kiss him. It's the most passionate kiss I've ever had, behind it everything we feel, everything we need, everything I am so afraid we'll lose.

I lean back and look at him, studying the face I see in my dreams. My voice is thin when I say, "I think I'm falling for you, too."

We lie back on the dock, our hands just barely touching, and watch the stars sparkling above. Every once in a while one of us sits up to have a sip of the sweet, bubbly liquid. It tastes like the summer that's just beginning to arrive.

I shift closer to him, and for a moment it feels like this might not have to end. That this—this giddy, happy, amazing love—might go on forever.

"I miss the city," he says.

"Mmm, me, too."

"I miss waking up with you...showering with you."

I wonder if he can see my smile in the dark.

"Not just the sexual stuff. I mean, I love that, but if we're careful, we can do that here. But the little moments like this... I wish we could have more of them here. That we didn't have to hide."

"Me, too."

I give him a peck on the cheek before sitting up to grab the bubbly. I tilt the bottle up, but only a few drops spill out.

"Champagne's gone."

"Really?" He sits up, as well.

"Yeah, it—"

Before I can finish my sentence, his lips are on mine, kissing me feverishly.

I break away to catch my breath. "Okay." I laugh and set down the bottle, and then kiss him back.

He slips a hand in my hair as we kiss more deeply. I pull him closer, then swing one leg around him. He lets out a moan.

His hands travel to the nape on my neck, then down my back. I weave my hands through his hair, and his hands slip under my shirt, brushing across my waist and upward to cup my breasts over the lace of my bra.

I lean back and lift my shirt by the hem, pulling it over my head and dropping it on the deck beside us.

He takes me in, running his finger along the black lace, which contrasts against my fair skin, even more so in the dark of night.

"You're so beautiful," he murmurs.

I smile and kiss him again.

"You're not so bad yourself."

"Thank you." He kisses me lightly on the lips again.

I lean back. "You know what we should do?" I can feel the mischievous smile on my lips.

"What?" he asks.

"This." I stand up and slide off my skirt so it pools around my ankles.

I'm wearing tiny black lace underwear that barely covers my ass. My pale skin shines in the moonlight, and the air is colder than I thought it would be now that I'm exposed and no longer in his warm arms.

And even though he's seen me naked, I feel a bit self-conscious.

I look over my shoulder, and his gaze on me settles all my nervousness, replacing it with a new kind of thrilling feeling in my heart.

I reach behind my back to undo my bra, then slide the straps down my arms and let it fall to the dock.

I reach toward my underwear, and hear a sharp intake of breath from behind me as I shimmy the lace down my legs and step out of them.

I turn around and smile flirtatiously before jumping into the water.

The water is colder than I expected but feels nice. I'm definitely very aware that I'm not wearing a swimsuit, but it feels very…natural. There's something animalistic about it that's so hot.

I come back up for air, smoothing my hair back.

"Well, what are you waiting for?" I ask.

Jordan smiles and stands, pulling off his T-shirt.

———

We spend most of the night asleep in an old boathouse, cuddled up in a canoe, using some towels as makeshift blankets. I sleep well.

Until I wake up around sunrise, when there's enough light to see the effing spiders.

After I wake up a sound-asleep Jordan with my screams, we decide to head back to the house to get some real sleep.

It's full light in my room by the time I get there, but I climb into bed and crash without even changing or getting under the covers.

I wake up sweating, the sun in my eyes. Looking out my window, I estimate it must be around noon. I slide out of my bed and walk over to check my phone, but it's dead. Wiping the sweat off my forehead, I dig through my desk until I find the charger, then get down on my hands and knees to plug it into the outlet placed so conveniently under the desk.

After standing up, I head to my wardrobe, looking for a cute sundress to wear. Jordan and I made plans to get lunch in Palo Alto, but I don't know if the white lacy one or the floral one is more cute-but-not-trying casual.

My phone buzzes once, indicating it's turning on. I mean, it's gotta be floral, right?

My phone buzzes about fifty more times.

What the…?

I walk over and grab the phone. Seven missed calls and a voice mail from an unsaved number in New York, New York.

Oh my God.

My hands shaking, I click on the message.

"Cassie, this is Carl, and I'm so sorry. I've been trying to reach you for hours. Steve won't budge on the story. In fact, they pushed it up a week because there's a companion piece they want to run it with. By the time I reached him it was already being printed. He couldn't have stopped it even if he'd wanted to. It comes out tomorrow. I'm so sorry, Cassie. I really wish I could have helped but—"

The phone falls to the ground, bouncing twice on the carpet.

My brain is going off in so many different directions, but I have only one coherent thought: *I need to find Jordan.*

I fly out of my room. *Maybe if I find him before he reads it, if I can explain the situation, if he hears it from me…*

I throw open the door to his room, but all the bunks are empty.

I rush down the stairs and burst into the common room, and for the first time since I moved in, it's dead silent.

Most people get up and leave when they see me; others just shake their heads at the floor.

"Have any of you seen Jordan?" My voice sounds like I'm crying, even though the tears that sting my eyes haven't fallen yet.

Behind me, someone clears his throat.

I turn around, and there he is, leaning against the back wall, a copy of *America Weekly* in his hands. He looks like someone just slapped him.

"You lied…to all of us."

"I…" My voice starts out weak and fades to nothing. I doubt that syllable even makes it across the room.

"There's nothing to say." I've never seen his eyes like this. They are usually dark in a rich and warm way, now they look like a stormy sky. For the first time I wish he was looking at anyone but me.

I look around, but everyone else has fled the room.

"I—I tried to be fair, balanced. I say some good things."

"It doesn't matter *what* you said. I trusted—*we* trusted—" In his eyes I see what he can't say inside the house, where someone may overhear. You lied to *me*; all of this was a lie. I thought I was *in love with you*, and it was a lie.

But it wasn't a lie. I lied about so many things, big and small. But not the way I felt about him.

He throws the magazine down at my feet and storms out. And just like that, I'm alone, the sound of the slamming door ringing in my ears.

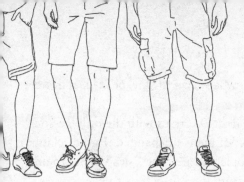

chapter fifty-two

I'M IN SHOCK THAT THEY DON'T KICK ME OUT ON my ass, but in a way it's even worse. My life quickly reverts back to the way it was for my first days living in the house. But worse. It's not just that everyone acts like I'm not there; they actively avoid me.

In September I would sit awkwardly as conversations buzzed around me. Now people get up and leave their meals behind when I sit at a table. Or they talk about me in front of me.

Jackie refuses to answer my calls. Even Duncan and Bambi retreat from my life. Duncan with a "wtf dude" text, Bambi with a tearful plea. "We were the three musketeers, you and me and Duncan—how could you do this to us?"

Jordan says nothing.

On Tuesday morning I get an email from Peter. Since I technically didn't break any rules in my report—I didn't describe any secret handshakes or rituals—there aren't grounds to officially kick me out of the house. But I think it's best if, for now, you look for somewhere else to stay, or at least avoid common areas.

I start eating all my meals at Dionysus with the only person on campus whose opinion of me is unchanged. I go to class, where I sit alone while people whisper, and I sleep in my room with the door locked, waiting for a knock that never comes.

That's it.

Actually, sleep has become the highlight of my life.

To just close my eyes and pretend this hasn't happened, that Jordan's arms are wrapped around me, that this house is still home to me and any second one of my friends will stop by, yell at me to rally and throw me a beer.

But voices rumble past my door on the way to study or party or hang out, passing by like it's just a blank wall.

Then I find out how good I had it when my door and I were just ignored.

Coming home late from studying in the library, I find my "Welcome Pledge Title IX" sign is gone and in its place *Bitch*, *Liar*, *Feminazi*, *Traitor*, *Shrew*, you name it, have been spray painted in red across the green door.

Well, that's certainly consistent with how my life is going.

I ignore the insults and head inside to flop onto my bed.

Eventually I meet with Professor Price. I made this appointment when I was frantically trying to stop the article, and this was "the absolute soonest she could meet," according to her secretary.

There's really no point now. But I guess it's rude to stand up a Nobel laureate, even when nothing matters anymore.

"Cassie!" Her smile feels warm, even now. "Come in—it's good to see you. Would you like some tea?"

I nod. "Thank you."

She hits a button on her phone. "Georgia, would you please bring in a kettle?"

She reaches down, pulls two ceramic mugs from a drawer and then opens an antique Japanese tea box.

By the time she puts a tea bag in each mug, there is a knock at the door. A young girl comes in and fills the cups with steaming water. The purple-red color of the tea starts to disperse through the water like smoke.

The girl leaves, but not before giving me a smile, her eyes full of pity. Or maybe that's just in my head.

I pick up my mug for a second, letting it warm me, before I take the first sip. "This is delicious."

She nods. "It's my favorite. I like to save it for special occasions."

"I don't exactly feel like celebrating." I twiddle the tag of the tea bag between my fingers.

"I mean, important moments, good or bad. Times when you need to be centered."

I take another sip.

"How are you doing?"

"I've been better." I set down my cup.

She closes her eyes and nods. "This is not how I wanted things to go for you."

I look down at my cup. "It's not how I wanted them to go, either. And, honestly, the way people have reacted…sometimes I'm not sure I should've done this at all."

"Why's that?"

"I've lost almost everyone who matters to me."

We're both silent for a moment.

She exhales. "You know, I didn't start as a gender activist."

"Really?" I'm not sure what this has to do with my situation, but I'm happy for the distraction.

"Yes. I was finishing my PhD when Rodney King happened. I had just published my first big paper, and it was on police brutality. Suddenly I was on every TV station, the young black author and professor with the Ivy League education. I was the perfect counterimage to put up on-screen next to footage of the riots.

"Of course, that was the first time I lost the support of people fighting the same fight as I was, when I became the Brooklyn girl fighting from the ivory tower instead of protesting on the streets like someone who was really invested in the cause.

"But I wrote about racism for a long time, and I still write about it almost every day. And then in 2006 Coretta Scott King died, and I wrote an article about straight men in the struggle not always acknowledging those who also fought alongside them against oppression. Not acknowledging the different ways racism and misogyny affect black women and LGBTQA people of color. I argued for intersectionality, for a united cause against these forms of oppression that were so clearly connected. I wasn't saying don't talk about Dr. King—I was saying also talk about Coretta Scott, also talk about Marsha P. Johnson.

"But many of the people I had worked with for years and years heard my words as attacking black men for the way they treated black women. Said I was dividing the movement, causing distraction.

"Some people came back around, realized that I was still going to be there for Oscar Grant, for Ferguson, even if I was also there for the wage gap and female education and transgender housing discrimination.

"But there are still friends I've lost." She takes a sip of her tea. "My father still doesn't support a lot of what I do. He doesn't buy my books. To hit the *New York Times* bestseller list, to know strangers have probably mentioned my books in front of him, not knowing I was his daughter, and knowing my father, the one who marched on Washington and taught me how to fight in the first place, will pretend he doesn't know who I am...that's still pretty hard, even now.

"So the way I look at it, you've got two problems. One is that you lied. And, honey, we all knew that was wrong when we began. Those boys welcomed you into their home and offered you friendship, but you and I both know you were approaching them under false pretenses. And we knew the sin was worth the good we'd be doing, but you can't expect them to see that from their perspective, especially when they're just finding out now. Hell, it's sometimes hard for me to see that, and I was one of the adults who told you to do it.

"So that's the first thing these boys are mad about, that you lied to them. And it's okay that they're mad.

"The second is what you had to say. And you can *never* apologize for that—do you hear me? There are men in that house who, from what you've told me and from the research we've done, we both *know* are misogynistic.

"And lie or not, no matter how objective you were in what you wrote, they *will* hate you, for questioning their way of life, for saying that some of their behavior is causing so much hurt that it should stop. And more important, you are a woman who thinks, and that threatens them more than everything else. They won't admit it, but I think that's the secret fear that motivates them. They're worried that if there's an equal playing field, they'll lose.

"Those are the ones whose hate tells you that you're doing your job right. It still hurts, but you can't let it stop you.

"The good news is the ones who are just mad that you lied will come around. They'll forgive the means because of the end. The ones who never come back aren't worth it."

I look down at my tea. "I hope you're right."

"I hope I'm right, too." She smiles. "Worst-case scenario, you've got me and all these friends." She reaches into her desk drawer and pulls out a thick stack of papers, all different colors, folded all different ways.

"Some are letters, others are emails we printed out." She flips through them. "Your generation doesn't seem to be much of a fan of real letters. Young feminists and quite a few women who just realized they were feminists. A surprising amount of sorority girls." She pulls one out of the stack. "This one's my favorite. I highlighted a part you might like."

The paper she hands me is pink and smells good. The letter is written in swirly handwriting.

"This is like my life. I mean, I'm not in a frat, but this is what it's like to be a girl in college. It's not always easy to know the feminist thing to do, but I guess I'm not the only one that has a hard time. I'll keep trying. Thank you, Cassie."

For the first time in a long time, I smile.

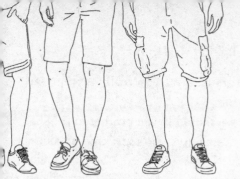

chapter fifty-three

THAT NIGHT I WALK UPSTAIRS AND STARE AT MY closed door, pressing my key a little too hard into my palm. When I open my hand there's a small indent in my skin.

I look back to the door, and the word *Bitch* screams at me. The dripping red paint looks like the sign on a cheap haunted house.

Enough is enough.

Shaking my head, I shove the key in the lock and push open the door. I barely throw down my bag before I'm out the door again, heart pounding as I run down the stairs. For the first time all week, I'm full of energy.

After trying three half-empty closets, including one stocked solely with red cups and a mop, I find what I'm looking for.

I run back up the stairs, the bucket—rag and soap inside— banging into my hip at every step. I fill the bucket up in the bathroom sink, add the soap and start scrubbing.

The *B* in *Bitch* smears until it's just a big red blob. *Fabulous.*

A voice echoes up the stairs. "Are you really saying you want her to stay?"

"Are you really saying we should kick a brother out?"

I close my eyes and try to imagine who's speaking, to identify the voices, but I can't.

A nasty kind of laughter echoes up the staircase. "She's not exactly a brother."

I hear the sound of footsteps, and then Peter and Sebastian round the landing.

Well, that answers my question.

I mean, kind of. I still don't know who said what.

Bass avoids eye contact as he slips into his room. Peter looks at me like he's a small child who got caught doing something he shouldn't.

Yeah, that's right. I heard you guys talking shit, I want to say.

But I just turn back to my quickly failing project, trying to make sense of what I heard.

Peter *was* the one who told me to move out soon if I can. But Bass has never liked me.

And what about the whole brother thing?

Peter is always the one who corrects *brother* to *sister*, who uses gendered pronouns, even in big speeches, so he had to be the voice against me, right?

So…is Bass *defending* me? What has the world come to?

I shake off these thoughts and stare at my progress, or rather, lack thereof. The door is beginning to look like some sort of modern art project. A tie-dye design in red and green.

Like Christmas.

Except for on Christmas you usually don't see the smeary but still totally legible remnants of curse words on the decorations.

There's a noise behind me.

I turn around, and Peter's standing there with a rag and spray bottle in his hand.

He clears his throat. "You, uh, gotta use this stuff."

He offers me the bottle.

Goof Off Graffiti Remover: Removes the Tough Stuff!

There's a company that specializes in this? But I guess if you need it, you really need it...

"Oh. Thank you."

I expect him to set down the bottle and run, but he sprays the door and begins to scrub.

"Well, don't just stare at me," he says. "Here." He stretches out his arm and sprays the words closer to me. "Work on your side."

We scrub in silence, him on his side, me on mine. Every so often he sprays a new spot for me and then goes back to scrubbing away at his.

When the door is basically done, he says, "This doesn't mean anything, I just care about the house."

I watch him as he walks away.

Still, I think, *it's an improvement*.

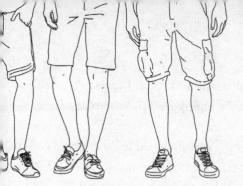

chapter fifty-four

I'M ON MY WAY BACK FROM A SHITTY TEST I HAD TO get up at eight for, opening my door and wanting nothing but to lie in bed and watch *Friends* all day, when the door across from me opens.

Bass lunges forward and laughs in a way that sends chills down my spine.

"Why is it that every time I leave my room, *you* are here?" He reeks of booze, even though it's only noon.

Something in his eyes makes me feel uneasy, so I step to the side, thinking of my waiting bed.

I just need to keep my head down and avoid whatever confrontation Sebastian is gunning for.

"Bitch," he spits. "Why are you still here?" He steps in front of me. "You were never supposed to be here, but your feminazi friends put us in an impossible situation."

I stare down at his shoes, way too expensive for a college student. Italian leather, maybe.

Hopefully if I just let him finish his rant, I can say a quick, "Yeah, you're right" before slipping into my room and locking the door.

"This was the only fucking place we had left for men. Free from all that PC, affirmative action, give me some of what you *earned* for free bullshit. First the blacks wanted in, and then the fags and now you stupid bitches. Gonna ruin the whole damn thing."

I look up, fire in my eyes now. I don't want to get past him anymore. Now I'm ready to fight.

"Fuck you, Bass." It's all I can manage. A million more-intelligent comments fire off in my head, but in the emotion of the moment, the big *F you* is all I can muster.

"Should've known this was all part of some liberal-agenda bullshit." His eyes are glassy and mean.

I bite my lip. *Don't argue with the delusional; keep yourself safe.*

I step around him; this time his reaction is slow, like he's moving through syrup, or maybe Jack Daniel's.

"Hey, bitch! I'm talkin' to you." He grabs my arm, his fingers digging in.

I try to pull it back, but he yanks harder, spinning me so I face him, then stumble backward.

"Look at me when I fucking talk, you bitch."

I lunge forward and step on his foot, like they taught us in self-defense class, and his grip loosens enough for me to pull my arm away.

Stepping toward my open door, I exhale. I'm okay. I reach for my key, my hands shaking. Repeating: *It's okay. It's okay. It's ok—*

Hands seize my shoulders and push me from behind. The wall flies toward my face.

———

I open my eyes, and the first thing I see is feet. Dancing around. Waltz music plays in my aching head to accompany the dance. One-two-three, one-two-three.

They shuffle around, weaving toward each other and away, fancy leather loafers and beat-up Nikes.

Beat-up Nikes with "JL" written on the heel in Magic Marker.

What the…?

I snap back into focus, becoming aware that I'm lying on the floor, my cheek against the carpet.

I push myself up with one arm.

And the hallway shifts like it's on a tilted axis, the floor rising toward the ceiling.

Then things go back where they belong, and I realize the feet weren't dancing. They were fighting.

Jordan, a large red welt over his eye and an expression I've never seen before on his vote-for-me-for-class-president-perfect face. Rage.

"Stop!" a voice says from above.

I turn in slow motion.

Duncan is barreling down the hall, yelling something about trust funds and lawsuits and losing scholarships.

Duncan is pulling Jordan off Sebastian when everything goes dark again.

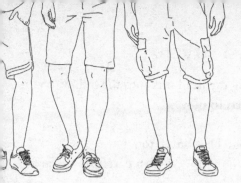

chapter fifty-five

A FLUORESCENT LIGHT AND A BEEPING SOUND.
For a moment, this is all I know. I blink and the light goes away, but the beeping persists.

I blink again, and my eyes focus. I take in the window with industrial curtains, the old television suspended from the ceiling, the linoleum floor, and carts and machines full of wires and screens, the twin bed with a scratchy blanket I'm lying on.

I'm in a hospital room.

I turn the other way and see a doorway, and a woman running by in scrubs.

And then I see... Peter. Sitting in a cheap hospital chair, staring at me.

"What are you doing here?"

He laughs. "Well, that's one way to say thank you."

"Thank you." I squirm, trying to sit up. "I meant—sorry, I'm just a little—" My hand goes to my throbbing head.

"Confused. Yeah, I bet." He laughs. "Sit back. You're fine."

I nod, my brain knocking around inside my skull.

"Shit." I lie back, letting my head sink into the pillow, trying to keep it still. "It hurts to move."

"I bet."

I laugh up at the ceiling. That hurts, too.

Keeping my head on the pillow, I turn carefully toward Peter. "What happened?"

"Concussion. They did a CT, and there're no bleeds or evident damage, but you definitely have a pretty good concussion. You'll be fine. They just wanted to keep you because you went unconscious at the time of the incident and then kept wanting to go back to sleep, but some of that might be because you were exhausted before it happened. But yeah, I'm sure the doctor can tell you more, and Duncan can tell you about what sort of precautions you should—"

"No, I mean what happened after I passed out?"

He laughs. "You mean the title bout that broke out in the middle of my house? Don't worry—your boy's fine."

"He's not my—"

"Cassie, I've known since January."

Oh.

I stare up at the ceiling.

"So I guess I'm really kicked out now." He can't have a house divided, fights every day, in-house dating...

"Why would I do that? I've voted for you to stay at every point this year."

I whip my head around. *Ow.*

"Wait." I hold up my hand. "You're the one who gave me a *zero*."

His brow furrows. "How do you know that?"

Shit. "I...uh." I avoid his eyes, trying to think of a lie.

"Whatever." He chuckles. "Those things don't matter at all, except for pledge shots, I guess. It looked good to the guys, balanced out my pushing for you in the ways that really matter."

"But why couldn't you give me good reviews everywhere?"

"You were a pledge. Do you really think you getting different treatment, being president's pet, was going to help you?"

I stare at him. "You're like an evil genius."

He laughs. "I like to think I'm more a rough-around-the-edges, deeply-troubled-but-ultimately-good hero."

"Okay, Han Solo." My eyes roll so far back into my head I think I can see my beat-up brain. "So wait—I'm not gonna get voted out?"

"Nope." He leans back and puts his feet up on my hospital bed. "Sebastian, on the other hand, was booted this morning. Unanimous."

I smile, a movement that for some reason doesn't hurt at all.

But then I remember something. "Uh, Peter, not to be insensitive, but I mean, after my article, is there even really a frat for Bass to be booted from?"

He grabs a newspaper off my bedside table and throws it in my lap.

"This came out this morning. I wanted to show it to you, but you'd left for your test by the time I got to your room."

I brace myself for the "Frat Gone Forever" headline, then notice it's not the school newspaper. It's the opinion section of the *San Francisco Chronicle*.

What the…?

On the Future of Fraternity
My father believed there was nothing more American than Delta Tau Chi. He talked dreamily of football games and toga parties, and of sorority mixers—one of which was where he met my mother. He claimed he could still recite the secret pledge at a moment's notice and made

most of his adult friends through the DTC alumni network. The Delta Tau Chi name on his application got him jobs and, later, was the reason he hired a large number of his staff. To him, his frat could do no wrong.

And he's not alone in that opinion.

To many, Greek Life is like a religion.

In Texas, where I come from, there are stores in the middle of town that sell nothing but clothes and knick-knacks with Greek letters on them. Students pick colleges based on what Greek organizations are available, mothers sing lullabies to daughters about joining their sorority and to sons about being a frat man who loves that sorority just like their fathers did.

To so many, these are Great American Organizations that can do no wrong.

But like so many American bastions of pride, the Greek system also has a dark history of discrimination.

It continues to promote the idea that women can only be friends with women and men with men. Although there are a lot of interactions between frats and sororities, many of those are sexually motivated and focused on inebriation. Few people form as strongly meaningful relationships with opposite gender members of the Greek community as they do with those in their house.

But sex is just one way the Greek system discriminates.

Ridiculously high dues discriminate against most socioeconomic groups.

Fraternities and sororities have historically discriminated by race, religion, and sexual orientation. It's all too common in the Rush room, when the debate should be about the character and values of the candidate, for people to be rejected without discussion based on background or sexual identity.

This kind of thinking has no place in higher education. And it especially has no place in a community that pledges itself to a mission of character, sincere friendship based on common interests and loyalty.

So the question is how to preserve all that is good about these organizations that so many people love without also continuing these abhorrent practices.

I would prefer no Greek Life to Greek Life that continues in a way that marginalizes minorities of any kind.

However, I am a firm believer that a fair and just society, and pranks and finesse in beer sports, are not mutually exclusive.

It's time to create communities based on common personality traits, not common privilege.

To create frat-rorities that include both men and women, people of all backgrounds, and orientations.

It's simply the right thing to do. It's the only way that Greek members can continue to speak proudly of their organizations into the future.

But if you need more proof, talk to any of the brothers of DTC at Warren. A lot of controversy has surrounded our chapter this year, most notably with the admittance of the first female member to an American fraternity, and the subsequent study she recently published in *America Weekly*.

But anyone who really takes time to read Cassie Davis's story will see not only the ignorant behavior that has people up in arms but also the progress she documents. They will see minds opened and respect built.

They will see how living with people who have a different perspective—in this case, someone of a different gender—helped our members to understand what women go through, and, more important, how their own actions contribute to this culture of discrimination, and how they might change.

A lot of people thought that as a prominent member of the chapter, I'd be outraged reading that article. But by the last page I was proud. Proud of Cassandra, but also of many of the brothers whose behavior she documents.

Cassie's article definitely proved American fraternities have a long way to go. And, I'm sorry, Dad, but it also showed that DTC can do wrong.

But it also showed that these beloved organizations are able to evolve and come into the twenty-first century if they are open to change.

In other words, if we want to continue this American pursuit of frattiness, our great traditions of college fun and lifelong kinship, we must first live up to our American promise of equal opportunity.

Peter Ford is president of the California Alpha chapter of Delta Tau Chi at Warren University. He is a political science major, ROTC cadet and a member of the Young Democrats. He aspires to run for political office one day.

Pictures accompany the article: our group picture from initiation, and then the rest are of…me. At parties, philanthropy events from last semester, moving in, at Rush.

I look up. "How long have you been planning this?"

Peter shrugs. "You were always good for PR. Why do you think we threw you a bid in the first place?"

I'm dumbfounded. This whole time I was worried about lying to them, and they were playing me, too.

Peter struts out, but then pokes his head back in. "Oh, there are some people here to see you."

I pull myself out of bed, relieved to find that my hospital gown is the kind that covers my butt, and walk tentatively to the door.

The small waiting room across the hall is packed.

On the left side, taking up the chairs and leaning against the wall, are Alex and Jackie and a few girls from my feminist studies classes.

On the right side is most of my pledge class, a clear line of demarcation running through the room, with the exception of Duncan and Jackie, who are holding hands over the coffee table.

Everyone turns when I approach, relieved to see me walking. Or at least to be freed from making awkward small talk anymore.

I'm swamped with hugs and questions.

"I'm fine. I'm fine," I say, but no one seems to hear; they're all so busy asking how I am.

"They wouldn't let me in," Marco says. "The lady said family only. Peter got in, but for *some reason* she wouldn't believe we were brothers."

I laugh and pull him into a hug.

"Good thing Jordan was in his room and heard what was going on when…*it* happened," Bambi said. "I would have beat him up, Cass. But I was at class, found out after."

I smile. "I appreciate the thought, Bambi."

All the greetings and thoughts of concern wash over me.

"Thank you for coming," I repeat. "I really appreciate it. Thanks. Thank you."

I smile and hug, the whole time looking for one face that's noticeably missing.

When Alex hugs me, I bury my head in her soft blond hair.

"I was so worried," she says.

"I'm fine."

"It's okay if you're not." She leans back, her arms still around me and her eyes shining.

"I am. Thank you, though." I smile. "Hey." I bite my lip. "Jordan hasn't stopped by, has he?"

She laughs. "He's getting his hand looked at down the hall."

"Really?"

"Yep."

"I'm just gonna go…" I gesture over my shoulder.

"Yeah, I thought so." She laughs. "I'll catch up with you in a few minutes."

I wander down the hall, eavesdropping, and figure out where they have him. I'm about to go in, then pause for a second, wondering what to say. I mean, really, what *is* there to say? He ended it, he hated me, and then he risked his scholarship, risked everything, to help me.

I'll never be ready for this. I take a deep breath and walk in. Hoping I'll see his face and just know.

He's sitting on a bed, a nurse standing in front of him, wrapping his hand.

She's blocking his face, so I can't see his reaction to me walking in.

The nurse whips around. "Excuse me, miss, but you can't be in here."

"I'm sorry, I—"

"She's fine." His voice is strained. I wonder if it's from pain, or if he's still mad at me.

"Humph." She finishes fashioning the gauze around his hand quickly. When she's done, she pushes past me on her way out.

We're silent for a moment, the only sound the nurse's retreating footsteps.

I remain standing, practically against the back wall, giving him as much space as possible.

He looks up. "It's broken."

My eyes go wide. "Really?"

"Yep."

"Oh God. How did you…did you break it on his face?" I imagine what Bass must look like. I try not to be too happy at the thought.

He looks down. "No, uh, on the wall behind him."

I laugh. "Well, maybe we can tell people it was on him?"

He smiles. "I like that idea."

The moment of laughter fades, and we're back to our tentative silence.

"What does this mean for soccer?"

"Well, luckily you don't really use your hands in soccer." He winks.

I roll my eyes.

"But…yeah." He exhales. "I'll be out for a little while as it heals, but it's not career ending or anything."

"That's good." I look down at my shoes. "Thank you for… what you did."

"Don't worry about it."

I look up. "Also I, uh…" My throat feels tight. "I was hoping we could talk. I wanted to say—"

He just shakes his head and cuts me off. "Me first."

I brace myself for what he might say. "I'm still feeling a bit dizzy. Maybe you can lead the way to the house this time?"

I just smile and nod. "I only have ten percent battery, but I think I can manage it."

"Cool."

I breathe again. "Wait. Dizzy? I'm the concussed one."

"Hey, he got you once. He got me, like, three times."

I shake my head. "You're ridiculous."

"But that's a good point—you should lie down." He pats the mattress next to him.

I cross the room and lie down next to him on the cramped bed.

He starts to put his arm around me, then winces. "Nope, nope, that doesn't work."

"Here," I say. "Lie back."

I nuzzle into the little nook his neck and shoulder create.

He kisses the top of my head. "Look at us, both infirm. How will we ever make our way home?"

I laugh. "We can help each other."

"I like that plan."

I tilt my head up and scooch closer. He kisses me on the lips, softly, like he's worried he might hurt me.

I kiss back harder, as if to say it's okay, and readjust so we're closer.

I used to think he was too good for me. That I was too messed up, and needed to find another heart that was broken like mine, while he was this living, beating whole heart. That maybe I wanted him because I couldn't really have him, and he wanted me because he didn't realize how messed up I was.

But I was wrong. I didn't need him so I could move forward every day.

My day was just…kind of great when he was around. Like, really, really great.

He made me feel sunny, like a younger version of myself, or maybe that's not quite right, because I don't feel naive, but like I've gone through all I have and still can be as happy as I was when I was young.

He doesn't need to fix me; he doesn't "heal all my wounds with his love," or something like that. He just helps me be happy even though those wounds exist.

And that's just one of the reasons I love him.

"Oh, no, no way, not in my hospital, one patient per bed."

I look up to see the nurse is back, standing, arms crossed, in the doorway.

Sheepishly, I slide off the bed.

"It's all right. We were just leaving anyway," Jordan says.

"Not until you're properly discharged. Your forms are at the desk."

She stands in the doorway and watches us while we readjust our clothes and make our way out. I head back to my room to get dressed.

"Turning my hospital into a damn frat house," she says as I move past her. "There are sick people here!"

Once we are both dressed and ready to go, we head to the waiting room.

"He survives!" Peter yells as we enter.

The brothers whoop and holler. I look over my shoulder, hoping the nurse can't hear them.

A few of the girls ask if he's okay.

"Yeah, I think so." He examines his hand.

"Don't be a pussy—it's not your head," Alex says.

Duncan tells her not to use the word *pussy* in this way because it associates female with weakness in an untrue way.

The jaws on the left side of the room drop. Jackie smiles.

Jordan stands with me, arm around my waist, as we fill out the paperwork to check out.

My phone buzzes. I pull it out of my jeans pocket to see an email alert from the Stevenson Fund.

Project Proposal for Next Year: Deadline approaching

I close it. I have plenty of people to brainstorm with tomorrow, I think as we rejoin our friends.

"Free?" Duncan asks.

"Free."

Everyone stands up.

Jordan turns to me. "What now?"

I take his hand. "Now we go home."

★ ★ ★ ★ ★

ACKNOWLEDGMENTS

The book that *Frat Girl* is today, and the person that I am as I write it, is thanks to the support and wisdom of so many amazing people.

First I must thank Nicole Resciniti, who has at times been my cheerleader, therapist, mentor and friend, but is formally my agent. You believed in me when the phrase "I'll finish up the draft after prom!" was one that made sense, and have encouraged and guided me from that day to this one.

Thank you so much to the team at Harlequin TEEN/Inkyard Press and HarperCollins at large, including Natashya Wilson, Margaret Marbury and Siena Koncsol. As well, a special thanks to Leslie Wainger, who took a chance on me when *Frat Girl* was still just a few paragraphs, and Michael Strother, who just totally *got it* from our very first conversation and helped bring *Frat Girl* from rough draft to a much stronger version of itself. The amount of stress I am going through—and raw cookie dough I am stress eating—while writing this, the only part of the book that you will not touch, is a testament to what you have done with the rest.

Thank you also to the authors who have been so welcoming to me, especially Joelle Charbonneau. To meet a writer you're a fan of is incredibly exciting. For them to encourage you with your own writing is downright surreal.

I would also like to thank by name some of the people the dedication alludes to: my college friends.

Thank you to Nicolas Lozano, who really did run across campus when a boy was mean to me and has been one of my best friends ever since. And to AT Hall, a Hagrid-sized football player who would need no redemption story line because he is as gentlemanly and kind today as the day I first met him. Thank you to Carrie Monahan for your weird-awesomeness, insights on feminism and example of true female friendship.

Thank you to Graeme Hewett, for all your inspiration and support—this book would probably not exist if I didn't get to Skype you after I finished a chapter. And to Maddie Bouton, thank you for countless conversations that challenged my perspective on many things, beginning with how a blonde Southern sorority girl could also be a tattooed, bass-playing philosophy major. Lastly, thank you to Maddie Bradshaw, passionate feminist, brilliant business mind, wearer of Raise Boys and Girls the Same Way T-shirts, and expert dancer on tables—you are my person.

And even more than my "college family," it was the support of my real family that made this book possible.

Thank you so much to my parents, who let my summer job be "I'm gonna write a book!" Twice. You have been incredibly supportive and I cannot thank you enough for all you have done for me.

Thank you to my brothers, who kept me from taking myself too seriously and gave me my first insight into the pizza-rolls-for-dinner, laundry-once-a-month-if-possible world of boys in their natural habitat.

Thank you to my sister, the first reader of this book, whose stamp of approval meant the world to me. You are younger than me but inspire me daily, as you are unapologetically smart, athletic and outspoken in a world that tells you to be otherwise.

Finally I would like to thank my teachers—including Ms. Rodogno, Ms. Garcia, Ms. Waz and Ms. O'Mara—and my editors and mentors at *The Mash* and *Huffington Post Teen*, including Morgan Olsen, Phil Thompson, Michelle Gonzalez Lopez, Taylor Trudon and Elizabeth Perle. I'm sure that telling teenagers to write is hard. But helping them to write what they really care about, and encouraging them toward the best version of their own voice is truly an amazing feat. I am just one of many students who cannot thank you enough.

Turn the page for a sneak peek of
the witty and wonderful new novel
THE DATING GAME
by Kiley Roache
available wherever books are sold.

Part 1

GAMIFICATION

chapter one

Roberto

IS THERE A FUN FACT ABOUT ME THAT MIGHT IMPRESS a billionaire? This is what I wonder as I sit in the first lecture for Professor Dustin Thomas's class. Which is actually my first college class, ever. At the beginning of the hour, he asked the class to go around and *say your name and a little bit about yourself.*

As the minutes click by and the chance to speak snakes through the room, getting closer to me, I have only a big, fat blank.

I'm beginning to think I might be in over my head. That applying for this class might have been a mistake. That applying for this *school* might have been a mistake.

The question has reached the guy sitting in front of me. He stands up, introduces himself as Joe. He takes a second to mention the place he was born before moving on to all the places he has interned.

I can't blame him. If I wasn't a freshman whose job experience included mowing lawns, scooping ice cream and sorting the book drop at the library, I would probably do the same. When else are you gonna find yourself in the presence of Dustin Thomas?

After all, he is not just a billionaire, but a billionaire-maker. A venture capitalist, Thomas was an early investor in companies like Instafriend. Yep, that Instafriend. He's the guy who helped turn a group of kids working out of a dorm room into tycoons.

Now he's pretty much retired and tells all the tech blogs that he just wants to teach one class a year about the work ethic required for entrepreneurship, and research how the study of human behavior can be harnessed for marketing.

We are all here pretending we care about those topics so that we can be in the same room as him. And maybe be around when he decides to come out of retirement.

The next person stands up. "Hi, I'm Megan, and I went to a little school in Cambridge, Massachusetts, before coming here to Warren University to get my master's." She winks and points to her Harvard crew sweatshirt, just in case she was so coy that we didn't know what she meant.

I've seen one-upmanship like this all throughout orientation, and it's not that I don't find it irritating; it's just that I don't have time to care. Of course, I want to grab some of these kids by the shoulders, tell them how ridiculous it is to debate whether Exeter is better than Andover when so many schools in the US—including the one I went to for K–8—are straining to afford books and basic supplies. But I can't exactly do that.

If I want to carve out a piece of that golden pie for myself, and even more important, for my family, I know I need to operate in this world, under their rules. In my notebook, I jot down a few things I could share, like my magnet school acceptance, and the community service recognition I got at high school graduation. I stare down at the paper. Neither seems like enough.

"And, what was the last thing I was supposed to say—a fun fact?" Megan asks, tapping her chin. "Um, well, last summer I received the award for best intern when I worked at Apple, so that was pretty fun!"

A small laugh erupts two seats over, but it is quickly concealed by a fake cough.

I look down my row. The guy who laughed reaches under his seat for a water bottle. Maybe to cover up more laughter, or maybe because he's hungover. After all, he's wearing sunglasses and a baseball cap inside the auditorium.

He slips the bottle into the side pocket of a backpack bearing the large seal of what I assume was his high school. The logo includes a gold shield and a founding date that means his school is older than the country. *Fancy.*

He leans back and props his feet on the chair in front of him. This guy is either so rich that he doesn't need this class, or straight-up stupid.

"Hi!" A cute blonde shoots up like her second-row chair is on fire. She straightens her shoulders. "My name is Sara Jones, and I'm a freshman studying computer science."

"Great," the lounging dude mutters. "Hermione Granger is in this class."

I'm not sure if he's talking to me, but I kind of hope he's not.

I am actually grateful for Sara, the only other freshman who has stood up so far. At this point, it seems that most of the students are upperclassmen, if not graduate students. I am trying my best to remember everything my high school guidance counselor told me about not letting anyone make me feel like I don't deserve to be here because of my age or where I come from. It's a bit easier to do so knowing I'm not the only freshman. In that small way, I am not alone.

Sara collapses into her seat, as if that sentence exhausted her.

Professor Thomas gestures for her to continue. But Sara just looks from side to side.

"What?" she says, her voice even higher than before.

"Your fun fact," the dude next to me yells, still practically draped across the chairs. He looks like a heckler at a comedy show.

"Oh." She stands again and straightens her skirt with shaking hands. "I, uh…"

My heart sinks to my stomach on this girl's behalf. I know what it's like to feel intimidated, like everyone around you is summing you up, just waiting to academically eat you alive. I've been in rooms where I am the only kid who looks like me, the only one who speaks two languages at home, the kid who's "only" here because of a scholarship, who's from that neighborhood your parents tell you to avoid when you drive back from the airport. People find this out about you, and it's like they smell blood in the water.

Of course, I have no idea what this girl's story is, or why she looks like she might cry in the middle of this class right now. But I feel for that isolation.

"Um…today I learned that twin sheets do not fit on twin extra-long mattresses." She forces a smile and sits down as a few people laugh, including, thankfully, Professor Thomas, who musters a chuckle.

I decide I like this strategy, to say something that isn't a thinly veiled résumé check. When it gets around to me, I say, "Hi, my name is Roberto, but most people call me Robbie. I am a freshman and will either major in computer science or electrical engineering. I haven't decided yet. And my fun fact is when the last Harry Potter book came out, I stayed up all night and read it in two days."

I sit back down. I guess that still was kind of a humble brag, depending on how you look at it. But it's from elementary school, so I think it's okay.

When the introductions are over, Professor Thomas moves his coffee cup before sitting on the desk at the front of the room, a causal gesture at odds with the fiercely competitive atmosphere in the auditorium.

"People often ask me what makes an entrepreneur," he begins. "What sets aside the man who has the type of success where he enters an industry, climbs to the mid or upper-mid level and retires fine, with the kind of mind that alters an industry completely, leaving a mark for decades after he's gone. The kind of mind that takes an idea born in a garage and turns it into the kind of thing my colleagues and I trip over each other to invest in."

At the HP Garage reference, half the room scoots farther up in their seats. It's Silicon Valley, after all.

"The answer is failure." He pauses dramatically. "Sure, all successful people experience setbacks. They are passed up for a promotion or don't get a job. But some successful businessmen can *make* it through good careers without experiencing terrible failure. Catastrophic failure—down in the gutter, debt piling up, not sure if you can keep the lights on another week failure—that is where an entrepreneur *lives*. If you are innovating, you are coming up with an idea that either people have tried and failed to succeed with before you, or is so ridiculous that no human has even thought of it before. You will be laughed out of rooms. You will spend hours, if not months, building prototypes that fall apart.

"You joined this class because you want to be entrepreneurs. But from what I could gather from the…illustrious introductions you all just gave, very few of you have ever failed. You've worked incredibly hard and jumped through the right hoops, checked the right boxes. But the thing about innovating is that you will work one-hundred-hour weeks, not for the six-figure checks you'd get if you went into established industry, but for doors to be slammed in your face. You don't work hard and then succeed. You work hard and then you fail, you fail, and then you fail again. And then, finally, just when you want to give up for the three hundredth time, you succeed more than you could ever imagine.

"I teach for *this* school and I make this class application-only because I don't waste my time with students who aren't worth it. I ensure that those who make it through my class leave having gained something, and I advocate passionately for my past students. But if they don't have what it takes—the intelligence and technical skill, yes, but also the willingness to fail—they don't get to have me as their teacher. You proved you had the first two in your application. Now let's see the latter." The professor stands up and steps away from his desk. "Over the next three weeks, you will form groups of three or four and come up with a product that you will pitch to me, as if I were a VC, the next time our class meets."

A murmur ripples through the room. The professor continues, unfazed. "There are no well-worn paths here. There are no test prep books or study guides for innovation. You must go forward, maybe for the first time in your life, with no clear direction set out for you. You can reach out to mentors, read books and do research, but in the middle of the night, when part of your project isn't working, you have just you and your equally blind teammates to count on. With that in mind, I hope you choose wisely." He walks behind the desk and picks up his briefcase.

"I expect you to sink, but try to swim. This is, after all,

worth a third of your grade for the class. Go ahead and get working. I'll see you in a month." With that, he walks out the door in the front of the classroom.

The lazy dude sits up with a start at the sound of the closing door.

The rest of the class is in stunned silence.

A few rows up, Sara stands and looks around, a stricken expression on her face.

People begin to murmur to those around them, and there's an awkward laugh here and a "Nice to meet you" there. Students start to stand and ask about being in the same group, for clearly there's nothing else to do but to assume Professor Thomas was being serious.

More and more students venture from their seats. They reach a critical mass and rapidly it seems like the whole room is power walking, introducing, teaming up and swarming together. They move like a school of fish rushing upstream, and I feel like a tiny minnow being tossed around.

"Are you in the MBA program?" A man in a suit pushes through two young women talking to reach another guy wearing a tie.

"Who has a master's?" a brunette woman yells into the crowd.

My mouth feels like sandpaper. I slide my notebook into my backpack and reach for my water.

Down the aisle, the lazy dude stands and turns to the row behind us.

"Hi, Braden Hart." He reaches out his hand to a bespectacled, white hipster-looking guy, who has teamed up with an olive-skinned, preppy-dressed girl in the row behind us.

"How many languages do you know?" the guy asks, skipping any introduction.

"Three." Braden crosses his arms with confidence.

The hipster guy raises his eyebrows. "Which ones?"

"French, Span—"

"Coding languages, you idiot," the girl snaps. The hipster guy just blinks at Braden.

"Oh." Braden steps backward. "I don't really…uh…"

The hipster guy scoffs. "Get out of my face." He holds up a hand.

I slide out of the row and walk up to a group of older-looking students. I could've tried for the group behind me—I do know three coding languages—but I don't want to work with anyone that rude.

A girl with a pink stripe in her hair smiles as I walk up.

"Hi, I'm Roberto." I clear my throat. "Robbie," I add.

"Hey, I'm Rebecca," she says.

"Chad." The guy reaches for my hand, and as I shake it I can't help but notice he's wearing both twine bracelets and a Rolex.

They ask me about my skills, and I nod along as I walk through my experience. They seem less interested when I mention my passion for social impact, but they don't tell me to get lost or anything.

"Do you have any experience at a start-up?" Rebecca asks.

I start to answer, but my attention is pulled away. On the other side of the room, Sara is speed walking from group to group, her heels clicking. She barely makes it a few syllables through her high-pitched introduction before she is turned away. And turned away. And turned away again.

I bring my attention back to the people in front of me.

"I don't, but I was in the prebusiness club at my high school," I say.

Rebecca nods. She leans over to whisper to Chad.

Around us, groups lock together and push upstream toward the exit like mini tornados, probably trying to get from the classroom to the library without losing any members.

"We're really sorry, but my thesis coadvisees want to join and that would make us five," Chad says. "You're the only undergrad, so it's only fair if you're the one we cut."

"Sorry!" Rebecca shrugs sheepishly.

I nod and say thanks anyway. Looking around the room, I count group members, looking for any that have an opening. But in a flurry of business cards and iPhones, the room has thinned. Just as quickly as it exploded with sound, the auditorium is quiet. Practically empty.

Sara is stalking a group of three headed toward the exit, yelling her high school GPA as the door swings shut in her face. She turns on her heel, her shoulders falling.

I stand in the aisle, mystified.

Braden, who has taken a seat in one of the last rows, looks up from his phone. "Well, I guess it's just us, then."

Look for The Dating Game
only from Kiley Roache
and Inkyard Press!